Paul Werner

THE LEGACY OF THE YELLOW DANCER

adventure novel

Bibliographic information published by the Deutsche Nationalbibliothek:
The Deutsche Nationalbibliothek lists this publication in the
Deutsche Nationalbibliografie; detailed bibliographic data are
available on the Internet at http://dnb.dnb.de.

TWENTYSIX – The Self-Publishing Company
A cooperation between the publishing group
Random House and BoD – Books on Demand

© 2017 Paul Werner

Manufacture and publishing:
BoD – Books on Demand, Norderstedt
Cover artwork and typeset:
uc graphic, Heidelberg
Illustration: Evelyn Mantei

ISBN: 978-3-7407-3209-7

FIRST CHAPTER

1. The Rock

The woman swims for her life. Her naked arms thrash the boiling sea in a languid rhythm whilst her torso keeps rolling left and right in tired succession. Panting, her gaping mouth desperately gasps for air before her head disappears again. Wave upon wave seizes the woman and lifts her up with sudden force onto the frothy crest. Hovering there for seconds on end, the blast of the roaring gale hits her with devastating might. Foaming white spray lashes into her face like a thousand needles and causes brief spells of agonizing blindness. Then, corpse-like, she again falls into the dead calm at the bottom of the waves and seems forever lost in their narrow black canyons. Her arms and legs are becoming leaden, her desperate lunges for breath ever shorter. Like merciless hammer blows, her pulse resounds through her head all the way to the tips of her dark gleaming hair. Her lungs are distended to bursting point. Her stomach cannot hold the swallowed salt water any more. Time and time again the woman chokes, coughs and throws up. Her eyes hurt as if slowly gnawed away by gush upon gush of hydrochloric acid. Her skin burns as if on fire and comes off in flakes here and there like scorched parchment.

It's been some time since the woman had her last clear thought. At present, she is driven by nothing but her stubborn will.

"Keep going," one of two voices is shouting at her from somewhere in the raging darkness.

"Don't give up on me now! Don't go wilting away like a wretched pussy! Don't you dare drown the two of us like rats in this wet blue graveyard called the Aegean. You really want to end up as fish-food, a relish for eels, crabs, and worms somewhere in the dim depths of this corpse-saturated pond of a sea? Well, do you?"

Whenever she feels flat out and finished the woman turns on her back and, for a few blissful moments, abandons herself to the rolling billows. As long as she keeps breathing the sea will support her. Such are the terms of their tacit agreement. The freshly polished stars above are dancing like a million rhinestones on a cowboy riding the fiercest bull in a Saturday night rodeo.

"Don't even listen to her! Just let go, Sweetie, why don't you?" The lizard-like lisp of the second voice keeps whispering into her ear out of the dark. "Why won't you let go? I'll catch you alright, cross my heart and hope to die."

Helplessly adrift like this, the woman will be pushed further and further south by the combined forces of wind and current. As she knows full well, nothing but bleak emptiness awaits her there. With the half-choked death cry of a wantonly harpooned young whale, she turns back onto her stomach and continues her pointless fight.

Each time a particularly massive wave tosses her all the way to the roof of the sea, the wildly flickering lights of the Lesbos coast lure the woman on. Too far, she'll never make it there. Suddenly, the black hump-back of a massive shadow starts squeezing itself between the woman and the coastal lights. A writhing, glistening leviathan emerging from the unfathomable depths of the ocean, the shadow is towering right in front of her, blocking her sight, barring her passage.

Hesitatingly, the woman's alerted consciousness regains control. Painfully slowly, she begins to grasp what it is that is emerging before her: a tiny rocky islet, saddle-formed, a black elevation of volcanic stone, unlit, uninhabited, unheeded like so many other wood-devouring remnants of a world in the making. Scorned by fishermen, dreaded by sailors but at present her stalwart promise of rescue, her pledge of salvation. Like an ugly blot on a paling old photographic negative, it shows against the dark background of the northwest coast of Sappho's blessed island. A characteristic helmet-like bluff around the middle of the islet, hardly taller than a sailing-boat's mast, identifies it beyond doubt. The woman has almost reached it. Another twenty, thirty strokes and she will once again feel solid ground under her feet. Or would, if it weren't for the deadly grindstones of cliffs protecting the islet from the perpetual onslaught of the restless, never tiring sea. Razor-sharp edges of volcanic rock will be lurking just underneath the billowing surface. The bloated, half-eaten corpses of men, women and children drowned at sea and eventually washed ashore, are they not frequently disfigured by deep cuts and vicious bruises? Such gruesome tell-tale wounds give us but a vague idea of how the unfortunate victims' tragedy. In full sight of land, already eagerly filling their lungs with the invigorating scent of humid soil and lush vegetation, blindly following the shouts and cries of beachcombers allegedly rushing to their rescue, such victims of the sea's wanton irony ended up torn to pieces by the grey sharks' teeth of those impassionate cliffs.

As she comes up for air, the woman can already distinguish the lighter splashes of the surf from the much darker grumbling of the unwavering rows upon rows of billows tracking south like phalanx upon phalanx of a conquering army. As soon as the rolling waves hit the abruptly rising seabed, the water is no longer deep enough for them to complete their circle. As they see their passage blocked, their frustrated, mindlessly raging energy makes them rise like horses confronted with some insurmountable hedge. A human being unfortunate enough to end up between the "hooves" of the breaking surf and the anvil of the iron reef will be crushed like an egg falling off a wall.

The woman realizes the deadly danger, yet has little chance to withstand the sheer power of the sea. Helped only by the feeble light of the peeping moon's sickle behind her back, she makes a huge effort at freeing herself, but is found wanting. Persistent bursts of sheet lightning from the top of the Lesbos mountain range are effectively blinding her like misleading flashes from a piratical coast. At the renewed flashing of forked lightning she catches a glimpse of the tiniest, sorriest excuse of a sandy beach to her right, closing in at breakneck speed. Here and now, this is her only bid at landing on the islet in one piece. She mobilizes what little forces she has left to break the steely embrace of the surf and steer towards the sandy patch. For the briefest of moments, it looks as if she is not going to make it. But then her half-mangled body is lifted clean over the belt of cliffs by a last thundering wave and dumped like flotsam onto the wet abrasive sands.

For what feels like an eternity, the battered woman lies motionless in the thick, white froth of algae and the loose mats of seaweed that mark the transition from water to land. As if unwilling to let go of their prey, the long, wet tongues of the dying waves keep sucking at the woman's bloody feet and legs. Yet even the unfettered forces of the elements have to admit defeat at some point. Tonight, the sea cannot complete its grim work of destruction. Grudgingly, it surrenders the woman to the interminably raging gale that tortures her pickled body with the onslaught of a myriad of bullet-like grains of sand.

The silent thunderstorm yonder has slowly moved south. With the first shy twitches of her burnt-out muscles, life returns to the woman. Her hands trembling, she reaches down her leg and pulls out a large combat-knife with a saw-tooth blade from the sheath strapped to her right ankle. She seizes the handle with both her bleeding hands, lifts it above her head and rams its blade into the sand to the very hilt as if putting a stranded yet still breathing whale out of its misery with a final almighty blow. Then she pulls herself further up the beach, inch by inch. Over and over she repeats the process, drives the knife hard into the ground and crawls forward like some antediluvian creature hesitatingly leaving its ancestral habitat to venture into new territory. Finally, she reaches the foot of the bluff. The crumbling porous surface of its undulating volcanic rock-face offers her fingers a precarious first support. She succeeds in assuming a sitting position and leans her aching back against the abrasive stone that welcomes her with the faint memory of yesterday's sun.

She tries to stand up but her tired legs, suffering from cramp, refuse to obey her. She groans, half turns and eventually finds herself kneeling in front of the rock like a pilgrim, having taken unspeakable pains upon herself to worship some obscure orthodox martyr on the run said to have breathed his last on this godforsaken spot.

The woman's chest, bleeding from a multitude of raw bruises, is racing up and down like the glowing pistons of a tormented engine shortly before seizure. The starry skies are already fading at the mere suspicion of dawn's first rosy cracks as the woman eventually rises to her full height. Lean, dark-haired and endowed with the almost impeccable build of an amazon steeled in combat, she stands there in the wavering twilight. With that slight stoop of hers, she forms a perfect effigy of hounded Leto, barely delivered of her glorious Delian twins, Apollo and Artemis. An idol, as good as naked in her torn rags of shorts and tattered stripes of T-shirt, she leans against the wet and rough stone. Her legs still shaking, she gropes her way along the steeply rising rock-face as if looking for some crack or gap, some hidden Sesame that will miraculously open and allow her into the rock's secret womb. The gale now hits her squarely in the face and chest, rendering even the shortest of her steps hard and painful. The woman could do herself an easy favour by walking in the other direction, turning her back on, and eventually escaping from, the tireless sandblaster. On the other, leeward side of the bluff she is likely to find cover and protection. Yet perversely, she insists, unflinching in her battle to wrench inch upon inch of rock from the powerful grip of the wind.

At long last her fingers, long gone numb, feel a void. A sharp receding edge in the rock marks access to a low cave, hardly larger nor deeper than a blast-hole, witness of some half-hearted and quickly abandoned mining folly. Her peculiar insistence was not in vain and suggests that the woman knew about this cave. She stoops and disappears in the black hole into which the gale cannot follow her.

As her eyes adapt to the cavernous twilight, she catches sight of a dull shimmer next to her feet. She picks up a plastic bottle almost baked in sand, probably left here weeks or months ago by one of the rare visitors to the island. A marooned fisherman, maybe, having to sit out a gale such as this one, who, upon his hurried departure, carelessly left the bottle behind. With her bruised fingers, the woman is given a hard time by the red screw top, literally welded to the bottle by the heat of uncounted days and weeks of evening sun lighting up the cave that vaguely faces west. Eventually, she seizes the plastic with her teeth and turns the bottle with her hands, until the screw top gives in. The sickening foul smell emanating from the bottle twists the woman's stomach. But thirst beating nausea any time, she braces herself and swallows the lukewarm water in greedy gulps. Then she throws the empty bottle down and lets out a troglodyte's happy morning belch which, echoing from the cave's walls, seems to shock and silence even the gale if only for a second.

"Welcome to scenic Neanderthal," the woman murmurs, forcing a wry smile from her cracked dry lips. Then she bends down and crawls left on all fours. On the far side of the cave, she runs into a heap piled up on a wooden pallet as if readied for an imminent UPS dispatch. Wrapped in a military-style tarpaulin and covered by a net, it has been perfunctorily stuffed with a few withered twigs in a perfunctory effort at camouflage. As low as the pile seems, it takes the lion's share of the measly space proffered by the cave.

The woman pulls out her knife again and starts to cut, first the net and then the rope which firmly ties the tarpaulin. Suddenly she stops. A strange bulge in the tarpaulin betrays the presence of something underneath that does not belong there. A booby-trap maybe, meant to blow to pieces any inquisitive simpleton careless enough to lay an unauthorised hand on the pile. Very slowly and carefully the woman cuts the last knots of the rope and little by little pulls the tarpaulin towards her, which allows her to release it as soon as she happens to feel the slightest resistance caused by a ripcord detonator. Still holding her breath, she finally throws the tarpaulin aside.

The pile on the pallet consists of several layers of brick-sized packages, each wrapped in shiny plastic foil and sealed by bits and pieces of silvery tape. On the top layer, only a yard or so away from the face of the kneeling woman, a coiled-up snake is hissing indignantly at this blatant violation of its territory. Taking in the distance instinctively, it rises just high enough for its small, pointed fangs to dig into the intruder's hollow cheeks.

The woman does not flinch, betrays neither shocked surprise nor fright, but meets the snake's menacing hiss with a like sound. Her knife hand, hidden from the reptile's weakly sight by the pile, moves imperceptibly upward. The snake's almost human-like "brows" over both eyes identify it as a sand viper. Its bite, though painfully venomous, does not represent any mortal danger for a healthy adult, even if untreated for lack of an appropriate antidote. Should the snake succeed in plunging its fangs in the woman's head or throat, however, that would in fact worsen her odds of survival rather dramatically. More likely than not, the woman is aware of this. Yet once again, she displays that curious pig-headed resolve of hers, does not shy away from the bizarre battle of chicken and coolly returns the viper's stare.

Neither is the angered reptile the least bit disposed to relinquish its cave to the shameless intruder. Ever so slowly, the woman lifts her left hand and moves her fingers as in a shadow play meant to humour a grouchy child. When it finally comes, the snake's thrust at her fingers is right on target but just a split second too slow.

With lightning speed its would-be prey pulls away her left hand and, profiting from the thrust's own momentum, cuts the snake in two with a single well-aimed upward slash of her saw-toothed blade.

Using the tip of her knife, the woman picks up the snake's head with its still defiantly wide-open mouth and looks into its unseen eyes as if distrustful of its ill-famed kind even beyond death. Only when she has ascertained that all life has left the reptile for good, does she toss the head into the sea to be devoured by the crabs. The rest of the snake's body, still writhing in the sand like a severed live cable, she brushes aside.

Then the woman devotes her attention to the watertight bricks. She pulls one of them out of the pile at random, cuts a small slit in the plastic foil and takes a sample of the mealy white powder with the tip of her blade. A few milligrams melting on the taste-buds of her tongue seem to suffice for her to verify the quality of the merchandise. With a nod of appreciation, the woman re-wraps the package and pushes it back into the pile.

Meanwhile, daylight has broken and the islet's resident seabirds, flapping the ruffled feathers of their wings at the gale, meet the morning with their routine cacophony. The storm rages on undiminished, stripping the first rays of the glowing red sun of their habitual warmth. The woman dresses her wounds to the best of her abilities with bits and pieces of her torn garments. To avoid inflammation, gangrene, and tetanus during the coming hours, she will need a lot of luck since medical help of any kind will remain beyond her reach for quite a while.

A few deft cuts with the knife suffice to turn the stiff tarpaulin, soaking with the salt of the humid sea air, into a primitive, tent-like poncho, whose seams touch the ground. She slips the cape over her head and shoulders and looks around, as if searching for a mirror to tell her whether colour, size, and shape are commensurate with her type or whether she should not opt for something a mite tighter, racier, more in keeping with her untamed personality.

At last, the woman forces herself into a narrow crack between the back of the pile and the wall of the cave. Here, she feels protected against both wind, snakes, scorpions and the inquisitive looks of uninvited humans. Anyway, the shipping lanes to and from the Dardanelles give the rocky islet such a wide berth that there is no way anyone can discern coastal details from the bridges of passing cargo ships or ferries. Given the prevailing weather conditions, the appearance of foolhardy fishermen in the area should be just as unlikely. If the rocky islet impressed itself on drug traffickers as a convenient hiding place, this is very likely due to precisely its isolated location and gruff well-nigh inaccessibility.

The woman wraps the self-made poncho round her exhausted body, rams the knife into the ground in front of her and closes her eyes. She does not wear a watch. When she wakes up, the light of the afternoon or evening sun will allow her to assess the time of day. She wastes no thought on escaping from the islet. What with the storm howling and the last of her of physical forces spent, any attempt at swimming across the raging sea to the coast of Lesbos cannot but result in drowning. Only minutes go by until her head drops onto her chest and a low rattling snore comes out of her half-open mouth.

2. Three Gentlemen in White

None of the usual suspects in Yannis' Funky Pelican could tell with any degree of conviction exactly when the three strangers' nameless blue boat had arrived in the tiny fishing harbour of Mithymna. Gazing into the grounds of their thimble-sized coffee cups and flipping their komvoloi chains of prayer beads of coloured glass back and forth in their greasy, callused hands with a soft clicking sound that seemed to keep time with the ticking of the kafeneion's clock, they had discussed the matter at some length. Petros, the bearded owner of the recently opened local "hyperrmarket", claimed he had glimpsed it enter the harbour at dusk, or shortly after.

Now that was a great deal less precise than the patrons might have wished, for one thing. For another, Petros' credibility had seriously been called into question ever since he had called in the first batch of low-flying UFOs to the police at Mytilini. Nothing short of Petros being kidnapped and held at ransom by a Martian vanguard would redress that situation.

Never mind the three men's doubtful ETA, their presence was generally felt to have something awkward, unpleasant, vaguely oppressive about it. Despite their expensive-looking white suits, they looked a raggle-taggle threesome, as oddly out of place as an owl's cast on a tombstone. Their blue motorboat had been tied up fairly sloppily, to say the least. Its already battered and bruised aluminium hull took another beating, incessantly grinding as it was against the rough cement of the primitive quay in the swell. With next to no luggage, no oilskins and, it would seem, not so much as a single pair of life vests, they had to be city dwellers who, blessed with a handsome dose of ignorance, had ventured out to sea and probably very nearly perished.

They were no Turks, Yannis was absolutely positive. After many decades of rubbing shoulders with the "goat-busters" from the mainland opposite, he would have recognized, albeit hardly understood, Turks by their language. If anything, they looked more like Georgian money collectors, trained to break the legs of bankrupt yacht owners. One of them, their leader or spokesman, as it would seem, even sported a thick moustache vaguely reminiscent of Joseph Stalin.

The men's obscenely tight white pants lamentably unfit for keeping anatomical secrets, soon became the object of openly admiring looks on the part of local females of pretty much all ages and grudging comments on the part of Mithymna males. Talk of swings and roundabouts: the quantity of linen saved on their pants seemed to have gone into the shaping of their flapping oversized jackets. Both trousers and jackets were quickly covered with blots of sweat and dust. Whatever business they had at Mithymna, if any, they could not possibly have planned to stay for any length of time. Yet here they were, trapped, held hostage by the fickle summer gale the locals call meltem, sometimes blowing over in a matter of hours, often enough lasting for weeks on end. It was notorious for driving even locals crazy by its unrelenting strength and wantonness.

"Estragon, Thyme, and Origan," as Yannis would call them, had moved into the grubby bread-and-breakfast on the top floor of the Funky Pelican. Not because they had taken a spontaneous liking to its mildewed walls, ramshackle furniture and saggy beds, but because it was Mithymna's only accommodation available at that time of the year. Petros thought they might be mob hands, but Yannis begged to differ. True, what with their obvious lack of style and savoir-vivre, they would have qualified as mobsters. But your typical wise guy would not readily set foot in a motorboat, no sir. After all that regular ravioli, tortellini and capellini, a wise guy's stomach would be much too doughy for the rough motion of the sea, Yannis' compelling argument went.

On a more jocular note, he then once again treated the patrons to their favourite urban legend of the dead mafioso lying on the coroner's table. As the forensic pathologist opens the victim's skull with his whining oscillation saw and takes out the man's brain, he comes across an engraving saying, "Buy your pizzas at Paolo's". As such, the episode shed precious little light on Estragon's, Thyme's, or Origan's possible behest, but the veterans at the Pelican, who knew every word by heart so that they would anticipate certain passages by mouthing them before Yannis even got there, still appreciated it as if were the very first time. Judging by his uncanny ability to take his public to a joke's climax, Yannis would probably have made a decent stand-up comedian.

Maybe they were traffickers of human beings. More recently, the uninterrupted rush of desperate refugees, illegal migrants and destitute asylum-seekers venturing across the narrow Lesbos strait from the Turkish coast in all sorts of inflated craft had increased yet again. Or perhaps they were just common criminals on the run who had ventured too far out to sea and had been caught out by this sudden burst of a gale? For your average smugglers, they seemed too heavily armed and perhaps a little overdressed. They never did take off their jackets but, every now and again when launching into an argument over cards, they would wave their arms about like a bunch of dancing flamingos flapping their wings. It was on such occasions that the Greeks caught glimpses of the shiny pistol butts in the men's shoulder holsters. In fact, the men had probably bought their jackets oversize for the express purpose of discreetly housing their bulky artillery.

Dimitri and Vangelis, the local sheriff and his deputy, had preferred to put their regular visits to Yannis' kafeneion at the end of their regular evening rounds on hold for the time being. Though they did claim it had nothing to do with the strangers' sudden arrival, the coincidence was striking enough. At the Pelican, their move was met with silent approval. Handguns as packed by the men in white the two cops only knew from American gangster movies and gory TV series. Their own regulation firearms were just about fit for putting down packs of stray dogs getting hungry and aggressive during winter time. Their shells frequently got jammed in the chamber and the magazines had an awkward propensity of dropping on your boots after the first few tentative shots. With guns like that Dimitri and Vangelis were obviously no match for the likes of Estragon, Thyme, and Origan. Hence, as long as the strangers kept the peace and made no trouble, discretion was the better part of valour, as far as those two were concerned.

In his best pidgin English Yannis had tried to break the disconcerting piece of meteorological news to the men in white that the probable duration of the present bout of meltem was unpredictable even for himself. The strangers obviously did not understand Greek, and their own language, in turn, was an incomprehensible mumbo-jumbo to the Greeks. Which is why both sides had to resort to either basic English or sign language as practised by deaf-mutes. Only trouble was that even this wonderfully silent means of communication appeared to have different vernaculars.

The vague nature of Yannis' weather forecasts understandably did little to cheer up the sullen mood of the strangers. They probably felt that the privileged first-hand view of the wind-swept harbour and the boiling sea they enjoyed from their room above the kafeneion added insult to injury. The howling gale, the roaring sea, and the rattling shutters not only functioned as undesirable reminders but, on top of that, kept them from falling asleep at night. The lamps in their room burned until the wee morning hours, at any rate. Nevertheless, they were up before noon, probably in the vain hope of being able to leave again soon.

Other people, finding themselves in the strangers' present situation, might have felt tempted to profit from the time spent waiting by visiting some of the sights the area had to offer – other than the shabby, overcrowded refugee camp further east, that is. But the men in white seemed to foster the same kind of general contempt for their environment as they did for the Greek patrons in the kafeneion. For hours on end, Estragon, Thyme and Origan would ride their rickety wooden chairs like cowboys glued to their blazing saddles. Wiping their brows with grim determination, they would slam their cards on the table like fly swatters, while sweating booze big time.

Even though the strangers picked no fights with the locals, the Greeks felt increasingly unnerved by the frequent quarrels of the three. On one occasion, Estragon was apparently accused by the other two of dealing the cards falsely. On another, Origan would seem to have played out the wrong card at the wrong moment and on yet another, Thyme had forgotten to announce the colour of his game quickly enough. Thus, it went on and on. In their general state of frustration, they simply didn't miss a single opportunity to pick a fight. Estragon, a tall, lean man with scarecrow limbs, who Petros was pleased to nickname "Tiny", was the worst of-fender. Nervously lifting and dropping his shoulders whenever he got excited, he would never accept defeat in good grace. Thyme and Origan, both of average height, the former bald and plump, with a pit-bull face and the latter lean, moustachioed and beady-eyed, had a better grip of themselves. "Curly", as Petros mock-ingly called the bald guy, would take a long time before raising his voice, but when he did eventually, the other two would shut up all the more quickly. "Chucky", Petros' favourite because of his remote likeness with the child-demon of the horror-movie, was the calmest of the three. Petros wagered that butter wouldn't melt in that man's mouth, but dared not put him to the test either.

Their language was a mystery. Not even Kostas, who had seen many parts of the globe during his almost life-long career as a truck driver for many different hauliers had any idea in what bi-zarre lingo these strangers conferred. In his usual convivial man-ner, Kostas had addressed them first in English, then in a sort of French, and had finally even ventured his hand at some German, ignoring the irregularity of some of its more complicated verbs. All he had got for his considerable pains, though, were dark-ish looks and silent shaking of heads. If there is truth in Oscar Wilde's saying that the despised do well to look despising, the palikaria of the Funky Pelican were doing the right thing ignor-ing the strangers as much as they felt ignored by them. If they insisted on being left alone, that, too, could be arranged.

Tourists might have objected to the strange manners and possessive attitudes of Estragon, Thyme, and Origan, but this was a little too early in the season for tourists to find their way to this windward side of the island. Besides, frequent media reports on the chaotic situation of Arab and African refugees in quickly hammered together Lesbos camps had given the island a bad karma, so that sun-seekers and holiday-makers from abroad were likely to be looking for alternative destinations this year.

On the morning of the third day the meltem stopped almost as abruptly as it had started. Once the wind had died down, it took only minutes for the boiling sea to follow suit. As they came blustering down the staircase, the strangers, complete with large Gucci shades, dark three-day stubble, sweat-soaked shirts and creased jackets, seemed bursting with renewed energy. Small, bald headed Thyme pulled out a roll of ruffled green presidents and held it under Yannis' nose. The Greek, using only his thumb and index finger as if asked to collect a turd, daintily picked three ten-dollar bills and ironed them out on the table, still damp from being wiped down with a wet cloth only minutes before. When Yannis saw that Thyme did not bother to even look at the bills, his disappointed face showed how much he regretted not having charged more.

The three men stepped out into the street. To all appearances, they were really in a hurry to shake the Mithymna dust off their Italian designer shoes. When they arrived at the harbour, Tiny went about pouring fuel from the several jerry-cans they had brought with them into the tank of the nameless, nondescript blue-hulled boat. Since he did not take the trouble of using a funnel, and did not have a particularly steady hand either, it did not last long for an overflow of fuel to trickle down the side of the hull and drip into the harbour water. Immediately, an oil film, iridescent with all the colours of the rainbow, began spreading at great speed. Chucky, impatiently waiting for his tall companion to finish the refuelling operation, eventually turned the ignition key before Tiny had even had the time to screw the lid back on the tank. The engine did not start right away, a fact which came as no great surprise to the Greek fishermen standing by. The spark plugs were probably moist with fuel. Petros suspected the starter battery, but since the engine had performed a few slow turns before going back into a coma, the battery was acquitted by common consensus.

After a short break, Tiny tried again. A few reluctant coughs and that was it, as though the engine was not quite ready to run but, at the same time, was loathe to disappoint the onlookers whose numbers had almost imperceptibly increased. Then it apparently had second thoughts and burst into sudden life with a series of shotgun-like backfires and a solid cloud of blue smoke. The three strangers slipped their mooring lines, performed an elegant U-turn around the mole-head, pushed the gas-lever down and roared off in a northerly direction, skipping over the residual swell like a flat pebble over the smooth surface of a lake. At each bound, the men's wide open jackets flapped joyously in the air.

The villagers made three miniature signs of the cross in quick succession and stared after their bizarre visitors' speeding craft. Before long however, their interest in the presumed destination of the trio gave way to relief about their departure.

A slightly more patient observer might have concluded that the strangers were heading for the Turkish coast, whence they prob-ably had come in the first place. Their little open boat with its limited fuel reserve would hardly take them much further, any-way. Which was probably just as well, since they seemed not to possess so much as an inkling of navigation.

"At least they are lucky as far as weather conditions go," Pet-ros said on the way back to the kafeneion. Whatever destination lay at the end of their little odyssey, the sea was not likely to cause them any trouble today. In normal times, they would have had to beware of the coastguard patrols, yet the times were anything but normal. The rising number of refugee craft sinking or running aground were giving the coastguard ships on the Eastern side of Lesbos enough of a headache as it was. After a series of hefty budgetary cuts, the coastguard had neither the necessary staff nor the financial means at its disposal to do more than perform as many rescue operations as they could handle. Meanwhile, for boats passing west of Lesbos, all was plain sailing. In the case of the three men in white, this state of affairs may actually have been for the better of all parties concerned, since, who knows, had they been intercepted by an eager patrol, Estragon, Thyme, and Origan might have felt sufficiently unnerved by three days of useless waiting to let the coastguard guys have a taste of their fine artillery.

3. Dead Man's Hand

Hardly has the blue motorboat reached the north-western cape of the island and is effectively hidden from the sight of the Mithymny villagers, it veers sharply to port and heads for the open sea. For an hour or so it stays on its westerly course until, even for someone scanning the sea from one of the peaks of the Lesbos coast, it has effectively dropped beneath the horizon. Apparently, the men in white do not take chances and want to make absolutely sure no-one can watch them from the shore. Only when that is ascertained beyond reasonable doubt do they steer southeast. After a while, the hazy silhouette of a low-lying saddle-shaped rocky islet with a helmet-like hump ever so gradually emerges from the haze.

A light breeze from the north and the south-setting current in this part of the Aegean combine forces with the boat's engine to drive the craft on at a brisk pace. Once alongside the saddle, the men in white deaden the boat's speed and slowly circle the islet. Either they are naturally distrustful or else they are not quite familiar with the islet's miniature topography and need to look for a suitable landing spot. Finally, they discover a gap in the belt of barely visible cliffs. They allow the engine to peter off and run the boat's keel onto the sands of this little speck of beach. With that eerie crunching sound feared by every sailor's ear, the craft comes to a jerky halt.

Curly, who has placed himself at the bows with the noose of a rope in his hand, underestimates the force of the impact and almost topples over headlong. Then, his balance restored with some difficulty, he hops over the railing, yet makes his second misjudgement of the day and lands with both feet ankle-deep in the creamy algae scum and sticky bladderwrack. Swearing blasphemously, he blames his two mates for ruining his expensive Italian designer shoes. Following the instructions of his grinning mate at the helm, the bald man ties the loose end of his rope round the nearest boulder in a rather perfunctory way.

He asks his chums to throw him his jacket, takes off his shoes and socks and clumsily trudges through the wet sand towards the cave, whose access is clearly visible now that the sun has cleared the hump on his way west. Meanwhile, the two men in the boat keep a look-out for anyone stupid enough to show up in the most unfortunate place at what would turn out to be the worst, and last, moment of his life.

Curly has just about reached the mouth of the cave when the pile of drug bricks wrapped in plastic foil comes into his sight. He hesitates, realizing that there is neither a tarpaulin nor a camouflage net. Whoever dumped those packages on this uninhabited islet would not have left the place without protecting the pile, albeit sloppily, from wind and weather. Nor would they have cast off again without hiding it from the looks of fishermen, a race of people passing by the oddest of places in the pursuit of their prey such as the popular red snapper or the rock-bound Aegean lobster. To pile up the packages on the sand without placing them on a wooden palette or at least shoving a few wooden boards underneath constitutes a further breach of precautionary diligence uncharacteristic of experienced smugglers and drug-traffickers.

The gale had raged for several days alright, but a tarpaulin fixed with a rope doesn't just grow wings or evaporate into thin air. Something untoward seems to be going down here. Curly whistles through his teeth as if summoning a dog. Turning his head over his shoulder to face the boat, he pulls out his shiny gun from the shoulder holster. With a few rapid movements he checks the magazine, chambers a round and releases the safety catch. His two mates in the boat, whose line of vision to the cave is blocked by the bald man immediately do likewise. The metallic sound of the pistol slides gliding back and forth still lingers in the air as, from somewhere near the top of the hump, a huge bird of prey pounces, claws first, onto the man underneath with a cry that makes his blood curl. "Stalin" remains paralyzed by shock just long enough for the harpy to ram her knife into his neck upon landing. Thus, the moment her feet touch the ground, her first victim is already dead and done with.

The two others have only fractions of a second to overcome their utter amazement. The frightening figure in her flapping poncho wings seizes the slumping "Stalin" with her left arm and aims his gun with her right hand at his two mates. While on her knees, she holds the corpse in front of her as a human shield and pulls his cold trigger finger. Six shots resound in quick succession. Two bullets hit "Stalin's" corpse, the remaining four home in on the men on the boat. Tiny falls over board backwards and smashes into the shallow water which immediately turns red with blood. Chucky manages to fire two pointless shots in the air and collapses over the steering wheel.

Pulling her knife out of his neck, the woman with the poncho pushes "Stalin's" corpse aside like a discarded crash-test dummy. She searches his clothing and grabs the short-barrelled Smith & Wesson back-up she can feel hidden in his ankle holster. She empties his pockets but finds no papers nor ID that might give clues about "Stalin's" origins or nationality.

Stepping into the boat, she unceremoniously pushes Chucky overboard and greedily gulps down the contents of two plastic water bottles stuck under the helmsman's seat. A cool box in the stern holds some stale sandwiches and a plastic bag with half-mildewed oranges. She turns the box upside down and hastily bolts down whatever edibles fall out on the floor. Then she sits down in the sand, belches and slips out of her poncho. Naked, she offers an even more horrific sight, if anything. Her thighs, arms and chest are covered with bad bruises that have formed clods of dried blood. Her left biceps must have been grazed by a bullet during the short skirmish with the men in white. On all fours, she crawls to the bald corpse, tears his blood-stained shirt to strips and, with loud moans, ties them round her fresh wound.

For a little while longer she sits in the sand as if mesmerized by the unreal decor. Somewhere out at sea the low humming sound of a distant boat's diesel engine cuts through the excited chatter of the gulls circling with anticipation. The woman shudders out of her trance. On the rocky islet, she will not remain undiscovered for long, that's for sure. Not now that the gale has passed. Were she to be found in the company of three massacred men and a large quantity of dope, however, it would take a lot of time-consuming explanations for her to get away scot free.

Seizing him by the collar, she pulls Tiny's corpse out of the water, turns him on his back and drops him on the sand. Once she has rifled through his clothes she undresses the man and spreads his pants, shirt and jacket, all nailed to the sand with knives, to dry in the sun. "Chucky" gets much the same treatment but is at least allowed to keep his clothes on. It's obvious that none of the three could have proved their identity to either police or coastguard, which leaves but one conclusion. Wherever they came from and were headed to, the three gentlemen in white never intended to be taken by the law alive. At least that part of their plans could be said to have come out right.

Eventually, the woman drags the corpses over the sand into the cave and places them with their backs to the wall right at the entrance. Turns out Tiny got two in the chest whereas Chucky displays some two reddish-black holes where his beady eyes used to be. The sea-gulls, always going for the eyeballs first, have a disappointment coming. A black spot of burnt sand and pieces of charcoal are all that is left of the pallet and proof of the fact that, at some stage or other during her enforced stay on the islet, the marooned woman must have succeeded in lighting a camp fire of sorts.

In Tiny's jacket pocket she finds a deck of cards which she now re-arranges with the "faster-than-your-eyes" shuffle of an inveterate casino hand. To the hummed sound of Kenny Roger's

Gambler the woman deals everyone his hand of the day. Then she bows backwards out of the cave and straightens herself to her full height. "Gentlemen, the name of the game is seven-card stud," she instructs the three corpses, "and don't even think of pulling any fast ones unless you want me to come back to punish you, which I'm pretty sure you don't." Then she leaves the three to their fate and turns to the pile of drugs.

Brick upon brick she throws into her spread-out poncho and pulls the lot across the bloody sand down to the water's edge. Three times she repeats the process, until all the packages are stowed away in the boat and covered by the tarpaulin no longer standing in as a poncho. All guns and knives she hides in the cool box. Tiny's shirt, trousers and jacket have sufficiently dried so she puts them on. "Pret-a-porter sucks," she murmurs, as she tries to roll up the sleeves of the jacket and the legs of the pants, so as not to look too much of a scarecrow on shore leave. The improvised bandage on her upper arm has come loose and blood colours the jacket's sleeve.

The woman takes a last long look around, very much like an artist critically mustering her finished work before signing it with a flourish and releasing it for auction. When she turns the ignition key, the engine, still warm from the past effort, jumps to life immediately. The woman taps on the electronic fuel-gauge to her right a few times and gives a satisfied nod as the indicator ever so slowly moves in the direction of "half".

The woman in white gets out and is just about to throw off the noose of the boat's rope when she suddenly stops. Once again, she crawls into the cave and fiddles with the poker cards. At last she throws the three corpses a farewell kiss, frees the rope and slowly pushes the boat away from the beach. As it gets into the deeper water and is being seized by the first gentle waves, the woman just about manages to hop aboard before it drifts off irretrievably.

In reverse she manoeuvres the motorboat away from the cliffs until there is room enough to turn and go full ahead. A school of dolphins with high expectations welcome the boat as though it were an acquaintance of old and go through the rigmarole of jumps and zig-zag swerves. When no reward is forthcoming, the disillusioned animals move on, crackling and whistling with frustration. Soon the boat is but a darkish blot dancing on the shiny blade of the Aegean.

SECOND CHAPTER

1. The Heiress

"...and since you obviously lack your father's experience, you might wish to profit from the competent support of an excellent manager such as Peter Hansen, at least in the short and medium term, eh, medium term. Peter Hansen, I hasten to add, enjoys the unqualified approval of both our business partners, represented here by their respective attorneys. Thank you for joining us, Gentlemen. On top of this, I dare say the man has done a brilliant job whenever standing in for Robert, eh, for your father, as you well know. May I take it then that, in view of his outstanding track record, he will be welcomed here by you too? Eh, Laura? Laura, are you alright?"

Dr Sanders, the company's chief legal representative of long standing, contracted his nimble eyebrows over his rimless progressive-lens glasses and interrupted his routine presentation with a touch of irritated bewilderment. As he kept staring at his female opposite with a slight frown, an awkward silence fell across the small conference room. Finally, Dr Sanders resorted to clearing his throat somewhat ostentatiously.

Laura Forster blushed like a school-girl caught secretly exchanging WhatsApp messages with a friend by her notoriously distrustful maths teacher. Progressively sedated by Dr Sanders' sonorous voice, she had allowed herself to sink into a mild stupor and now straightened herself in her chair with a sudden strong jerk that caused its upholstered back to crackle like a dry branch under the foot of a clumsy redskin. She nervously tore at a notoriously unruly strand of her thick darkish hair that was tightly brushed back and braided to a sumptuous bird's nest of a bun at the back of her head. As she did so, the tiny scar over her left eyebrow, hardly visible until now, seemed to turn pink.

"I'm sorry, what was that? I mean, yes, certainly, definitely. You will have to excuse my brief spell of absent-mindedness, I just don't sleep well at all these days, you see." The stern baritone of the firm's legal eagle instantly transformed itself into a velvety crooning contralto.

"But of course we sympathize with you, Laura. I am sure, we are all of us most understanding, eh, understanding. Even though I suspect some of us would prefer your catching up on your sleep some other time, once the dust has settled again, if I may say so."

Obviously, Dr Sanders was the kind of lawyer used to having his audience, or jury, riveted. On behalf of the dimmer section of the parties involved, he had acquired the habit of repeating certain key elements of his rhetoric so as to make them stick. Laura had never quite got used to Dr Sanders' cherished idiosyncrasies, rhetorical or otherwise. She did not mind his vaguely schizophrenic manner of calling everybody by their first name, if he knew it, yet at the same time treating them on family name terms, as it were. No, what really got to her was his affected use of foreign languages, preferably French rhetorical dainties which, as a rule, did nothing to elucidate the gist of his train of thought but rather were picked to gloss over the sheer banality of many of his assertions. You did not have to be a fanatic linguistic purist to frown on such linguistic snobbery.

Right at the start of this important meeting, devoted to the execution of the entrepreneurial legacy of Robert, Laura Forster's suddenly deceased father, Dr Sanders had stressed that he would take a dim view at both lack of focus and time-consuming loquacity. Time was money, he repeated several times, lest someone forgot. Strictly speaking, as chief legal representative, he had no official leading function in the running of the company's daily business and even lacked procuration, as Laura had recently discovered with some surprise. Yet, during the formative years of the forwarding agency founded by Robert a generation or so ago,, he had managed to capture and occupy vital strategic corporate high ground. And, due to his extensive first-hand knowledge of, and insight into, both the company's official records and its less well documented underhand dealings, he had time and time again stood his ground against the repeated onslaught of promising aspirants to his throne.

"Yes, as I said, all of us here can relate to what you must be feeling so shortly after this cruel loss, which, need I remind you, is ours as well. That said, I suggest we take a short break at this juncture. Figuratively speaking, we are not on the run, are we now?"

He was the only one to smile at his pathetic little quip. Granting his nimble eyebrows a rest, he went for the intercom button. Pushing it was the sign for his secretary residing in an adjacent room to have coffees served by the young blond intern who was everybody's darling these days. The attorney got up and opened one of the high, narrow windows a crack. Though situated on the fifth floor, the conference room was immediately invaded by the humming, screeching, and hooting orchestra of the city traffic. From somewhere far off, a solemn church bell started ringing. Four light chimes were followed by eleven darker ones. Laura felt goose-pimples forming on her skin and blamed the wet cold of this Hamburg April day.

"We're not on the run," she murmured to herself. "Or are we?" She wasn't quite so sure about that. After having a virtual ton of bricks falling on her so recently, the idea of a strategic retreat had a lot going for it. A retreat where to? She lifted her head from the heap of files piling up next to her laptop and looked out of the window as if the answer was to be expected from over there. All morning, surprise bursts of pale sunlight had fought a losing battle against the persistent fall of vicious icy rain. This year's foul April weather appeared determined to confirm its dubious reputation.

Laura picked up her black Prada jacket from the adjacent chair. Sven Larsen, the rather good-looking company's fiscal expert and Robert Forster's private investment wizard, helped her to drape the jacket round her shoulders. On other occasions, Laura would have minded neither Sven's matey smile nor his tender touch on her shoulders. Under present circumstances, however, both his facial expression and his gesture were out of place since they suggested an affective intimacy that did not really exist - not as far as Laura was concerned.

For the length of the ninety minutes that the conference had lasted so far, Laura had found it very hard to stay on the ball. She would never confess to it, but in her heart of hearts she felt blatantly overwhelmed by events. Which was a novel experience for her, who used to be feared in many circles as a merciless control freak. True, her expensive education, with economic and entrepreneurial studies and internships both at home, in England and in the US, had been aimed at preparing her for precisely this contingency of taking over the management of her father's company at some far-away point in the future. But at the moment this concept proved both a lot less remote and far less abstract than she had always assumed, Laura found herself shying away from the crushing weight of responsibility like some female version of Atlas asking to be excused because of a suspected acute hernia. Seriously, how is anyone to prepare for something they hope with all their might is never going to happen?

She had been looking forward to being shown the ropes of the trade gradually, one by one, and had had every reason to, because with all the hindsight in the world, no-one could have even vaguely suspected her father's sudden fatal heart attack. Least of all Laura, who was closest to him. There had never been any one of the usual harbingers of coronary doom such as ventricular fibrillations, palpitations, frequent bursts of cold sweat or repeated chest ache, not one. On the contrary, after two decades of sustained effort and supreme personal sacrifice on behalf of the firm he had built up from scratch, her father had, more recently, seized every opportunity to take time out and absent himself from business. For three or four weeks in a row, he would absent himself, "bugger off", as he called it, and maintain his one and only cherished hobby, yachting.

His favourite sailing grounds were the West Indies, he said. Over the years, he must have gained the notoriety of a pink elephant over there, Laura had often thought. She could, of course, have asked him to take her with him on his sprees now and again. Yet, to begin with, Laura was not particularly fond of sailing, to put it mildly. On top of that, she had understood at an early age that a merry widower still harbouring a host of libidinous appetites such as Robert was likely to find ways and means of relief and relaxation in the Caribbean which he would not readily want to impart, not even to his daughter. Particularly not to his daughter.

Whenever he returned from one of his ,wet safaris', as he called them with a grin frequently bordering on the lascivious, he would appear fully recovered, free of stress symptoms of any kind and with a deep-fried tan to boot. Whatever nagging headaches he might have taken with him to the other side of the ocean, he must have left on the Caribbean beaches like so many cracked or wilting coconuts.

And then this proverbial bolt out of the blue. After attending a routine morning conference, he had stepped down from the old-fashioned paternoster he had always obstinately refused to get replaced by some modern contraption, and had collapsed dead or dying on one of the Persian cleaning ladies' trolleys. Just like that, in a matter of seconds. No famous last words, on whose deeper meaning Laura could have mused for months and years to come. The sad truth was that, on this unspectacular April Wednesday, the Grim Reaper had put on his glasses, checked in his black book and ticked off the name of a certain Robert Forster, Esquire. Curtains. Neither his moderate drinking record nor his restrained though admittedly gourmet eating habits had bought Robert a ticket for longevity. As for smoking, he had already given that up shortly after the even more untimely death of Laura's mother Frederike, some twenty years ago.

"You can't look inside a man," had been the quizzical comment of the doctor from the hastily summoned LC ambulance once it had become obvious that any further attempts at resuscitation would be in vain. "You can't look inside a man." What exactly the nervously blinking medicine man had meant by that would remain his secret. Presumably a consecrated formula of embarrassed resignation he resorted to whenever he had to offer a quantum of solace to the inconsolable.

Of course, Laura fully understood that a going concern such as ROLA Logistics Inc. was in dire need of a refurbished management structure after such a brutal cut. T's had to be crossed and i's to be dotted as fast as possible. The logistics business was a proper shark pool, Robert had always insisted. Anyone caught hesitating, flapping, flailing or fidgeting, was instantly devoured. A destabilizing event such as the death of a company's figurehead was a gilt-edged occasion for predators circling with intent. Some competitors were financially well enough equipped and only too eager to swallow firmly established ROLA, thus permanently ridding themselves of a loathsome rival on both the domestic and international front.

All of this stood to reason alright. But so shortly after the funeral, which, due to Robert's peculiar status of a lonely child without surviving next of kin of any kind other than his daughter, of course, Laura had had to organize practically single-handedly, she felt incapable of such strategic considerations. The death of Laura's dearly beloved mother had turned her mourning husband and daughter into a sworn conspiracy of two against the rest of the world. Irrespective of the thousands of miles which often enough separated them from one another, Robert and Laura had kept in touch almost daily via the modern means of communication, social media and the like.

Days or even weeks spent together in their villa in Blankenese were few and far between and hence, all the more cherished by both of them. Laura was painfully aware of the fact that her father looked upon her as a substitute for Frederike in more ways than one. It flattered and, at the same time, frightened her. Frequently, she had asked him whether he hadn't half a mind to re-marry, making it perfectly clear by the same token that he would certainly not have to fear any resistance or mental reserve against whoever he might happen choose as his second wife or permanent companion. A promise which, on reflection, she hadn't been quite sure she would be able to keep. But that was beside the point and, anyway, the idea had never seemed to catch on with him. If any promising female comets had crossed his lonesome orbit more recently, Robert had not let any hints drop. This she took as an expression of his deep respect for Laura's staunch sentimental attachment to her mother.

There was no escaping the conclusion then that, all said and done, Robert Forster preferred to remain his cagey, reserved Northern German self, rebutting any attempts at dissecting his present state of mind or, perish the thought, at discussing his pre-nuptial past that seemed to consist of one whooper of a black hole. If Robert Forster's mask were to drop one day and reveal the face of the bionic third-generation Martian that he really was, it would hardly come as big surprise to anyone at the company. His local Freemasons' lodge might want to disown him in a hurry whilst some ladies of loose morals from this or that more discrete Hamburg erotic speakeasy would claim they had always known but alas, had never been asked.

Meanwhile, Laura acted the part of his consultant in matters of dressing, coiffing, styling, eating and drinking and occasionally even in helping to clinch such business transactions whose conse-quences she could trust herself to grasp. Leaving aside for a mo-ment Robert's enigmatic past, there was practically no subject un-der the sun the two of them would have considered taboo in their discussions. Most certainly not Laura's first tumultuous sexual experiences and early experiments with cannabis and all sorts of synthetic leisure drugs. If the former were an inexhaustible source of mirth, the latter could provoke the odd row. When it came to drugs, Robert had an uncanny way of slipping into the role of a stern police officer or irreconcilable drug-enforcement agent.

"Milk, sugar?" The blond intern had started serving coffees. Laura took hers black, as her father used to. Right now, she would not have sneezed at a wee dram of French brandy or Scotch whisky either, but dared not stand out as a sore thumb knocking it back at this early hour. Whoever was to become the future CEO of ROLA plc, it had better not be somebody with the reputation, albeit un-warranted, of a seasoned alcoholic. Despite its self-awarded repu-tation of a gateway to the world at large, rumours spread as fast as they would in Hicksville, Arizona. Basically, Laura hated the would-be ,free and Hanseatic' city with its wet cold, humid heat, eternally rainy westerlies, annihilating floods and its hypocritical political caste just as much as she suspected her father had done.

"Why the blazes don't you sell up the whole lot so we can move to Florida, or to the Caribbean, some place with palm trees, a splendid beach and no cell phones, tablets, PC's, CEO's or DJ's?" Laura had more than once tried to tease him. "Surely, you must have made enough money by now to last you for the rest of your natural life. Why this sentimental loyalty to the capital of stiff shirts and dead souls?"

Even though her father had agreed in principle, something about the firm and the city must have been stronger than himself. Who knows, despite his occasional walks on the wild side, he may have needed the structuring element of daily routine business. Anyway, to imagine a Robert Forster in lacerated jeans, plaid cotton shirt, flappy Stetson and shiny cowboy boots sitting on a speeding airboat chasing alligators in the snake-infested swamps between Micanopy and Lake Okeechobee would require a bit more imagination than Laura could muster.

If there was one thing he hated, it was half-finished business and loose ends. He never rushed to conclusions, but he didn't waste precious time unnecessarily either. Whenever he saw a chance to beat a competitor to the post, he would do so without much hesitation, move in for the kill, figuratively speaking. How else could he have succeeded in multiplying his starting capital at such an amazing pace, almost miraculously turning a fledgeling forwarding company into the logistics ,empire' he now bequeathed to Laura, albeit somewhat earlier than planned.

"Very well, ehm, outstanding. Now, how about carrying on? I'm sure we all have other business to attend to."

As long as Laura could remember, Dr Sanders had been her father's right hand and legal oracle. The man counted himself among Hamburg's ,leading one hundred' and derived not a little pride from the fact. Justifiably so, since he had not earned this privilege on the tennis courts and golf greens alone, as might be said of some of his colleagues, but by putting in a lot of round the clock labour. Robert had not embarked on many private or business ventures without asking the man's opinion first. Had a woman appeared on the marital horizon, Robert would presumably have presented her to Dr Sanders first, requesting a preliminary expertise.

Curiously enough, however, Robert did not seem to trust his chief counsel any further than he could have thrown him. How her father managed to straddle this paradox like the two wings of an open bridge without falling into the water, Laura could not begin to guess. But his admonitions to follow his example once she "wedged her ass" into the driver's seat had fallen on fertile soil. The legal eagle was no stranger to anything human, least of all to man's unflinching pursuit of profit, one of two instincts you could always count on blindly. When it came to fiscal legislation with its deliberate loopholes or inadvertent incoherencies, he had long acquired pundit status. Like an insatiable caterpillar, he would literally guzzle his way through every bit of juicy fiscal foliage and sometimes exude solutions that had not even found their problem yet.

"There comes a point at which the Dr Sanders' of this world will feel they can walk on water," Robert had told her. "It is at that juncture that you want to split. Economic organizations," he would get into his argumentative stride at this point, "do not fundamentally differ from those of criminal structures, not when it comes to their ways and means: intimidation, exhortation, blackmail, even assassination, you name it. Why should they, indeed, seeing that they share the basic objective of their respective activities, maximizing profit by minimising, preferably eliminating, competition?

In this general context, personal betrayal is commonplace. Both in the world of business and crime - and I'm deliberately leaving out politics at this stage - it's a favourite device, perversely so, but there you are. You want to finish someone off, better approach him with a smile and stab him in the back. It will infallibly be your best friend, or most intimate counsellor, in other words, the person you would least suspect who will approach you with malice aforethought. In my case, I suspect, the knife in my back would have Dr Sanders' fingerprints all over its handle. That's why I profit from the man's skills and knowledge to my advantage but never turn my back on him for long."

"The so-called Brutus syndrome, is it?"

Robert had burst into one of his rare hearty laughs. "I guess so. Except here, we're talking the Doctor Brutus syndrome, to give the beast its correct title."

Against that background, Laura had known the attorney from her childhood days. It was no coincidence she belonged to the privileged group of people authorized to call him by his first name, at least in private settings. In case of open conflict on corporate matters, she would be no match for him as yet, given his extensive insider knowledge of the company's sometimes questionable business methods. On the other hand, she could not possibly be seen simply to submit to his present supremacy. Not if she wanted to retain enough latitude for manoeuvre in the company and be respected by her future staff.

Presumably, he thought of her as generally weak and malleable, especially now, in her destabilising predicament. A man of his mental complexion would have no moral qualms using that to his own advantage. Maybe he was already paving the way for a hostile takeover by one or another of their competitors, and wanted to install the innocuous Mr Hansen, not so much as managerial tutor for her, but as a reliable source of information for him, a mole that would keep him abreast of her plans at all times.

Be that as it may, what Laura needed now was a respite. Time for reflection and planning, time to prepare her one and only shot. She had to put some mileage between herself and the company without losing face by making it look like she was scampering off the battlefield at the first resounding echoes of enemy bugles. A plausible reason would help. "Dr Sanders, please listen to me." Laura had to get on top of this resumed conversation quickly before the attorney, who was just closing the window, had time to get his show back on track.

"I am extremely grateful for what you are trying to accomplish here, for the company and myself, I really do, believe me. Also, I could not think of anyone better suited for the job than Mr Hansen. My father used to speak of him in terms of highest praise." Whenever Laura had finally identified and locked on to her target, she was perfectly capable of lying, stealing, or borrowing without blushing.

"And I am perfectly aware of the urgency of the matter, I really am. Hence, it is with some trepidation I plead my case. Thing is, I need breathing space, coming up for air, know what I mean? In my present state of mind, I would not trust myself with any far-reaching decisions, anyway. Hence, my usefulness would be marginal at best. No, I feel I must ask for your help and understanding, once again."

With a nervous gesture, Laura tried to fix her stubborn mesh of hair behind her right ear and took a sip of water. She was waiting for someone or other to contradict, protest energetically to try and change her mind. Then she understood. They had taken this contingency into account, of course, and had prepared their moves accordingly. The attorney would pull out his plan B right away for the others "reluctantly" to agree. Laura felt that what was left of the badly mauled Light Brigade had to charge again, immediately, or all would be lost.

"Things are moving a little too fast for me here. My father has hardly been under the ground for more than a week and I think I'm entitled to ask you to respect that. I am convinced you're all motivated by the best of intentions. But then, I need not tell you what the way to hell is paved with."

This was an unauthorized dip into Dr Sanders' treasure chest of trite sayings and futile commonplaces and would not be lost on him if only for that matter.

"How do you expect me to get ahead of things so quickly without practice, without experience, without sufficient knowledge of how the company runs its affairs? Mr Hansen's competence notwithstanding, but when push comes to shove, the decisions will all be mine and so will the blame. For me, it's a you win or I lose kind of situation."

The attorney's nimble weasels started moving about frantically again. "Now, take off your glasses," Laura thought. And, sure enough, that's what he did. Laura could read him like an open book. Translated into plain English, the glasses gesture meant

something like, yes, I am all ears, but don't for a moment flatter
yourself into thinking you can surprise or convince me.
"I would slow down the corporate train unnecessarily. No, really,
I think the best solution would be for Mr Hansen to be in charge
temporarily, with a contract of limited duration, that is. Always
assuming of course that he would be game."

Laura leaned back in the chair with an air of ill-concealed triumph. This had been a smart move for a rank corporate recruit
such as herself, she found. No competent, self-respecting manager would consent to work under such precarious terms. So, if
Hansen agreed, it would be one more piece of evidence that there
was more at stake here than the Doc had let on, so far.

"Hm, not an ideal solution, I have to say," the Doc fretted, "not
by a long chalk. I can try and convince him, of course, but I suspect it won't be easy."

She secretly felt this round would be hers on points. She was
no stranger to the fact that Dr Sanders was given to taking such
daring counter-proposals as a slight, if not a downright insult.
Laura didn't care. Her poisoned arrow had homed in on his
bared flank. But the attorney would not be where he was, were
he in the habit of fostering petty resentment. This, then, was not
a moment for triumph but one for compromise. So what. Another hour gone, and an unprejudiced observer would have come
away with the impression that Laura's proposal had really been
Dr Sanders' brainchild all along.

Laura sighed with relief. She had stood her ground, got her
respite and, to all intents and purposes, had acted in both her
father's and her own interest.

Even the free and Hanseatic rain stopped pelting down momentarily to allow for celebrations. The measly April sun had managed to drill a few pale rays through the black and violet clouds
for longer than just a few symbolic moments. One bundle of rays
came to rest on the tiny red blossoms at the top twig of the crown
of thorns which had been banned to the remote corner of the office
by the cleaning lady. It seemed to stretch its thorny arms with the
two drops of blood in a vain gesture of heart-rending protest.

This was as far as they would get for the time being. Dr Sanders wound up the meeting in his elegantly polite manner. Everybody went back to their offices. Everybody, that is, except Laura and the fiscal counsellor. The blond poison of an intern collected the empty coffee cups and opened the window. Sven Larsen waited patiently for everyone to disappear single file with their laptops and briefcases. Then he squatted rather than sat down on the table, drove his fingers through his greasy hair and gave a sigh.

"Come on, now, is that all you have to say? How was I?" Laura asked him. Of course, she knew that from the day of his recruitment, Sven Larsen had developed more than just a crush on her. Discounting a few visits to the opera, two or three dinners and accidental encounters at parties, nothing much had come of it, so far. This was at least partially due to the fact that in flagrant breach of the company's time-honoured procedures, Larsen had been "short-circuited" by Robert himself.

He should have known better. A woman of Laura's IQ was not to be fooled that easily. At an early stage, she had resigned herself to the necessity of lowering her standards concerning men somewhat, lest she ended up a spinster. But that didn't mean she was ready to acquiesce to match making quite yet.

On top of that, Larsen had the distressing habit of cracking his knuckles whenever he got impatient and he got impatient quite frequently. To compound his ruinous karma, he was fond of U2 music. At a pinch, Laura might have put up with the latter, but a husband who nervously cracked his knuckles on all sorts of occasions including the most intimate ones would be unbearable. Which was not sufficient reason to discourage him altogether. Laura never rushed to conclusions and loved to keep her options open as long as humanly possible. Besides, in the course of the two years he had been on ROLA's payroll, Larsen had proved a competent, sociable and, above all, discreet operator whose services as a financial advisor might come in handy for Laura one fine day. Today, for instance.

"Excellent, eh, outstanding! I knew you have the steely resolve of a Lady Macbeth. What I didn't know was you could be as diplomatic as all that while turning the dagger in his wound with such unconcealed relish. But you must be aware of Messrs Sanders and Hyde having an elephantine memory, especially when it comes to rare defeats and humiliating slights. All I'm saying is, as from this moment, look over your shoulder every now and then!"

"I thought watching my back was more in keeping with your role," Laura replied and gave him what she took for her most seductive smile. Then, she pulled a file marked ‚Private' out of the pile. Larsen understood that she was in the working mode. He jumped off the table, opened his laptop and filled the minutes of waiting with a few cracks of his knuckles. "Okay, let's go to it, shall we. The sooner we're done, the better."

He may not have been in the mood for running up and down endless columns of figures, but he had learned not to allow his personal feelings come in the way of his career prospects. Hence, during the ensuing half-hour, he juggled with the numerous items of his late master's belongings. He presented Laura the lot wrapped in suggestions for mind-boggling amortization ploys, promising investment options and excruciatingly complicated cascade participations, all levelled at preventing internal revenue from taking the lion's share of the late Robert's, and now Laura's, sizeable fortune.

At some stage, the entire office furniture started turning like a merry-go-round in front of Laura's eyes. Larsen realized his nervously twitching and fidgeting client was getting dead tired and probably out of her depth with all those figures, notions, and options. He interrupted his presentation.

"You know something, Laura. Why don't I get us a little champagne to grease those synapses. Not the company stuff proffered to unsuspecting visitors, mind, but a bottle from Dr Sanders' private stash. His secretary stumbled across it only recently and told me in a moment of, shall we say, blissful abandon. I think we owe this much to ourselves," he said, imitating the well-known Jane Fonda TV commercial to such ridiculous perfection that Laura had to guffaw again.

He vanished and re-appeared just moments later with the bottle in hand. Obviously, he had foreseen this moment and prepared his devious move. He opened the bottle and filled Laura's glass. Then, the two of them drank a toast in a relaxed mood a little out of keeping with the sad occasion.

"I would never have thought fiscal advisers had that kind of humour," Laura smiled and took a sip of the golden effervescent liquid.

"Well, strictly speaking, I am presently wearing the hat of your financial counsellor. Apart from that, you are doing my profession an injustice. Considering all we get from our clients, day in, day out - present company excluded, of course - it's a miracle we ever stop laughing, actually. But, on a more serious note, there are a few pro-memoriam items left we should quickly run through, come what may, if that's okay with you."
He changed the USB stick on his laptop and opened the programme entitled ‚Robert's cornucopia'. "To wit: the leased-out farm, the summer house in Breege, the custom-built Porsche Carrera, the Yellow Dancer and the family jewellery, the largest part of which has already been in your possession ever since your mother's death."

As always, the mention of her mother alarmed and hurt Laura. Frederike had caught cancer of the breast, refused to undergo chemotherapy and died when Laura had just reached thirteen years of age. Laura had loved and idolized this proud woman, so full of confidence and natural self-control, with all her heart. In her turbulent puberty, Laura would have profited from her advice particularly much and, for years on end, had not been able to overcome her loss. As for the farm, this was but a small rundown croft of sorts handed down by Frederike's parents. It represented little financial value but, during her childhood, Laura had turned it into Pippi Longstocking's Villa Villekulla for the length of her summer holidays and would have liked to keep it.

"Leased out, to who?" Laura asked with some palpitation.

"Yes, well, your father thought that there was no need for it to stand vacant. Anyway, the tenant has been duly notified that we may have to discontinue the contract because of projected personal use. At present, he works the place under deteriorating conditions, as it were."

Laura felt disappointed, nevertheless. The farm stood for an important part of her family's history and was very close to her heart. On the other hand, she could not and would not just kick out the present tenant either. She would have to think of a mutually acceptable formula, a form of staggered retreat. One more headache she didn't need.

"I don't want to appear a heartless monster," she turned to Larsen, pretending not to hear another one of his deep sighs, "but all things considered, you have to admit that…"
Laura stopped. She felt as if some low tune like that of an opera overture had slowly gained in tempo and volume. More and more instruments had joined the initial handful of strings and contributed to turn what started as a trickling stream into a mighty river no longer to be ignored.

"For Pete's sake, Sven, stop cracking your knuckles and tell me, who or what in heaven or hell is a Yellow Dancer?"

2. The Great Escape

"Premié fwa Gwada?" Wearily, Laura looked into the pair of large bloodshot eyes twinkling at her like grained glass beads glued to the silvery slit of the rear-view mirror. They evoked a childhood trauma which it had taken her years to shake off. An elderly lady, generally considered confused, who lived close to their Blankenese home, had made it a habit to snoop on practically everybody in the neighbourhood. The methods she employed were as simple as they were effective. At times, she would hide behind one of the chestnut trees along the avenue that formed the dividing line between public park and residential area. Armed with her cute ancient mother-of-pearl opera glasses, she would watch people's daily routines and draw God knows what conclusions for herself. Dogs were her personal bane. Frequently, she would pursue innocent dog-owners walking their fastidiously tree-sniffing pooches all the way down the avenue. Whenever she caught one in the act of leaving its mark on a piece of lawn or, worse, on the pavement, she would turn her umbrella into a lethal weapon and smack both the terrified creature and its owner over the head or shoulders.

In the case of the Forster family who were often away from home and generally difficult to pigeonhole in a roster of any kind, the old lady had apparently felt both obliged and entitled to resort to more invasive measures. One evening, she had climbed up the stairway to the massive wooden entrance door of the Forster villa, pressed her ear to the belly of one of the two beautifully carved lions and listened for signs of life from inside the house. When there had been none for a while, she had lost patience and, using her ball-pen the way she seen some peeping tom or other do in a movie, had lifted the lid of the mail slit to look through it.

As a child, Laura was frequently left alone at home, since both her parents were devoted theatre and opera-goers holding numerous subscriptions and had to attend to all sorts of parties populated by influential Hamburg citizens and local politicians. Laura did not mind that. Rather on the contrary, she enjoyed zapping her way through all the different TV channels undisturbed or, even better, roaming the place, pretending she was the resident ghost on her midnight round to the tune of Michael Jackson's Thriller on her MP 3 player. That night, as she had prepared herself the kind of peanut butter sandwich anathema to parents but irresistible to kids, she had suddenly caught a strange noise from the entrance door. When she stepped out into the long dark corridor, she had found herself inadvertently staring into a pair of big, round zombie eyes that gazed back at her with an expression of surprise that matched her own. Crying out in sheer horror, Laura had run upstairs and hidden under her quilt.

When she told her parents about it later, they had called on Mata Hari and told her in no uncertain terms to lay off. If there was something specific she was dying to know about the Forster family, she was always welcome to ask.

In the years to follow, Laura had befriended the old lady, who she used to run into every now and again in one or the other of the small shops that still studded the area at the time. She had quickly grasped that the woman was not half as disturbed as her unfortunate, if self-inflicted reputation would have it. If the little lady had one outstanding talent, it was reading out loud to children. Whenever she recited one of her own drummed-up fairy tales with great aplomb, extraordinary shebang and dramatic gesticulation, she would kindle her audiences' imagination and capture their otherwise short-lived attention for hours on end. The aftermath of such magic sessions lingered on even today, when Laura would fall for the sonorous timbre of a gifted seanachie with a knack of resuscitating the fanciful world of fiction.

Such was not the case with the black taxi driver, whose red Peugeot car had waited first in line at Pointe-à-Pitre's Pôle Caraïbes airport. Even though his melodious, ingratiating creole was not totally devoid of quaint charm, as far as Laura was concerned, it might as well have been Klingon.

"Welcome to Guadeloupe, Mrs Spock," Laura murmured absent-mindedly. This strangely corrupted form of French was enough to cure the likes of a Dr Sanders of their linguistic hubris. On the eve of her departure from Paris Orly, Laura felt she had still managed quite well with her all but fluent A-level French and had even tried to emulate the exalted pronunciation of the female airport staff. Which wasn't all that easy, since, to her ears, they sounded like the valves of some ill-tuned organ, whose worn-out stops would keep on hissing spent air long after the word hinging on a final vowel had nominally ended. You wouldn't want a woman like that having an orgasm next door to your hotel room, Laura thought. Now she realized, however, that she had heard nothing yet. Guadeloupe was likely to confront her with much steeper linguistic challenges or so it would seem.

The continuous blare from the car radio, though vaguely irritating, had the comforting effect nipping any conversation in the bud. Gwo-ka music, as produced on the island, was not to everybody's taste, to put it mildly, but Laura didn't mind. If only she could be spared Bob Marley shooting both the sheriff and his deputy, she felt she could handle it. Marley's dreadful lyrics and slurry music she detested.

Not to appear totally impolite, Laura forced a wry smile which the taxi driver might interpret as he pleased. The hot humid air of the island took some getting used to. She wiped a few drops of sweat from her brow and thought she caught a funky whiff from her own armpits. Time for a shower in the hotel room.

For one thing, she had to bequeath her black pant suit to Oxfam as quickly as possible. Her dark ‚mourning rags' would draw the bulk of subtropical ultraviolet flak that would make her melt like butter sizzling in a frying pan. The driver was shaking his curly black hair in a measured rocking rhythm. What the metal oil barrels had done for the steel-bands of Trinidad, the wooden ka drum had achieved for the blacks on Guadeloupe. The real McCoy complete with animal hide and all the rest of it had been banned all over the Caribbean at an early stage, Laura had read. The colonial masters suspected their slaves imported from Africa of trying to exchange secret information, something that could not be tolerated. On ‚Gwada', where no crude was found and no steel barrels needed, the blacks had to find other basic materials. They took to collecting discarded wooden herring casks and transformed them into primitive drums fit for playing the Gwo-ka, which was more rhythm than melody, more mood than music.

"Super, Gwada, tu verras. Moi, jsuis né ci."

Laura felt at a loss. She did not really understand the man and would have preferred to be left to her own thoughts. Besides, she hated verbal intimacies from complete strangers, never mind their status or colour of skin. In Laura's experience, chatting with taxi drivers abroad was as laborious as it was pointless. Often enough, all the drivers had in mind was trying to find out quickly whether or not their respective customers were familiar enough with the place to notice on what kind of unnecessarily circumstantial ride they were being taken. Having only just touched down on the other side of the Atlantic, Laura wished to relax and enjoy the scenery of this Caribbean harbour town in a bit of peace and quiet rather than having to make futile conversation. "Pointe-à-Pitre" she mouthed with her lips in the dark of the taxi's rear, trying to open and shut the Parisian ,valve'.

Having done that several times over, she found she somehow kept stumbling over the cacophonic array of consonants. When you thought about it, the name seemed neither here nor there. ,Piter' was what the inhabitants of Russian St. Petersburg aka Petrograd aka Leningrad called their beautiful city on the Neva river. Yet, more likely than not, Tsar Peter the Great had never even heard of the place, let alone visited it. It must have been some other, less famous Peter, who had given the town its name. No Pierre, no Pedro, Padrino, but a Piter. Sounded like a Dutchman, rather. Maybe Guadeloupe had originally been called Gouda-loupe and been a centre of Caribbean cheese production? Holland, in turn, would be faintly reminiscent of the Russian tsar-cum-carpenter again, who loved roaming German and Dutch shipyards incognito to admire the voluptuous shapes of both Teutonic ships and women.

Would Peter the Great have enjoyed the old Guadeloupe with its sugar-cane plantations and black slaves, taken from African kraals and shipped here under revolting conditions to cut sugar cane or pick cotton for the rest of their lives? Then again, Russian tsars weren't exactly known for their delicacy and social empathy either. The climate would probably not have bothered him unduly either, both St. Petersburg and ,Pitre' having been erected hastily on mosquito-ridden swamps.

Day-dreaming, Laura pushed the side of her head against the cool windowpane and looked at the city lights flying past on the right-hand side of the four-lane highway that connected the town with its airport. Graffiti, executed with great artistic flourish, did their best, or worst, to hide the whitish plaster on the saddening facades of one tall social housing block after another. In some places the sprayed-on colour had come off with the flakes of plaster underneath and left gaping blanks in large-scale portraits or political slogans, defacing the former and turning the latter into syllabic charades which Laura tried to solve in passing.

Bed linen, towels, T-shirts and unexciting items of underwear were flapping from almost all the balconies and terraces like so many flags waving in a welcome parade. Here and there, the brownish green crowns of palm trees trembled and rocked like giant feather dusters, cleaning the tropical sky to make it fit for the all-nightly splendour of constellations such as the Southern Cross. Ranks of fast-growing ferns and bushes with broad dark green foliage shimmering wet would break the monotony of the facades every now and then. Had it not been for such specimens of subtropical botany, Laura might as well have been driving through yet another of the dull Paris suburbs that she passed on her morning bus ride between Charles de Gaulle and Orly airports. All that was missing to complete the typically French faubourg atmosphere was a few incinerated car wrecks, battered and bullet-riddled dustbins and the odd road-side pyramid of dug-up paving stones, ammunition deposits for the next nightly riot.

The phoney reflection of the fast-sinking rosy Caribbean sun in the glass fronts of some uninspired office buildings acted as a reliable hydrograph indicating the degree of the local atmosphere's moisture saturation. Already at the airport, the hot wet air rising from the lush vegetation of the Guadeloupe rain forests had crept into Laura's pores. That said, her prolonged stays in Florida and Louisiana had taught her that, in the longer term, her sensitive skin reacted more favourably to this kind of climate than to arid heat. She would never forget the excruciating pain she had gone through on the occasion of a school excursion to Santiago de Compostela, Spain.

Fortunately, yesterday morning's plane had been on time, although, incredibly, the bus ride through the metropolis had taken almost as long as the flight from Hamburg to Paris. Orly airport looked like a huge aquarium, its toilets smelling as much of chlorine as any Hamburg indoor swimming pool she had ever tried. The regular users of this busy airport were a colourful mixture of elderly tourists and people from the French overseas territories. Some escaping from the precarious Central European April weather at advantageous late-season rates, the others heading home again after finishing their private or business chores in or around Paris. Sooner or later, they all converged in front of the check-in counters manned by badly paid, ill-tempered airline staff. It had to be frustrating, Laura thought, to sit by all day helping people to fly to all sorts of exotic destinations without being able afford even a weekend on the "littoral", as they would call the coast.

Islands such as La Réunion, Martinique or Guadeloupe enjoyed such popularity with the French, not least because during their stay there they need not forgo such venerable traditions as dunking their limp morning croissant in the lukewarm liquid they called coffee. Nor did they have to give up sipping their afternoon pastis or knocking back the inevitable coup de rouge, briskly refilled glassfuls of inferior claret. Hence, they could travel far without changing the accustomed matrix, which had the added advantage of fostering the illusion of an empire upon which the sun never set.

There were further rewards to look forward to, such as the dubious marronages her father had told her about. With that endearing term evoking the convivial image of someone frying edible chestnuts on the beach, the French somewhat euphemistically labelled the sexual exploitation of ebony "natives" by ivory tourists and ebony 'natives' as organised pretty much everywhere on the islands. Some habits die harder than others.

Island ladies, who had, God knows how, wrapped their truly voluptuous forms into stupendously colourful clothes as if only too eager to present them to potential takers, had been pushing mountains of luggage about, cursing the jamming wheels of their overloaded trolleys going in all but the desired directions.

On her numerous travels, Laura had learned to deal with wayward trolleys. The ploy involved some degree of psychological delicacy. If your ultimate target was the queue at, say, gate number 34, your average trolley would make for the shopping mall instead, as a matter of course. Resistance during this preliminary phase of the conflict would be a waste of time and energy. What mattered was to lull the trolley into a deceptive sense of triumph and supremacy. So, you followed it, as it were, in a state of despondency, only to suddenly turn to, say, gate number 38 close by. Very probably, your trolley would then veer off to gate 34 out of sheer spite. By the time, it realized that this was where you were headed in the first place, it would be too late.

With her black pant suit, Laura had formed a kind of Island of the Dead in a sea resplendent with all colours of the rainbow. On two occasions already, she had been addressed by travellers asking for some piece of flight information. From that she had concluded that people looked upon her as the stewardess of some unusually morose airline. "Thank you for choosing Allied Funereal Intercontinental for today. In your AFI in-flight information you will find a list of warmly recommended crematoria."

Yet, to change her clothes already at the airport, Laura would have felt to be an irreverent and disrespectful thing to do. Her father would have been the last one to mind. He usually paid no heed to hollow symbols. But Laura Forster wasn't just anyone, as her father had never tired of reminding her. Infallibly, some old acquaintance or another, whom she hadn't seen for ages and would probably never run into again this side of oblivion, would materialize out of nowhere and express his or her honest condolences, only to bandy Laura's ‚frivolous' attitude about exhaustively immediately afterwards.

A cowardly flight from reality? Was that what Dr Sanders had called Laura's quickly decided trip? Well, what did she care. She needed a change of scenery. It would help her to see things from a different angle and bring some order into the chaos of her conflicting feelings. Had her father's death been the natural consequence of a long ailment during which she could have prepared herself for the inevitable, well, yes, that would have been a different story altogether. But literally steamrollered by recent events, she found her plea for time out more than justified. If he wished to call that a cowardly escape, well, so be it. She had always been a firm believer in the saying that discretion was the better part of valour.

In a ladies' rest rooms, Laura had taken a hard look at herself in the mirror. Mourning and reverence should be perfectly compatible with discrete makeup and a well-kept coiffure, she felt. What little cosmetics she used ought to, at the very least, cover the little scar over her left brow which had kept her company for as long as she could remember. Thirty was another ‚critical' age. Come to think of it, any milestone passed as from age 12 or so could be considered ‚critical' for a female. Almost undetectable small lines here, budding cellulite there, the occasional bags under her eyes - if you didn't pay early enough attention to such vital signs, you were bound to lose your bid for beauty. The number of patches in need of repair had a nasty habit of increasing almost as fast as a woman's girth.

One way or another, the bun had to go. Why would she make herself look older than she was? She couldn't bring back Robert, as it were, in exchange for her youth. In Pointe-à-Pitre, she would let her hair down to fall loosely on her shoulders. Or maybe, for practical reasons, have it cut quite short. Her thick, full hair had misled many of her student colleagues in the States to think that she had Southern European or South American roots. She probably owed it to one or the other of Robert's ancestors, since her mother had had much thinner and slightly reddish hair, which had turned grey prematurely.

In the tropics, dark sunglasses, a sun hat or foulard and sun blocker - protection factor 100 - were absolute musts for people with darkish hair such as herself. At that moment, Laura's mirror image had smiled at her so encouragingly that she had decided to give in and undo the silly bird's nest there and then. With renewed determination, she had brushed her hair, first to the right, then to the left and had been quite satisfied with the result. After all, there was no telling what radiant male she might happen to sit next to in the plane's obscenely expensive business class. Laura sighed. With her luck, probably not George Clooney's hitherto unknown brother, kept under the lid by plotting George because the bro was even better looking than the original. No, with Laura's luck, she would surely be placed next to a sweaty, fat estate agent who would try to talk her into buying the late Coluche's vacant mess of a residence at Des Haies.

"Pa ni pwoblem. Voilà kaz la." The taxi stopped. As far as she could judge, the driver had resisted the temptation of doing a couple of extra loops but had taken her straight to the hotel. That called for a generous tip. By the time Laura, stiff and aching from sitting, had swung her behind out of the car with the agility of an octogenarian, the driver had already circled the taxi, popped the trunk and started to align Laura's luggage on the pavement next to the hotel entrance.

Laura looked up. She stood in front of a three-storey mixture of Art Déco and colonial memorial style. As if ashamed of the extrovert canary-yellow paint it had been covered with very much against its will, the facade of the double building had discreetly withdrawn into the shadow of two large terraces adorned with intertwined cast-iron ornaments. The space between the two residential towers was only just wide enough to allow for the external elevator shaft. This was inversely ‚U'-shaped with a crowning rosette at its rounded-off peak.

Laura paid the driver and stepped into the small reception hall while a local boy took her luggage. "The Saint-John Perse hotel welcomes you in Pointe-à-Pitre and wishes you a pleasant stay," the receptionist greeted her like a talking doll provided with a personalized tape. Yet, as Laura immediately responded with a grateful smile, the tape, if it was one, continued in perfectly intelligible French, "If you wish to dine or need anything else…...?"

Laura shook her head in the negative and had the boy accompany her to the second floor. She tossed a few coins in his palm and waited patiently until the door's lock had clicked shut behind him. She took a quick look around. The room did not differ dramatically from what she had hitherto been exposed to on her travels. Clean, airy, with a double bed, TV set, telephone, WiFi, shower and toilet. What more could you wish for? She pulled a small green Perrier bottle from the minibar and drank the water in hasty gulps.

"St. John Perse," she murmured, imitating the bionic receptionist's voice. Yet another strange name complete with awkwardly positioned plosive consonants surrounded by nasal vowel trip-wires. Had St. John, the travel addict among Christ's disciples, really made it all the way to Persia? She wouldn't have put it past him. But why? And in what way did that reflect on Guadeloupe or the Caribbean at large, for that matter? Even more important, which of the two Johns were we talking about, John the Baptist or John the cryptic apocalyptic?

And why not "Jean", since she was still in France, in a manner of speaking? Wikipedia had it that this St. John was the Anglo-French pen-name of a diplomat with a poetic vein and a soft spot for the Germans. Having fallen out with the Vichy government - not because of his outrageous lyrics but because of veneration for the Germans - he had opted for the US during the 1940s. On Gua-deloupe, his birthplace, he was considered the most famous of the island's prodigal sons which must number among the thousands. "St. John" had turned his back on Guadeloupe still something of a toddler and had made it a point never to return, not even for the briefest of calls. They don't come much more prodigal than that. His thin volume of Dadaist poems, entitled Anabase, arcane as it was, had nevertheless earned him the Nobel Prize in literature. Which, at the time, had lent new substance to the question of what the members of the Stockholm Nobel committee had been smok-ing during their confidential selection deliberations.

The subtropical night had descended upon Pointe-à-Pitre al-most without any twilight foreplay. Laura had crashed onto the bed like a palm tree felled in its prime by a devastating flash of lightning. Once again, she experienced that eerie sensation of some heavy shadow rolling onto her body, stifling her, pushing her deeper and deeper into the mattress. She was gasping for air, yet found herself paralyzed, unable to shake the shadow. It was a recurring nightmare of hers, a kind of near-suffocation experi-ence that had kept revisiting her for many years.

Is this how the Prince of Darkness came to claim you, Rob-ert? Her father did not reply from the dark and dusty depth of Hades. The living should abstain from summoning the dead,

Laura knew. If they did not, the waking dead were susceptible to show themselves, but alas, like small children, they never came unaccompanied. And a merry band of French-talking zombies with hissing valves for mouths was all Laura needed to round up what had already been a terribly exhausting day. Without recovering consciousness, she stretched out and fell into a deep, dreamless coma.

3. The Buffalo Soldier

Next morning, woken by a persistent knocking on the door of her room, Laura reluctantly opened her eyes only to close them again quickly with a loud groan. Her room looked east and, since she had fallen asleep the night before without drawing the curtains, the glaring Caribbean morning sun shone right in her face now. She tried to sit up, but immediately fell back on the bed like a puppet whose strings had been cut. The irritating knocking sound was not coming from the door, either, but from inside her head. A pulsating ache behind her temples reminded her that migraine was part of her genetic heritage on her mother's side. Hardly a day had gone by without Frederike complaining about headaches that would frequently be accompanied by nausea and temporary near-blindness.

Her arms held high above her head, Laura rolled her body to the edge of the bed as if bereft of the use of her limbs and started hectically rummaging through her handbag in search of sunglasses and the little silver pill box she had inherited from her mother. When she could not feel either, she turned her bag upside down like an impatient thief and spread its contents on the carpet. Then she swung her legs out, staggered across the room to the window and drew the curtains. Was the local tap water fit for drinking? She doubted it, but if she had to fight her headache at the price of an upturned stomach, well, tough titty, Miss

Pretty. She dropped the effervescent tablet into a glass of water and drank the lukewarm sizzling liquid before half of the tablet had dissolved. One of the three or four glasses of rum punch that had practically been forced upon her by the caring business-class stewardess must have been way past its expiry date. She looked herself over in the mirror and quickly covered her face with both hands. The creature staring back at her was on manifest hair alert and had a make-up melt-down to boot! Were there any hairdressers in Pointe-à-Pitre apt and willing to handle anything but local favourites such as extensions, French plaits, cornrows, or dreadlocks? And what about her pant suit, which she had not had enough energy to take off yesterday? She looked like a ruffled and bloated Jane Doe just picked from a ditch somewhere by the roadside. Her mourning attire had outlived its welcome, served its purpose. Now it had to go.

First things first, however. She badly needed a cup of proper black coffee. Not your average French dog bowl sloshing with some tepid milk and a drop or two of anti-coronary decaf. Afterwards, a shower would work wonders. Hot water first, then the ice-cold aftermath, to crank-start her blood circulation. Finally, dress up and hit the kerb. Laura accorded herself a generous thirty minutes for her comprehensive re-boot.

An hour and a half later, freshly showered and filled to the hilt with caffeine, she stepped out into the near-empty street. All parts of her body that either were or else might conceivably be exposed to the perfidious Caribbean sunlight were safely embalmed with a sun blocker giving off an embarrassing whiff of stale coconut milk. Better than the pungent floor polish she had once put on in New Orleans, Laura thought as she looked left and right for direction clues. In lieu of her black pant suit, which would henceforth be donned by the hotel's leading cleaning lady, Laura had put on her white jeans with riveted pockets and a rhinestone-studded black belt, country and western style. Her reddish-blue blouse had been bought at the Orly Airport's Zara boutique. The shop assistant had been positive that it would work as a fork-lift for Laura's slightly slumping breasts. When she had looked herself over one more time in the hotel foyer's mirror, Laura had found the assistant's daring prognostics confirmed. Comfortable, light sandals and the expensive YSL foulard, a last gift from her late father, completed her safari outfit. As she stood there in the street, slightly lost and vaguely agoraphobic, she might as well have carried a sticker on her chest saying "I (heart) being ripped off!"

She held her Vuitton handbag, with passport, purse, and cosmetic first-aid kit, under her right elbow. Normally, she would also have packed her pepper spray, but the irritating security people at Orly had been impervious: no knives, handguns or pepper spray on board the plane. Stripped of her habitual means of self-defence, and dropped off so far behind enemy lines, Laura felt an easy prey to pickpockets, sex or dope fiends, and cut-throats of any description. The crime rate in Guadeloupe was said to be lower than that of Martinique alright, but what individual takes comfort in statistical averages?

Come on, bitch, pull yourself together, she pepped herself up.

"Which way Central Frigging Court?" she shouted playfully at the crowd of noisy seagulls clinging to the rain gutter as if waiting for the Wimbledon final. "Pa ni pwoblem", the receptionist had responded to her question about how she might get to the local high street on foot. On the map, which the receptionist had shown her, it looked easy enough to find and in walking distance, anyway.

"Pa ni pwoblem" appeared to be the local mantra. Laura did not pay much heed to such light-hearted assertions. For her, they rather had the opposite effect of alarm bells ringing: you had better start worrying now! For one thing, Laura's migraine had gone. On the flip side, her next ovulation could not be far away. Which made a visit to some pharmacy a matter of priority. Why on earth she had forgotten to pack the Tampax plugs escaped her. But on the face of it, the place was swarming with women, so Laura got under way cheerfully, almost buoyantly. The hot, humid air smelled of marshy soil, sea salt, algae and some undefinable spice. Laura felt like Atlas feigning a hernia to be rid of the globe for a while. Her decision to give Hamburg the slip and go for this "safari" had been the right one, of that she was more convinced now than ever.

"The strong are most powerful when left to their own devices", her history teacher would comment whenever she caught one of the girls consulting her neighbour during written tests. Laura doubted that. Here and now, she would have welcomed a strong partner to lean on. Even though the prospect of passing one or two weeks alone in the Caribbean did not exactly cause her panic attacks either. She felt confident she had lived through worse during her stay in the States. No, her present situation was more that of a snake shedding her old skin grown too tight without her new outfit being quite ready for the wearing. Maybe there was a skilled snake charmer out there somewhere, courageous enough to approach a German-born black mamba with some of the deadliest fangs around. Or, to put it in Robert's cherished marine terms, someone who knew how to shake the barnacles of idleness off a middle-aged woman's sex.

Pitre did not seem to encourage any hopes in that direction. Its apparent architectural chaos confusing the newcomer was something the place could hardly be blamed for. The town's foundations had been laid on a chalk plateau smack in the middle of a swamp during the late 18th century. Successive earthquakes, volcanic eruptions, conflagrations and no end of hurricanes had time and time again flattened Pitre, whilst numerous cholera and other deadly epidemics had repeatedly taken a huge toll on its population. A little roly-poly of a Caribbean harbour town, that's what it was, drawing heavily on French and European Union financial support, too.

The oppressive humidity of the day put not only human stamina to the test. As Laura strolled along, she came across several instances of stray dogs seeking the cooling shade offered by the rear ends of parked cars. She only hoped they would wake up in time to avoid getting run over by the reversing car later during the afternoon. At one of the small sugar-cane chariots, she stopped and lingered undecided. Its owner stuck some pieces of loose cane rejects into the chariot's mill, gave it a few turns and presented Laura with the squeezed-out juice collected in a plastic cup. Laura took a cautious sip as if having been handed a hemlock infusion. When she was satisfied that it did not taste as abominably sweet as she had feared, she gulped it down in one thirsty go. The man did not ask for money, but Laura pressed some coins upon him all the same.

An ominous grumbling sound made her stare at the sky. A threatening black cloud with yellow and violet rims had occupied the entire northern horizon and quickly spread over Guadeloupe, causing a sudden eclipse of the sun. Laura slapped her forehead. The possibility of an occasional tropical shower had failed to occur to her when leaving the hotel. Some light plastic cape with a hood she could have stuck in her handbag would have been useful now. She looked around for shelter and finally made for the roofed-over spice market, which welcomed her with a thick cloud of aromatic Caribbean ingredients, making both her eyes and mouth water. She had hardly reached the market when a real whopper of a shower, as she had only witnessed in the south of the US, broke loose. Raindrops the size and elasticity of table-tennis balls came pelting down and seemed to ricochet right back into the air. Solid gusts of wind would have mauled Laura's umbrella, had she thought of bringing one. As rapidly as this monster of a cloud had approached, however, it now moved on westward and left the virtual steam bath of a town behind.

Laura walked slowly past the spice stands. She was no great cook by any standards. If someone twisted her arm, she might have managed to prepare a decent meal in the tradition of the pedestrian northern German cuisine. Notwithstanding, she found the temptation of handling and tasting some of the thousand island flavours irresistible. Ginger roots grown crooked and awry; black glistening nutmeg; thick cinnamon sticks rolled like so many dusty cigars; black vanilla pods; analgesic cloves; bloodred saffron threads; fenugreek, cumin, Colombo powder and all kinds of pepper almost took her breath away.

After several vain attempts at verbal communication with the pacotilleuses, dressed in Madras-coloured clothes and bonnets,

Laura gave up creole as a regular write-off and resorted to sign language. She soon found that in the expressive gestures department, she had a lot to learn from the local ladies. Decency, it would seem, was not on their list of chief concerns. Pressing past her in a flurry, one of the pacotilleuses ever so lightly stroked Laura's behind with her fingertips and called out something that sounded like "Prima bonda Man Jack.' Her colleagues' shrieking laughter shook the roof-tops. Laura needed no translation, nor was she truly angry about the remark. What really got to her was the horrible thought that the woman might be right, after all, and Laura's backside possibly on the wrong side of conventional size values for her respective age group.

As far as lush colourings went, the women's clothing was only just beaten to the post by the ,poisonous' lemon yellow, bloody crimson and mysterious jungle-green of their bottles, tinctures, and glasses with rum, punch and other kinds of alcoholic beverages and cures. Some of the roots and mixtures even promised to work as Caribbean Viagra. Laura pretended not to pay any more attention to the obscene allusions of the women around her. An attitude which they, in turn, commented on with sombre shakes of their heads, ironic whistling and scornful hoots.

If she was to be cruelly honest with herself, those women were not that far off the mark either. Her sexual life had withered away of late. Her wild student days with their bouts of drug abuse and freewheeling sex were too far away to serve as reference points any longer. In the immortal words of her favourite song writer, "nothing much had happened since". Her single relationship of relatively long standing with a rather hopeless physicist had been doomed from the beginning, both by his embarrassing erection problems and abominable musical tastes. As for Sven Larsen, he had crushed the first shoots of a possible common future with the crackling of his knuckles. Since her latest one-night stand, several months had elapsed unexploited. Or was it already close to a year? Anyway, what business had she to share such highly intimate dire balance sheets with the pacotilleuses, edifying as their sexual insights and pieces of advice might have proved.

"Vêtements!" Laura tried a long shot to move her search for new clothes into the focus of their haphazard exchanges not exactly helped by mutual misunderstandings. The local ladies again laughed aloud and nodded as if critically appraising Laura's exquisite taste in clothing. That way, she would obviously get nowhere. Holding a handful of cinnamon sticks that one of the women had made her an unwanted gift of, Laura soon found herself standing in the street again which was still steaming away here and there with evaporating rain water.

"Can I be of any assistance, Ma'am?" Quickly stuffing the embarrassing cinnamon sticks into her bag, Laura turned around to look at the person who addressed her in English, and in such unexpectedly polite terms too. Standing in front of her, yet keeping a respectful distance, was a colourful bird of paradise. Male, as far as she could tell. A tall, anorectic looking Caucasian individual in his late thirties, early forties with ‚golden' curls, medium-rare tan, pink shirt with old-fashioned wide-open collar, gold chain and amulet across an apparently hairless chest: the entire lot wrapped in an impeccably whitish linen suit with pink breast-pocket handkerchief. His pleasantly dark voice had a slight nasal twang to it, which made it sound a mite effeminate, with a dash of half-ironic haughtiness. If she had been asked to translate that man and his voice into a cocktail, it would have to be a chalice of Sex on the Beach, though probably not with a woman. In Hamburg, Laura could see him accompany local fashion legend Karl Lagerfeld on the terrace of an Alster café or at the rumbling ‚Village People' daintily sipping their daiquiris. After running the gauntlet of the lewd and unabashed pacotilleuses, a little cultured conversation couldn't hurt. Besides, Laura felt she did need help.

"Yes, I mean, I think so, thank you." She told the bird of paradise, who introduced himself as Martin, that her French wasn't that hot and that she was looking for clothes shops.

"But no problem, Madame," Martin gave a bright smile, bowed politely and offered Laura his arm. "Allow the Buffalo Soldier of Pointe-à-Pitre to show you what he can do as a tourist guide and pilot you through the dazzlingly colourful world of Guadeloupe's pret-à-porter. Yes, I notice your incredulous little sneer. But let me tell you, Madame, our local couturiers may not be the stuff that Vogue's or Vanity Fair's centrefolds may be made of, yet, don't you know, the Old World establishment chooses to ignore the creative forces of the Caribbean at their commercial risk and peril. With your kind permission."

He took Laura's left hand, lifted it over her head as if striding along in a courtly minuet and spun her round her own axis so that she ended up facing the part of town she had just come from. Then, Martin offered her his right arm and paraded her down the road in a kind of gangster-rapper jive-walk, something Laura had, so far, only seen in rather ridiculous American films and never suspected to experience in a real-life situation one day.

Two blocks further on, they turned into Rue Nozières, where Laura immediately hit on two promising boutiques. In his modest presentation, the gay Buffalo Soldier had been guilty of gross understatement. He turned out to possess an amazing competence in questions of current fashion, in the ladies' as well as gents' department, and would have won any shopping drag-queen contest hands tied behind his back. He did not let Laura out of his sight, approved or disapproved of her choices the Roman gladiator way – thumbs up or thumbs down. Also, he took it upon himself to pluck a bit of seam here or pull out a piece of collar there and helped Laura to save a substantial sum of money by dint of shrewd haggling. Laura was literally basking in the nasal sing-song voice of this well-educated and obviously widely travelled young gentleman, who appeared to know the town like the inside of his pocket. Which, it is true, wasn't saying much in so small a place as Pitre.

Laura would have liked to book him as her escort for the whole of the coming week but feared he might take that as an insult. "Just my kind of luck," she thought. She had hit upon her snake-charmer, only to find he was not into women in any sense of the word.

"May I thank you for your kind help by inviting you for lunch?" she asked him about two hours later as she left the last shop with two big glossy paper bags in her hand.

"Only on condition you leave the choice of restaurant to me," he replied.

"Because, you see, I dabble in haute cuisine myself," he added smilingly and made a gesture as if adding salt to a virtual bouillabaisse simmering away on the invisible stove.

"Hence, I am very appreciative of a meal prepared with love and impeccable craftsmanship. It does not even have to be all that humble, either, if you see what I mean. Therefore, I should like to recommend the Café de Paris at the Place de la Victoire, if it's all the same to you. Allow me."

He took hold of her bags and directed her back towards the harbour. Laura was bushed. Her feet had started hurting from the unusually long walking she had done during the morning, so she craved to sit down soon somewhere, anywhere.

The terrace of the Café de Paris looked pretty crowded already. Its cuisine must enjoy a good reputation not only with Martin. The local competition wasn't exactly cut-throat, it is true, and its location next to the central square of Pitre's inner city unbeatable anyway. Be that as it may, the Café de Paris was radiant with an atmosphere perfectly commensurate with the establishment's ambitious name.

One of the two waiters, wending through the lines of tables like experienced slalom racers, replied with a dismissive "non, désolé" when Martin asked him for a vacant table in French. To the extent Laura could understand, the waiter explained that it would be better for the two of them to come back, say, an hour or so later when the table situation would be far more relaxed. Whereupon Martin's affable nasal twang assumed a touch of unexpected steely abrasiveness, as he insisted they would vastly prefer to eat here and now.

Even in the general hubbub of buzzing conversations, shoving of chairs and clinking of china, forks and knives, the change of tone was not lost on the waiter. He stopped and turned around. Recognizing the Buffalo Soldier, he immediately became a model of almost abject servility. He excused himself profusely and led Laura and Martin to a table right at the entrance to the restaurant's interior. He removed the little white ‚Réservé' card with a sheepish smile and straightened the chequered cloth at the table's corners. Then, he saw to it that Laura was comfortably placed in her chair and presented the two of them with a menu. Laura was not a little impressed by the impact Martin's seemingly calm but determined approach had had. Whatever his trade, he would have to be a person of some local consequence. Their table at the entrance had the double advantage of being close enough to the rest room, yet far enough from the street and the exhaust fumes of the cars. The traffic was modest but of irritating regularity.

"What does someone like you do in Pointe-à-Pitre, when not helping lost foreign ladies with their choice of clothes?" Laura asked Martin.

The Buffalo Soldier smiled as he looked up from the menu.

"Let's just say I try to make myself useful wherever I'm need-ed. And the funny thing is, I seem to be needed practically every-where. May I ask you whether you are into spicy food?"

No, teutonically dull would be fine, Laura thought. But that would have broken the spell of their unlikely encounter.

"Of course, love it" she lied, at the same time asking herself what ‚spicy' translated into in the West Indies. A burnt throat and punctured stomach wall, to start off with, presumably.

"In that case, I would recommend you to chance your hand at the Assiette Créole. I mean, you've got to be tired of Choucroute d'Alsace with sausages and pigs' trotters. Pasta again, with due respect, should only be eaten at an Italian's, that's how I feel about it, anyway."

Laura apprehensively did as she had been advised and or-dered the plate of creole food with a glass of Pinot Gris. Secretly, she regretted not having dropped by the pharmacy to get a box of activated charcoal. She was very hungry by now, in fact, and would have preferred something really plain and filling. Chou-croute d'Alsace with sausages or pigs' trotters, for instance.

She looked around. The restaurant's clientele consisted almost exclusively of whites, as did the staff. The few tourists who in-sisted on visiting the Caribbean at this late time of year must feel cornered by the local business community and administrative staff having their lunch break together.

In France and assimilated regions of the world, restaurants, Laura knew, fulfil the same vital social functions as pubs and clubs in Britain or bars in the States. They are institutions of national standing. Without them, public life would have to look for other, less convivial spaces to unfold. Robert had once told her that far from all business, private or political decisions in France were taken in restaurants - only the important ones. Newcomers to foreign diplomatic services in Paris quickly understood that office hours were of little consequence there. Instead, such youngsters spent months trying to find out and memorize which influential journalist, official or politician was in the habit of dining where, and when. "It is so deeply embedded in our neighbours' DNA that, for quite some time, I had taken the famous Code Napoléon to be a cook-book in so many volumes," Robert had laughed.

Laura smiled at the mere memory of it.

"Where and when did you learn English? I mean, no offence, but the French I had the pleasure of getting to know weren't exactly paragons of foreign language learning. It's considered unpatriotic, isn't it?" Martin laughed.

"Yes, I guess you're onto something there. I guess I must have picked it up as I went along."

He pointed at the square.

"You know, some two hundred years ago, we would have been diverted by the spectacle of selected members of the local landed gentry literally losing their heads," Martin said and pointed towards the centre of the Place de la Victoire.

"The glorious Victory in question doesn't refer to a war, but to the Revolution, even though it is debatable. But never mind, a moot point. The winning side spared no trouble to prove its ruthless thoroughness and dismantled an original Paris guillotine, transported it here and had it re-erected on the square. The message being, you can run, but you cannot hide, I suppose. Locals of high standing, who could not or would not pay the heavy bribes, had to face the apologetic hooded executioner. Many of my fellow-countrymen make no secret of the fact that they vividly regret the softening of manners that ensued as a consequence of successive pussy-footed penal reforms in France."

"That's the kind of spectacle I can do without." Laura had always opposed capital punishment most violently. In the US, that had caused her many a heated discussion with her fellow students. As much as she had enjoyed the States - when it came to American religious fundamentalism in its various manifestations, she lacked both sympathy and understanding.

The Assiette Créole turned out quite a mouthful, literally. In Edinburgh, Laura thought, it would have been ushered in like a plate of haggis by a tartan soldier complete with folkloristic headwear and wheezing bagpipes. The dish was composed of seafood such as mussels and crab, salad, some vegetables and generously spiced grey and black "boudins" or sausages you could either suck to death or finish off with fork and knife.

Setting aside her momentary qualms, Laura dug in to her heart's delight, but soon found herself overwhelmed by the concentrated intake of oil, protein and spices. Martin had just ordered a humble toast-like Croque Monsieur which he washed down with a glass of local beer while watching Laura's valiant efforts with suppressed chuckles.

"How did you come by your nickname?" Laura asked Martin, partly out of genuine curiosity, partly because she felt on fire and needed a breather.

"Which one? You mean Buffalo Soldier?" Instead of a lengthy explanation, he just pointed at his curly hair. "The Bob Marley song, you know." He struck up the first few chords low key and, as far as Laura was any judge, betrayed quite some talent in this area as well.

"Buffalo soldiers. That's what they called the blacks filling the ranks of the Union army during the Civil War. Because of their curly mats, vaguely reminiscent of buffalo hide. An original insult that was converted, over time, into an expression of respect. Military slang abounds with those."

"But you are neither black…"

"Nor much of a soldier, you're right. Some things have a logic of their own. Here, in the West Indies, it don't matter if you're black or white." This last part he sang again, this time slipping into Michael Jackson's shoes.

"The Caribbean is a big melting pot. Much more so than the US, in fact. The Americans are clans people very much in love with their Civil War. They hate to let it go. We have no such hang-ups."

He took a swig of beer and raised his eyebrows in mock despair.

"Now it's my turn to pop a question, if I may. What wind blew you across the ocean and dumped you on our island? You are German, aren't you?"

Laura nodded and wiped her greasy fingers clean on the napkin.

"Yes, I am. What wind blew me here, honestly, I'm not so sure. A breeze of sheer curiosity maybe. Yes, I think that's it, unmitigated curiosity."

"It's said to have killed many a cat..." Martin laughed and raised his right hand.

"I need another beer. Can I get you one more glass of wine?"

"That would be nice." Laura had no intention of letting a total stranger, charming though he was, become privy to her plans which, so far, had not taken distinct shape anyway.

"Be that as it may, if ever you need any help do not hesitate to call upon the Buffalo Soldier. I should..." He stopped abruptly in the middle of the sentence and stared over Laura's left shoulder at something or someone that seemed to disquiet him. Laura put down her wineglass and tried to use the restaurant window behind Martin as a mirror, but could not make out anything unusual. A small group of tourists seemed to be haggling over the prices of trinkets with a tall streetvendor. The fly-pitcher's colourful clothing had only met with one serious competition in the form of a male tourist's beetroot-red P & S windbreaker, the kind that Robert used to wear on occasion.

"I'm terribly sorry, Madame Forster. I would have liked to accompany you to your hotel, but something seems to have come up. Tell you what. I'll leave you my card. As I said, if you need any help do give me a call. Waiter, the check please!"

Laura accepted the card and lifted a hand in protest.

"No way!", she said. "You're my guest. Thank you once again. I'll hang around in Pitre for a while, I suspect. Maybe I'll have to take you up on your offer yet."

Martin nodded and smiled absentmindedly. Clearly, there were other more important matters calling for his attention. He got up hastily, threw his napkin down and took his leave from Laura with a polite bow. The next moment he seemed to have vanished into thin air.

Laura had an espresso with the check and studied the visiting card Martin had very casually left with her. Actually, it was not a card of his own but that of a Paris nightclub called At the foot of the Volcano. On the back of the card he had scribbled his mobile phone number. A pleasantly polite man, Laura thought. A real pity their conversation had been curtailed at the very moment that it proposed to become interesting.

"Jackie Sparrow? Is that what you just called me, Jackie Sparrow? Well, let me remind you, bitch, that'll be Captain Jackie Sparrow."

Upon her return to the St. John Perse, a Laura Forster somewhat under the influence had a serious word with the impertinent mirror image smiling back at her with an unabashed, nay, coquettish sneer. Back in her room, she tried on the foolhardy outfit she had bought piecemeal in the six or seven boutiques. The linen pants in navy blue threatened to be swallowed by the greedy cleft between her buttocks. So, from an objective point of view, it could be argued she should rather have taken one size further up the scale, but that would have meant admitting defeat in the war she had been waging with her stubborn BMI for the past months. The material was likely to give, anyway. Her blouse was pure Madras. A reminder of the Indians who had been among the first to try and make their living in the Caribbean, but had long since gone under, commercially speaking. The tips of the blouse, Laura had tied across the two bare folds of her tummy.

The nec plus ultra, however, was the headscarf. The shop assistant had shown Laura how to tie it and trim it according to local custom. This innocent-looking accessory, the assistant had told her, actually had tell-tale properties for those who were in the know. All according to which way the two little ,horns' on top of the foulard were pointing, its wearer would declare herself married, single, widowed, in love, available or what have you. Now there was only the matter of her hair. She had not had the time to pay a resident figaro a visit, unfortunately. So maybe she should just let it hang down. In this kind of outfit, not even her own father would have recognized her, never mind the coiffure. Thinking of Robert sobered her instantly. Looking at it now, the most recent discussions about the question of succession seemed to have taken place on some other planet light years away. Dr Sanders would no doubt be scandalized at her Caribbean masquerade. But his despotic jurisdiction ended at the European coasts of the Atlantic and thank God for that.

Nevertheless, where was she to go from here? Laura sat down on the bed and thought it through as best she could under the circumstances. Perhaps it would be wiser to take the next plane, return to Hamburg and assume the responsibility that everyone seemed to think was hers, instead of fooling around on Guadeloupe. What would her father have done in a situation like this? Obvious, dear Watson. He would not have got himself into some mess like this in the first place. Either way, there was unfinished business to be taken care of.

During a summer holiday spent in Greece, young Laura had one day played around at the edge of a stream near their rented summer house and come across a big stone. Upon turning it over with some difficulty, she had found a coiled-up thin green snake that had been hiding next to the stone, on its sunny side. A perfectly harmless grass snake. Still, it had given Laura a shock and frightened the wits out of her suddenly to look into the impassionate tiny yellowish eyes of the reptile.

"Take a lesson from that," her father had told her with a strange insistence, "and remember that some stones are better left unturned. You never know what you will find." "You should be so lucky!" Laura shouted aloud. Whatever she was going to decide about her leaving or staying on in Guadeloupe, it had absolutely no bearing on her resolve to unturn the one stone going by the intriguing name of Yellow Dancer. She had already prepared a few hard questions for that person and did not give a damn if, this time, the coiled snake proved to be a venomous viper. If it was true that curiosity killed one cat, dozens of others might have found the very lack of it their undoing. Whatever happened, Robert Forster would not be allowed to take this one with him to his grave.

Yet, there was no hurry. A little rest, a short siesta was what the doctor would have prescribed. As a child and youngster, Laura had frequently poked fun at her father because of his siesta obsession. The older she got, the better she understood him, as far as such basic physical needs were concerned. Besides, even though her biorhythm appeared to have adapted to the local set-up and her acclimatization seemed almost complete, her prolonged walk, getting in and out of new clothes, heeding a host of irregular French verbs and digesting highly inflammable Caribbean food, had all but completely sapped her power reserves. Laura kicked the sandals off her feet and stretched out on the bed. Whatever he or she was, the Yellow Dancer wasn't likely to be going anywhere. That was one of the few perks of being in a small place surrounded by lots and lots of water.

THIRD CHAPTER

1.The Phantom

The taxi stopped right in front of a semi-circular, one-storey red brick building on the waterfront. To the right, a big iron gate blocked the entrance to a coarse cement quay and, branching off to the right, five or six floating pontoons packed with moored yachts, most of them looking wrapped up in anticipation of the hurricane season's uncertain beginning. Laura got out of the car, paid the driver and asked him to come back and fetch her again in about two hours' time. "Pa ni pwoblem?" He seemed to have understood.

She had overslept her siesta and, for a moment, had been in two minds about her scheduled visit to the marina. Maybe it would have been better to postpone it till tomorrow, since today had practically ended already. She should have set the alarm, just hadn't counted on sleeping that long. Sod it. She had quickly donned her Jackie Sparrow costume, without the communicative headscarf, though. If she took a taxi, she might still make it there and back without floundering about in the dark.

The drive to the marina, picturesquely situated below the remains of the old fort that had once guarded the harbour entrance, had taken only a few minutes. Past the wooden huts and corrugated iron shacks of one of Pitre's Bidonville slums, the taxi had swung sharply to the right and reached the waterfront almost immediately. Hanging round all alone now like a woman stood up by her unreliable lover, Laura realized that the marina staff must long since have packed it up and gone home. European office hours clearly held no sway in the Caribbean.

While she was walking up and down, at a loss about what to do or how to take it from here, the seaward evening sky literally burst into colour. Someone must have taken it upon himself to prove that nothing in the world could beat "Gwada's" glossy sunset. Due to the various layers of moist air, the last rays of dying sun made the sky go through the entire spectrum of different hues of red: from salmon to raspberry, from fire to wine and deep purple, winding up in the neighbourhood of a papal kind of violet. Laura could not take her eyes off the hallucinatory spectacle and eventually had to force herself away from the evening sky to look for the marina area called Blue Lagoon. When she found no signs with that name, she decided to put her trust in a half-naked man, who just left the separate sanitary complex with a towel over his shoulder and a small bag under his arm. The man gave a short explanation in miserable English and murmured something unintelligible about "Turks".

Laura thanked him cordially none the less and took the direction he had indicated. Before long, she passed a row of sailing and motor yachts of various types, colours, and sizes, all with their stern turned to the quay. Then she wound her way through the animated café and restaurant complex and followed the narrow road, which led her away from the water in a sharp bend.

Apparently, the road had only recently been newly paved. On Laura's right-hand side, it was lined with high palm trees. To her left, Laura soon discovered a row of melon or Turk's cap cactuses, at whose sight she understood what the man with the towel had been on about. The round red tops of the three-foot high plants did bear a striking resemblance to the Oriental headwear called a fez, popular with the Turks until Mustafa Kemal had banned it as a blatant symbol of past Levantine backwardness standing in the way of modern Turkey's way west. Notwithstanding, to this day, the peculiar item would stick, if only on funny postcards and caricatures. The "Turks" archipelago forming a union with the Caicos islands south of the Bahamas, owed its name to these funny cactuses.

The next moment, Laura jumped and gave an involuntary startled noise. Out of the twilight, a solitary dog came scampering towards her. Not your stray bag of fleas, but a seemingly well-kempt cinnamon-coloured Labrador retriever, a family dog with necklace, tag, and pedigree, by the look of it. Laura was generally not afraid of dogs and loved retrievers, counted among the more intelligent and affectionate canine races. So, when the Labrador, that seemed a little long in the tooth, was almost abreast of her, Laura stretched out her hand and leaned towards it, addressing it in a gleeful voice as if recognizing an old friend of hers. But the animal seemed in a hurry and would not be diverted, let alone stopped. Its brief sideways glance appeared to be saying, "not now, Honey, can't you see I'm busy?" The next instant, it had disappeared into the dark.

It could not be far now to the Blue Lagoon since the funnel-shaped marina basin was getting narrower all the time and would soon present her with its cod end. Further down the paved road, the mast tops of more sailing yachts could be glimpsed over the thicket. Laura took them as wayposts and minutes later found herself in a place that, even with darkness descending for good now, was more of a Green Hell than a Blue Lagoon.

Mangroves, palm trees, agaves, aloe vera, and other exotic plants bitterly fought one another for the best places close to the darkish green water. Creepers, as thick as adult pythons, entwined and suffocated the withering trunks of defencelessly dying sycamore trees. Dangling almost imperceptibly in the soft evening breeze, Spanish moss hung from the outreaching branches of venerable oak trees like tousled black lametta. Swamp grass, bamboo, and wild reeds bowed to the occasional squall as if genuflecting in dignified reverence to the weather gods. The lush plant life of the place was surely bound to be gradually winning the upper hand in the Lagoon and seemed to push the shallow salt water further and further back due to the irresistible force of botanic patience. A couple of hissing swans was chasing a mother duck through the long grass, almost swallowing up its frantically chirping young. To get to the yachts, Laura would have to step on a ramshackle wooden jetty, which had been knocked together rather ham-fistedly with cudgel-like logs differing both in length and girth. Not the most confidence-inspiring piece of workmanship Laura had come across lately.

Darkness was precisely what she had wanted to avoid. Especially now, when she did not have her pepper spray on her, which would at least have given her the welcome illusion of safety. Yet she felt she had no choice in the matter. She took off her sandals, picked them up and cautiously stepped out along the jetty, balancing, her arms slightly stretched out like a circus artist high above the breathlessly watching crowd. Somewhere in the darkness, a resounding flourish with cymbal clashes was introducing her Barnum and Bailey's special act. "Ladies and gentlemen, tonight we proudly present the great, the incomparable, Laura Forster, all the way from Germany, Europe, to perform her unique death-defying tightrope walk." The jetty wobbled and swayed, but seemed prepared to bear her weight.

When the imaginary circus flourish had died down, a magic kind of hush fell over the unlikely scene. Not even the suspicion of a breeze, no chirring crickets - nature seemed to hold its breath. Even the indefatigable ocean swell, always eager to creep into the tiniest cracks of even the most jagged of coastlines, exhausted itself somewhere far out at sea that night. Seething surface patches and the occasional slashing sound of invisible fins betrayed the eerie presence of prowling predators profiting from the dark. The unseen world beneath the surface was probably not nearly as peaceful as the moonlit one above it. Barracudas were restless, relentless night hunters, shrewdly chasing their prey into the blind alleys of harbours and marinas.

Laura stood still and listened almost in awe to the brushing of the palm fronds above her head and the creaking of the wood beneath her feet. She did not regret having come here, after all, even though an ominous prescience weighed upon her chest as if she was only seconds away from a coronary. The serene nocturnal spell of the Blue Lagoon carried more charm than she could have bargained for. There was no artificial lighting here except for the few background street lamps whose weakly flickering bulbs were eclipsed by myriads of flies, moths, beetles and mosquitos. What few bungalows there were lined up along the banks stood vacant, their shutters closed at present. Each time the silently drifting clouds allowed the full moon to take a fleeting glance at the earth, its glaring silvery light would reflect on the oily black surface of the water, languidly washing around the boats' hulls like freshly tapped crude.

Unusually big bats were swerving this way and that on their hunt like the dark shadows of unusually nimble spacecraft in a nightly battle of the galaxies. As she tried to follow their breakneck shifts of height and direction, Laura spun on her axis a couple of times, almost toppling over and not far from falling backwards off the jetty. She had already passed two large sailing yachts, apparently locked up for the season, when one of the slimmer cudgels under her feet broke with a dry, crispy crackle. Once again, Laura lost her balance but caught herself quickly and laughed about her display of clumsiness. Putting down her feet with even more delicacy, she continued her tripping tightrope walk.

When she had reached the third and last sailing yacht near the head of the jetty, she stopped. It was an unspectacular single-mast sailing boat with, as its only special feature, a yellow hull. Most of the yachts Laura had seen so far, here or elsewhere, had been blue or white. Yellow was rather original, unusual, a marine version of the proverbial pink elephant. The dubious aesthetic merits of the colour aside, the outside appearance of the boat was that of an almost brand-new showroom exhibit. Its mooring ropes were not yet covered by slimy green algae, an infallible accessory typical of older, more neglected yachts. Her deck was of teak, as Laura recognized at first sight. A wide dark blue stripe ran all around the upper third of the side and the transom. Inlaid into the stripe with yellow ornamental letters were the name of the yacht and that of her port of registry. With the next short burst of moonlight, Laura managed to read both quite clearly: Yellow Dancer, Pointe-à-Pitre.

So that was her father's yacht, lying moored in the Blue Lagoon as Sven Larsen had found out by dint of a few phone calls at unusual hours. The very boat about whose existence Robert had deemed it wise never to breathe so much as a word. Laura, for her part, had never really wasted much thought on the organizational aspects of Robert's sailing sprees. Why would she? She had always assumed that, in line with thousands of other sailing enthusiasts, he would charter boats in the Caribbean. There must be enough to go round, surely. Only now did it occur to her that, for someone like Robert, who could afford to come to the Caribbean rather regularly, the purchase of a yacht must have been both more practical and more economical than chartering. Which made it all the more peculiar that he had never felt tempted to mention the Yellow Dancer at least on occasion. Most of the other yacht owners Laura had come across in her life hardly ever stopped getting into a lather about their boat, its performance under such and such weather conditions, the prices of sails and spare parts, whatever.

No, your Honour, circumstances oblige me to rephrase the question. Why was it that the accused went to such extraordinary lengths to keep the yacht's existence a secret? Only one logical answer, your Honour: the yacht represented something that, in the judgement of the accused, would have affected his relationship with Laura Forster deeply and lastingly. In other words, the Yellow Dancer was no mere means of transport, but an instrument of time travel. Yes, indeed, your Honour, allow me to insist: a time machine, which, once set in motion, threatened to unveil some of the less glorious aspects in the life of the accused. To bandy her about would have invited a dangerous loss of control uncharacteristic of someone used to keeping his cards close to his chest all the time.

Laura laughed aloud and shook her head. Talk of frying pan and fire. Shirking a vital entrepreneurial decision at home, she had come all the way to the Caribbean to manoeuvre herself into an even more disquieting private dilemma. Not a bad move, Laura Forster, do keep it up.

Then again, nobody obliged her to unturn that stone. The yacht had presented her with an excellent subterfuge to turn her back on Hamburg and the company for a while. Thus, as far as Laura was concerned, it had done its duty and was free to go. Tomorrow or the day after, she would place the yacht with all its material and immaterial contents in the hand of a local agent, to have it sold on commission, and that would be the end of it. If it did hide any dark secrets, some other owner would perhaps be only too happy to stand in for her father in what may have been his sugar-daddy role. An agent worth his money could even turn this into a compelling sales argument: yellow-hulled yacht with built-in marronage for the taking.

"You should be so lucky," Laura called out aloud and was immediately taken aback by the eerie sound of her own voice breaking the silence of this sanctuary. When it came to the point, what other option did she have now but to step on board? The taxi she had asked to return would be gone by the time she had reached the marina building on foot. If indeed it had ever come back in the first place, that is. Her mobile telephone which would be a definite asset now, she had forgotten at the hotel, of course.

"Hence, your Honour, to all intents and purposes, my client was practically condemned, eh, condemned not just to set foot on the Yellow Dancer but to spend the night on her, lest she was to expose herself to the incalculable risks of a subtropical night."

A barrister is what she ought to have become. She felt she would have had the knack for it. On the other hand, considering what treading the hamster wheel of legal reasoning had done to pundits of the profession such as Dr Sanders, she was not so sure any more.

How the Seven Seas' curse was a body supposed to get aboard this contraption anyway? At the time of her studies in Florida, Laura had been invited to no end of boat parties and even attended some of them. But those had taken place on monstrous high-tech transformers of motorboats, ironically termed "gin palaces" by the locals. Even handicapped by a long evening dress, you had no problems getting aboard via hydraulically operated gangways. By comparison, the hull of the Yellow Dancer looked small, narrow and derisively low-tech. No sign of a gangway to be seen anywhere. Taut steel wires the diameter of a pencil ran around the deck to form taffrails like a misplaced farm fence. Were they live? Metal supports fixed at regular intervals kept the wires about knee- and hip-high, respectively. Were you expected to crawl underneath the wire, like cabbage-faced Rocky Balboa entering the ring? Laura took a few steps further towards the bows. When she arrived at about the foot of the mast, she saw a gap in the taffrail, obviously meant to facilitate stepping onto and off the deck. Laura put her sandals down, tossed her handbag aboard and, grasping hold of the taffrail supports to the left and right, half pulled herself, half jumped on deck. As the yacht reacted to the sudden movement with amazing sensibility, "nodding" towards the jetty as if to welcome her late visitor, Laura almost fell off the boat backwards even before having completely boarded her in the first place. But since the Yellow Dancer righted herself immediately, Laura finally found herself standing with both feet firmly on the yacht's deck. On legs as stiff as wooden stalks, she walked towards the stern and, squeezing her chest past the wet white tarpaulin of the sprayhood, she climbed over the bench into the cockpit. Here, everything looked a little cramped and smelled of wet wood, ropes, salt, sweat, alcohol, and diesel fuel, not unlike the old disused Route 66 gas stations more recently converted into smack shacks.

The small, double-winged bulkhead leading down to the living quarters of the boat was locked, as Laura had suspected. Nor did she see a doormat or flowerpot that might serve as a hiding place for the key. But when she bent down to take a closer look, supporting herself with her right hand on the hatch, the wooden lid slid forward just a little under her pressure. Peering down into the "crypt" through the narrow gap between bulkhead and hatch, Laura could discern next to nothing. A torch would have worked wonders now. Why hadn't she thought of that? Probably, because she had been in a hurry to get here and not taken the time to think it through. Once more, she pushed against the hatch, this time with as much force as she could muster. The resulting gap was wide enough for her to open the lock from the inside.

Again, she hesitated - not because of any qualms or mental reservations, but because she suspected foul play. Why lock the door yet leave the hatch open? If someone as little versed with boats as Laura could get inside the Yellow Dancer that easily, what about experienced thieves? There were no visible traces of forced entry with a crowbar or anything like that. Maybe someone had done a repair job and forgotten to first pull the sliding companion hatch all the way to the stops before turning the key. Sloppy job, but a perfectly plausible explanation.

Tolerably satisfied with her conclusion, she looked into the black hole in front of her. She felt a bit like an actress notoriously weak on text gazing into the ominous void of an exceptionally empty prompt box. The only thing she could clearly make out, and instinctively disliked, was the incredibly narrow, steep companionway that seemed unfit for the ascent and descent of human beings of average height. Did they hire hobbit crews on such boats? Surely, there must be a light-switch somewhere? Even the magic display of her mobile could have helped. Cautiously as a cat following a rabbit into its burrow, she set her naked toes on the first narrow step, grasped the edge of the hatch in front of her and pulled in her left foot. Then, a true cascade of things seemed to be happening all at once.

Laura's humid feet slipped on the moist, splintered wood of the steps, so that she lost her balance and, her sweaty fingers slipping off the hatch under the weight of her body, slid down the rest of the companionway very much like a rubbish bin tumbling down a staircase, briefly touching each step with a resounding rumble. She had hardly thumped down onto the ground, crying aloud with the sharp pain in her coccyx, when all the lights around her suddenly came alive with blinding force as if, in falling, she had triggered a motion detector. But there was no acoustic alarm. Instead, two giant hands hairy and powerful like those of a gorilla grabbed her under her armpits and threw her torso onto the table like a sack of flour. Again, a piercing pain flashed through her body as if it had been hit by lightning.

One of the gorilla hands seized her hair and bent her head backwards over the edge of the table, so that Laura feared her neck might snap any moment like a dry twig. It all happened so fast, Laura had no time for defensive moves. And even if she had been able to react, what resistance could she have offered to stay this hominid apparently escaped from some nearby zoo? Her attacker was practically lying on her like the huge dark shadow in her recurrent nightmare. And precisely like in her dream, she seemed perfectly unable to move. When she felt the broad serrated edge of a combat knife against her throat, Laura was sure her end had come. The banal circumstances of her father's decease had demonstrated to her that, when in a hurry, death did not indulge in pathetic opera finales but made short shrift of humans, never mind their merits and status. But to get killed as unceremoniously and pointlessly as all that was scandalous, she felt.

"You can't look inside," were her last ridiculous thoughts. But the knife did not move, just maintained its pressure and thus kept its victim motionless. The firm hold on her hair relaxed a little. The light of the ceiling lamps blinded Laura. She tried hard to turn her head a little sideways and closed her eyes. When she opened them again, the ugly face of her attacker slowly moved between her eyes and the lamps like the disk of the moon during an eclipse of the sun. The man's sweaty, darkish face was literally covered with the scars of bad burns like irregular gaping craters. His bulging upper lip bore a cut right under his nose, betraying a cleft palate. Even though his eyes were no more than slits, Laura recognized his pupils to be of the dark blue lapis that had always been her favourite semiprecious stone.

His blond hair was lengthened by filthy-looking dreadlocks and hung down on his broad shoulders. The man was a ghost, a phantom, a misshapen messenger of Hades. His hideous face had been botched up in such outrageous manner as to be quite fascinating again, in a macabre way. Nothing seemed to tally there. Mother nature must have set about this fanciful piece of creation in a moment of tiddly exuberance and, consequently, had come up with a Gothic gargoyle of a face. His scars reminded Laura of photos of Indian women whose husbands had poured acid in their faces to avoid the cost of divorce.

Laura turned her head further aside to avoid the disturbing sight of the man's face and the rum-saturated smell of his sickening breath. But her attacker was not having any of it. He pressed his body so close to hers that she could feel his erect member against her thighs.

Was he going to rape her? Laura almost fainted at the mere thought. Particularly now, when it was her time of the month. She would rather die right away then.

The man pulled her head back into the light, lifted the edge of his knife off her throat and brushed her meshes aside with such rash violence that the tip of his knife almost grazed her left eye. Then, he took a long, hard look at her, as if to decide whether a touch of cosmetic surgery would not promise sustainable improvement. His eyes, or what was visible of them, expressed amazement, surprise, disbelief, with, as absurd as it seemed to Laura then, a bizarre touch of tenderness. For all she knew, Laura was the "white woman" of the silent films looking into King Kong's bloodshot eyes.

Finally, the phantom let go of Laura's head, sheathed his knife, and, mumbling something incomprehensible to himself, turned around in a flash and jumped up the companionway steps with the speed and bounce of a true tree-dwelling ape.

Laura felt the yacht bow briefly to the side of the water but heard no splash. Dazed and rigid as if shock-frosted by events, she nevertheless registered every tiny detail. Thus, shortly after the man's disappearance, she heard an outboard engine come to life and a small boat speed away into the night. While the dinghy, which Laura had had no chance to discover from either the jetty or the deck, kept on sending its bubbling wake to the hull of the Yellow Dancer, heavily wheezing Laura was lying where the phantom had thrown her, staring into the dazzling lights like a patient on the operating table.

It took quite a while till she felt she had herself under control again. Now that the shock had receded, the piercing pain in her coccyx, back, and neck started pulsating at such a rate that she could not hold back her tears and was afraid she might have to throw up. With a loud gasp, she righted herself to shun the lights. Thus, she sat for a while without moving, hung her head down and let her legs dangle from the edge of the table.

Had all that really happened just now? Or was it yet another figment of her sick imagination, fired by the theatrical magic of a feverishly hot Caribbean night? Hardly. Her throat bore witness to the reality of the attack. The man's razor-sharp blade had left a superficial cut that trickled a little blood onto her bare chest. Coming aboard the Yellow Dancer she had counted on the likelihood of unpleasant surprises alright, but had not imagined she would be looking into the ugly mug of Satan himself. With a shudder, she slid from the table and immediately cried out loud again. If nothing else, her coccyx would probably remind her of this episode for the rest of her life. She just hoped it was not broken. Coming home to Hamburg with a damaged ass didn't seem very heroic, now, did it? The accompanying story would be taken as cock-and-bull hardly worth a thought. To the left of the companionway was the Yellow Dancer's galley. With trembling hands, she opened the lid of the spacious fridge, half expecting to stare into the broken eyes of a frozen corpse of some earlier victim of the phantom. But there was none. Thank God, a merciful soul had thought of stock-piling plastic bottles with drinking water. She poured some of the cool liquid on her head, neck and wrists. Then she drank the rest of the bottle's contents in short controlled swigs. Opening the first-aid kit fixed against the hull over the sink, she took out some disinfectant and adhesive dressing. She managed to stop the bleeding and dress the wound as best she could. Then she sat down on the bunk, which was upholstered in a tasteful dark blue, and closed her eyes.

What in God's name was it the phantom had been looking for? He could not possibly be a thief. If he was, he must be of the rare pedantic sort who hated to leave a mess behind. Nothing indicated that somebody had rifled through the cupboards and drawers in search of valuables. On the contrary, everything looked as if he had passed by with the express intention of rendering the yacht's interior shipshape. It didn't make sense to Laura, none of it did. The laws of logic seemed suspended in the Caribbean.

Had he been looking for a place to stay and hide from the police or rival gangsters hard on his heels? What motivated his initial brutality, his absolute killing intent? What could Laura have sued him for? Trespassing, damages and minor injuries. You don't kill anyone for that. Even if she had been as vindictive as to pursue him in court, the police would have to get their hands on him first. Which, by the look of Mr Uglymug's amazing agility, was probably not the easiest of tasks.

But once he felt he had to kill her for reasons of his own, why then had he aborted his attempt? What had brought him to his senses all of a sudden? If anything was fathomable by reason: this man was a natural-born killer driven by instinct and drugs rather than reason, Laura felt certain. He must be at home in worlds and dimensions perfectly alien to normal human beings. Maybe an element of superstition? Women were anathema not only in practically all traditional religions. Whatever separated minor sects, secret orders or obscure religious communities, the one thing they surely would have in common was their irrational persecution of women. No, there was more to it than that. Laura had had the impression of looking into the eyes of a beast of prey slashing out at a victim by way of an irresistible reflex, realizing only at the very last moment that it was about to kill and devour its own offspring. Should she not call the police? But how would she do that without her mobile phone and without any knowledge in the handling of the boat's radio installation? If she got it wrong, half the yachting world of the Caribbean would be alerted for no reason. Besides, what could she expect the police to do now, at the dead of night? Draw a phantom portrait? Laura laughed.

The man would not return in the course of the night, of that she was sure, as she tried to put herself in his shoes. He could have no knowledge of her technical communication problems and, consequently, had to count on the police waiting for him here to turn up. Hence, she would probably be safer on the boat than outside in the dark.

Pain, as well as physical and mental exhaustion, made her collapse on the bunk like a punctured silicon doll. Half sitting, half lying, she closed her eyes. A gently swaying Yellow Dancer rocked her into sleep. Soon, her head fell backward. Her lips parted slightly and a few Blue Lagoon bats particularly keen of hearing would catch a low snoring sound from inside the yacht with the yellow hull and momentarily wonder, as they shot by, what to make of it.

2. One-Eyed Jacques

Laura was sinking, plunging ever deeper into the lukewarm blue sea. She had tripped over a rope on deck and fallen off the cruising Yellow Dancer. When nobody had heard her cries for help, she had desperately tried to follow the yacht in her wake, but had soon been hopelessly distanced. As she had fallen further and further behind, with the yacht only a dot on the horizon, she had given up hope, stopped fighting and let gravity do the rest. Although quickly getting her head under water, she had felt neither suffocation nor panic, strangely enough, but had even been quite relaxed: if this was death by drowning, there was nothing much to it, she had thought. Now, tens of yards further down, she was still pretty much alive and hovering blithely somewhere in mid-sea. The water pressure did not seem to grow and, instead of getting colder with increasing depth, the sea appeared to become warmer, in fact. A school of inquisitive clown-fish were circling her at one stage, nibbling away cautiously at the tips of her fingers and toes. When Laura started giggling, the clowns flurried away through the rising cloud of air bubbles that Laura produced every time she opened her mouth. A giant squid slowly spread its long tentacles, spat out a jet of black ink and, in the face of much evidence to the contrary, insisted on being a starfish. The glitter of the sunrays on the silvery scales of the fish dashing this way and that became gradually duller, with all the colours of the spectrum being progressively reduced to a ubiquitous pale blue. Yet it was still light enough for Laura to watch her immediate surroundings.

At long last, Laura's backside landed gently on a soft sandy bottom between two ragged rocks. Her long dark hair kept standing up for a little while longer like undulating kelp. Then, it slowly sank down, too, mesh upon mesh, and clung to her face as lightly and tenderly as dark candyfloss.

So she sat for a while and listened to the amazing cacophony of the deep which turned out to be a lot noisier than she had ever suspected. When she slowly turned round, eventually, she recognized the silhouette of a big walrus hobbling towards her as if in slow motion. The massive male with its two long, pointed, awe-inspiring tusks wore the same glasses as Dr Sanders. In fact, the closer it came, the more it resembled the legal advisor of ROLA Ltd.

"I always assumed walruses to live in the Arctic," Laura said, when the animal had closed in on her and looked her over with a mixture of curiosity and irony, prompted both by its awe-inspiring age and unquestionable physical superiority.

"Is that so, young lady? Well, let me assure you, it's not the last surprise you have coming. That said, I always assumed humans to live on land, eh, on land, primarily," the walrus answered and mischievously glanced over the rims of its glasses.

"As for the Arctic, well, it's what it is, very white, cold and just a wee bit boring, on the whole. Especially in winter time. Months and months of depressing darkness. Personally, I prefer to travel and widen my horizons, as they say. Especially since my wife died four years ago. She was a manatee, the gentlest of souls."

Laura realized that she was dealing with a specimen of such extraordinary shrewdness and remarkable quick-wittedness as was last encountered in The Jungle Book. In the light of this preliminary assessment, any sarcastic comments touching on such delicate subjects as fighting excess weight and heeding one's BMI that might have lingered at the tip of her tongue had to be swallowed then.

"I'm sorry for your loss. May I ride on you?" she tried a more jovial approach. "My feet are killing me, you know."
The walrus took off its glasses and stared at Laura with genuine indignation.

"Ride on me, young lady, are you kidding? I believe you're mistaking me for a sea-horse, a hippocampus circensis."

"Hippo, horse, walrus, what the heck, to me it all comes down to very much the same thing," Laura exclaimed.

"Not even close," the walrus protested with a cunning smile and a disapproving shake of its mighty head. "Might I remind you that we are proud descendants of the whale family and hence, entitled to a certain amount of respect, eh, respect. More specifically, we stem from the toothed branch. Originally, we were called whaleruses, you see. Due to dyslexic Charles Darwin, one of your doomed species, we unfortunately came to be handed down to posterity in a bawdlerized form, as walruses."

"In fact, my great-grandfather on my mother's side was a narwhal, complete with tusk and blow-hole. No anaemic vegan pussy, either, let me assure you. Which is why nature provided us with these beautiful ivory tusks. Where else in the animal kingdom do you have that ingenious combination of tooth and toothpick rolled into one? Evolution has its bright moments."

Laura felt she was being had. She must not allow this animal, generally reputed as thick, slow and clumsy, to deal with a representative of the masters - and mistresses - of creation in such an inadmissibly condescending manner. Maybe the unusually warm water had gone to the walrus's head. If so, it had to be put back in place. Laura decided to demonstrate her superior intellect by rubbing the animal's nose in what looked like an obvious contradiction in terms to her.

"If what you say is true, and, no offence, that's a very big if, as far as I am concerned, you ought to be able to speak your ancestors' language."

Well, touché, that should do it, Laura thought. But the walrus appeared less than impressed.

"And who told you I can't," it replied with even greater dash. The walrus' attention was straying at that point because it had discovered a sea cucumber, which, upon becoming aware of the walrus's giant shadow spreading all around it, sped away as fast as its short cucumber legs would allow.

"Strictly speaking," the walrus resumed, "strictly speaking, it's none of your business. But let me assure you, for entire centuries, walruses have acted as dragomans, or interpreters, for their barnacled cousins and brethren. In exchange for the eyes of giant squid, big as plates. Not the squids, their eyes. The whales regularly bring them up from the unfathomable depths of the ocean. Breaded and deep fried, they are a great delicacy, squid eyes are. You should try them in a sweet-sour sauce with a bottle of dry white wine, superb."

The walrus resettled its glasses on the ridge of his nose, rose on its hind flukes with astounding dexterity, pursed its lips, formed a cup around its mouth with the front flukes and howled with a penetrating falsetto, "Hiiijaaawaaaathaaaah!"

Laura thought that was the poorest imitation of a blue whale's mating cry and covered her ears with an expression of intense pain. Whereupon the walrus stuck out its tongue as if to mock her.

"You see this? Is this your typical whale tongue or what? Would you say it belongs to a penguin, eh, penguin?"
Laura made a serious effort to keep a straight face.

"Since you ask me, I should rather think it was a half-digested salmon fillet trying to escape…."

"A what? A salmon…?

Having reached the end of its intellectual tether, the walrus apparently changed tactics and relied on its physical advantage instead. Still balancing on its hind flukes, it started turning in circles like an underwater Nureyev a little out of shape because of lack of exercise but still capable of performing the occasional en pointe. As the walrus was spinning round and round, it kept singing the popular Eskimo nursery rhyme, The lonely little whale young with its pretty bluish whale-tongue, howling at the end of each verse like a clobbered seal.

Laura had had enough of this. The impertinent walrus had to be silenced. She got up and approached the insolent animal, to let it have a piece of her mind. But the walrus grabbed hold of her arms and spun her around to the rhythm of its song. Then, it pulled Laura even closer and started licking her cheeks, making smacking gourmet sounds and oinking like a pig. "Hmmm, squid's eyes, yummy squid's eyes. Hmmmm, gimme more, gimme all."

Its tongue was long, cold and mildly abrasive, a bit like a a salmon fillet fried on the skin, actually. Not all that unpleasant, really, if it wasn't for that fishy breath. Laura tore herself away from the walrus and covered her face with her two hands.

"Stop it!" she shouted again and again and wanted to run away. But the water slowed her down and her feet were caught in the kelp forest, so that she fell headlong into the sand.

She woke up with a piercing pain in her coccyx. Dizzy as if still half-drunk after a night of unrestrained debauchery, she was groping for a hold. Graham the Sleeper couldn't have been more at a loss waking in a world 200 years on than Laura coming to in what might as well have been the lavishly furnished insides of a whale. And she wasn't alone here, either. Right opposite her, whimpering, wagging its tail, and panting with its tongue hanging out on the side of its soft lips, sat a cinnamon-coloured Labrador retriever with brown eyes and some white age-patches around its nose.

Laura wasn't sure her dream had really ended. Had the walrus transformed itself into a dog? Which side did this peculiar animal belong to? Probably it had been the dog's tongue that Laura had felt on her face while she was half asleep. Very gradually, she started to realize where she was and what had happened. She had passed the night on the yacht and dreamed a lot of rubbish towards morning as she was wont to whenever her brain caught her consciousness unawares. Then she had had her face licked by a dog, slid down from the bunk and fallen on her already aching backside.

But what business did the dog have on the boat in the first place? Was the Yellow Dancer a kind of free-for-all? A floating asylum where dogs, bums, thieves, just about anyone popped in and out whenever they pleased? Anyway, at some stage, the dog must have noticed that he was bestowing his reverential caresses on the wrong person and taken fright. Laura recognized the animal now. Surely, this was the Labrador that had materialized from the twilight and come running towards her the night before at the "Turks". Talking to him in a calm, friendly manner, she stretched out her hand to make contact.

Outside, she heard someone stumbling, huffing and puffing, over the wobbly jetty. "César," a man's hoarse voice called out in French, "viens-ici, espèce de brute." The animal yawned out of embarrassment, as if to say, "Sorry, but I have to take that one." Then César, if that was his name, got up, stretched, first his hind legs, then its forelegs, like a sprinter seconds from the start, and bounded up the companionway. Laura heard his paws pitter-pattering over the deck and pulled herself up on the bunk to her left and the table to her right. Someone knocked on the boat's hull like the postman on a bungalow door. She felt tempted to call "Do come in, everybody else does." But then she thought better of it.

"Allo, ya quelqu'un?" Again the man's hoarse voice. Laura pulled her blouse into shape, brushed her hair back with her hands, wriggled her throat bandage into place and climbed up the first few steps of the companionway until she was just able to glimpse over the rim of the cockpit.

Outside on the jetty stood a man of about 60 years of age, lean to bony, dressed in comfortable but somewhat old-fashioned leisure wear that looked a size or two too big for him. The one thing lamentably out of place was the burnt pancake of a beret he had rather coquettishly pulled over his left ear as if that needed special protection from the ultra-violet rays of the sun. His right eye was covered by a black patch and his upper lip decorated with a vaudeville toothbrush-style moustache of the kind which even Frenchmen were increasingly reticent to cultivate these days. In lieu of the habitual yellow, saliva-soaked yellowish fag-end of a plain Gauloise glued to his lips, he had a small, bent pipe sticking in the corner of his mouth. Ejecting almost as many blue fumes as an outboard engine with serious carburettor problems, the pipe would not have been allowed in Hamburg's inner city on smog days. His khaki shorts covering the thighs of his thin, prickly legs, seemed to give away the retired army colonel who had practically been born into his uniform and was consequently at a loss when it came to choosing appropriate civvies.

He couldn't be married, Laura thought. No woman in her right mind would have allowed him to leave home with that ridiculous pancake on his head. Why men would want to wear shorts off such places as the football ground or rugby pitch, tennis court, beach or outdoor swimming pool, had always been a source of bewilderment to Laura. Did they ever bother to take a hard look at the mirror? A George Clooney was likely to remain his seductively virile self even in Japanese sumo diapers, to be sure. But the pitiful rest of manhood, Laura found, was as attractive in shorts as a woman with cellulitis. Why did men of all nations not emulate the Italians? They would not want to be caught dead in shorts, ever, and knew perfectly well why not.

The dog leash with the empty collar in the Frenchman's hand would have made him the cinnamon Labrador's owner even if the dog had not sat next to his right foot, waggling his tail and wheezing in Laura's direction. Were older dogs affected by Alzheimer's syndrome, too, and if so, did they get confused about people's identities, Laura wondered. Because this Labrador clearly seemed to mistake her for somebody else.

"Mais ça suffit. La ferme, César!" The one-eyed man hit his dog lightly over the back with the leash, whereupon his dog bit the leather and, with a sudden jerk, tore it out of his hand. Laura remembered that typical Labrador reaction from another specimen she had once taken care of for a few days. Bird dogs are supposed to fetch shot-down ducks, quail or any other fowl, and, if necessary, put them out of their misery by breaking their necks with this sudden sideways jerk. In a playful tug-of-war over some silly rag, they would not easily give in but hold on for dear life even if you lifted the dog clean off the ground with all its weight hanging by its teeth. Laura snapped out of her thoughts and tried to pull herself together, even at this early hour, to welcome the man in his own language.

"Bonjour Monsieur! Je m'appelle Laura Forster." Holy cow, didn't she feel abominably silly with that idiot sentence from lesson number one, French for Dummies.

The one-eyed man seemed taken aback for a brief spell, took his crooked pipe out of his mouth, stroked his toothbrush with his thumb and then addressed her in almost impeccable English.

"Good morning, Madame Forster, enchanté. Allow me to present myself. Jacques-Pierre de Hougmont, Jack to my friends. Of whom, I regret to say, there are not that many left. That's the way of the world, isn't it."

He bowed with the ceremonious elegance of a slowly fossilizing sexagenarian and stuck his pipe back in the corner of his mouth, which seemed shaped for this very purpose. Laura fleetingly mused about what it must be like to kiss him but quickly shunned the outrageous idea. His French accent in German was barely perceptible and as for the tripwires of syntax, he avoided them with greater ease than Yoda the Master Jedi.

"Am I right in assuming you are German? I seem to have picked up a Northern German tinge in your otherwise excellent French. City of Hamburg, I presume?"

Laura was not as impressionable as all that.

"Which borough?" she retorted.

The quaintly moustachioed one-eyed Jack laughed. "Let me think. I'm taking a wild guess here, of course, but yes, I think I'd put my money on the borough of Blankenese."

This time, Laura was downright nonplussed. Her surprise probably showed on her face, because the Frenchmen promptly laughed out loud again. How could he do that without his pipe falling in the water, Laura wondered. His laugh reminded her of the cascade-like bleating of goats on the Geesthacht farm.

"You must forgive an old man for his silly pranks. At my age, anything to impress a young lady, especially one as attractive as yourself, with due respect."

Again, the ritual of the pipe coming out, the toothbrush being stroked. His Labrador, used to the somewhat cruder welcoming routines of the canine world, showed signs of growing boredom. Profiting from the situation, he strolled down the jetty and disappeared in the bushes without his master even noticing.

"Here's the thing. I happened to be an acquaintance of your late father's, Monsieur Robert's, as he was generally called down here. He had let me know he came from Hamburg Blankenese and I thought it would not be such a long shot to assume that his daughter… Sorry about that. Anyway, whenever he wasn't here, but back in Hamburg or God knows where else, I used to keep an eye on his Yellow Dancer, the good eye, of course." He pointed at his left eye and laughed again. Laura wagged an admonishing index at him.

"I was already half convinced you had compensated for the loss of part of your eyesight by sharpening your hearing. Would you care to come aboard?"

Jack bent down and knocked the bowl of his pipe against the jetty so the embers fell in the water with a sizzling sound. Then he straightened himself again with faint crackling of his rusty joints. He bowed again. "I'd be delighted to, but what about the dog?" He looked down at his feet, then gave a despondent sigh.
"What dog? Restless old soul, much like his master. Probably caught the whiff of a loose bitch roaming the lagoon, I suspect."

He literally swung himself aboard with surprising sprightliness. His every movement told Laura that the man was a habitué of boats in general and another frequent visitor on the Yellow Dancer. She would not be surprised if he could found his way about blindfolded.

"Do you know any German at all?"

"Used to, in fact. You see, I grew up in Strasbourg, where you tend to hear more German than French in some quarters. Later, during my time in Paris, most of it went down the drain, unfortunately, as was probably to be expected. Here on the island, I frequently offer my services as a guide to tourists, both in French, English and German. It helps me to keep up a kind of basic German vocabulary, but I vastly prefer English. Or French, for that matter, no offence."

"None taken. So you know my father died?"

Jacques looked down on the deck.

"Indeed, Madame Forster, so I do. And I am still in shock, believe me. So very young at heart and positive in all he did and said. I am truly sorry for your loss, since, to some admittedly lesser degree, it is mine, too."
He paused and fumbled with the end of a rope that had not been properly sorted out.

"Yes, well, some pieces of news reach us faster than you can blink an eyelid. Rumble in the jungle, you know. Other things remain a secret forever and a day. That's the Caribbean for you, paradise or hell, depends on what you make of it. Your late father could be said to have made the best of it, from his point of view, anyway. Had a lot of friends over here, too. I may be flattering myself counting myself among their ranks. Whatever I can do to be of service to his daughter… just say the word."

Laura would have liked to confirm that her father had practically never stopped telling her about this old Caribbean friend of his, the one-eyed Jack. But had that really been the case, she would have to have recognized the man at first sight from his descriptions and not needed any introduction. Nothing but his appearance would have left no room for doubt. Jack would no doubt come to the same conclusion and look through her polite lie. On the other hand, Laura saw absolutely no reason to open herself up and betray her total ignorance concerning her father's "Caribbean side", closely connected to the Yellow Dancer, as it would seem. They climbed down the companionway and Laura offered the Frenchman a glass of the orange juice she had found in the fridge.

"Sorry, but I forgot how to activate the gas stove, otherwise I would brew us a good German filter coffee."

Jack raised his brow and protested.

"Don't even bother, Madame Forster, I can do that. In fact, had I known about your arrival, I would have joined you with a bagful of croissants, as behoves a true Frenchman. If you like, I'll just rush over to the nearest baker's, and…"

Laura shook her head. "No need for that, thanks anyway. But a coffee would indeed be appreciated no end."

"Did you notice my arrival last night?" she asked the Frenchman, while he was firing up the stove. Apparently, he knew perfectly well where everything was, since he didn't have to look around to find either matches, coffee powder, a can, two cups and spoons.

"No, unfortunately I didn't. Had I seen you wandering around aimlessly, as it were, I would certainly have presented myself to you and offered my services. A good thing you at least knew roughly where to look for the yacht. No, this morning, I just followed the dog about, something I seem to be doing most of the time. Seen from that angle, he's regularly walking me instead of the other way round. César knows the boat, of course, and probably heard or sniffed someone aboard. May be to him, you smell like your father."

Laura laughed. "I hope not. Did César occasionally lick his face?"

As the water came to the boil, the Frenchman took off the kettle and poured two cups of powder coffee.

"You mean to say… No, not that I ever noticed. As a matter of fact, I have never as yet seen him do that to anyone, very strange. He must have a crush on you. Well, as a French he-dog, he has a reputation to live up to."

Again, the goatish laughter broke loose.

Jack plunged his hand into his trouser pocket.

"Your father deposited a set of keys with me, which I should like to pass on to you. Though I take it you have your own?"

Laura answered in the negative and bit her lip at the same time, realizing that she had made a first mistake.
The Frenchman hesitated.

"May I ask you, then, how you got in last night?"

Laura could not make up her mind whether she should tell Jacques about the attack she had suffered on the hands of the phantom the night before. Jacques' professed friendship with Robert could be a lie. How was she to know that the Frenchman was not in fact an accomplice of her attacker and had been sent to test whether the coast was clear.

"I found the hatch unlocked," she replied.

"Really? Unlocked? I'll be…" Jack seemed genuinely surprised.

"I could swear I turned the key after my last inspection visit, what, three days ago. After that, nobody went aboard, not to my knowledge. Had the lock been forced?"

Laura answered in the negative.

The Frenchman thought it over a little while.

"Ah, well, old men are forgetful. Or rather, their osmotic brains can no longer tell the important from the accessory. Past and present become inseparably intertwined because the axis called future has dropped out of the system of coordinates. We are constantly being overwhelmed by meaningless childhood memories and forget why we've gone to the supermarket. Progressive loss of orientation, that's what it is. Without the permanent guidance of reason, our brain is lost in the thickets of our synapses like the proverbial babe in the woods."

He sighed and raised both his arms as if in despair.

"I must have been in a hurry three days ago, and forgot to pull the hatch all the way to the stop. Do you take sugar or milk?"

"No, thank you, I'll have mine black, please."

The Frenchman carefully placed two cups with hot coffee on the table and sat down on the bunk opposite Laura with the table between the two of them.

"You don`t really seem to know your way about the boat that well, do you?"

That was more of a rhetorical question, Laura thought. Obviously, you don't forget the operation of a gas stove that easily unless you are a complete moron. This one-eyed Jack was closing in on the truth like a wolf on its not yet totally defenceless prey - in ever tightening circles. She had to be on her guard with him.

"No, not really. My father always promised to take me on one of his excursions, but somehow never got round to it. Why the name Yellow Dancer?" she asked, to shift the thrust of the conversation, but also because the thought didn't stop preoccupying her.

"Cruise," Jack insisted. "We call it cruise, not excursion. Sailors have their own terminology and are ridiculously meticulous using it. No big deal, you'll learn it in a jiffy. Why Yellow Dancer? Well, it's the name of a flower, actually, a particularly beautiful yellow lobster claw, as its popular name goes. Widespread in the US and the Caribbean. You do like flowers, now, don't you?"
Laura nodded. She had made the acquaintance of the particular species with its blossoms shaped like lobster claws, always looking slightly waxy, in Florida, perhaps the most artificial place in the US except Las Vegas, of course. And Ocean City. And Salt Lake City. And Hollywood. Curiously enough, now that the Frenchman had mentioned them, Laura seemed dimly to remember having seen a bunch of Yellow Dancers on Robert's grave without really paying them any attention at the time. Yet, somehow, the Frenchman's answer did little to elucidate why Robert had given his boat that peculiar name. Laura did not recall her father to display botanic interest in anything other than hemp.

"Then you must give me a chance to let you in on the secrets of handling the Yellow Dancer. She is a Hallberg, as you will have noticed. Not a very fast ship, but a really seaworthy one."
He seemed on the brink of starting the first lesson right away, but thought better of it.

"Unless, of course, you have come to put the yacht on the market. In which case, you can leave it to an agent to press the Yellow Dancer's many virtues on a small crowd of potential buyers. These people know their trade, and the brand is well known all over the world. You will have no problem selling her at a reasonable price."

"But what about the colour?"

The Frenchman laughed and stroked his moustache.

"Yes, that's something, isn't it? As a rule, Hallberg's are very partial about anything that might reflect on their time-honoured image. But Robert had insisted on the yellow hull, and finally had his way, as he was wont to. Giving the boat a new lick of blue or white paint is no problem, however."

Laura told him she had not yet decided what to do with the Yellow Dancer.

"Superb. Well, I shouldn't really outstay my welcome, should I. You look fatigued, if I may say so. Jetlag, heat, humidity, it all wears us down, obviously. Incidentally, what have you done to your throat?"

By mere reflex, Laura's hand went to her throat and nestled at the bandage, which had loosened again and slid down a little, allowing a glimpse of her cut.

"Oh, well, that's nothing, really, an insect sting or spider's bite, whatever. I must have scratched myself a little too violently in my sleep."

"Don't underestimate trifles like that, Madame Forster. People die of less, believe me. Rupert Brooke, a young English poet and gentleman of the last century comes to mind. He was eventually sent to his grave by an infected mosquito bite. Happened during the Gallipoli campaign, curious incident, when you think about it. And, somehow, a stupidly unheroic way to go. May I have a look at that?".

"Are you a medical man?"

"Used to be, yes. I no longer practice, not officially, at any rate. But a mosquito bite should still be in my range. No, let me do this, please."

He removed Laura's hand from her throat and cautiously opened the bandage. When he saw the wound, he gave a low whistle through his teeth.

"Doesn't look like a mosquito bite to me, honestly. I don't wish to be nosy, but did you try to kill yourself?"

Laura laughed almost hysterically.

"No, certainly not. And if ever I did, I would not do it by cutting my own throat, I don't think. No, as I said, I must have scratched too energetically with my long fingernails."

Of course, Laura knew full well that any person with a smattering of medical knowledge would immediately recognize her wound as what it really was, a cut from a sharp knife. This would no doubt apply to Jack, who came across more harmless than he probably was. But she didn't feel like launching into lengthy explanations at this juncture. Every square inch of her body was aching, her ovulation time had positively set in and what with the few hours of rest she had had the night before, she felt gelatinous with fatigue. All she wanted now was for the Frenchman to be gone so she could have a shower and maybe catch some sleep.

"Right, now, that should protect you from inflammation," the Frenchman concluded his perfunctory treatment and smiled somewhat ironically, it seemed to Laura.

"Perhaps you ought to get your fingernails clipped a little shorter then, one of these days, Madame Forster."

Laura looked at her nails, most of them broken when her fingers had slipped the hatch last night.

"Thank you very much. And, please do me a favour and call me Laura, will you. Whenever you address me as Madame Forster, you make me feel like my own mother."

"Enchanté, Laura." Outside, on the jetty, the pitter-patter of a dog's paws on the planks was to be heard.

"May César come aboard, too?" Jack asked.

"Of course, he already knows his way about, doesn't he?"

The Frenchman gave a single low whistle, which made César jump on deck and climb down the companionway. Laura filled a bowl with water and placed it on the floor. The thirsty dog immediately rushed to it and started licking the water up with his tongue curved like a soup spoon.

"César asks me to thank you for the water. But as soon as he has finished, you will finally be rid of us. We have taken up too much of your time, already. But you must join me for lunch on my catamaran, the Perséphone II. I have an excellent cook, you will see. My yacht is moored right next to the marina building, the one you must have passed on your arrival yesterday. You can't miss her, even though she does not have a yellow hull. Hers is a slightly faded white. Shall we say at one p.m.? Would that suit you?"

Not really, Laura thought. She would have preferred the entire afternoon at her own disposal and was afraid to have to spend it listening to an old man's rambling life story. But to refuse, even in the politest of terms, would have amounted to an unnecessary insult. Also, the man might prove useful.

"Yes, great," she replied. "I spotted some wine while you were making coffee. I'll bring a bottle then, red or white?"

"If I may be impertinent enough as to suggest the 1969 Pinot Gris d'Alsace, a favourite of your late father's, but that you will know better than me."

The Frenchman and César took their leave and hopped onto the jetty. To Jack's order, "without step, march!" the two of them walked, or rather stumbled and tripped along in a cloud of blue smoke. Laura waved after them and climbed down the companionway, backwards this time, having realized from the Frenchman's example that this was a lot safer.

About an hour later, Laura had taken a shower, shaved her legs and "caulked" herself anew. Now she was sitting at the chart table naked, with a cup of cold coffee in front of her. Fortunately, she had found a full Tampax box in the boat's pharmacy. Exactly why Robert had felt it necessary to have that aboard, she didn't even want to know.

The yacht's interior pleased Laura, even though she had found the Yellow Dancer very small and narrow at first. Cherry wood, mahogany and other first-class hardwoods had been employed with great craftsmanship and rendered the entire living quarters warm and cosy. Unless you had to share them with an ugly freak of the netherworld, that is.

Her father had always been a stickler for cleanliness and had certainly made no exception when it came to the boat. The smaller a place, the more quickly it adopted a chaotic look. Nothing of the sort around here. Wherever Laura passed the tips of her fingers over wood or metal, not so much as a speck of dust. In some of the cupboards, she came across Robert's pullovers, oilskins, T-shirts and the odd pair of trousers, socks, and boots. Robert's presence was ubiquitously palpable. Articles of women's clothing weren't to be found. And even though she didn't pick up any female scents, either, her instincts told her that some woman or other had been aboard the yacht, at least intermittently. Men on their own were not likely to keep things in such an impeccable state for long, not in Laura's experience.

She looked at the heap of charts, handbooks, tables and operating manuals in front of her. A chart table was something like the skipper's desk, apparently. When looking for information on the yacht, her owner, her voyages, and the people who had sailed in her at some time or another, the chart table was hence the best bet.

She brushed the heap of papers aside and lifted the wooden lid. There were more IMRAY charts of the wider Caribbean, all the way up to Puerto Rico and Hispaniola, transparent navigational triangles, compasses of different sizes, and all sorts of odds and ends, like in most office desks anywhere. Laura also found the ship's papers, flag letter, insurance documents, and Robert's navigational licence stating that its owner had the permission to skipper ships up to 100 tons deadweight anywhere on the globe, without restrictions. Seen that the Yellow Dancer would hardly displace more than ten tons, in Laura's laywoman's judgement, that left a wide enough margin.

There was a black logbook for the current year, too. It contained all kinds of useless information such as GPS positions, courses, harbours visited, weather conditions encountered, manoeuvres performed and the like. The only blank column was the one that should have contained the names and addresses of guests or crew. Unfortunately, that was precisely the piece of information Laura wanted most. The rest could have gone into the shredder right away as far as she was concerned.

Unwilling to leave it at that, Laura groped in the corners under the covers left and right. As her fingers touched a package of notes or letters, she had a presentiment she might have struck a vein of pure gold. She pulled the package out from underneath the cover. It was letters alright, still in their envelopes, tied with a yellow ribbon, what else. Trying to open the ribbon, she broke two more of her fingernails on what was probably one of those silly sailor's knots, complicated to tie, impossible to open. Cursing aloud, she took a knife from the galley's drawers and cut the ribbon in two places.

Absent-mindedly, she rifled through the envelopes as if through a deck of cards. The addressee was always the same, to wit, Robert Forster. No mention of the sender or senders, however. Laura had always hated envelopes you had to open first to know who or where they came from. The clumsy handwriting apparently common to all of them seemed to indicate that the sender was either a very young person or someone not on speaking terms with the Latin alphabet.

Laura was getting truly excited. She sensed she had found no less than the ignition key to the time machine called Yellow Dancer. Did the legal protection of postal confidentiality extend beyond the grave? Surely not. But even if she was legally entitled to open the envelopes, there was the moral dilemma. How would she like some insensitive relatives of hers to browse through love letters or other intimate exchanges of hers post mortem? Not a pleasant thought. Then again, these letters might contain items of information of commercial ramifications. Not very probable but not impossible, either. Looking at it from that angle, she was not only entitled but practically obliged to learn what was in them. She opened the first red envelope, already bleached somewhat by repeated exposure to the Caribbean sun, and unfolded the sheet of coarse notepaper. Then she stared at it only to refold it and put it back almost immediately. The moral issue could be put to bed. The letter was in some alphabet and language unknown to Laura: Greek or Cyrillic, she guessed, in a totally illegible handwriting that might as well have consisted of ancient hieroglyphs. Of course, she thought, that's why the addresses looked so clumsy. The author, probably female, was quite simply not in the habit of using the Latin alphabet.

Half-heartedly, she opened the other letters one by one, only to find her assumption confirmed. They were all in Greek or Russian.

Laura hadn't known her father to be conversant in either. Laura, at any rate, wasn't. If she wanted to extract whatever morsels of information they contained, she would have to have them translated first.

The letters carried no dates, but the stamps on the envelopes bore postmarks with partially smeared and almost illegible ciphers in them. Thus, armed with a magnifying glass of sorts, Laura would probably be able to establish a chronology, by and large. With a bit of imagination, she thought she had managed to decode the respective signatures, though. In what seemed to be the earlier letters, it was a "Penelope Z", which obviously pointed towards Greece. The more recent ones were signed by the "Yellow Dancer".

Especially this one was hard to decode, since the English name was spelled in a funny kind of transliteration probably based on the phonetic values of Greek letters. If you did not know the one, you would have a hard time understanding the other. Either way, you did not have to be an experienced graphologist to realize that all the letters had been written by one and the same person. Which allowed the conclusion that Penelope Z was the Yellow Dancer. This boat hadn't been baptised after a flower as insinuated by some crooked one-eyed Frenchman, but after a woman Robert had known and cherished.

3. Persephone's sheaves

Jack had not promised too much. His Perséphone II was very easy to find indeed. The slippery cold bottle of Pinot Gris d'Alsace, which Laura carried in her right hand, had spent several hours in the fridge and now started sweating heavily. When she approached the marina building, watchful César came running and danced all around her wheezing with joy. Laura clasped the frolicking animal and let him escort her to his master's yacht.

The Frenchman stepped out of the door of his catamaran. As opposed to the Yellow Dancer, the Perséphone II was not moored alongside a pontoon, but turned her stern to a concrete pier, while her bows were probably held by either an anchor chain or a mooring line. Besides, hers was not a transom stern such as the Dancer's, but one with integrated steps, which made coming on board and stepping ashore appear much less of a hassle. No gangway, plank or crampons needed here.

Laura had never been on a multihull of this client-friendly design and was quite astonished about the abundance of space it seemed to offer. Even from outside, everything seemed bigger, more spacious, more comfortable, starting with the door which would not have looked totally out of place on a bungalow and literally dwarfed the Yellow Dancer's unwieldy bulkhead-cum-hatch affair.

"I'm glad you like her," the Frenchman replied, when Laura commented on the design of his yacht.

"So do I, in fact. But comparing her luxurious layout with the Yellow Dancer's prim frugality would be grossly unfair. You see, there's an important difference in the underlying concept. A yacht like Robert's is made for roaming the oceans in all kinds of weather conditions. Which means she must be absolutely, hermetically watertight. Any apertures she is given by way of compromise need to be restricted to a bare minimum both in number and in size. My Perséphone is more of a floating Peony Pavilion with limited operational capability, not necessarily at home on stormy seas. Perfectly seaworthy, but you would feel less comfortable in her in a gale, I daresay."

By the look of it, Jack had laid his beret back in the cupboard where it belonged and changed into a pair of white long-legged linen trousers that stood him in much better stead than the silly happy-camper shorts. His dark blue blazer on top of a light blue polo shirt bore some sort of club script embroidery on its breast pocket. On the whole, he looked much more the elderly gentleman as advocated by Vogue and seemed perfectly aware of it too.

"César, to heel! I must admit I had nearly failed to recognize you, Laura. What must I do for you to share your magic formula with an old man? Superb, your colourful combination, and the shades and sun hat look like they were made for you."

Laura thanked him for the compliment. She had found the hat on board the Yellow Dancer. It had belonged to Robert no doubt, but suited her as well, as the mirror had confirmed. She handed Jack the sweating bottle over the taffrail.

"Well, well, you don't look half bad either, if I so may say. I admit I was clutching to the illusion I would be the most elegant person aboard, yet I see, I underestimated the Perséphone's owner. Thank you very much once again for your kind invitation. I'm looking forward to lunch and would like to hear more about your years as a disciple of Hippocrates'."

Jack waved his hand as if brushing Laura's remark aside.

"Hardly worth mentioning. Do come aboard, by all means."

While Jack was reaching out for Laura's hand, to help her over the utility cables and pipes connecting the Perséphone to the shore, a nasal voice that seemed familiar to Laura called from inside the catamaran.

"Don't you believe a word he's saying. It's not for nothing everybody here calls him the Toubib."

Laura could not look far enough inside, but felt sure she had identified the voice of the Buffalo Soldier from the day before. That little tinge of arrogance was unmistakable, inimitable.

"No need to present you my master chef and precious partner, I take it. Not after what he told me about your recent shopping spree." Laura had landed safely on the wide stern platform of the boat, so Jack had a hand free again. He used it to beckon the Buffalo Soldier to come out and join them. Martin stepped into the open. Instead of his white suit with pink handkerchief, he was wearing a yellow apron, with the inscription "Ti Martin" inscribed on its upper part.

"Yes, we've already had the pleasure of each other's company," Laura told her host as she shook Martin's hand. "In fact, without him, I would probably never have seen the end of my shopping efforts. Everybody is being very polite, but either I don't understand them or they misunderstand me, it's fairly frustrating."

Martin smiled at Laura.

"Well, like I told you, I feel needed in many places around here."

"One of them being the Persephone's galley no doubt," Jacques shouted," and on the double, too, because I just caught the whiff of something burning."

Martin ducked like a wounded animal and disappeared again inside. Laura sat down on one of the wobbly camping chairs that Jack had grouped around a little round table with three champagne glasses on it.

"Ti Martin was kind enough to prepare a little hors d'oeuvre sublime. He is a man of many talents, as you had occasion to witness yourself, and a true wizard with the pan and barbecue, I assure you. He turns the cooking spoon into a magic wand, quite extraordinary."

Another thing Martin had prepared was an ice bucket with a bottle of champagne resting in it. When Laura had sat down, Jack expertly opened the bottle without any vulgar popping of the cork or spilling of any of the stuff on the floor. Then he poured everyone half a glassful. Martin came back from the galley and seized his glass for the toast.

"Santé," Jack called out, as the three glasses touched with a tinkling sound. "Let's drink to Robert's memory and Laura's future, shall we." Laura took a sip of the golden bubbly. It was first rate, as far as she could judge. The two men apparently had no nagging financial problems and knew how to enjoy life's little compensations.

"I can see you do your best, or worst, to live up to the reputation that precedes your fellow compatriots," Laura said. "What was it Martin called you, Toubib?"

Jack glanced at his partner with mock seriousness. Laura couldn't help smiling with empathy. The two men were like an elderly couple way past their first passionate years, but not any worse for it, as it seemed.

"You see, that's what comes of your misguided indiscretions. I wish you had kept your peace, instead of letting a total stranger in on our most intimate secrets."

Martin shrugged his shoulders and squinted sheepishly into the sun.

Laura was full of admiration for the ease with which Jack hopped back and forth between the two languages and cultures. He would have made an excellent interpreter, she thought.
"Well, you'll learn all about that some time or another, anyway. Better have it come from the horse's mouth than from some donkey's ass, beg pardon. As I told you this morning, I used to practise as a family doctor, a general practitioner in Paris, where I had a kind of little clinic near the Gare de l'Est. Many years ago, in a different life. One fine day, somebody in the profession felt the cup of my unorthodox methods had runneth over. The occasional illegal abortions I carried out in my place became my downfall, as was to be expected. To cut a long and rather tedious story short, my medical licence was eventually withdrawn. The profession had insisted on its pound of flesh and got it." His one eye turned skyward and he took a swig of champagne.

"All of this not so much because of medical considerations, mind you. There had never been any complications, not once. No, my major misdemeanour had been to treat women, girls who had neither sufficient means nor any insurance coverage to speak of, free of charge, every now and again. That frivolous attitude went directly counter to that section of medical ethics, which expects a doctor to extract as much money from his patients as possible. Athenian Hippocrates, you must know, has effectively been bullied into retirement to make place for his greedy Spartan nephew, a certain Hypocrites."

Laura nodded sympathetically. The unabashed pecuniary leanings of German medical doctors had always been a thorn in Robert's flesh, as well. Fortunately, he had rarely been ill, before dying, an ideal state of affairs, at least from a financial point of view. Laura regretted having brought the delicate subject up at all since it threatened to taint the serene atmosphere with the reminiscences it seemed to evoke for Jack.

"So, I left my beloved Paris and moved to Perpignan, in the south of France. But my occupational ban followed me there, too, like a persistent rash in the groin."

He stroked his moustache and tugged at the blind patch, something of a nervous tic of his, as Laura had already registered.

"Hence, I decided to go the whole hog, as they say, cross the Atlantic and settle here in the Caribbean, land of the freed, home of the bizarre. Not least, because I was confident my rheumatism would profit by the same token, to be honest. I bought the Perséphone from a retired professor of classical Greek literature at the Sorbonne. Didn't even have to haggle much over the price. The man was what we call a penguin - someone too clumsy to even change a light bulb, you know the type, I guess. He had acquired the yacht in a fit of momentary lunacy, as he put it himself, because the name had appealed to him. Now he was only too happy for me to take her off his hands quickly and painlessly.

Splendid guy, Apostolos, the professor, very erudite and pleasant as well as informative to talk to. Could make a synopsis of Oedipus Rex sound like a Leone spaghetti western, unbelievable. For the rest, he was an avowed disciple of Socrates and his midwife's method. Never contradicted you, never ventured any sweeping assertions. Kept undermining the seemingly obvious by asking questions instead, not unlike a child pestering you with things like 'why is the sun hot, grandpa?' Answering to the best of your knowledge, you would soon be hit in the face by your own ignorance or fall over your contradictory premises. On balance, though, you came away a wiser man. A good thing, he never ventured out to sea with Perséphone. Probably wouldn't have found his way back. Unless he performed and completed a proper circumnavigation. I can almost see him discussing with himself for weeks and months on end, never paying much attention to time and space until, one day, inevitably, he would hit Guadeloupe again thinking, 'Hey, Apostole, wait a minute, this place looks uncommonly familiar. Is it possible I've been here before?'"

Laura was all ears. She was no real believer in the Socratic method. Asking so many questions was poison for a woman's mind, she felt.

"Could I meet professor … Apostolos, is it?"

"Not unless you have a hot line to the next world. Apostolos was inconsiderate enough to move on last year already. I like to imagine him promenading along the Milky Way with all the Platos, Socrates, Homers and what have you around him in a never-ending symposium, discussing, gesticulating, drinking, as was his wont. Having him nearby saved you the trouble of building up a library of your own. Or resorting to Wikipedia, for that matter. Had but one deplorable flaw, the man - did not deign to admit defeat, which made playing chess with him a little painful. Do you play chess at all, Laura?"

"Very little. My father repeatedly showed me some of the basic moves, but wasn't around either often or long enough for me to cultivate it further."

"Yes, you know I have this theory about women and chess." Jack leaned forward as if on the brink of divulging a dirty secret.

"Whenever someone mentions typically 'male' sports, most of us probably think of, I don't know, stuff like boxing, rugby, rowing, things like that. Yet most of these erstwhile male strongholds have long since been gate-crashed by women. With very few exceptions, chess being one of them. Or do you remember a single woman among all those grand masters of chess we witnessed duelling in recent decades? I don't. Look up a list of the 100 best players in the world and ask yourself why there are next to no women among them."

Laura had not given it much thought, nor did she really care, if she was honest.

"Maybe a question of the different ways in which women and men take their respective decisions."

"What do you mean?"

"Well, in my experience, men are slow breeders. Confronted with a problem, they keep tossing it this way and that till the square pegs finally fit in the round holes. For a mind accustomed to moving along algorithms, chess would be the ideal playground. Women's minds are more accustomed to following the lines of sewing patterns, which is why we favour quick, communicative solutions. Applied to chess, it means that before making her move, a woman would call a friend or two and talk the different options over with them, you see. That's why chess isn't really in our domain, never will be. Personally, I like to think it's a game for borderline sociopaths with autistic leanings, no offence."

"Wow! That's something of a mouthful. But no, none taken. I must admit, I have never seen it in this light, so far. Anyway, where was I? Right. These days, I do what I can to make myself useful in the small local community of liveaboards, the homeless of the sea, as it were. A festering abscess here, a persistent diarrhoea there, nothing more complicated. No more abortions, thank you very much. By the way, how is your mosquito bite?" Laura nervously pulled at her neck bandage and forced a little smile. "It's okay, thanks again. Toubib?"

"Pardon me? Oh yes. Well, it's an Arab word, derived from tip, 'medicine', and simply means doctor. Came to Europe in the wake of tropical diseases during the 19th century, I believe, and pushed roots in French military jargon first. Like many other nicknames of its kind, it's characterized by the paradox of condescending appreciation, if you like. Soldiers, members of the foreign legion and so forth traditionally live on borrowed time, don't they. Hence, medics, doctors, nurses are the last persons they wish to see: bad karma, ominous portent, whatever. Personally, I think of it as a secret sign of distinction, a title of honour, and should like to drink to it."

He raised his glass and sniffed the air like a dog.

"Ti Martin, my friend, I seem to smell something irresistibly spicy, a cloud of reinforced curry and pimped peppers, am I right on track?"

César, coming back from another one of his excursions in the neighbourhood, started barking, seemingly without reason. There were noises from inside as from someone hastily pushing saucepans around.

"Good old César. A retired ex drug dog, would you believe it. Not surprising, with his olfactory sense. The longer a dog's nose, the more whiffs it can pick up and identify, you know. That's why bloodhounds will track a man right across a town with thousands of other people crossing its path and no end of other confusing smells trying to throw him off the scent. Amazing, isn't it? And once at the end of their tether, they will scratch the licence number of the get-away car into the tarmac with their paws to boot."

He broke into another laughing goat imitation and waved his hand.

"Rubbish, of course. As for César, I succeeded in turning him around, converting him into a double agent. Now, he'll bark whenever an undercover drug enforcement officer is anywhere near. Or whenever there's a fire. Burglars, on the other hand, are perfectly safe with Labrador retrievers. They are self-confident creatures, not afraid of humans, and so they can't be used as watchdogs, hopeless, eh, César?"

The dog started wheezing as if in confirmation.

"And why Ti Martin?"

"Ti is local patois for petit, little, small. An adjective turned into some sort of prefix. Very popular in these parts. A diminutive expressing inherited humbleness as well as affection. You didn't just ask your massa for a loaf of bread, say, but tuned it down to a ti pain, which made it sound less preposterously assuming. Small people love diminutives, haven't you noticed? Anyway, Ti Martin would be something like Little Martin, in English, an affectionate diminutive."

"Does everyone have a nickname like those around here?"

"Not everyone, but many. Whoever decides to settle somewhere on a Caribbean island will sooner or later be rubbing shoulders with what we call Pègre in French, the criminal underworld, if you like. These islands just aren't big enough for both communities to permanently avoid one another. And so, certain habits and practices encroach upon one another, not much to be done about that. In criminal circles, it's customary to exchange your civilian name for one which the Pègre will eventually provide for you, if they feel you're worth it. Compare it with entering a monastery, if you wish, or a convent, in your case. Someone enters as, say, a Monsieur Pierre Maurois, and turns into Brother Melchior upon taking the final vows. He won't be allowed to pick his patron saint himself, but will be given the respective name by his elders and betters and will be expected to come to terms with it."

Well, that sounds a little too difficult and occult for me. Maybe I can get away with calling you Doc, how about that?" Laura laughed.

"Certainly," Jacques nodded. "I quite like the sound of that. Reminds me of Doc Holiday, the gun-slinging card sharp, though he used to be a dentist, as far as I remember."

"And suffered from tuberculosis." Laura added.

"Yes, is said to have coughed his lungs out. Didn't prevent him from shooting straight, though. Was maybe rather looking forward to that final bullet to put him out of his misery, who knows."

"What would I be called, any idea?"

"No, that depends on a number of different factors, the kind of image you project of yourself, for instance. Besides, you probably won't stay long enough to come into contact with the local Pègre, I suspect. Their loss entirely."

"Doc, you give me the impression of someone habitually slightly distrustful, always very much on his guard. How come you seem so credulous when it comes to my person? I mean, I could be just anybody posing as Robert Forster's daughter, to, I don't know, take possession of the boat, for instance. What makes you so sure I am who I say I am?"

"An unmistakable part of your anatomy," the Doc smiled.

"You see, Robert once told me of an accident, involving the two of you. He had apparently taken you along on his motorbike and promptly missed a bend because of a thin layer of loose sand on the road, as he said. The bike crashed into the shrubbery, and because of that fall, your right arm was almost crushed. As a consequence of the operation, the genuine Laura to this day appears to be holding her right arm just a wee bit askew, very much the way I observed you to do."

"Oh, don't worry, a layman wouldn't notice it. Never, not even a future husband of yours, I don't think. Unless you were to marry an attentive orthopedist. Anyway, it's not something you could easily feign, like, say, a stiff leg. I hope you never wished to play the piano?"

Laura shook her head. This Frenchman seemed to have an eerie surprise potential. She had no recollection of the accident herself, but as it was related to her, it had very nearly cost her father's life. By comparison, Laura had been rather lucky, even though she had to undergo the odd corrective operation in later years. Her unorthodox posture of her right arm, which not many people had either noticed or commented on, appeared to have psychosomatic rather than orthopaedic causes. One way or another, she had never ever sat on a motorbike again.

"Apart from this," the Frenchman leaned forward again, "I do not exactly take everything as read. I think we both know that thing on your throat is not a mosquito bite, don't we. I would have to hand in my freshly forged new licence if I believed that." Laura sighed and cursed her "evil deed". Anyone wishing to make lying their career needed a better memory and a lot more imagination than Laura possessed. She knew she had better come clean or else would only work herself deeper and deeper into the quagmire of her own myths. Besides, she might have to depend on the Doc's and Ti Martin's help. Telling them the truth would hopefully be taken as a sign of appreciation.

"You're right, it's not a mosquito bite, of course. But it's a long, dreadful story I really don't want to bother you with." The Doc was fumbling in his pocket and pulled out his pipe, at last.

"No problem, Laura, I love stories. For me, they just can't be long enough. It's the child in us, don't you think. It never really stops craving for fairy tales. One night, I listened through Apostolos' rendering of large parts of the Iliad, the one great fairy tale that defines our western culture more effectively than the Bible, when it comes to that. In ancient Greek, the whole programme, with some of his students as an audience. I did not understand a word, of course, but the experience was nevertheless awe-inspiring. An incredible human achievement, language. What Apostolos was reciting - all by heart, I assure you - was probably still a long way from Homer's original Ionian dialect, but the mere sound of it, the rhythm, the euphony! You would have to imagine this in the acoustic atmosphere of the gigantic Epidaurus amphitheatre. Which, incidentally, has a genuinely medical raison d'être, you know, the largest amphitheatre of antiquity. Thousands of spell-bound spectators, and you could still hear a pin drop. Funny we came to know the underlying concept in its Latin form as mens sana…"

"Yes, very impressive, I'm sure. But they didn't have chewing-gum then, nor popcorn or nachos with sweet-sour salsa, did they? Chewing sunflower seeds makes less noise. Anyway, in my case, you would have to be satisfied with discordant English."

Thus, Laura started, hesitatingly at first, telling Jack aka the Toubib about her experience with the phantom from the night before. To the extent that the Frenchman kept refilling her glass, Laura soon got into the swing of it and became more and more loquacious, though not necessarily more coherent. The one detail she deliberately left out of her account altogether, was her attacker's erection.

The Doc listened with great attention, while filling, lighting, and smoking his pipe. When Laura had finished, he stroked his moustache pensively.

"What did the man look like? Can you describe him at all?"

"Nothing easier and, at the same time, nothing more difficult than that," Laura replied. "I am not likely to get his abominable physiognomy out of my head, ever. He looked like a creature from the netherworld, his face covered with all those nasty scars. Darkish skin, blond hair, blue eyes, whose expression…"

She stopped in mid-sentence. The jocular serenity of ten or so minutes ago had suddenly given way to a sombre, menacing atmosphere which was reflected in the Doc's "coroner's" tone of voice.

"A phantom, you say? Well, I'm sure he wouldn't be delighted to hear that. Although, come to think of it, he must have been given worse names than that."

Laura was surprised. "You know him?"

The Doc nodded gravely.

"If I am to trust your excellent description of him, and I really do - yes, I unfortunately happen to know him. Not as the phantom, though, but as Ignace, Ignace le Chabin. A sort of Mack the Knife of the West Indies. Many who enjoyed his company as briefly as you didn't live to tell the tale. As for myself, I owe him this little souvenir." He pointed at his eye-patch.

"An accident, nothing I could blame him for. Still, I should prefer never to have made his acquaintance. You have been very lucky."

"Ignace le… Chopin?"

"Chabin. That's what mustees like him call themselves. They don't like to hear it from others, though. Not surprisingly, after all. How would you like to be characterized as the offspring of a billy-goat and a sheep? That's what the word really implies. Not very flattering, is it. Which brings us to the subject of colour. You'll never hear the end of that one in the Caribbean, I'm afraid."

"To cut it short. On those West Indian islands that had plantations, such as Guadeloupe or Martinique, you'll find all possible shades of black and brown. At the beginning of the 20th century, someone actually took the trouble of establishing a kind of melanometric scale, a kaleidoscope of colours and hues somewhere between ivory and ebony. For what specific purpose, I have no idea. Maybe he was just bored stiff and needed something to do. Anyway, at about hue number 110, he gave up, threw in the sponge."

"And whereabouts on what scale would Ignace be sitting, close to ivory, as an albino?"

"No, not really. It's way more complicated than that. Albinos are creatures the Almighty clean forgot to provide with any colour pigmentation. Can't always keep every little detail in mind when creating a universe, can you?"

"As for chabins, on the other hand, they are the result of indecision rather than forgetfulness on the part of the Almighty. Black man, white man - decisions, decisions. He may have grown tired and finally decided not to plum for either. Let's have a mixture, half negro, half Caucasian, why not. Didn't rally catch on with the rest of humanity, though, and was largely discarded by evolution."

"But what about those terrible scars?"

"Those are man-made. Can't blame the Almighty for everything now, can we."

He laid aside his pipe and emptied his glass.

"It was pretty obvious from the start that a boy with his mug would have a hard time never mind what. Any action engenders reaction, or so the physicists and sociologists tell us. And Ignace lived up to it. As an adolescent, he already sported a rap sheet that would have stood a Sicilian wise guy in good stead. Because of his juvenile age, much of his prison time was remitted or shortened. Not least, because he had quickly come into rather large sums of money and learned to re-invest it in the form of bribes."

"One day, however, he had the misfortune of falling into the hands of an enemy gang. Those lads' knowledge of juvenile penal law was scant at best. They had therefore made it a habit to dish it out with both hands. They stripped the poor boy and tied him to a manchineel tree to let him swelter for several days and nights. You have heard of manchineel trees?"

Laura shook her head.

"They are botanic thugs, about the most poisonous thing our regional flora has to offer. Its little apple-like fruit is deadly. You think you're eating it while in actual fact it's eating you, starting with your liver. Its resin leaves deeper scars than most run-of-the-mill acids. Even its shadow has repeatedly been under investigation, they say: lack of evidence, so far."

Ti Martin appeared in the open door and made a sign that lunch was ready. The Doc let Laura precede and took the champagne glasses with him. Inside, Laura had a quick look around and found her first impression of comfort and spaciousness confirmed. Cleanliness was another matter, however. No trace here of the pedantic orderliness and almost clinical atmosphere of the Yellow Dancer. Somebody, probably César, had torn open a box of popcorn or cornflakes and spread its contents all over the floor only recently. This morning's dirty plates and cups piled up in the sink and some of the cupboards could not be closed because they bulged with old brochures, cheap paperbacks and last year's magazines. A housewife's loving would work wonders with the place, Laura thought. The luncheon table had been laid tastefully and rather voluptuously. It all betrayed Ti Martin's sense of form and colour which Laura had come to admire during their shopping spree.

"Do you have any pets?" the Doc asked.
Not that I know of, Laura thought. But if she were to spend another couple of hours in this interesting environment, she might take some new friends home with her.

"No, I haven't. I'd very much like to keep a dog, but you know yourself what kind of burden that can be for someone travelling as much as I do. Besides, the dog probably wouldn't be crazy about it either."

"Yes, well. Let's start with fruits de mer, if you like. Do help yourself, and, as we say in French, give us news, in other words, tell us what you think about it."

The Doc started noisily opening an oyster, while Ti Martin befriended half a lobster. Some peculiar crabs with one big right claw and an infinitely smaller left one caught Laura's attention. She took a specimen and held it up in the air like a vital piece of circumstantial evidence in court.

"That's our friend, the it's-my-fault crab. Sand-fiddler, I believe the English call it. All day long, they are fiddling away with their big claw, calling out, all my fault, all my fault." Laura laughed and very carefully tried to dismember the thing.

The Doc helped her and showed her, how to suck the flesh out of the shell.

"Yes, our Caribbean menu is quite something, isn't it. Take breadfruit, for instance. Towards the end of the 18th century, the British sent the Bounty to collect breadfruit seedlings from Tahiti, where James Cook had discovered them some years earlier. They were supposed to be taken to the West Indies to make cheap food for black slaves in the plantations. When they finally did arrive, after a series of bizarre mishaps, the blacks turned out to despise them, preferred burgers instead. I don't blame them; it's an acquired taste, breadfruit. Though why anyone would want to acquire it, beats me. Same goes for the fruit of the sausage tree, reputed to enhance the, you know, male pride."

"I take it you are not referring to the male brain, now, are you?" They both laughed. Laura briefly thought of Ignace. Maybe he had had an overdose of sausage tree fruit with cinnamon before going aboard the Yellow Dancer. With a jolly swig of rum, if his breath was any indication.

"Sweet potato mash with sockets, another good one. You know sockets?"

"Not edible ones, no."

"That's what they call pig's snouts in these parts, because of the two parallel holes. An affordable delicacy even for less well-off families."

Laura shivered at the thought. Was there any part of the common pig that humans wouldn't eat, from trotters to head and ears? Did Jews and Muslims have any idea what they were missing?

"Coming back for a moment to Ignace. How did he survive this treatment?"

"Wasn't supposed to, that's for sure. But killers have friends, too. Help each other out every once in a while. Turns out Ignace had contracted the assistance of the worst killer elite of the tropics – coconuts."

Laura looked questioningly, while gulping the oyster that Ti Martin had opened for her.

"Remarkable fruit, coconuts. Indestructible. They can drift along in the warm seas close to the Equator for months on end, without losing their ability to germinate. Up in the Bahamas they've found coconuts with shark's teeth-marks in them. Belligerent, too, knowing to defend themselves. An estimated 300 people each year are killed in the tropical regions by coconuts alone. Sharks don't even come close to such success rates." The Doc poured chilled Pinot Gris all round.

"Now, this gang that had caught young Ignace, exposed him to the sunlight during the day and the acid rain from the tree at night. You should see his back. Or rather don't. He would not have survived the ordeal had it not been for the gang losing interest. They went about their business and left only one guard behind. That stupid individual allowed himself to doze off under a palm tree, never to wake up again. Can you imagine. An average coconut of some, say, three kilos, falling from a height of, say, 200 feet, at a rate of some 40 miles per hour, packs no less than a ton on impact. So, the guard's head was simply smashed like the shell of a raw egg being hit by that of a hard-boiled colleague."

"Ignace was able to free himself unobserved and escape. Not one member of that gang survived the following few months."

The Doc scratched his head.

"So much about that. What I don't understand, though, is what he was doing on board the Yellow Dancer when you arrived. Were you smuggling cocaine, heroin, or crystal meth?"
Again, he burst into his goat's laughter.

"Of course not, a joke. But the thing is, though, wherever Ignace shows up, drugs are seldom out of reach."
"Yes. Another thing I don't understand is why he let me off the hook."

The Doc sighed and waved his hand.

"There may be many reasons. Who can look inside that man's head, or would want to. He may have been on amphetamines, or on God knows what. But you were lucky, that's for sure. Nobody knows precisely how many murders he has on his conscience, or would, if he could afford one."

"Of course, one would have to allow for the attenuating circumstances of his youth. To be called a freak and worse from early childhood leaves scars on a man's soul, as well. And scars, as any medical man will tell you, cause insensibility. Ask your heart or liver. Well, I'm sure he had found whatever he had been looking for on your yacht and won't be back in a hurry."

Laura was wondering at the affirmative overtone in what the Doc said. How could he be so sure?

"Shouldn't I report the incident to the police all the same?" she asked.

The Doc passed the question on to Ti Martin with a straight enough face.

"What do you think, Buffalo? Should she go to the police?"

Then, the two of them simultaneously hollered with laughter, as if the Doc had cracked a prime joke.

Police was something, Ti Martin did not need to have translated and the context was apparently clear for him, too.

"Well, you probably do know that Guadeloupe is a French overseas territory. In a way, you are in France here, in other words. So, if you manage to smuggle whatever stuff you wish to transport onto a ship in Pointe-à-Pitre, it has practically already entered Europe. Which makes this unassuming little harbour an important turnstile for drugs, among other things."

"Drugs register a gigantic value added at each processing stage. Take heroin, for instance. The peasant in Afghanistan who grows the poppy gets a mere pittance. Once it's turned into wholesale cocaine and smack, we're already talking millions. And once the stuff hits the Amsterdam, Hamburg, London or Paris markets, you might as well add another fifty percent. So, we are talking millions and billions. Wherever that kind of money is at stake, you can bet your string, I mean you can be sure, that someone or other in customs, police or DEA is on the take. And do I blame them? If you are confronted daily with sums such as these and cannot help comparing them with your own measly wages in a high-risk job, it takes superhuman resilience not to be tempted. No, believe me, the police would be the wrong address entirely."

The Doc sang from the same hymn book.

"I wouldn't even claim there are no honest policemen. There are, I'm sure, but that's not the issue. One rotten apple, well you know the saying. The drug industry receives most salient pieces of information in real time, and the honest cops keep wondering forever why their surprise raids and staff-intensive searches somehow don't seem to surprise anyone and yield no results."

"And Ignace, he's one of the drug barons?"

"No, he is more of a mercenary, a tradesman in lead and steel. If you want to lose a competitor or traitor for good, you call Ignace. But enough of that creature of the dark. Let's not allow him to sit at our table this afternoon. May I ask you, Laura, whether you have come to any conclusion as far as the Yellow Dancer is concerned?"

"To be honest with you, I haven't yet. Originally, I had come here to take a look at her and then put her on the market. Now, I'm not so sure any more. She meant a lot to my father, so, to just let her go like that...."

"If I may make a suggestion: why don't you leave her here, in the Caribbean? That would give you all the time in the world to think it over. Selling her will never be a problem, as I told you. But you would have to find a bolt-hole of sorts, some place where she is safe from cyclones passing through. And it would have to go down soon, because the hurricane season starts earlier each year."

The Doc stuffed his pipe again.

"I happen to know a boatyard on Antigua specialized in storing yachts in special hurricane-holes on their premises. If you like, I'll have a word with the owner, to see whether there is still room, and let you know."

The Frenchman's proposal appeared reasonable to Laura. She agreed and thanked both men for the delightful meal and pleasant company.

Ti Martin gave her mock-darkish look, because she had neglected some of his more exotic delicacies. A simple steak with chips would have done the trick, too, Laura thought, but pretended to have stomach ache. The Doc promised to give her a call first thing.

She bid them farewell, and let César escort her to the marina building. Here, she paid the mooring fees due up to now and received Robert's keys. Then, she hailed a taxi outside and asked the driver to take her back to the hotel.

FOURTH CHAPTER

1. The March of the Ten Thousand

"Hi Laura. Thank God I finally got you on the phone. I tried three or four times before, but you seem to have been very much on the move."

Dr Sanders sounded his authoritative self. Laura nervously reached for her handbag and dug for her pen and a slip of paper. He wouldn't call if he hadn't got some kind of message she had better jot down.

"Well, yes, I'm sorry. It's nice hearing from you, although we had agreed on keeping radio silence, had we not?"

Dr Sanders seemed unperturbed by the mildly reproachful overtones in Laura's voice. Apparently, he wished to lose no more time than necessary with whatever it was he wanted to get off his chest.

"I just wanted to make sure that you didn't learn about this from the papers. Yesterday morning, there was a pile-up on the autobahn near Stuttgart, hell of a place at the best of times, as you know. One of our lorries was involved and the driver was killed, unfortunately, as did two or three other people with no links to ROLA. We thought it fitting for you to send your condolences: your heart going out to the family, everything possible will be done to help them overcome their material plight, the human factor. We prepared a text for you, all we need is your electronic signature."

"Pa ni... I mean, no problem, I agree of course. Do you foresee any problems with the insurance? Is the family being looked after properly?"

"We're doing what we can, obviously. As for the insurance people, you know their reticence to dish out money. We'll have to wait for the results of the police enquiry, I suppose, and see what happens, prepare a file to take legal steps, that's routine business. Meanwhile, we should advance the necessary relief sums. I take it that's alright with you?"

"Naturally."

The company's legal eagle was right. Accidents with or without loss of life will happen in companies that move a hundred thousand tons of goods of any description all over the globe, day in, day out, by any means available. The ensuing bureaucratic skirmishes had more recently taken on such proportions as to keep a whole department at their Hamburg centre occupied almost round the clock. Laura's father had always put great emphasis on the human factor and had made it a point to put in personal appearances at funerals of company staff killed on the road or wherever. That wasn't always possible, of course. Fortunately, Laura thought with a touch of egotism, because at present, she did not really feel up to the paraphernalia of yet another funeral. But a personalized message of condolence was the least she could do.

"Was that it?"

"As far as I am concerned, yes. Larsen wants to have a word with you too, though. Just a sec, the secretary will put you through. I wish you a pleasant time for the rest of your stay, none the less. You will be back the fifteenth, though, won't you?"

"Absolutely, you can count on that. I already feel homesick," she lied. "See you then."

Dr Sanders pushed a button. There was some irritating atmospherics, but before long Sven Larsen picked up at the other end.

"Hi Laura, how are things with the Caribbean?"
He did not wait for an answer. Laura was sure she could hear Larsen's knuckles. Unless someone was listening in on their conversation.

"I'll come straight to the point, if I may. Looking through your father's private affairs as recorded on that cute little USB stick you slipped under my door before your departure, as it were, I came across some bizarre money transfers inexplicable to me."

"Really? How? Maybe I can contribute to elucidating them."

"That's what I was hoping. Robert seems to have sent regular sums to the Caribbean. Did you know about that?"
Laura was thinking fast. Once again, she got caught with her trousers down.

"Well, yes and no." Her second lie today, Laura thought, and she hadn't even had breakfast yet.

"He may have mentioned it, fleetingly as ever. At the time, I probably wasn't paying any attention. I thought it had something to do with his sailing expenses in the Caribbean. How much money are we talking and who is the lucky winner?"

"It started with some 2,500 US, increased at more or less regular intervals, indexed, as it were, and stands at roughly twice that sum at present. To me, it looks like concealed subsistence payments, voluntary ones. If they weren't, they would have left deeper footprints."

"Well, voluntary maybe, but not as minor as all that, then. Subsistence payments for whom, Pippa Middleton?" Laura made a lame effort at sounding casual.

"I'm afraid we're dealing with a phantom beneficiary. The payments were always made into the same HSCB account on Antigua. These people there are not in the habit of leaking names. Certainly not on the phone, anyway. Since you happen to be in the area, you might wish to make a few cautious enquiries, grease some palms, do whatever it takes to extract information. If you feel it important enough, that is."

Laura grinned. Yes, she did feel it important enough. In fact, she would have given her right arm to know. Parts of it, anyway.

"Would internal revenue be likely to make it an issue?"

"Only if they were to hear about it. If you like, I'll classify the respective files."

Laura grinned again. "Classify" was his standard euphemism for "burying".

"Yes, I'd prefer that. But do let me have the number of the account, please. I might wish to poke around in the haystack, just for the hell of it."

Laura jotted it down and finished their conversation with a few saucy remarks on the local set-up.

This was getting ever more intriguing almost by the hour, she thought when she had hung up. What more surprises did her father have in store for her? 5000 tax-free greenbacks were peanuts or a minor fortune, all according to which way you looked upon it. A less than extravagant individual should be able to live rather comfortably on a sum like that, even in the Caribbean. Had Robert been blackmailed? Hardly. Extortionists were much too greedy to be satisfied with a monthly "salary", indexed or not. Besides, the period in question was too long. Every day that went by would have increased the blackmailer's risk of either getting caught or else losing the compromising basis of his or her transaction. No, Sven was probably right, those had to be alimony payments.

Laura knew she would not get any answers today. The same applied to the letters she had found on board the Yellow Dancer. The hotel had no scanner, but an ancient steam-operated fax. Laura had discovered the address of a translation office in Hamburg and had sent them the letters. Let them sort it out and render the lot into intelligible German. To accelerate things, Laura had promised to pay double the usual tariff.

For the moment, that was all she could do. She felt like having another look at the town. Chances were, she would never come back to Pointe-à-Pitre, so why not try and pick up some lasting impressions beyond the high-street boutiques. Besides, she was on hold as far as the yacht's Antiguan berth was concerned. And so, she dressed and walked along the harbour in search of the tourist highlights.

Most if not all of those came back to St. John the wandering poet. Local government had devoted a whole colonial-style building to Alexis Leger aka St. John Perse, the town's and island's most famous prodigal son. It did not take Laura long to find the building and stroll through its neatly decorated rooms and corridors. The poet-diplomat's thin booklet called Anabasis, though anything but a best-seller, had nevertheless earned him the Nobel Prize. The flyer, which Laura had picked up at the entrance, had it that the work was based on a classical model, the extensive notes of the renowned general and author Xenophon, hence the Greek title. At around 400 B.C., this ancient jack of all trades had inadvertently found himself in the role of a military leader having to bring up the rear, as it were. After a protracted campaign of attrition ending in what would appropriately be termed a Pyrrhic victory, it had fallen upon Xenophon to round up the scattered remains of the Greek legions and march them back to the Aegean through hundreds of miles of heavily mined enemy territory. An admirable feat of military strategy and logistics, which Xenophon hastened to make known to the wider public in his outstanding descriptions entitled the March of the Ten Thousand. Suspiciously round figures such as these had to be taken with more than a grain of salt, Laura knew. But even if the ten thousand had shrunk to much fewer on closer inspection, that would not have seriously belittled Xenophon's astounding performance because en route, the Greeks were repeatedly set upon by hostile tribes treating them as insolent trespassers. Xenophon's account came to serve as a model not only for writers and poets such as Alexis Leger, but also to creative talents of other art forms. In a modern film version, for instance, it was exploited by the makers of the 1982 American thriller The Warriors. Here, a small group of Coney Island youths has to quite literally beat their way back home after falsely being held responsible for a murder on the margins of a Central Park jamboree. In every one of the Big Apple's hoods they have to pass through, the Warriors are attacked by baseball-bat swinging local toughs and repeatedly effect their escape and journey but by the skin of their teeth. Laura had seen the cult film in a student cinema in Florida and had been literally spellbound by the voice of the charismatic female radio commentator who keeps all interested parties abreast of the pugnacious pilgrims' progress Greek chorus-style.

In its literal sense, Laura knew Anabasis to refer to the simple act of going ashore or, in semantic extrapolation, of coming home. In its figurative, symbolic sense, the word could stand in for someone's painstaking search for his or her true self after many a dangerous battle with the legions of adversity. Laura felt that, little as she enjoyed St. John's esoteric poetry, she could very well relate to that latter aspect of things.

Back in the street, she walked towards the fruit-and-vegetable market. All of a sudden, she had the creepy sensation of someone tailing her. Just a dull gut feeling, nothing she could put her finger on. Enough, though, to give her goose bumps all over. A volatile shadow, always keeping the same distance, sometimes on the opposite, sometimes on the same side of the street. As soon as she stopped in front of a shop window, the elusive shadow would stop, too. When she continued, so would the shadow.

It could not possibly be the phantom. Marked men like him would be well advised to avoid populated areas, at least in broad daylight. Perhaps the Doc had secretly provided her with a bodyguard, a sort of guardian angel, who was to make sure that no ill would befall an old friend's daughter.

Who else could possibly have an interest in her movements? She remembered the inquisitive lady from Blankenese. She smiled at the hilarious idea of her having followed Laura across the Atlantic - from her grave, too, since the old soul had been dead and buried these twenty years.

If her soul kept marching on like John Brown's body, it might be wearing the bright red windbreaker Laura thought she had repeatedly caught a glimpse of for a few seconds at a time. Laura's instincts, never truly dormant, had certainly been wide awake ever since the phantom's attack on her in the Blue Lagoon. To shake the shadow, she had to blend into the crowd, that she had learned from Robert. But what crowd? Pitre wasn't Manhattan Central, not even the Hamburg town hall square. The only place that came anywhere near to housing a crowd was the market.

She had hardly entered the roofed rectangle when the rich choice of tropical fruit and vegetables instantly fought for her attention. Piled up to form red, green, yellow, or brown pyramids, sprayed with water from time to time to preserve their fresh looks, there was no end of coconuts, oranges, kiwis, avocados, bananas, papayas, corn, sweet potatoes, and tomatoes. The apparent luxury could not fool Laura, who had read that many basic foodstuffs such as rice, flour, potatoes, pasta, and others not on display, had to be shipped here from Europe at forbidding though subsidized freight rates. The same applied to simple objects of daily use, from hoover bags to shock absorbers, from the popular mopeds to medical appliances. These were business prospects no logistics enterprise would sneeze at, but more likely than not, the French were sitting on it.

The gap between such expensive overseas products and local income levels, the Doc had explained to Laura during their luncheon, had frequently been the source of considerable social unrest both on Guadeloupe and Martinique. In the 1960s, a general strike in Pointe-à-Pitre had even cost some workers' lives. To "accelerate" the crushing of the revolt, the mercenaries deployed to reinforce local police had fired into the crowd.

In a lame attempt at confusing her shadow, Laura veered to the left and to the right between stands a couple of times, and, leaving the market, finally squeezed herself into the unlocked entrance of a grey tenement building. Her heart beating audibly, she kept the door ajar and waited in anticipation for the things to come. Pepper spray! She had to try and get some here. Ti Martin would know where to look. Nothing happened, though. If the mysterious shadow was worth his money, he had probably smelled a rat and was patiently lurking somewhere himself. Whatever. Laura slipped back into her childhood role of the spoilt little brat who would declare a game of hide-and-seek over as soon as it stopped going her way. Without so much as looking back over her shoulder, she made straight for the hotel.

When she reached the St. John Perse with broken blisters on her feet, she was handed the message she had been hoping for. The Doc had been lucky and booked a berth for the Yellow Dancer in the Jolly Harbour boatyard on Antigua. But time was of the essence, he wrote. Joe Grady, the boatyard's owner, would not be able to stall other interested parties for more than a few days. The yacht had to be transferred to Antigua right away, tomorrow if possible. The Doc suggested that Laura come along with him and Ti Martin. Thus, she would witness the Yellow Dancer going through her motions and learn how to handle her - on the outside chance that she might wish to keep and use her, at least on occasion.

The prospect of having to spend a whole day at sea was daunting for Laura. But then she remembered the phone call. On Antigua, she might find someone who could be persuaded to part with the name of the beneficiary of Robert's payments. She doubted it, but giving it a try would do no harm. She was sure she could have gone to Antigua on one of the small Pipers circling the Pôle Caraïbes airport. But the Doc and Ti Martin might take offence. So she called the Doc, told him she would be coming along alright and asked his advice on the kind of clothing she might need for the trip.

When she searched both her suitcases and the cupboard with his suggestions in mind, she found an ugly suspicion confirmed that had impressed itself upon her the moment she had entered the hotel room again. Someone had gone through her belongings during her absence for sure. It wasn't just the expression of a paranoid persecution complex either. Robert had once shown her a simple trick in case she felt spied upon at home or abroad. It consisted basically in arranging certain harmless objects of everyday use such as hair brushes, cosmetic articles, minor pieces of clothing and the like in a precise yet unobtrusive manner. Thus, she would be likely to notice at one glance if someone had touched them. Of course, the maid had gone through the room during her absence, but she would have no reason whatsoever to file through her things and then carefully re-arrange them in what she thought she remembered to be the right order afterwards. Maybe the uninvited visitor had been kept informed on Laura's movements by the "shadow" she had sensed following her about. To get in and out of the hotel unseen by the receptionist would be an easy task for an experienced burglar or spy. The same applied to picking the lock of her room, no doubt.

On a rapid superficial check, she ascertained that none of her few valuables had been taken. She could have used the room safe for her money and items such as her Tissot watch, her gold rings or her rather precious-looking collier. But after that stupid incident with a number safe of this kind at a Miami hotel many years ago, when her forgetfulness had caused her a lot of trouble involving locksmiths and painfully unnecessary expenses, she gave such contraptions a wide berth. Besides, she had heard of cases where spying hotel staff had teamed up with burglars on a regular basis, providing them with the respective safe numbers as set by the guests in the maitre's or page's presence.

Thus, she understood how, but, while having a prolonged shower, kept speculating on the "why" in vain. On the face of it, she could not for the life of her see no earthly reason why someone would go to all that trouble yet be prepared to leave empty-handed? For the second time, too, after the incident in the Blue Lagoon.

2. Twilight at the Bridge

"Are you a good swimmer, Laura? Yes? Even so, humour me, please, and put on the jacket, so you know how to do it should you really need it one day."
The Doc handed Laura a surprisingly heavy lifejacket with a collar that promised to keep the wearer's head over the surface at all times.

"It will not protect you from passing out, but will save you from drowning while unconscious. It's self-inflatable, theoretically speaking. The triggering mechanism works with the Alka Selzer effect. As soon as it comes into contact with water, an effervescent tablet inside will dissolve and release a pin to punch a gas cartridge. If the automatic system does not work, you pull this ripcord like a parachutist in mid-air. Should that fail, too, you still have this mouthpiece to blow the jacket up with the air from your lungs. If that fails, you will have to pray and wait for the next friendly dolphin to pass by. Here in the marina and harbour areas, such precautions might seem a little over the top, but the quicker you get used to wearing the thing, the better for everybody concerned. Ask César."

The dog was already wearing a cute miniature jacket with his name on it as if to avoid a serious risk of confusion in an emergency. Howling and yelping, he kept jumping all over the cockpit and couldn't wait to get under way.

The same did not apply to Laura. That morning, she had cancelled what remained of her original hotel booking period and had her suitcase and a bag brought on board the Yellow Dancer. The aft cabin, traditionally reserved for the owner, was too low even for Laura to stand fully upright. "Teaches you a little humility," her father had laughingly retorted when Laura had occasionally referred to the permanent "nun's walk" smaller boats would force you to adopt. The width of the cabin wasn't exactly comfortable, either. Basically, it consisted of a large bed surrounded by all sorts of smallish built-in cupboards. It reminded Laura of the urban legend of rooms in some Japanese hotels: irrespective of the corner you picked to have your heart attack, you were always sure to drop on the bed.

As far as the weather conditions were concerned, the Doc had had a hard time talking Laura out of her misgivings. Official weather forecasts in the Caribbean were few and far between and hardly as reliable as most of the European or American ones. Besides, by the end of April, beginning of May, the general weather situation around the West Indies began to destabilize and, hence, was getting even harder to predict. Violent thunderstorms and rain showers were becoming frequent, almost regular afternoon and evening features. In the Tropic of Cancer area, the first hurricanes would be forming in June, when the surface temperature of the Atlantic Ocean approached the critical threshold. Yet global warming was moving the goal posts so that early hurricanes were getting uncomfortably close to Whitsun.

"Don't worry. The first cyclones are still way off," the Doc had tried to waive Laura's respective misgivings.

"Maybe so, but I happened to experience both hurricanes and tornados in the US. They scared the hell out of me. Also, I volunteered for the big clean-up in New Orleans after the passage of hurricane Catherine, so I have first-hand knowledge of what kind of damage hurricanes can wreak."

"Oh I see, well, that must have been something of an experience, I'm sure. But unlike seismic events such as earthquakes or volcanic eruptions, hurricanes are not unforeseen ordeals but slow-moving, permanently monitored features. Even if one were to form in mid-Atlantic this very day, it would take quite some time to get here. As fast as the masses of air inside the maelstrom will be whirled around, accelerating all the time, the whole wind machine as such travels not much faster than an ambitious sailing yacht. Besides, as a rule, hurricanes go ashore much further up north, in Florida, the Carolinas, sometimes even as far up as Jersey and New York. Once cut off from the water, they lose steam and degenerate into a series of stray tropical storms and tornados."

It had done little to make Laura feel more at ease. But once she had agreed to the Doc's proposal, she had to abide by her word. That, too, had been one of her father's lessons.

"From a business point of view, your word is part of the company's goodwill. Once you start giving your partners reason to doubt your commitments, your business is finished and so are you. Hence, never give your word lightly, not to anyone."

Not to waste time, the Doc had suggested taking the shortcut via the so-called Rivière Salée. This should limit the voyage to some twenty-four hours and was, hence, both Laura's and the Doc's preferred solution, even though the specific modalities of the strictly regulated passage that would take them through the "Salty River" were less than agreeable.

Once at Jolly Harbour, they would hang around until they could be sure that the Yellow Dancer was safe and properly looked after. While Laura was going to take a plane home via London Heathrow, Ti Martin, the Doc and César would be looking for a ride on a yacht going south or, if that failed, take a small plane back to Pitre, at Laura's expense.

Thus, around noon, Laura's crew had shown up in the Blue Lagoon and stepped aboard the yacht with their hand luggage. After an improvised luncheon, the two men had prepared the Yellow Dancer for the trip which, essentially, was no more than a crossing. Among other things, they had hoisted the sails to check whether the sun, moths or mould had done them any serious harm. Everything was found in working order, if a little marked by wear and tear. The engine jumped to life almost immediately and hummed away smoothly, without coughing black or blue clouds of smoke from the exhaust. Both water and fuel tanks were reasonably full up, the batteries were a "go", the electronic devices blinked, beeped and hissed reassuringly, in short, the Yellow Dancer was cleared for take-off.

In late afternoon, the men had cast off the boat's moorings and Yellow Dancer left the Marina Bas du Fort. Even though they were in no particular hurry, it was essential to stick to the time schedule that the Doc had sketched out for them.

As Ti Martin had shown Laura on a chart, while the Doc did his first turn at the helm, the so-called Rivière Salée was not really a river, but something of an artificial cut, separating the two wings of the butterfly-shaped island. "Here, in the East, you have Terre Haute with, as its centre, the port of Pointe-à-Pitre. In the West, you see Terre Basse with the island's official administrative capital, Basse-Terre. Unlike many other channels or canals, the Rivière Salée is tidal, inverting its direction twice a day."

Laura nodded and said she was familiar with such patterns from the largely tidal Elbe river at home. What confused her no end, though, were the local place names. Why would someone in his or her right mind call the eastern part of Guadeloupe, flat as a pancake, highlands and the glaringly mountainous western half with its volcano lowlands? Had the original settlers been as blind as a bunch of bats or was it an expression of their quaint sense of humour?

Ti Martin showed sympathy and told Laura that he, too, had first had to get used to such mysterious Caribbean misnomers.

"The Humpty-Dumpty syndrome," he smiled. "In the Gwada vernacular, a word means precisely what the locals want it to mean. In this case, High doesn't stand for "elevated", as it does for the rest of the world, but rather for above the wind. The same goes for low which stands for below the wind, see? This kind of derived usage applies to places, individual islands, just as much as to entire archipelagos."

"The two parts of Gwada," Ti Martin went on, "are linked by two separate freeways, one in the North and the other in the

South. Both cross the Rivière Salée once. The two resulting bridges are bottlenecks for road- and incoming or outgoing boat traffic
alike. Passing under them while they are closed is possible only
for very minor craft. To let the other yachts, and, in particular, the
sailing boats with their masts sail through, the bridges need to be
opened. Which, in turn, brings the road traffic to a complete halt.
In order not to let this happen during busy working hours, the
bridges are opened only very briefly once a day, at a time when
no God-fearing and law-abiding citizen should be on the road
anyway, at 5 in the a.m."

"No kidding?"

"No kidding."

Whoever missed this critical moment had Hobson's choice
between waiting for another twenty-four hours or picking the
much longer route around Terre Basse, which, for yachts beyond
six feet or so of draught was inevitable, anyway, seeing the very
shallow nature of the cut. To avoid oversleeping, the Doc had
suggested mooring the yacht at one of the buoys laid out for this
very purpose right opposite the bridge that marked the entrance
of the "River". Should they still miss the critical moment, they
would have only themselves to blame.

That's why they were here now, at the extreme western cod
end of the harbour basin. It lacked the Blue Lagoon's magic
charm but was calm and quiet enough. They had lots of time on
their hands to eat, chill and talk at leisure. Laura thought it was
an appropriate moment to kick-start her investigations in the
case of The People vs. Robert Forster. The witness Jack aka the
Toubib aka the Doc being practically nailed to the stand for quite
a while, Laura could profit from the occasion and grill him at her
heart's delight. Like an experienced DA, she decided to quit beating about the bush and came straight to the point.

"Doc, who is Penelope Z? And why would she call herself the
Yellow Dancer? Was the yacht called after her or vice versa?"

She had not really counted on taking the Doc, sitting opposite
her in the cockpit, by surprise. After all, he had already proven
himself a sharp customer, presumably not shaken easily. And he

seemed to live up to her impression of him. As if her words had been blown with the wind, he took out his pipe and laboriously started filling it with tobacco from his pouch.

Laura had little or no patience with smokers. She did not tolerate the wafting clouds of cigarette smoke, hated the revoltingly sweet aroma of cigars, and despised the barbaric stink of pipes. What kind of pleasure men found in this sorry surrogate of a baby's dummy escaped her altogether. Even conceding, for the sake of argument, that there was something vaguely sexy about pipe-smoking, the pleasure to be derived from it couldn't but be seriously affected by the facetiousness of pipes going continually out. It vaguely reminded her of "her" physicist, the one with the erection problems. Once finished for good and laid aside, the pipe kept giving off the pungent smell of smouldering wood for hours on end.

So, normally Laura would not have allowed smoking on board the Yellow Dancer. With the Doc, she made an exception. His tobacco smelled disturbingly of a whore's cheap perfume, but for the time being, as long as she had no translation of the letters, the man with his eye-patch and silly moustache held the one and only spare key to the Time Machine. To make him talk, Laura would have endured a lot more than his pestilence of a pipe.
The sun had already sunk beyond the visible horizon. Its bloody red evening hue was flickering a last time like the melting butt of a spent candle. The Doc had placed himself on the convexly shaped seat behind the huge, leather-clad steering wheel and was staring absent-mindedly at the compass as into a fortune-teller's crystal ball. César had tucked himself in at the Doc's feet and started hitting the air with all fours in some canine dream of hares or rabbits zig-zagging across autumnal stubble fields. Ti Martin had stretched himself on the starboard cockpit bench with a glass of punch and a lit joint. At present, he seemed lost in the purple folds of the western skies.

Laura leaned with her back against that part of the forward cockpit wall on top of which there was a small provisional chart table. Originally designed for eyeball navigation in the treacherous waters of the Scandinavian skerries, it had proved equally useful in Caribbean coastal waters studded with reefs. The night stretched out its cool, pale hands to caress both land and sea. Almost imperceptibly, the ever restless tide wrapped itself around the Yellow Dancer's hull as if to carry her away with its gentle current.

Laura repeated her questions, even though she had no doubt whatsoever that the Doc had heard her the first time around. The man had lit his crooked pipe and huffed and puffed away like a human steam engine. Laura half expected smoke to come out of his ears, as well. When he had nearly disappeared completely in blue smoke like a genie hoping to get back into the bottle, he took the pipe out of his mouth and stroked his moustache with his thumb.

"So you have found the letters," he said, finally. Laura saw it more as a statement than a question, and didn't comment.

"Well, I already thought so when you manifested a curious interest in my late partner at chess. Why would anyone look for a professor of ancient Greek in the Caribbean? A pity, come to think of it. The man would no doubt have taken it upon himself to read you the letters aloud in German with all the likely pathos of the original. He would have convinced you of the letters having been written by the original Penelope, Ulysses' faithful wife, I'm sure."

"Then again, ours is not the world of epics, is it? Has it occurred to you that epic protagonists are terribly type-cast, never change so much as an iota, irrespective of what situation they happen to be involved in? Achilles is always the ruthless killer, Ulysses always the cunning sailor, Penelope always the faithful wife, et cetera. What change there is, comes from the intervention of gods more flesh and blood than two-dimensional humans."
He stuck his pipe back and puffed a little more. Laura patiently waited for the pipe to go out on him.

"Ours is more the world of the novel, a genre which carries the promise of change in its very name. But I am digressing, am I not? You know, I wish you had not broken the spell of this magic evening by asking questions as prosaic as those. Also, I was confident that, given some time, you would find most of the answers yourself. Curiosity, your name is woman. Isn't that how the saying goes?"

There it was. The Doc's pipe had gone out. Laura did not take his mild reproaches to heart. A good investigator must grow a thick skin or change professions, she had once read. Also, you had to be extremely observant. When interrogating someone, you had to be able to interpret both that person's choice of words, inflection of voice, facial expression, gestures, and other involuntary body language. The Doc touching his eye-patch like he did this very moment meant he was feeling uneasy, nervous.

"You see, I have to confess I'm neither a Homer nor a Marlowe. So, you should not set your expectations too high. Besides, there's a paradox to be taken into consideration. To wit: Penelope's story lacks depth and plausibility without the background knowledge of Robert's past. The full facts of that, however, are Penelope's exclusive domain. So, the only thing yours truly is able to contribute are sporadic episodes, bits and pieces, sometimes connected, frequently unrelated. Your father's early life and times as they reflect on Penelope. Most of it is taken from hints, remarks, and innuendos I later deduced and tied together myself. You know best, I presume, how little information about himself he would readily part with. So do not hold me responsible for any gaps or inconsistencies that may strike you. Like I say, to tell Robert's story in a coherent manner, you would need Penelope, but alas, that is not to be."

The Doc stopped as if sorting out conflicting images before his mental eye.

"And, with all that in mind, here comes my one crucial question to you, Laura. Are you sure, I mean, are you dead certain you want to hear this? Remember Oedipus Rex and what good it did him to learn about his parents' past. I would hate to see you blind yourself in despair."

"You're frightening me. Is that another trick of yours to make me let bygones be bygones? But no, or rather, yes, I am positive I want to hear it, all of it. I feel it to be part of my father's legacy and since I am his only heir…"

The Doc looked up from the compass glass and, glancing at Laura, realized that it would not be in him to change her mind, come what may. "Very well, then. But allow me to remind you of this little exchange of ours when the time comes. And come it will."

He pocketed his pipe and sighed. Manifestly, he did not quite know where nor how to start. If you keep testing my patience, Laura thought, you will find me no oyster. Just pick up the bloody thread somewhere, anywhere, for God's sake, it can't be all that difficult.

At the same time, she had serious misgivings. When she had asked her questions, she had expected to get some straightforward, if unpleasant, answers. Why this elaborate introduction? Was he trying to lend more weight to his tale than the whole thing warranted, to make himself important? Did he really think that Laura couldn't stomach the coming to light of one, two, or whatever number of lovers, female or male, Robert may have entertained here in the West Indies? He couldn't possibly believe her to be that naïve, that frail.

On the other hand, the Doc she had known so far was not given to playing to the gallery, after all, so there must be more to it all than had hit Laura's imagination. The more emerged, the greater the risk that it was no longer limited to Robert and this Penelope, but encroached upon other people's lives - not least Laura's own. All the more reason for her to squeeze this crumpled lemon of a Frenchman for any single piece of information he might be both able and willing to divulge.

"Maybe you ought to consider pouring yourself a solid glass of rum or have the chef prepare you a Ti Punch, meanwhile. Tell him it's Doctor's orders."

3. The Unsinkable

"Laura, you give me the impression of a perspicacious, bright young lady. I cannot believe someone like you never asked herself where your father's initial assets, his seed capital came from. You know, his Monte Christo treasure chest that enabled him to found his forwarding company and quickly develop it further into today's impressive logistics empire."

Laura nodded and took a sip of the rum punch Ti Martin had handed her.

"Yes, I did. Rather frequently, too, I daresay. At least in the beginning. But he was forever evasive on that subject. I felt like an unlucky archaeologist hitting granite rock wherever she stuck her spade. Now and again, it is true, the soil would yield the odd pieces of earthenware, so to speak, but they never even seemed to belong to the same period. He just didn't give me a chance to put two and two together, never showed me any photos, kept changing the reference points to blur the outlines. In the end, I just gave up, left him to roam the maze of his memories on his own."

"And you never had a nagging gut feeling you might not have liked what you risked finding, if someone provided you with Ariadne's thread? I daresay Robert knew only too well why he kept you at arm's length. You see, if I told you he was hiding a nice array of skeletons in his secret cupboard that would be no mere figure of speech."

The Doc rummaged in his pockets for a match. Despite his intensive efforts at whiffing, the embers in his pipe had gone out again. Maybe this was part of a stratagem, Laura thought, as she watched him with amused detachment. A frequently extinguished pipe would give him the relative satisfaction of smoking without unduly harming his lungs. Shrewd, but beside the point since pipe smokers' favourite cancer was that of the tongue, as far as she knew.

"Well, I mean, let's face it. After all I could gather, Robert must have come from altogether humble origins. Which would make his life achievements that much more extraordinary, of course. Or so it would, if experience didn't teach me that, often enough, business success and meteoric social rise are not only the result of puritan work discipline combined with sheer luck, as many faked tycoon biographies wish to make us believe so we do not lose faith in the American dream, you know, that ridiculous rags-to-riches mythology. The end of the rainbow? Hardly. Try monomaniac ruthlessness, uncompromising brutality, criminal involvement, instead. It all goes by no end of despicable euphemisms, but I prefer to call a spade a spade. Take it as a sign of my appreciation of your intellect, if you will."

"And so, putting two and two together, Laura, there's unfortunately no escaping the fact that young Robert Forster was a criminal. An uncommonly skilful one no doubt, but an outlaw who had a lot to answer for and didn't."

Laura sat motionless as if shock-frosted by the sudden passage of an Arctic front system. She was horror-stricken and couldn't make out what shocked her more, the significance of the message or the sheer banality of its delivery. She refused to believe what she had just heard and yet could not see what kind of objective this French one-eyed fool could possibly pursue by vilifying her father who he had called his friend. Could he be right in insinuating she had always had bad feelings about the origins of Robert's funds? The accumulation of assets by illegal means was something she might have made her peace with. But the Doc appeared to be suggesting that at least some of those assets consisted of what they didn't call blood money for nothing. That was plainly monstrous. She took a swig of punch whilst the Doc continued, unmoved.

"Now you know the name of the game and will be wondering about Robert's hand. Well, it all boils down to the concept of trafficking. The clandestine transport of merchandise or people. No offence, but I don't think Robert Forster had a salesman's gifts. He was not the kind that would convince Saudi sheiks of the merits of importing sand to the Arab peninsula. Robert's strong point was his uncanny sense of anything to do with moving things from A to B. A wizard of the trade's three h's: hiding, handling, hauling. In short, he had the logistics' gene. As a true natural he would probably have made a very successful career at all events, only not half as fast."

Ti Martin had finished his joint and slouched below to prepare supper. César, always looking for titbits from the tables of the rich, had woken from his slumber, put the rabbits on hold and followed Ti Martin down into the galley. Laura glanced at the two of them, without really seeing. She felt like cutting the Doc short to put an end to his slanderous tale. But somehow, she couldn't bring herself to do it, seemed unable to speak or move a limb. As she sat motionless, she could relate to the paralytic captain of the Titanic once it had become clear that she would be a goner. Contrary to what Laura had been made to believe ever since she had developed a consciousness of her own, it would now seem that Robert Forster was not unsinkable.

"Has it ever struck you," the Doc continued, palpably warming up to his subject matter, "that ever since the construction of Noah's ark, logistical infrastructure has been the key to the success of any major undertaking in the history of mankind? Irrespective of the respective discipline: military, commercial, cultural, criminal, you name it. The building of the pyramids, the erection of the tower of Babel, the siege of Troy, the Persian Wars, Alexander's, Napoleon's, or Hitler's campaigns - take away the logistics of it, and it all collapses like a house of cards."

"That logistics should be of vital importance for trade is self-evident, I believe. That this applies even more so to its illegitimate brother, smuggling, is perhaps less obvious to the uninitiated. Looking at it from a purely technical point of view, smuggling consists in moving high-value merchandise, frequently perishable, as fast as possible and as unnoticeably as feasible. It's a bit like, I don't know, crossing a fresh snow-drift in the mountains without so much as leaving a footprint. If it is a craft at all, it's one that touches upon the artistic, believe me."

The ardour with which the Doc was delving into the technicalities of trafficking made Laura suspect that he himself was perfectly at home in this secret world whose topography he charted in such vivid colours. Presumably, she was listening not only to the disclosure of Robert's past, but, by the same token, to the Doc's valiant attempt at exculpation.

"The ranking of Logistics within the overall structure increases with the value of the merchandise to be moved. In any discussion of wholesale drugs business, what immediately crops up is the image of the almighty scar-faced Columbian drug fiend with hands dripping blood and insatiable murderous appetites. That's a romantic if disgusting make-believe as cultivated by Hollywood. I'm not saying such people don't exist. What I'm saying is they are a negligible entity. You don't seriously believe now, do you, that financial high rollers looking for illegal money outlets in our time and age would feel inclined to leave their billion-dollar investments in the hands of unpredictable psychopaths? Nowadays, drug trafficking is masterminded by pin-striped managers in fully air-conditioned towers of glass and steel."

The Doc broke off and started staring hard into the darkness of the harbour basin. A yacht, probably another sailing boat, was approaching from the direction of the marina entrance. She displayed a red and a green light on her sides close to the water line and a white light midway up her mast. The Doc picked up the binoculars dangling round the compass column and looked through them with his sound right eye by holding the instrument upside down instead of vertically. Whether his sudden interest was motivated by general curiosity or habitual caginess, Laura could not tell. At any rate, as he continued his terrifying tale, the Doc would never lose sight of the other boat.

"Now, as much information as we may be offered on the historical front figures - emperors, kings, generals, gangster bosses, what have you, we learn next to nothing about the logistics experts behind it all. Same applies to trafficking. The logistics specialist is the notoriously invisible man. He works behind the scenes, largely unknown even to otherwise well-informed circles. Sometimes, he goes by some flowery alias, such as the Provider, the Dispatcher, or the Hauler, the Transformer. Notwithstanding, they are key players in the game. Restlessly moving worker ants, always on the look-out for inconspicuous hiding places and unsuspected transport modes, forever two steps ahead of both customs and drug enforcement agencies. Unlimited discretion, detailed technical knowledge in many different areas, unlimited flexibility, unconditional reliability, lots of imagination, and, inevitably, networking ability are among the most vital skills expected of this category of criminal strategist. In his time and age, young Robert belonged to the vanguard elite of multifunctional organizers. He was clever enough to learn by doing, and flexible enough constantly to adapt to changes and to think out of the box."

By now, the second yacht had almost reached the Yellow Dancer. Suddenly, a strong searchlight was switched on, its blinding beam turning first on them, then on the row of mooring buoys. Laura and the Doc shielded their eyes with their hands. The searchlight was quickly switched off again.

"Don't forget what's at stake in drug trafficking. If and when the logistics guy gets it wrong and a batch of 'bricks' is burnt, sunk or seized, a fortune is lost. The man held responsible will not be dragged to court, but stuffed into a barrel of acid, dropped overboard with his feet in a bucket of concrete or put to sleep in a freshly cast foundation. That's where henchmen like Ignace come in. As with all other business aspects, the profits are a function of the risks involved. If all goes well, you get rich faster than in any other line of business."

The Doc made a break, no doubt to give Laura an opportunity to come to her senses again. To learn that your private as well as professional existence rests on the quicksand of criminal machinations is not an everyday experience to anyone. To even start digesting what she had heard, Laura, whose mental agitation clearly showed in her face, would need time, lots of it. If she ever was to get over it at all.

Laura finally understood the Doc's precautionary remarks. She appreciated his efforts to cushion the shocking facts in innocuous imagery, to display them in the softening light of technical specialization, as if drug trafficking was not that much different from building engines or peddling real estate. It did little, however, to mitigate the overall impression that, at least in his younger years, her father, her great idol and role model, had been a hardened criminal. Not some gentleman-thief on the roof-tops of Nice, delivering rich elderly ladies from the weight of their jewellery. No latter-day Robin Hood, either, but a common drug runner, the vermin of modern society, living albeit indirectly on the hopeless addiction of thousands of lost souls. On the scale of societal values, you could not sink much deeper than that. Laura rested her head on both hands as if the newly obtained knowledge threatened to make it burst.

"You remember now what I told you at the outset? Oedipus Rex and all that?"

Laura lifted her head. The Doc looked at her with a mixture of pity and impotence. It was a difficult task she had forced upon him, a walk through the maze. Obviously, he had wanted to break the news to her as gently as possible, without leaving her in any doubt about the true nature of her heritage. By and large, he had succeeded.

It seemed the other yacht was preparing to moor on buoy number three more to port, to keep her distance from the Yellow Dancer. To all appearances, there were only two persons on board. One man sat at the wheel, the other stood at the bows with a rope in his hands.

"At the time, a large part of the drugs mainly from Afghanistan or Central Asia was shipped via the Middle East or Turkey," the Doc, apparently satisfied with the handling of the neighbouring yacht, opened a new chapter.
"From Turkey, the merchandise was transported either on the Black Sea route to Bulgaria and the eastern Balkans, or across the Aegean, Greece, and the western part of the Balkan peninsula. Since the shipping could not always be effected without the odd hitches and wrinkles interfering, the smugglers had a lasting interest in all sorts of hiding places, where a specific lot of merchandise could temporarily be stored without the risk of seizure

or pillage. Robert had repeatedly served on the Aegean route and thus come to know his way around there quite well, and even learned conversational Greek into the bargain. His most important discovery had been the small, innocent-looking Greek island of Leros, close to the Turkish coast."

Ti Martin appeared on the top steps of the companionway, holding two bowls of steaming hot stew in his hands. He offered one of them to Laura, who was taken aback by the strong smell of many different spices. The other one he handed to the Doc. They both thanked their chef, who promptly went one step further and presented them with two glasses of white wine he had deposited on the steps before coming up.

"Like some other Aegean islands, Leros had been at the centre of fierce fighting during the last phase of the Second World War. The natural local harbour of Lakki Bay counted among the best and safest deep-water ports in the whole of the Mediterranean. Reason enough, first for the Italians, then for the British and, finally, for the Germans to try their worst and gain a foothold there. Each of the three successive occupying forces dug their own bunkers, fortified their depots and enlarged its subterranean storage facilities for ammunition, spare parts, fuel, and provisions. Given a few more months, the place would have been turned into another Gibraltar."

The Doc clicked his tongue in appreciation.

"Hmmmm. Nothing beats this Cajun Gumbo of Ti Martin's, sublime."

Laura had lost her appetite. She remembered the red-hot gator food of the rugged Louisiana swamp-dwellers and saggy-pants moonshiners only too well and knew that her stomach would not take it lying down at the best of times. Which the present one wasn't.

The other yacht had moored at the buoy. The crew of two had disappeared below without so much as waving or shouting a perfunctory "hello". There was light in the yacht's saloon, but dark blue curtains gave sufficient privacy. The Doc still kept his wary good eye on the neighbour.

"After the war, this maze of subterranean facilities fell into oblivion. Stripped of its strategic importance, doubtful even during the war, the port of Lakki held no more attractions for the new powers that were. During the 1980s, Robert, on the other hand, had not been slow to realize the logistics potential of the island. There were hideouts galore, a well-established network of asphalted roads, ferry connections, no end of unqualified but willing and not particularly inquisitive manpower with no trade union representatives around. In short, the island of Leros appeared nothing short of tailor-made for the requirements of Robert's shy trade. What local law was present could be bought at ridiculously low rates, and the Greek government was too far away and too preoccupied with other matters to give a damn about this fly-blown fluke of an island at the other end of the Aegean. Robert took advantage of the situation and, for a while, turned Leros into a prime depot for Turkish-Asian drugs on their way to the civilized world."

The Doc gave the hollow laugh of a disappointed goat staring down an empty well.

"Whenever Robert spoke of Leros," he continued, "tears would well up in his eyes. Of course, this was not only due to his recollections of the days of past logistical glory."

Laura felt like a shipwrecked passenger, clutching the barnacled hull of a capsized lifeboat, surrounded by patiently circling sharks, whose half-open teeth-studded mouths were already watering with anticipation. It would not take long now for the air bubble under the hull to fade away, leaving the boat with no buoyancy reserve. Still, she did not find it in her to interrupt the Doc and cut the thread of his sombre account. Uncharacteristically, the Frenchman had been guilty of an understatement. He was no Homer alright, but then, who was. Notwithstanding, narrative talent did form part of the Doc's genetic heritage. Perhaps Laura, by some intricate mechanism of psychological sublimation, had found a morbid pleasure in listening to this profligate story-teller and convinced herself somehow that his lavishly adorned rhetoric had absolutely no bearing on either Robert's or her own life? A story lifted from the One Thousand and One Nights, albeit presented with inverted roles - one-eyed, pipe-smoking king Shahriyar doing the narrating and a badly rattled Sheherazade the listening? Laura took a last sip of punch and put the empty glass down on the floor.

"Want Ti Martin to fix you another one?"

Laura shook her head. She felt dizzy enough already. One more punch, and she would come to regret it at sea tomorrow, of that she was sure.

"Anyhow. Warehouses, depots, and bunkers were not the only vacant spaces in those days. Barrack buildings that had housed Italian, British, and German troops during successive periods had no more tenants for a while. Word of their availability eventually reached Athens. The then Greek government, unrestrained by moral qualms, decided to put those convenient facilities at the country's far eastern outpost to some practical use. Political, social, and medical outcasts all over the country were rounded up and shipped to the island. Orphans of world or civil wars, leftist dissidents, or the mentally handicapped, all those unwanted ones wound up in the Leros barracks, which quickly became the quintessential symbol of squalor and desolation.

At the beginning of the 1980s, western European journalists suddenly got wind of the Leros concentration-camp set-up. Scandalized articles unveiling the appalling conditions under which the Unwanted had to live there and be treated worse than animals alerted public opinion and threatened to harm the financial interests of the Greek tourist industry. Robert and his collaborators had no problem with that. On the contrary, the more shocking the news about the unwanted, the lesser the potentially pernicious interest in his own murky activities."

The Doc looked at Laura's untouched bowl and frowned.

"I can fully understand your lack of appetite, I really do. But as a medical doctor, I have to insist you eat something. Do us both a favour, Ti Martin will be inconsolable if you don't do his food justice. He can be very touchy about that, you know."

Laura gave a bitter laugh, more like a nervous cough.

"Inconsolable" because of a rejected bowl of gumbo? Well, there were worse afflictions than that, to be sure. Who was it again who said that consolation was the deaf sister of blind hope?

"To remedy the situation, the Greeks had to send more paramedical staff to Leros in a hurry to take care of the Unwanted. Among the trainee nurses idealistic or destitute enough to answer the Government's call and seek that kind of employment, there was a young girl of very pretty looks and totally obscure origins. Born somewhere along the Turkish Black Sea coast, the region the Greeks call Pontus, as she herself had declared. Apparently, she had spent some time in Istanbul, as well. That was just about as much as she herself or anybody else knew. The kind of alien that used to be quite common in those turbulent days. Even her name was a mystery. The girl insisted on calling herself Penelope. Since there already were some other Penelopes around, this one was called Penelope Z. Partly because zita, the sixth letter of the Greek alphabet, was next in line, as it were, and partly because the spelled-out letter forms the verb to live, which seemed to fit Penelope to a t."

"If you really won't eat your gumbo, would you mind if I gave it to César? Without Ti Martin noticing, of course. The Doc pointed at Laura's bowl. Were Caribbean dogs endowed with asbestos entrails? Dr Sanders' long-haired Chihuahua bitch would probably have been blown to pieces by her first mouthful of this inflammable mush.

"And wasn't she alive, our beautiful Penelope! Not surprisingly, Robert had been infatuated with this blossoming young lady ever since he had first set eyes on her. What with her thick black hair, framing her pale face like that of a Madonna on an orthodox icon, her white nurse's uniform and bonnet, her firm round breasts… You see, even someone like myself who doesn't easily fall prey to female charms, is still carried away by Robert's descriptions, sorry about that. Anyway, from what I could gather, she must really have been something of a sight for sore eyes. Unfortunately, he never so much as showed me a photo of her. But I think we can take his choice to have been an excellent choice."

Like a shiny loaf of Dutch cheese gnawed at by celestial mice, the incomplete moon peeped through a gap between two dark clouds and projected its light on the yachts gently bobbing at their moorings.

"I'm sure that Robert wooed his Penelope with all the passion of his youth. But there was a complication clouding his paradise. Not surprisingly, a Turkish business partner of the drug traffickers who Robert was working for at the time had also taken a fancy to Penelope. His name, or nickname, was that of Suleiman the Silent, to be precise. He had earned it by his position in the hierarchy of Turkish drug barons and his uncanny way of closing in on his victims by stealth. This refers back to a time when he had not yet reached the top and still had to do the odd killing himself It was said that when you heard him coming, you would already have his knife at your throat or the barrel of his gun at your temple."

"Suleiman the Silent was probably three times Penelope's age, but that did not daunt him a bit. Why should it have? Where he came from, a girl aged 18, say, would already be something of a shelf-warmer, or a prostitute. Baby snatching and enforced marriages are commonly accepted practices in the Anatolian parts the Sultan came from. So, the Turk had Robert at a socio-cultural disadvantage, as far as Penelope was concerned. Didn't do him much good, though. Robert took Penelope with him to Thessaloniki, in northern Greece, thus making himself another deadly enemy for life. Turks in general tend to be both touchy and vindictive, indulging in simplistic Oriental patterns of thinking: somebody not my friend is an enemy, somebody not believing in Allah's supremacy is a heathen, and so forth. It's a reflection of ignorance and lack of education, facilitating life in a world growing ever more complicated, by the same token rendering intercultural communication impossible, to my mind."

"How about some bread and cheese?" the Doc shouted in the general direction of the galley.

"Coming up right away," the slightly nasal answer resounded like a waking ghost's rumbling voice from an ancient crypt.

"Robert lodged her with some ethnic Russian couple, friends of his in Thessaloniki, Youry and Masha, I believe they were called. Penelope kept their daughter, of roughly the same age, company, and finished her last remaining years of apprenticeship, which she had apparently skipped while still in Turkey. Robert would obviously pay her regular visits and after little more than a year, they married in a Greek Orthodox church, though he at least didn't confess to that creed. An ill portent, perhaps."

"So they didn't live happily ever after?" Laura murmured.

"Well, I wish they had. True to his name, Suleiman the Silent left no stone unturned to track Penelope down. He probably felt dishonoured. His 'property' had been taken from him and he had lost face, hard to tell which was worse. Not a laughing matter for any one of us either, I suppose. For a gangster, it can mean annihilation. Once your competitors lose respect and fear of reprisals, you become an outcast among outlaws with no-one and nothing to turn to, a walking corpse. Anyway, the Sultan of course wound up unearthing Penelope and kidnapped her during one of Robert's absences, which, due to the host of his then professional obligations, were often rather prolonged. Another one of those cherished Levantine marital rituals, kidnapping the would-be bride. Normally a matter of the bridegroom being unable to pay the bride's parents. This move of Suleiman's was special, though. It must have hit Robert all the harder, since Penelope was already pregnant then, as time would show."

The Doc knocked his pipe out on the steering-wheel, which rang like a small church bell muffled by a silencer, and almost ceremoniously stowed his smoking equipment in the half empty tobacco pouch.

"Robert must have been literally shattered upon his return to Thessaloniki. But be that as it may, the kidnapping of Penelope became the decisive turning point of his life. His beloved wife was held captive somewhere in the dusty Anatolian plains. His western European principals were not a little miffed about Robert having estranged one of their most important Turkish providers. Despite glasnost and perestroika, both Nato and the Greek armed forces were about to develop a fresh interest in those old installations on Leros, which had lain fallow and gathered dust for so long. And, more recently, Robert's face had started turning up more frequently on Greek, Turkish, and international mug-shot galleries. In short, a rapid and lasting change of décor was what the family doctor would have ordained."

César had emptied the gumbo-bowl and started barking, very low at first, but rapidly growing louder. He rose on his hind legs, rested his forward paws on the cockpit frame and seemed to have picked up an intriguing scent emanating from the neighbouring yacht.

The Doc tried in vain to calm him down. Soon enough, though, Laura came to understand why César had grown so restless all of a sudden. Seemingly out of nowhere, a dog easily twice César's size appeared on the yacht next to them. Looking at it, one would have the impression of facing a bear young of last year's brood, Laura thought. She had never yet set eyes on a dog of that obviously quite powerful race.

"Stop that noise," the Doc called out to César. "Haven't you learned anything at all from my tale of sorrow? No woman, no cry? Yamaaan."

Ti Martin came up on deck with the dog's collar and tied César to the taffrail lest he jump overboard and swim to the neighbouring yacht. Over there, nobody but the snarling bear-like dog seemed to be on deck. Suddenly, a loud whistle rang through the silence of the night and the grizzly young disappeared below.

"Thus, one fine day, Robert came to Hamburg, where nobody knew him and where, thanks to the small fortune he had accumulated by smuggling dope, he was able to make a fresh start on civvy street, as it were. Nor did he waste any time licking his wounds, but soon threw in his fate with Frederike, daughter of a well-off Danish merchant. Strictly speaking, a case of bigamy, of course. But where there is no plaintiff... My personal impression after many talks with Robert is that, despite his seemingly frivolous attitude and life-style, his marriage with Frederike was not a cool calculated step to gloss over his bumpy past and help him to acquire fresh respectability. It was rather the case that Frederike had managed to conquer what little niche there was left in his heart after the Penelope tragedy."

"Which would be corroborated by the fact that he had a daughter with her, to wit, yours truly," Laura finally interrupted him. She felt her presence of mind returning like the use of an arm or a leg that grown numb momentarily. Her father may have been the villain the Doc had depicted - her mother's monument, even this dubious Frenchman could not, would not touch. She must have been as ignorant and blind about Robert's past as Laura had been.

"Yes. I guess you could say that."

"Did my father ever see Penelope again?"

"He tried his level best and almost managed, too. One day he learned from one of his numerous sources, which he took great pains to keep reasonably functional, that Penelope had to go to hospital in Istanbul for a few days. A matter of treating some medical complication to do with her having given birth to two girls under medically doubtful circumstances. They were Robert's daughters, that much was for sure, non-identical twins, only a year or so old at the time. Of course, she would have been accompanied by Suleiman, who never left her out of her sight for long."

Laura's attention strayed. Maybe her brain was suffering from an overload and had decided to suspend its function for fear of blowing a fuse. Somehow absent-mindedly, Laura watched the neighbouring yacht while half listening to the Doc's voice. At the yacht's stern, she saw the figure of a man crouching. He had turned up the collar of his oilskins jacket, even though the night was rather mild and only the faintest of breezes caressed Laura's hair.

Either the light wind or the tide had veered the two yachts round their moorings in parallel, so that Laura perceived the man's silhouette now against the background of some street-lights on shore as in a black-and-white paper cutting. The one thing that caught her attention was the curious shape of the man's skull. It seemed pointed at the top and reminded her of the cactuses she had seen in the Blue Lagoon. Minus the thorns, of course. The man sat down and lit a cigarette, probably his last one of the day before turning in. Laura tried to spell out the yacht's name and managed to do so after a while. The boat was called Yakamoz, home port Büyük Ada. Or was that the other way round? Neither meant anything to her and the yacht was just a little too far away to address the man in a normal volume to start a chat. To shout at him like a Greek lass talking to her sister across the street wasn't quite her style.

"Robert decided to act and prepared his move like a master-piece of logistics, as he would," the Doc continued. He had followed Laura's glance, but from where he sat he could see only the smoke rising from the 'cactus' on board the Yakamoz.

"This was before he met Frederike, by the way. In Istanbul, the Sultan held the high ground, obviously. Robert could not under any circumstances allow the Turk to mobilise his troops. That would have put paid to his plans right away. After Penelope's release from hospital, Suleiman and Penelope, or so Robert had heard from his source, intended to pass a few hours on some island near Istanbul, in the Marmara Sea, paying a visit to some of Suleiman's next of kin. That would open the critical window of opportunity. Some Turkish men Robert had hired would dress up as policemen, intercept Penelope and the two girls on some pretext or another, and take them to a motorboat waiting near the ferry quay before Sultan could smell a rat. From there, they would head for the shore close to Atatürk airport and put them on the next plane to somewhere in Europe. As always in logistics, sticking to the time schedule was of the essence."

Once again, the Doc took a close look at the neighbouring yacht from bow to stern and back, without interrupting his flow. But he did not appear to discover anything untoward. To think they would be alone waiting here for the dawn to break would have been facetiously naive, anyway.

"All went well, at first. Penelope and the girls gave Suleiman the slip thanks to Robert's carefully picked men. The motorboat was already on its way to Yeşilköy, a good stone's throw away from the airport. But, as Shakespeare I believe has it, there is many a slip twixt cup and lip. A nasty wrinkle turned up. At full speed, the boat hit the chain of one of the numerous cargos usually riding at anchor in this sea area. A ship like that should always be passed by the stern, never by the bows. The chain, normally quite slack, can become taut, for instance, by the onslaught of a squall pushing the ship astern. Maybe the man on the wheel had not known or heeded this or had simply not paid sufficient attention. Either way, the motorboat rammed the chain, capsized, and sank within seconds."

The Doc fell into one of his irritating intermittent silences. Laura waited for the narrative to resume at this dramatic juncture, but it didn't.

"And so? What happened to Penelope and the girls?" she finally asked, obviously annoyed .

The Doc rose from his uncomfortable seat at the wheel and downed his last remaining sip of red wine.

"That, young lady, may be revealed in the fullness of time, as they say. Anyway, some have it that all three of them perished in the accident. Others maintain they are still very much alive. What else do you expect in Levantine fairy tales that always open with that consecrated formula of Once upon a time – or maybe never?"

Laura was deeply vexed. She felt as if she had been watching an exciting though deeply disturbing film whose climax had been destroyed because the idiot projectionist had been smoking on the job and irretrievably burnt the inflammable material. She was perfectly convinced that the Frenchman knew a lot more than he had divulged so far. Then again, she already had enough on her plate to last her for quite a while, as it was. And any further insistence on her part risked being thoroughly counter-productive with the Doc, if she read him right. There would be another opportunity to loosen his tongue.

FIFTH CHAPTER

1. Salty River

Somebody was shaking Laura's arm. She opened her gummy eyes with some difficulty. The cabin was pitch-dark. She could smell a whiff of somebody's tobacco and rum-tainted breath in her face. Ti Martin lit a torch, shone it first in his own face to identify himself and then on the wristwatch he held under her nose.

"Ready when you are, Laura. The Toubib says you need not really get up at all yet, you know. We can handle this between the two of us, you know. It's up to you."

Laura switched on the reading lamp above her head and looked at her own watch. Half past four. Secretly wishing everybody had overslept or fallen into a coma, she could not but commend the ruthless reliability of the Yellow Dancer's waking service.

"I'll be up on deck right away, give me a minute or two, please." Ti Martin nodded, switched off the torch and vanished. Shortly after, the engine, separated from Laura's bunk by little more than a heat- and sound-insulated bulkhead, jumped to life. Its running at low revs made the hull vibrate to the rhythm of the pistons. Laura slipped into her father's pullover and oilskins, grasped her life-jacket and climbed into the cockpit like a zombie reporting for duty aboard the Black Pearl. She felt dead tired and beat. Still, the quiet excitement and eager anticipation of the start weren't altogether lost on her.

"Hello there, young lady, did you sleep well?"

The Doc stood behind the wheel and looked forward, whilst César was literally all over the cockpit again, jumping up and down the benches, frantically wagging his tail. Laura shook her head. No, sleeping well felt different. Almost all night, she had tossed about in her bunk and tried in vain to reconcile the villain's image that the Doc had sketched of her father with her own memories of him. Close to morning, physical and mental fatigue had got the better of her tormented brain. No, she had hardly slept at all. Now she looked forward to being absorbed by the boating routine. Anything to keep those pestering ogres of the parental past at bay.

"Free!" Ti Martin's nasal voice rang from the bows. He had taken in the rope that had tied the yacht to her mooring buoy. The Doc cautiously revved up the engine as though afraid it might strain a tendon or tear a ligament if seriously solicited at this un-earthly hour. With the engine in gear, the hull seemed to relax and stopped vibrating. Ever so slowly, the yacht drifted away from the buoy and then approached the small bridge that marked the beginning of the "Salty River".

On shore, everything was dark and quiet, not so much as a stray cat around. The Doc completed a first waiting loop and steered the Yellow Dancer, bows first, into the gentle sea breeze that was wafting in from the ocean yonder this very instant. A car was heard approaching the bridge at a brisk speed, its headlights flashing through the dark like two groping fingers. Then the lit-tle Fiat-like vehicle came to a screeching halt at the bridge, cut its engine but left its headlights on. Two men got out and slammed the doors shut. As the car lights captured the little Cyprus tree on the opposite side of the bridge, they gave it a silvery, almost white glow. One of the guards opened the bridge keeper's cabin, entered and switched on a nervously flickering naked bulb. His colleague emerged with some solid fenders that looked like they meant busi-ness. He hung them from the bridge's right-hand side. Meanwhile, the other yacht with her strange name had also slipped her moor-ings and had started circling almost parallel to the Yellow Danc-er. The two men on board had pulled their hoods well over their heads. The one at the wheel had lit a cigarette, whose wisps of thin blue smoke were blown back into the hood by the breeze so that the man seemed on fire like a vampire consumed by the first rays of the morning sun. Ti Martin helped Laura to get into her stiff unwieldy life-jacket which hung on her torso heavy and bulky like an early prototype of a bullet-proof vest.

An unexpected, painfully high-pitched ringing signal from the bridge resounded across the slumbering land as if calling upon the dead to rise from their graves. Two short, thin candy-cane booms were lowered until they had reached the horizontal position in which they would have blocked oncoming road traffic had there been any. Then, the causeway part of the bridge started pivoting round the single central pillar, thus opening two narrow boat passages. The Doc revved up the engine again, this time with even more conviction, turned the Yellow Dancer round and steered her smartly through the right-hand passage.

"The yacht behind us probably draws a mite more than we do, I guess," he explained to Laura and pointed over his shoulder with his thumb. "Hence, it's better for us to stay in front of him. Like that, he won't be in our way if ever he gets stuck in the mud further up the channel. Happens all the time."

There appeared to be no boat traffic from the opposite direction this morning. Yet a jolly good bore-like rip tide of Atlantic sea water pushed into the channel from the North, hit them like the bow wave of a Panamax cargo ship. The Yellow Dancer's hull got slapped about by the current and was jerked to starboard so sharply that the yacht would have sustained some solid scratches had it not been for the combined action of the protective fenders aboard and ashore. The Doc and Ti Martin gave the two men on the bridge a friendly nod and index salute. Then they were through.

Beyond the bridge, the salty "river" immediately became calmer, smoother. Laura looked over her shoulder. Having waited for the "bow wave" to spend itself in the harbour basin, the Yakamoz, if that was her name, passed the bottleneck with great ease. She had hardly cleared the bridge when the causeway pivoted back and the candy canes were lifted again to the repeated sound of the bell. The whole operation had not lasted long enough for the man at the Yakamoz' helm even to finish his cigarette.

Ti Martin untied the fenders and stowed them away. The Doc handed him the wheel. At its south end, the Rivière Salée meandered through the kind of swamp territory that must originally have dominated the entire area except for the low chalk plateau that was to form the town's precarious foundation. Laura wished this were the river Lethe, even though she wasn't sure she would have brought herself to drink from its murky waters to forget what the Doc had told her the night before. On the port side, the yacht was approaching some large bulging bushes with low stems and a crown of slender leafy twigs extending in all directions. At first sight, the twigs seemed heavy with white blossoms like oversized cotton. As the Yellow Dancer drew nearer, however, Laura realized that the cotton capsules were really sleeping birds which had tucked their heads into their snow-white plumage. What a racket a colony this size must make when waking to the dawning day, Laura thought.

The navigable channel was marked by smallish buoys blinking red to their left and green to their right. A good thing they were functioning alright, the Doc assured Laura. The bottom of the "river" consisted of thick, glutinous mud. Yachts overshooting the limits of the channel by albeit a few inches risked running aground immediately. Once stuck, a boat's chances of wriggling its way back into the channel in reverse were slim and the marine breakdown service might not be available for some time to come because of the bridges' rigid opening routine that tolerated no exceptions.

"In the Caribbean, the American rule of 'right red returning' applies," the Doc told Laura, pointing at the flashing buoys.

"Since we're not returning but going out to sea, we are back to the European system with green ones on our starboard side. Here, in the narrow channel, that's fairly obvious, anyway. The crunch comes whenever you meet an orphan red or green one. Then you'd better know for sure on which side to pass."

The numerous secondary channels branching off all along the route like so many minor blood vessels could only be explored by small craft with next to no draught. This made the area a true paradise for bird-watchers, anglers and reapers of all sorts of edible shellfish. The Doc pointed at the black mangroves, standing on their partially submerged stilt-like roots, transforming the "river" into a shady avenue.

"Very useful plants, mangroves. Did you know that their leaves have glands that can filter the salt from the water? Without them, the plants would not survive in this hostile environment. Skippers in desperate need of a hurricane bolt-hole will sometimes run their yachts right into the mangrove thickets as a last resort, put a few anchors out and start praying. It gives their boats a fighting chance of survival. If ever you come across what seem to be mast-tops sticking up from the muddy water between the mangroves, you'll know how they got there."

Many of the upper branches of the mangroves were bent under the weight of resident frigate birds, whose disproportionately short legs reminded Laura of penguin claws. With their red, puffed-up gular pouches, the males went out of their way to convince discerning females of their qualities.

"With those stumpy legs, they are sitting ducks on the ground," the Doc said. "And since they hate to get their plumage soaked, they refuse to swim, let alone dive as their cormorant cousins. So, they are practically condemned to spend their lives in the air. By way of compensation, evolution has lavishly equipped them for flight, much better than any other sea bird around. Relative to the size of their body, they have a true glider's wingspan. Besides, some of their bones are hollow, practically weightless. Such physical advantages make them naturally born pirates of the air. Leaving the dirty work to others, they swoop down on their victims in mid-air and harrow them with their strong jambia-like beaks till the suckers surrender their catch to save their skin. Spectacular birds to watch. Hopefully, you will see them in action yet."

Minutes later, Laura spotted something bright red among the mangrove spider legs. At first, she thought it was one of the male frigate birds that had perhaps overdone the huffing and puffing, burst and dropped dead into the murky water. As they by the floating object, Laura saw it was indeed a corpse, but not that of a bird. The human body floated on its belly, yet its brawny physique and short black hair suggested a male. Not Laura's first floater, either. She had seen and touched her fair share of them during those clean-up operations in New Orleans. But that was long time ago and hadn't come out of the blue like this corpse. The garishly red thing she had spotted was the same kind of windbreaker Laura remembered registering when having lunch with Ti Martin at the Café de Paris. She shuddered.

"As I said, the local Pègre is rather active."

The Doc put his left arm around her shoulder and turned her away from the dismal sight.

"But shouldn't we…"

"Call the cops or hoist him aboard? Forget it. Collateral damage. By tonight, he'll be eaten by the crabs and eel, the natural scavengers of the mangroves. Nobody gives a damn, believe me, least of all the cops."

Laura suddenly felt a fit of nausea as she thought of the crabs they had eaten aboard the Persephone. Behind, the Yellow Dancer's wake lifted the corpse and made him bob gently over the ripples.

After another half hour's leisurely motoring, the yacht reached the runway of the Pôle Caraïbes airport, where Laura's plane had touched down only a week or so ago. Hundreds of small red, green, yellow, and white lights marked the seemingly endless dark blue strip of tarmac moist with the morning dew. In the east, the sky above the horizon was beginning to display a deep crimson, daylight was returning with a vengeance. Yakamoz was following the Yellow Dancer at a short distance, so as not to miss the opening of the second bridge. The Doc went below to brew some coffee for the crew.

Bridge number two already came into sight. It was longer than the first, a wooden structure standing on several concrete legs with a cat flap probably remotely controlled by the men back on the first one. It lifted and let the two yachts pass without any delay. No oncoming traffic here, either. Anybody entering the "river" from the North had to either develop an uncanny sense of timing or would else have to spend the night amidst the mangroves swarming with clouds of aggressive mosquito females, a prospect that made the passage in a southern direction a decidedly unattractive proposition.

"Voià, qui est fait," the Doc yawned aloud. What followed after the second bridge was a one-mile leg of relatively open lagoon. The mangroves took leave of the travellers and granted them a glimpse of the wider landscape. Here and there, Laura saw first reefs only just breaking the surface. Where they didn't, only the darker colour of the water gave them away. To try and find your way here at the dead of night would be ill-advised. Ti Martin switched on the autopilot and let go of the helm. As he explained, not because he was lazy but since no human could steer straight with anywhere near the precision of a well-functioning mechanical device. By way of proof, he called Laura's attention to the Yellow Dancer's wake which looked indeed like it had been drawn with an invisible ruler.

At the sight of the next buoy, Ti Martin took over the wheel again and followed the crooked channel with a few swerves to the left and right. Finally, he manoeuvred the yacht through the gateway formed by two fully-fledged ocean buoys much taller than the rest. The Yellow Dancer dipped her nose into the element she had been conceived for, the open Atlantic Ocean.

While Ti Martin and the Doc set the sails, a disappointed César barked half-heartedly after the Yakamoz, which appeared to follow a course different from that of the Yellow Dancer. No doubt, the Frenchman's dog would have liked to get a closer look and sniff-up the little "bear" on board their former neighbour. But there was no time for such canine exchanges. Some 50 nautical miles lay ahead of the yacht. Which, according to the Doc, translated into some eight to nine hours' sailing. More, if they were unlucky and ran into a calm.

For the time being, that seemed rather unlikely though. The Yellow Dancer took a hefty squall squarely under her wings and rolled over like a dog expecting to be caressed. A few times, the pitching yacht lifted and dipped her bow in the rough swell at the critical borderline between the island shelf and the deep blue sea. When she appeared to have convinced herself to be right on course for Antigua, she accelerated with a sudden lunge. Ti Martin seemed to appreciate her spirited attitude and switched on the autopilot again.

"No way," protested the Doc, who had just come up with two mugs of coffee. "It's Laura's turn now to do her trick at the wheel. Oh yes, I insist, humour the skipper, I beg you."

He placed the mugs on the floor, took Laura's hand and led her behind the wheel to the helmsman's seat with the mock-pompous grace of a master of ceremonies. Then he switched off the autopilot and laid Laura's hands on the huge leather-clad wheel that covered almost the entire width of the cockpit.

"The ideal would be for you to sit down and relax. You will feel much more at one with the beast. Her movements will be yours, like in an elegant waltz. That's the ultimate pleasure which only a sailing yacht can provide, the exciting feeling of mystic unison with the boat and the sea. Steering a sailing yacht is pure, unmitigated Zen. Just let her have her way, don't reign her in, don't try to force your will upon her. With her sails once properly adjusted, she will stay on course forever. Or at least until such time as shifts in the strength and direction of the wind call for adjustments, which is rarely the case within reach of the Trades. Whenever you do feel you have to correct, do it gently, using two fingers, only, lest you overdo it. Are you a horse-woman at all? Same thing, or nearly. Talk to your boat like you would to your bronco, apportioning praise or blame in a low voice. You'll see, she will feel and obey you. Yes, well done, that's the spirit. Steady her, yes, like so, now you are right on the money. Remember, a yacht is not a car or motorbike. All her movements are much slower, more contemplative, like that of a whale. It's something you will have to anticipate. As in a game of chess, you always need to think two steps ahead and prepare your moves in good time. Out in the open ocean, under ideal circumstances such as these, nothing much can happen. But in difficult coastal waters or when entering a crowded harbour, you might only get one shot. You miss and your boat will both cause and sustain serious damage, be wrecked, people will get hurt or drown. The bigger and heavier a yacht, the greater her unwillingness to react to the rudder right away."

For a rank beginner, she seemed to be doing exceptionally well, Laura praised herself. The sea and her stomach had started a silent discussion on the question of compatibility, but that was something her tummy had to get used to, and would, she was sure.

"Once upon a time, when I had just joined the navy, I had to replace an experienced helmsman about to fall ill. So there I was, all of a sudden, with my hands on the wheel and five thousand metric tons of steel under my feet," the Doc launched on another stroll down memory lane, probably to make Laura feel more at ease and stop her from staring at the shifty compass needle.

"And when I say five thousand tons, I'm talking displacement, not deadweight, that's a world of difference. We were winding our way through the narrow waters of the Beagle Channel, not far from the Horn. Fascinating place, but hostile. Funny they should have baptized it Tierra del Fuego, the Land of Fire. Didn't really feel that way at all. Anyway, a ship of that size does not have much margin for error in those parts. At a critical waypoint, the officer of the watch told me to come up some four rhumbs to starboard. That's roughly forty-five degrees, a substantial change of course. I acknowledged the order and started turning the steering wheel accordingly, if a little shyly. Nothing happened, no reaction. It was as if the horse's mouth had gone numb and no longer felt the snaffle. I turned a little more. Again, no reaction. At this point, I started panicking and gave the wheel a further whooping spin. At some stage or another, the damned crate would have to veer, I thought. And so she did, of course, as if saying, ,Well, my boy, remember this was your idea, I'm just following orders.' She turned and turned and never stopped turning till we were running literally straight for a glacier. Having relieved his bowels, the sick number one helmsman returned, grabbed the wheel in a hurry and saved the day. Inertia is a bitch, pardon my language."

"So you served in the navy? For how long?"

"A few years, just to earn enough money for my medical studies. Wasn't my thing at all, the navy. Orders and unconditional obedience are all very well, I suppose. But for the rest, no end of time wasted in futile idleness. Playing soldiers is five per cent fighting and ninety-five per cent waiting. Waiting for just about anything: the enemy to move, your own company to decamp, new orders to come in, the grub to be dished out, this or that contraption to be repaired or replaced, you take your pick. Not much different in the navy, either. And those dumb robot rituals, like marching, standing at attention, and so forth, really got at me. Men reduced to puppets, if you ask me. Level hierarchies, that's more like us, am I right, eh, César? What can I say, a man who lets himself be pushed about by his own silly dog."

"Sorry to interrupt you, but what is this?"

Laura pointed over the Doc's shoulder at a darkish silhouette just rising over the horizon dead ahead. Because she had taken her right hand off the wheel, the Yellow Dancer immediately seized the opportunity to tease her by veering closer upwind. Laura stared at the compass again and, seeing the needle move to the right, reacted like a car driver, correcting to the left, thus dropping off the wind, almost provoking a jibe.

"Take it easy, Laura, no need to panic. She is just pulling your leg, you know, like a horse that tests your riding skills. You follow the movement of the compass needle with then wheel instead of counteracting it. Always takes beginners some getting used to. Better take your eyes off the needle altogether and look straight ahead, then you are much less likely to make a mistake. Besides, in this constellation of wind and sea relative to the sails, she will correct herself before long. It's a built-in safety mechanism, you see. Good boats are constructed in such a manner that, if let loose, they will always turn towards the wind, never away from it. A yacht lunging into the wind will slow down immediately and ultimately stop or veer to the other bow. A boat falling off like she did a moment ago in reaction to your helm will accelerate and risks getting out of control."

He turned round and peered ahead, following the direction that Laura's finger had shown.

"That dark thing on the horizon? That's where we are going, the island of Antigua. Looks a damn sight closer than it really is. Antigua has much less vegetation than Guadeloupe, you see. No real rain forest, hence no evaporating humidity, hence no haze, none of that eternal circulation of water that characterizes rain forests. That's why, even though Antigua is way smaller than Guadeloupe and has practically no elevations to speak of, either, you will spot it way earlier than the much bulkier and higher Guadeloupe or Martinique, hiding like gorillas in wafts of mist. Depends a little on the weather, too, of course. Low-pressure makes coastal features or islands look deceptively close. Don't fall for it. Anyway, I'll hop below to help Ti Martin with lunch. What with breakfast having fallen victim to our early start, I guess we'll all be ravenous before noon."

Laura was terrified.

"You must be joking, leaving me alone at the helm. I'd much rather volunteer for kitchen service."

"I don't see why. You are doing fine, and if something unforeseen happens, Ti Martin and I myself will realize it forthwith because of the yacht's erratic movements and we'll be up on deck in a jiffy. Any special requests? For lunch, I mean."

Laura nodded thankfully. "Nothing very spicy, please. My stomach won't take it, I'm afraid."

"Just concentrate on the helm. Try to steer towards the left edge of Antigua. Jolly Harbour lies somewhere not far behind it." Laura would not readily have admitted it, but the trust those two experienced sailors bestowed upon her by leaving the yacht in her hands filled her with not a little pride. Her father would probably have been very impressed to see his daughter confidently helming his Yellow Dancer.

The sobering thought of Robert made her disappointment and anger well up again. Who was this man she thought she knew inside out? And what about Penelope? Her name kept coming back at her like a pendulum. What had become of the woman, what of her twin girls? Legally speaking, Penelope's daughters were probably entitled to part of Robert's heritage, since he was their biological father, too, after all. Always assuming, that is, the Doc's tale had some truth in it. And on condition that at least one of the girls was still alive. The possible existence of two half-sisters out there, somewhere on the globe, was the one element of mild solace in the Doc's otherwise sombre account. Laura would very much have liked to get to know them. An only child, she had frequently felt at a disadvantage when it came to social skills and wished for a brother or sister of roughly her own age to talk to, confide in, whatever brothers and sisters do.

Suddenly, an ugly sound like that of a pair of tight pants coming apart at the seams cut through the silence. Laura came to shocked and confused. The Yellow Dancer rapidly lost speed and no longer reacted to the helm, not unlike a plane that had lost its engines. What had happened? Had she done anything wrong? Ti Martin came storming up the companionway, looked around and showed Laura a vertical crack running along the entire length of the genoa jib.

"Not your fault," he shouted nasally, as he took the helm from Laura. "Caribbean sun."

Then he started the engine and turned the yacht with her bows to the wind, so that sails, halyards, sheets, and all the rest of the rigging started beating, rattling, and whipping like mad. Impervious to the hellish din, Ti Martin reduced speed, switched on the autopilot, and called for the Doc, who appeared on the companionway with César hard on his heels. Working together, the men hauled in the genoa and folded it on the deck. The Doc said he had already been looking for a spare sail below but so far hadn't found any. They lowered the mainsail as well and stowed it away in the lazy bag.

"I suggest we have lunch first, anyhow," the Doc called out, as he revved the engine up again, and brought the yacht round on course for Antigua. All four of them went below, where they helped themselves to the scrambled eggs prepared by Ti Martin, a delicious affair involving onions, tomatoes, mushrooms and peppers.

"The ultraviolet rays are unforgiving in the medium and long term," the Doc explained while chewing on his slice of stale bread. "They eat at the very texture of sails and considerably shorten their lifespan, especially if they are not equipped with UV-protection strips. I had noticed the genoa was showing some clear signs of wear, but thought it would still hold its own, at least until we reached Antigua. For the next season, the yacht will need a new set of sails anyway, I presume." He shrugged his shoulders.

"The only temporary replacement, I'm afraid, is a number three jib. It's going to reduce us to lame duck status, alright. Except I can't even find that."

Ti Martin gobbled down his food and started searching for the evasive jib, finally finding it under the bunk in the front cabin. He opened the hatch and pushed the sail through so it came to lie on deck. Laura followed him up. She had to get some fresh air rather urgently. Under sail, the wind had kept the Yellow Dancer on an even keel. The yacht had been slightly heeling to starboard, gently pitching in the Atlantic waves. Now, under engine power, she was swaying round all axes, like a drunkard trying to co-ordinate the movements of his wayward limbs. Each time she rolled, the useless mast accentuated the movement with its seventy or so foot leverage. Besides, a strong smell of oil and diesel fuel blended in with the unpleasant exhaust whiffs from the stern, to form an alliance almost unbearable for anyone but the sturdiest sailors. On deck, Laura went down on her knees, clutched the taffrail with both hands and threw up to her heart's delight. Unfortunately, she had picked the windward side of the boat for her relief operation, so that her half-digested omelette, complete with discoloured onions, mushrooms, tomatoes came flying back at her and spread all over her oilskins.

"A shame about the eggs," the Doc called out. Both men kept a watchful eye on Laura, whilst sorting out the jib. Its smaller surface was meant for wind forces much stronger than what they had at present or could reasonably expect to get during the rest of the say. It would not only slow them down, but also make them look ridiculously over-cautious to any uninformed observer - of whom, it is true, there weren't all that many around at that moment. Still, as a stopgap, it would hopefully take them to Jolly Harbour all the same.

The Doc tried to comfort pale, sick Laura, who vividly regretted ever having set foot on the yacht.

"Don't worry. Sea sickness is rarely fatal, catches up with the most hardened of sailors sooner or later. I could have given you some preventive medicine, but thought that maybe you wouldn't need it. Anyway, once we have hoisted the jib and are under sail again, the Yellow Dancer will slip back into her ballet shoes and skim over the waves like Nureyev over the swan lake, I guarantee."

He proved right, if only halfway. Under sails, the yacht did get back to a somewhat more comfortable attitude, but was so much slower than before, as to make her pitch much more painful. The Doc advised Laura to go below and lie down on a bunk.

"It is a strange thing, seasickness," he told her.

"The only sickness victims recover from instantly on reaching terra firma. May have something to do with the lack of inter-organ communication, so to speak. The ears report movement. The eyes reply, 'not from where we sit'. The brain registers incoherent reports and triggers the alarm button: throw up now! That's what has been its panacea for all bodily disturbances since the creation of man. With your stomach empty, you cannot fall victim to the one evil that evolution identified as the most dangerous affliction of them all, poisoning. That's what needs avoiding, because for many centuries there used to be practically no remedy against it. Not all that stupid, evolution, is it, when you come to think about it."

"Down below, you will be at the deepest point of the boat, the one that moves least. Then you close your eyes, and put your brain at rest. Up here, you will only catch cold what with the wind chill, the loss of body liquid and all the rest of it. And you will continue throwing up, anyway."

Laura gave in. Beaten, sick and tired as she was, she had better try and catch some sleep.

2. Hounds of Hell

It was already close to nightfall. The looming Antigua coastline, which had seemed to recede into the background at about
the same pace at which the Yellow Dancer had approached it,
finally appeared to be fading altogether, becoming one with the
darkening sky. The yacht's progress with the small jib had been
absurdly slow. To make matters worse, they had been cut off
from the Trades the moment they had become shielded from the
wind by the bulk of the island, some two hours ago. The nervously veering gusts that replaced the Trades were decidedly unfit
for sailing purposes. And so, the Yellow Dancer had to furl her
sails and go back to motoring.

The Doc had shown Laura the Jolly Harbour marina outlay on
a chart. It had been built on what used to be extensive salt flats,
its shallow approach channel still bearing witness to this saline
past. On top of that, it was a little risky to try and thread your
way into the buoyed channel at night. Immediately north of its
approaches, some unlit rocks lay patiently in wait for the inatten-
tive or the intoxicated.

"No problem for sailing veterans such as Ti Martin and myself,
eh, le mousse?" the Doc gave his partner a jovial hug. Ti Martin
just made a dismissive gesture with his left hand, manifestly re-
fusing to give it so much as a thought.

At present, they kept a cautious distance from the coast with
its many invisible reefs and cliffs, lurking just offshore in the
dark. The two men obviously trusted the autopilot to take them
safely to the Jolly Harbour approaches.

Now that the sea had calmed down somewhat, Laura had ris-
en from her bunk and dizzily stepped on deck. She felt cold and
exhausted, impatiently waiting for the yacht finally to reached
her destination. Laura's first full day at sea seemed endless and
would not be remembered as an unqualified success, either.
Much rather, as another experience she could very well have
done without, all told. Sun and wind had joined forces to conjure
a lively red on her cheeks, yet at the same time had worn her out

beyond belief. Her persistent nausea had dried her out additionally and left her with a feeling of complete and total emptiness, a zombie-like human shell.

She was just about to go below again to try and make herself useful in the galley, when she suddenly noticed a dark pinhead-sized object performing what looked like a crazy jig on the narrow band of reddish glow of the western horizon. A shade darker than sea and sky, the "pinhead" must have turned the cape only seconds before. Now, it seemed to be heading towards the Yellow Dancer, closing in remarkably fast.

The Doc and Ti Martin had been busy taking out the torn genoa to re-fold it properly at their ease. When Laura drew their attention to the dancing little dervish on the horizon, they only gave it the briefest of glances and jumped into action immediately without uttering a word. Laura was perplexed and alarmed by both the rapidity and vigour of what seemed like an unwarranted over-reaction to her. Ti Martin disappeared below with one big leap down the companionway. The Doc switched off the navigation lights, disconnected the autopilot and reduced the boat's speed to almost nothing so the Yellow Dancer made no more headway but started swerving uncontrollably in the evening swell. His right hand let go of the wheel and disappeared under his glistening oilskin jacket. When it reappeared, it clasped the handle of something black and metallic that Laura immediately identified as a hand gun, probably a Beretta.

An active member of a renowned Hamburg shooting association and holder of all the requested licences, Robert had always kept several guns at home, safely under lock and key as prescribed by the law. Every now and again, he had showed one or the other to Laura, explained how they functioned and on occasion even let her fire the odd round in the provisional basement shooting range he had made for himself. The deafening blasts had scared Laura to death and the recoil threatened to break her wrist every time she had pulled the trigger. It had taken her some time to understand that, by the time the gun jerked upward like the hind legs of a kicking mule, the bullet had already left the barrel, so there was no need to aim at one's foot to hit the target on the opposite wall.

But she remembered vaguely what certain types of handguns looked like, and Robert's Beretta had stood out for her as an elegant Ferrari among so many Toyotas. Besides, she liked the sound of the Italian brand name. It was vaguely reminiscent of the mob, inter-gang shoot-outs, cotton-chewing godfathers and omertà, the universal snitching prohibition. When snub-nosed Pietro Beretta met his silver-barrelled German cousin Walther PPK, the shit would hit the fan in downtown windy city. She had had no way of suspecting then how close her hallucinating scenarios had really been to the reality of her father's involvement in organized crime.

Meanwhile, the Doc let the Beretta's magazine drop out of the handle, made sure that it was full, and slammed it back into place with a loud metallic click. Then he chambered a round by jerking the slide back and forth and flipped the safety catch. Laura was still very much at a loss as to what was happening.

"You'd better go below," the Doc told her in a tone of voice that did not invite discussion. Only then was it dawning upon Laura that they were apparently about to become the target of an attack and that every second counted. Still highly confused, she stumbled down the companionway and literally fell into Ti Martin's outstretched arms. The Frenchman also carried a gun in his hand and had stuck another one under the buckle of his belt.

"What's going on, for God's sake?" Laura gasped breathlessly.

"No idea. Maybe nothing at all. But if you hear shots being fired, better spread-eagle on the floor and lie still."

Then he pushed her aside unceremoniously and jumped back up on deck.

Peeping through the narrow, slit-like oval of a porthole, Laura could just about watch the pinhead she had been the first to spot. As it drew nearer, it turned into a blot and then into the silhouette of a motorboat's bows. As far as she could make out in the dark, it was an unlit craft with a black hull. At its present speed, its bow wave glistened like a silvery bone in the fangs of a rapidly approaching greedy predator that went for a new prey without even having quite finished with its most recent one, yet. The colour of the hull had probably not been chosen by accident or lack of imagination. Even at a short distance, it must render the boat virtually invisible already during daytime, so much more at night, in front of an unlit towering coastline. Laura had just been lucky to catch a glimpse of it the very instance it had, if only for a few seconds, allowed itself to be exposed against the backdrop of the dying day's twilight horizon.

Laura had started trembling uncontrollably. She felt they were in mortal danger with her having no idea what to do, how to defend herself. She had read and heard of cases of modern piracy alright, but had associated such incidents with the far-away shores of northwest Africa, the Somalia coat or the confusing maze of southeast Asian archipelagos. True enough, next to the Barbary coast of the southern Mediterranean, the Caribbean had once been the most notorious piracy stronghold with much-feared bottlenecks such as the Lesser West Indian passages. Yet she had thought that to be a thing of the remote past. The Henry Morgans, William Dampiers or Francois l'Ollonais of this world were as extinct as the proverbial dodo.

Besides, what kind of bounty was there to be had by seizing the Yellow Dancer, except for the petty cash and the few valuables the three of them carried between them? Nothing, at any rate, that would justify an all-out attack with the inevitable bloodshed that would entail. In her panic, Laura grabbed a long kitchen knife from the top drawer of the galley cupboard and placed herself on the companionway so that she could just glimpse over the edge of the cockpit.

"Come and get it," she murmured to herself in a vain effort to find courage and hope where in fact there wasn't much room for either.

The black motorboat approached the Yellow Dancer, by now lying dead in the water, without any shots being fired. A small number of black figures seemed to be crouching around the helmsman in the bow, prepared to board and take possession of the yacht. All held shiny objects across their breasts, probably no dancing scimitars but modern automatic weapons of infinitely more devastating effect. Laura tried hard to brace herself for the imminent clash with the raiders. Most probably, the Doc and Ti Martin were painfully aware of the fact that their odds in a gun fight with the apparently well-armed enemy were forbidding. A short-barrelled pistol was useful only at close range and to hit anything from the deck of a rocking boat with individual shots you would have to be extremely lucky. The raiders on their part didn't have to take aim. For them it was enough to just "spray" the Yellow Dancer with continued bursts of their automatic weapons. Hence, a shoot-out of any kind could not but have dire consequences for everyone on board. Full metal jacket bullets with hollow-point tips of almost any calibre would rip right through the glass fibre-reinforced carbon hull and cause a bloodbath.

Time for vain conjectures was rapidly running out. The motorboat was only twenty or so yards away, making for the Yellow Dancer's flank as if determined to ram her, bash in her starboard side and send her to the bottom of the sea.

Laura jumped down from the companionway, threw the useless knife into the sink and flattened herself on the floor. What self-respecting raider would shrink back from the image of terrified woman with a kitchen knife in her trembling hand? If anything, they would probably feel unnecessarily motivated to resort to even more violence. Besides, Laura was not at all sure whether, even in a desperate situation such as this one, she would find it in herself to stick a knife into a human being.

She heard a tremendous rush like a flood gushing out of a lock upon the sudden opening of its watertight doors, followed by an almighty bump. The massive collision caused the Yellow Dancer to quiver, shake, and tremble from keel to masthead. It would no doubt have knocked both Ti Martin and the Doc off their feet. Apparently, the man at the motorboat's helm had thrown the gas lever into reverse at the very last moment and simultaneously swung the bow away to starboard, so that the two boats collided side-on. The impact was so violent that Laura, although lying on the floor, already, was hurled against the fridge and sustained a gashing head wound over her right eyebrow. Blood ran over her face, into her eyes and down on the oilskins jacket she had not had time to take off. Shouts and César's frantic barking were heard in the darkness outside. The Yellow Dancer suddenly rocked to starboard. Heavy boots thudded across the teak deck. César kept on barking like mad, then suddenly yowled as if he had been kicked into silence. Something light splashed into the sea. Shouted orders gave way to a hoarse buzz of Jamaican English and patois French scraps. Somebody hit the deck with a loud cry of pain.

Laura was still lying on the floor trying hard to control her trembling limbs. The adrenalin shooting into her system made her heart race. Her mouth felt dry and furry like the inside of a kangaroo's pouch. Not a single shot had been fired, though: their attackers appeared to prefer keeping them alive for a little while longer, or maybe wanted to save the expensive ammo.

Any second now, the pirates would appear on the companionway. Laura could try and hide somewhere, but the men would no doubt turn the yacht inside out in search for whatever they were after and would soon pull her out of her bolt hole. So, she resigned herself to staying where she was and folded her hands over her head, as she frequently had seen it done by suspects apprehended by US cops. Above her, someone dragged a considerable weight over the deck and dropped it into the cockpit. The body of the unconscious Ti Martin came tumbling down the companionway like a sack of potatoes and landed in a peculiarly twisted position like a diver suffering from the bends. Ti Martin only half opened his eyes and gave a low groan. Then he apparently lost consciousness again.

The Doc was next. He came rolling down the steps with a whooping noise, but seemed miraculously unhurt. Then the raiders came marching down the companionway one after the other in rapid succession, torches in hand and guns at the ready in case they met with any resistance below. They seemed to know their way around boats and had no problem finding the light switch.

Their clothing was shoddy at best: torn jeans, threadbare pullovers, parachutist boots that looked ridiculously big on their feet. They were armed to their teeth but wore no masks or hoods. Two of them had stuffed their dreadlocks into woollen caps with the Jamaican colours on them and pointed their automatic weapons at Laura, whilst the third had hung his machine gun over his left shoulder and pulled out a pistol instead. All had handguns sticking in their belts and combat-knife holsters strapped round their ankles. As the raiders saw Laura holding up her hands, they laughed and exchanged remarks that left little margin for interpretation. Their Caribbean English stood out if only because of its peculiar intonation, something that Laura had not come across before, neither in the Mississippi delta, nor the Florida Keys.

While two of the men went through the fore and aft cabins, the third with the pistol seized Laura by her hair and brutally jerked her up from the floor. His bloodshot, restlessly wandering eyes, shying away from the light, as well as his coarse, pimpled skin gave him away as a hard drinker and junkie.

He swirled Laura round and started frisking her for weapons with unconcealed relish. Then he pushed her back to the floor again and told her not to move.

As quickly as the raiders had rushed aboard - once they were in full command of the situation, they seemed to have all the time in the world. They tied Laura, Ti Martin and the Doc hand and feet with plastic cable ties and told the Doc and Laura to kneel on the floor. The man who had frisked Laura guarded them, whilst the other two started searching the interior of the boat with a vengeance. The doors of cupboards were being bashed in with gun butts, wooden panels broken and pulled out, mattresses gutted, drawers turned over and emptied on the floor. The racket coming from the cockpit told Laura that at least one more pirate, left on deck as a lookout, was busy wreaking very much the same kind of mindless destruction to the cockpit locker.

Curiously enough, the pirates seemed not to be interested in Laura's money or the odd piece of jewellery that she had kept in her suitcases. Nor did they bother to frisk the Doc or Ti Martin for valuables. Clearly, they were looking for something specific of far more value to them than anything the Yellow Dancer's crew had to offer. Maybe they were after the smack that Ignace had carried off the yacht in the Blue Lagoon only days ago, when Laura had run into him. Laura's knees started hurting. Her forehead wound kept bleeding profusely. She felt like she would have to throw up again before long and the cable ties were cutting into her skin. Any moment now, she might pass out just like Ti Martin. She squinted at the Frenchman through the veil of her own blood. His ugly head wound had to be taken care of soon lest he died or suffered lasting brain damage.

Whatever vices the raiders could be blamed for, lack of assiduity and thoroughness were not among them. They had stripped the Yellow Dancer's interior to its bare bones but, by the look of it, failed to find what they were after. That risked rendering the situation even more dangerous for their victims, Laura thought. These devil's henchmen would not leave the boat just like that, empty-handed and with a friendly "parting shot" of a remark. They had not taken the trouble of concealing their faces and would probably not be prepared to leave eye-witnesses behind unnecessarily.

The three of them put their heads together for a brief deliberation. Then the one bearded pirate not wearing a woollen cap, probably the leader of the pack, pointed his gun first at Laura, then at the Doc, then back again at Laura. Each time he swung the barrel round, he shouted "Where's it at?" as if dealing with a couple of mentally retarded or deaf-mutes. For the second time in a week, Laura looked death in the face and didn't like it. Completely drained of all mental or physical energy, she suddenly felt as if a "tilt" sign had popped up in her brain which promptly closed shop. Her conscious seemed to take leave from her body and position itself next to her, playing the innocent by-stander. To her own amazement, she started laughing hysterically at that moment as though she found these three small black men in their weird Oxfam rags, hand-knit Xmas gifts of caps and outrageous accents irresistibly funny. Laughed and kept on laughing in the face of the bearded hoodlum with his gun barrel swivelling all over the place like a spinning bottle gradually homing in on the next person to undress.

The pirates were taken aback momentarily, probably suspecting this woman to have lost her marbles. In some less sophisticated cultures, the mentally handicapped enjoy almost religious veneration. Indian braves, for instance, Laura had read, wouldn't touch a demented person for fear they might end up bewitched by some evil spirit.

But these raiders weren't superstitious redskins. "Funny, eh?" the bearded monster had soon found his presence of mind and voice again. He put his gun down and drew his knife. Then he leaned forward and seized the moaning Ti Martin by his curly hair as if determined to collect the Frenchman's scalp. Then, the hoodlum placed the blade of his knife on Ti Martin's throat and shouted again, looking darkly at Laura: "Funny now?"

Laura was beside herself. The somewhat limited vocabulary of the bearded leader triggered another laughing fit. That was too much for the man. He straightened himself and pulled at Ti Martin's hair again, no doubt to lift his head and cut his throat. That was to be the last mistake he made this side of eternity.

The next moment, blazing hell broke loose. Volleys of shots resounded across the water. The bearded monster's head literally exploded, sending clods of blood, brain and splinters of skull bones in all directions. Outside, something heavy plunged into the sea. Bullets like fiery tongues tore through the upper parts of the Yellow Dancer's hull. Portholes burst, fragments of glass, wood and plastic rained down on the kneeling captives. All around, things seemed to pop, whistle, crash and hiss very much at the same time - a crazy symphony of death and devastation, orchestrated by some unseen Riders of the Apocalypse. The Doc wriggled and writhed towards Laura and rolled himself over her body to act as a human shield. Laura could hardly breathe, but it didn't matter. She had become totally apathetic and closed her eyes like a child who shuts out reality, hoping for reality to have the courtesy of ignoring her.

The intensive firing kept on uninterruptedly for what felt like an eternity but was probably no more than some twenty to thirty seconds. After the last shot, an eerie silence fell over the slaughterhouse scene. The Doc rolled off Laura and tried to get up. Laura opened her eyes. What had once been the comfortable, snug living room of the Yellow Dancer, now looked like the Wolf's Lair after Stauffenberg's failed attempt at blowing up Hitler and his chiefs of staff. A thick cloud of dust and pungent gun smoke blinded Laura, irritated her throat and made her cough and throw up again, simultaneously. The floor was littered with all kinds of debris that literally swam in puddles of blood. The hull was studded with holes big enough for cricket balls to pass, most of them above the waterline, fortunately. Whatever sea water was trickling in through a few lower holes, mixed with the pirates' blood to form pink rivulets. The automatic bilge pump reported on duty in a pathetic attempt at keeping the wreck of a yacht afloat. The ceiling panels hung down in tatters strewn with fragments of bone, brain, and blood. None of the three raiders had had the time to fire a shot. Which was just as well since the only targets they could have picked were their captives, already half dead and streaming with blood - their own as well as that of their attackers. The fourth pirate must have been hit in the cockpit and hurled overboard by the impact of the bullets. Whoever had opened fire at the Yellow Dancer from their vantage point somewhere out there at sea had shown very little discretion, to put it mildly. Anyone aboard could have been expedited by their wholesale volleys. Surprisingly enough, neither the Doc nor Laura had sustained as much as a graze. This was probably also due to the soft material around them: glass fibre, plastic and plywood absorbed the bullets and didn't cause many splinters or deadly ricochets. Hardly conscious, Laura thought she heard another motorboat, bigger and more powerful than that of the pirates, drawing alongside the Yellow Dancer. This time, the docking manoeuvre was carried out much more gently, as if someone was trying hard not to wake the Yellow Dancer's crew. Light, quick steps scurried across the deck. Ti Martin had come round as soon as the din of the fireworks had started. Now, he shook off the debris that had settled all over his body and tried to straighten himself. At that moment, a pair of boots appeared on the top step of the companionway. Not your regulation rubber affairs, nor anything near the clumsy combat kicks the pirates wore. Rather elegant, pointed boots of soft, dyed and thoroughly polished leather, as Laura had seen them on the feet of rich Texan cattle barons. The boots were followed by a pair of black corduroy trouser legs and a belt with a trophy buckle displaying a Jolly Roger. Finally, the upper torso of a man, totally dressed in black, and, as an anti-climax, the unmistakable pale mask of the scarred Blue Lagoon phantom. The devil had been out for a walk and come back to hell this very instant.

Ignace le Chabin was wearing a kind of helmet with tipped-up night visors no longer needed in the twilight shed by one or two ceiling lamps that had miraculously survived Desert Storm. Ignace lowered the barrel of his automatic gun, still smoking hot, which hung in a loop from his right shoulder. He squinted his eyes, switched on a torch he had brought and, letting its light travel all around, took a very close look at the shambles that were of his making. Apparently satisfied with what he saw, he touched his temple with his left index finger.

"Asking permission to come aboard."

He spoke with a thick American accent and the wheezing pronunciation of someone born with a hare lip. On top of that, a slow slur suggested to Laura that, as a child or teenager, he must have made a special effort to overcome a stammer. Still, despite his various handicaps, he had preserved a wry sense of humour, as it seemed. When nobody reacted, Ignace gave everyone a mirthless grin and added, "Hell, I do hope I'm not interrupting something, folks."

He then turned back to the companionway, looked up and nodded reassuringly to someone apparently standing in the cockpit, waiting for the chabin's "all clear" sign. Almost instantly, a second pair of cowboy boots, smaller and a mite more elegant than Ignace's, appeared on the steps illumined by the Chabin's spotlight. Next, a pair of narrow cotton trouser legs and a buckle depicting the wide-open mouth of a Bengal tiger showing off his ebony fangs. Lastly, the black cotton shirt and black-and-white leather vest of a woman of medium height and lean yet athletic build. One more step down, and her head, complete with visor helmet materialized. Her dark crew-cut hair and a reddish bandana were all that Laura could see from where she crouched in the galley. In her left elbow, the woman, vaguely of the same age as Laura, carried a wet and brow-beaten cinnamon-coloured dog complete with soaking miniature life-vest. César's stomach was still pumping frantically from the effort he had been forced to make swimming. Every time his tummy contracted, Laura caught glimpses of the butt of a huge revolver the woman was carrying in her belt. Its handle seemed clad with shiny mother-of-pearl. When the woman had reached the bottom of the companionway, she put César down on the floor. Then, she took off her night-visor, unwrapped the bandana, and wiped her forehead. Laura was familiar with the "flashy entrance" routine of film stars or self-important politicians. This lady was clearly over the top, though, she thought. Nor did she really have a crew-cut, but rather long rows of "corns". Between the individual rows of braided hair, furrows of brown scalp glistened like wet tarmac. She took a long close look at the battlefield around her and greeted the two men from the Yellow Dancer with a surprisingly casual air, as if they just happened to bump into one another in a sea-side piña colada bar on a busy night.

"Holy shit, ain't it a mess. Someone's gonna have to do a goddamn cleaning job, big time, what say ya, Chewy? Putain de merde, ça m'écœure." she said, turning to Ignace. Maybe to accommodate Ti Martin and the Doc, whom she seemed to be perfectly acquainted with, she spoke the same odd mixture of French and English that the raiders had used. Her voice was a pleasant contralto, clear, with a sassy edge to it. The voice of a woman who knew what she wanted and would take a dim view of anyone choosing or happening to stand between it and her. Although she could hardly be a day older than Ti Martin, she had addressed him as "môme", or "baby boy".

"Well, what can I say, folks. We had set our minds on a leisurely trip into the sunset, happy hour and all that, when Chewbacca here," she pointed her thumb at Ignace, "caught my straying attention with some gibberish about a dog floating by on starboard side. I says, so what, I says, dead dog drifts, don't it, now? 'Least till it gets swallowed by a friendly neighbourhood shark, anyways. Except, Chewy says, this here pooch is still alive and kicking. So we pick him up and I'll be damned if it ain't the Toubib's cinnamon retriever, creature named Cato or Cicero or something Roman, anyways. Can ya dig it, folks, Cicero? I mean, why not Napoleon, or Nixon, God help us? Anyways, minutes later, we come across the Yellow Cancer bobbing in the swell like a pair of tits in the bathtub. With a suspicious-looking guy on deck packing an automatic weapon, pas de blague, I'm telling you. Set me musing, it did. Curiouser and curiouser, is what I says to Chewbacca, n'est-ce pas?"

"Shouldn't we pay a visit?" he asks. "Well, ya know me. Waste not, want not, sure is my motto. Applies to ammo, too. At present prices, you might as well be loading your guns with sixteen grain silver bullets, mon cul. So, laisse passer, let it lie, is what I says. But before I know what's going down, he has already popped the guy on deck, just like that, the rash son of a bitch. After that, with one of the jolly fuckers down, we had no choice but to let the others have it, too. The way I sees it, we saved ya guys' bony behinds." When nobody offered any commentary, she added, "Mais pas de quoi, you're very welcome, folks, always happy to lend a hand."

Unwilling, as it seemed, to lose any more valuable time with lengthy explanations, the woman went straight on to her mental to-do list.

"Toubib, poor Ti Moun here looks to me like he might want a few goddam stitches in the head, wouldn't ya say? Quand-même, eh? Ya find disinfectant, needle and thread in the boat's first-aid tool-box, if I remember right. Same goes for bandages and pills, 'course. If not, we'll have to carry him on the Pas de Deux and patch him up there. Chewy, why don't you free these ladies from their handcuffs, the kinky play's over. The three headless gents here can go back on their boat, waiting for their Viking's burial later. Remember to stuff something into the Yellow Cancer's glory holes pissing water big time, so we don't sink just yet. Speaking of which, what the blazes is Snow White doing on board this sorry piece of floating yellow scrap?"

The question was addressed to the Doc. Its subject, indicated by no more than a vague nod in the direction of the galley, was Laura, of course. Even in her present precarious state, hurting all over, dripping blood and water and being generally ready to drop dead and be done with, Laura was not willing to let this kind of flippancy pass uncommented.

"My name is Laura Forster and the boat is called Yellow Dancer. Get it? D-A-N-C-E-R, and believe it or not I can speak for myself," she half-whispered.

The woman turned towards Laura very slowly, as if in disbelief, and confronted her head on for the first time since she had come aboard. Obviously, she had not expected to a retort of this kind, least of all by Snow White.

"My oh my, so I hear! Did ya get that now, Chewbacca, Snow White can speak."

Igncae giggled, wheezed and nodded.

"I likes her attitude, though," he said feebly as if commending a sheep's melodious bleating to a starved she-wolf.

Moving with the natural poise and elegance of a born predator, the woman approached Laura, who tried in vain to get up from the floor instead of practically having to kneel before her. But her limbs had not overcome the successive shocks of this tumultuous night and would not support her. The woman seized Laura under her arms and effortlessly pulled her up on her feet. As Laura looked in her opponent's eyes, she was startled and would have taken a step back had there been room enough to do so. Those weren't the bloodshot eyes of the bearded pirate, nor the narrow slits of the blue eyes of Ignace. The woman looked at Laura with curiosity rather than irritation, yet hers were the impassive eyes of a big cat who would kill in cold blood to survive and feed her young. No empathy, no anger, no discernible feeling at all, just cold, clinical curiosity. Her eyes seemed to penetrate Laura like laser beams. Which mother of what far-away planet had given birth to this female creature?

"Lau-ra For-ster," she mouthed Laura's name syllable by syllable with exaggerated clarity, the way an incredulous John Smith may have spelled the name of Pocahontas upon first hearing it pronounced by its bearer.

"Laura Forster. Is that what ya say? Sounds what, German, I think? Ya know, Laura Forster, I'm not in the habit of taking notice of the name of something bound to end up as fish food, anyways, feel me? Waste of grey cells, tu piges? Let's see how long ya last under the Caribbean sun. Oh, and my name, lest I forget, is Solitaire. Ya know, spells like Patience, of which I have very little, as you will find out, if you live long enough. The hairy monster following me about like a fucking shadow calls himself Ignace. But ya seem to have met, already, ain't that so?"

This last question was addressed to Ignace, who nodded in silence. The woman calling herself Solitaire put down her weapon and poured some water over her bandana in the sink. Then she pulled out a huge bushwhacker's knife from her right bootleg and cut Laura's ties. Her every movement looked perfectly controlled, studied, almost. She seemed in perfect harmony with her body, very much like a ballet dancer, only more powerful, in a subdued, menacing manner. Looking at Laura's face again, she tilted her head to one side like a dog trying to guess the intentions of its master.

"And ya really think Snow White resembles me? J'say pas. I don't think so, honest to God. But who knows what's hidden underneath all that gore and sweat and dirt."

She started cleaning Laura's face with the wet bandana in a strange gesture of motherly care which came so unexpectedly that Laura let it happen without resistance. It reminded her of what Frederike had done every time dirty little Laura had come home with the bruises of some fight she had had with the boys and girls at school. Much of Solitaire behaviour might be calculated, meant to impress and intimidate. But her weaponry was real, including her withering stare.

"Ya see, Laura Forster, you had no right to scare my collaborator of the month to death in the Blue Lagoon, shame on you. I take exception to that, even if he don't."

Ignace giggled again and wheezed some incomprehensible confirmation.

"I just hope he didn't come on to ya, Laura Forster?"

"Laura. Why don't you just call me Laura. Come on to me?"

"Why, thank you, Laura, with pleasure. Yea, come on to ya, ya know, sexually, I mean, pour niquer, feel me?"

The chabin had bent down to free the Doc and Ti Martin from their cable ties.

"Should you have felt his hard-on somewhere around your lower anatomy that night in the Lagoon, don't ya go flattering yourself just yet. Ya see, he looked at you and thought of me, always does, the fornicating bastard. Besides, he suffers from pra… Gotta help me out here, Toubib."

"Priapism, is what you mean," the Doc hoarsely called from the floor.

"Exactly, thank ya. It means he …"

"I know what it means, thank you," Laura interrupted her. Solitaire had finished rubbing Laura's face clean and took a step back to admire the result of her restoration effort.

"Ya know something, hot rod, I think we got ourselves a intellectual here. Too fucking good for the likes of ya, Chewy, I fear."

With that last quip, Solitaire's interest in Laura appeared exhausted, for the time being. She seized her automatic and held it up like a trophy.

"When it comes to cars and guns, your fellow countrymen are hard to beat, Laura," she continued as if discussing the pros and cons of some quality kitchen device.

"Heckler and Koch M 85 K, loses 900 bullets per minute. A birthday present from the blond stallion here. He must have misunderstood me big time when I told him I wanted a toy for bad girls. A good enough man, Chewy, make no mistake. Unfortunately, there is room for only one train of thought in his sparrow's brains. Which reminds me. Ya need to excuse me for a sec."

She put her gun down again and started collecting the pirates' firearms. Ignace had already carried one corpse up the companionway and dumped it in the cockpit. Now he did the same with the remaining two and, with the help of the Doc, transferred all three of them into the motorboat with the black hull.

"Maybe someone has a hand free to help me carry the armoury, that would be awful nice, méci," Solitaire, heavily loaded with firearms, called out.

"I suggest we all get our asses onto the Pas de Deux fast, because this sorry craft will hit rock bottom before long, I'm afraid. Sorry for sinking your ship, Laura, but she ain't gonna make it all the way to Jolly Harbour, not if I'm a judge."

Laura found the casual light-heartedness with which Solitaire disposed of the Yellow Dancer quite unacceptable.

"She was my father's yacht and must have meant a lot to him. I shan't leave her behind. I'd much rather go down with her, then."

Solitaire looked at Laura again with that same detached curiosity with which Darwin might have looked at a flailing Galapagos beetle on the tip of his collector's pin.

"Why, suit yourself, Laura Forster, I'm easy. Like I say, fish food in the making, anyways."

"Except I think we'll be keeping her company," the Doc cut in from the top of the companionway.

"Either we tow the Yellow Dancer as far as she will go, towards Jolly Harbour, or we'll drown all three of us. One boat, one crew..."

"One hell of a wet grave, is what ya mean. I see. Downright mutiny, no less. I swear I don't know how ya do it, Laura Forster, ma fois, but men seem to have a...proclivity for ya, un penchant, I mean. Okay, okay, suit yourselves. We'll take her in tow. But as soon as she threatens to go in deep, I'll cut her loose, that's a promise. Deal?"

Laura felt relieved. "Deal", she replied.

3. Snow White's Thong

"You could have massacred all of us last night."

Laura lay stretched out on the bunk in the saloon of the Pas de Deux. Against all odds, Solitaire's GRAND BANKS 49 had managed to reach Jolly Harbour with the Yellow Dancer still in tow. Twice, the rope connecting the two yachts had broken, since the Dancer had drawn more and more water and despite her bilge pump working overtime, had gone in deeper, and deeper, in clear defiance of Archimedes' law of displacement.

The Pas de Deux had done a great job. She belonged to a generation of American motor yachts built after the blueprints of exceedingly seaworthy fishing vessels like the Andrea Gail: ships that used to sail out of Gloucester, Bedford or Newfoundland ports to the Grand Banks and would come back heavily loaded with salmon, cod, tuna, and what have you. Until, one fine day, the Canadian masters of those splendid catch areas had decided that enough was enough and had closed the fishing grounds to give the many depleted stocks a fighting chance to recover. The Pas de Deux served Solitaire and Ignace as a mobile ocean home. With a yacht like this, maybe not the world, but most certainly the Caribbean was their oyster. The roomy cabins and living quarters allowed them to accommodate the Yellow Dancer's crew complete with dog and luggage, at least for a while.

At around the midnight hour, the slowly limping couple of yachts had reached Joe Grady's boatyard at Jolly Harbour. Joe had been waiting for them with a handful of his men. The Yellow Dancer had to be cradled by the crane immediately and drained of the sea-water by Joe's powerful land-based pumps before she could finally be lifted on shore. In the dark, a delicate enough operation that had taken the rest of the night and a good deal of the morning, too.

Once safely ashore, she had thoroughly been inspected by Joe for damage sustained inside and outside, clearly visible as well as hidden. When he had seen the bullet-riddled, devastated saloon, Joe's only comment was the silent sign of the cross. Ignace had explained how he had put the three corpses on the black boat, poured some fuel over its cockpit and deck and set fire to it with a signal rocket, as soon as they had put enough cable lengths between the boat and themselves. What Ignace hadn't told Joe was that Laura had been scandalized. The Doc's attempt at justification had carried little weight with her.

"Yes, maybe you're right and they would have done the same to us, had they had the opportunity. But that doesn't mean we have to sink as low as to employ their methods."
The pirate boat had burned surprisingly long, lighting up this part of the coastline like an eerie beacon of retaliation. When the final blast had been triggered by some spare ammunition, presumably, it had taken only seconds for the unreal spectacle to finish.

"Sorry, Snow White," Solitaire had shrugged her shoulders, "but we got no time for proper burials with prayers and speeches, pas question, ma biche. Those are the ways of the Caribbean. No loose ends, no unfinished business. Better get used to it or die a noble fool, your call."

"Remember these islands used to be strongholds of slavery not that long ago," the Doc had enlarged on the subject. "It's been abolished alright but the general contempt for human life that slavery engenders has lingered on in local people's minds and attitudes."

Laura felt her head reeling as if someone had stuffed her into the drum of a tumble-dryer running at top revs. This crazy rigmarole could not really be happening to her, now, could it? How could she activate the "delete all" function? What had gotten her into this world behind the mirror where everything stood upside down and common sense and logic held no sway?

"Scotty, you may beam me back now," she mumbled at herself while Joe Grady finished his sums mumbling and gesticulating to give her at least a rough estimate of the work to be effected if the Yellow Dancer was to put out to sea again one day.

In insurance terms, she was an economic write-off ready for the scrap- rather than the boatyard. If she was to be repaired notwithstanding, it was with the sentimental value she represented for Laura in mind. The yacht would have to be practically reconstructed from scratch at the price of a new one and no end of accumulated man-hours. But yes, it could be done if Laura insisted.

Much of what Joe had to say passed Laura clean by. She was deeply disturbed, shaken, depressed, washed up, deprived of her physical and mental capacities. Besides, she found it very hard to adapt to the confusing hodgepodge of languages, vernaculars, and jargons cultivated by her new acquaintances. The Doc and Ti Martin offered their services as interpreters and tried hard to give a plaintext synopsis of the most salient parts of Joe's barely comprehensible litany for her, but somehow, she did not grasp half of it. Her synapses had decided to go it alone and were at present exploring uncharted territory. Laura's past had effectively been carpet-bombed, her present was deeply disturbing, to say the least, and her near future she felt she had better not even contemplate. At some stage or other, she had no longer been able to keep her eyes open and had plunged into a long deep dreamless sleep.

When she had woken, the sun had just been crossing the local meridian. The Pas de Deux was anchored in an isolated, unpopulated bay of some scenic beauty on the heavily indented east coast of Antigua, itself an amorphous blot of ink on the chart. The boat and her owners were notorious in these latitudes. Which is why Ignace and Solitaire preferred to stay as far away from civilisation as possible. So much more so at present when, after most recent events, the Pas de Deux could easily have been mistaken for an IRA gun-running vessel. One way or another, her crew had every reason to avoid any contact with the law. Not because police, immigration, or customs of the double island republic of Antigua and Barbuda were noted for their uncompromising "zero tolerance" policy on drug-related and other crime. Rather, the troubled relationship between Antiguan law and the two "enemies of the state" were characterized by mutual respect, as the Doc had put it. Occasional generous contributions to the local cops' retirement fund made by Solitaire and Ignace had not failed to render the administration of local competences flexible enough for both sides to profit from. Still, over-zealous cranks in the services could not always be contained and made the balance of powers a precarious one. No need to tempt the beast by defecating right under its nose.

The Doc had looked after Laura's wound on her forehead while she had been asleep. Nevertheless, her head was buzzing and humming like a gyrocompass. Most probably, the Doc said, she would have to live with a small scar over her right brow, a little harder to conceal from the eyes of an observant wooer than the rather tiny one on the left side of her forehead. "Double brows", the Doc jokingly termed them.

Ti Martin was suffering far more than Laura. The Doc had stitched his scalp together again and sedated him with what drugs he could find aboard the Pas de Deux. Ti Moun, "little baby boy", as Solitaire called him, had no doubt been severely concussed and would need to stay in bed for a few days.

Solitaire and Ignace had prepared a brunch of sorts and were quietly munching their fried eggs and bacon at the table. The forward part of the saloon was taken up by the helm and a dashboard of navigational and other instruments which were doubled in the open cockpit upstairs, as was the helm itself. Thus, the yacht could be run from inside or outside, all according to wind and weather or the whims of the owners. Ignace' and Solitaire's table manners left a lot to be desired, Laura felt. Both used only their fork eating the proletarian way. Their lower left arm rested on the table up to the elbow so they would be closer to their food. With their fork hand, they shovelled the eggs down the hatch as noisily as two starved fishermen might have done after spending the night casting out their nets and hauling them back in heavy with fish or crab. Laura had swung her legs out of the bunk and decided not to mince her words when commenting on the reckless way these two had put everybody's lives on the Yellow Dancer at risk.

"Well, well, if it ain't Snow White. Woken from our beauty sleep, have we now, ma belle."

Solitaire stuck her fork in a piece of bread with a flash-like movement as if she had caught it in an attempt at escape. Then she let out a whooping belch that shook the lice from Ignace's filthy dreadlocks.

"'Scuse me all the way to hell. It's the bloody onions, they tend to revisit me something awful. Not a bloody thing I can do, either."

"But she's right, ain't she?" Ignace wheezed, his mouth full of egg.

"Like I told ya time and time again, ugly mustee: if I wants your opinion, you'll be the first to know, 'cause I be asking for it then, see. And whenever I ain't, it's 'cause I don't give a rat's ass. Here's the thing, Snow White." She turned to Laura again.

"We been expectin' ya at Jolly Harbour, see. The Doc here had been kind enough to let us in on his plans, or yours, whatever. When ya started looking like a no show, we got a mite worried and thought we'd better meet ya kind a halfway. Radio traffic is always monitored by some bored-to-death idiot or other out there, see, ya can bet your thong on that. Talking of which, and I am turning to the experts here: did Snow White wear tanga strings or edible thongs? Any bids at all?"

"Sure. My money is on the thongs. I bet it used to be a regular sight for sore neighbourhood eyes," Ignace offered his opinion with a chuckle, "Snow White's thong hanging out to dry next to seven little jockstraps."

"Well, didn't promise too much, did I? Anything in that area, trust Chewy to be in the know. No matter. Where was I? Radio silence, right. And most of the time, ya have no mobile network handy, either, not around these God-forsaken parts. Comes as a blessing or a curse, all depends on the circumstances, don't it now?"

She raised both her arms and described a wide circle with her hands.

"So, in the end, it had all the ingredients of a fucking cliff-hanger. No time for stealth and discretion. The lookout they had left on deck was facing the coast, his mistake. The moment he heard us and looked our way, that would have been the end of it. So, fatalement, once close enough to the Yellow Dancer, we had to let lie or let fly. I don't mind telling ya I was all for staying the hell out of it, none of our business, after all. Would have, too, had it not been for Chewbacca, who popped the guard before I could say Jack, let alone fucking Robinson. I'll be damned if he don't feel responsible for ya, Snow White. Dunno why, but on reflection, that's what I thinks."

She resumed her lunch and gulped down a stiff whisky that would have floored your average Dutch Harbour crab catcher unawares.

"Anyways. Here's the thing. We had used the Yellow Dancer for a smack job that almost went south, see. And ya happened to be served the check. I would a been good with that but Ignace thought it wasn't fair. What's fair got to do with it, I asks him. I mean, with a mug like his, ya would think he had long since banned that word from his hard drive, don't ya. But he wouldn't listen to reason, never does, the silly bastard. That's all there is to it." As if to put the seal of authentication on it, she let out another belch.

"Damn ya, Toubib, I said easy on the onions, didn't I? Why is it, nobody ever listens to me? As for killing everybody aboard. Yeah, now that you point it out, I gotta grant it to ya, that would have been a contingency. Remote, though. See, we had counted on those sorry scumbags making you go down on your knees. No, not for what you think, Snow White, not a chance. But low-life, crapules like that gets a hard-on when they can humiliate their victims before killing them. It's a kind a ritual, a conditioned reflex, ain't that what they call it? Which is why we aimed high. You kneel, you live. You stand on your feet, you die. Call it coarse, call it haphazard, gross, call it what you will, but it works. Most of the time, anyway. A good thing, the Yellow Cancer turned her port side, so we didn't hit the gas bottles. Woooom! What a almighty fireworks that would'a made."

She continued eating. The Doc hadn't touched his food. He, too, looked pretty much under the weather. Pale and visibly tired. If Laura hadn't known better, she would have assumed he had lost his eye in the fight the night before. A blue swelling under his sound one presumably restricted his already limited vision

even further and made him look like a French impersonation of
Buck the weasel. His right arm rested over the back of the chair
like that of a ventriloquist's dummy during remission. César had
collapsed in his favourite corner and was half-heartedly gnawing
away at one the Doc's Nike sneakers in blissful oblivion. From
where the dog lay, he could keep a wary eye on everybody in
the saloon. Laura knew that Labrador retrievers were excellent
swimmers. But without his miniature life-vest, good old César
would presumably have drowned the night before. As ill at ease
as the Doc seemed to feel in the presence of Ignace, he must be
aware of the fact the he owed him César's life as well as his own.
"Who were those pirates and what were they after?"

"Pirates my bony ass," Solitaire answered and spat out a tiny
piece of onion on the floor.

"Somebody's pathetic excuse for henchmen. Probably a drug
trafficker who thinks we stepped on his toes, God knows. It's a
fool's world out there, always someone hell-bent on laying a hand
on you. No concern of yorn, just for the four of us, n'est-ce pas."

Just in case anyone needed a drawing, she pointed her fork at
the persons round the table one by one and then in the direction
of Ti Martin's momentary sick-bed in the forward cabin, from
where faint whiffs of cannabis had started seeping through.

"But what a show, eh, Toubib? Two syringes like these," she
pointed at the automatic weapons deposited on the chart-table,
"are precisely what the family quack prescribes in case of tick-
attack, ain't it."

"I know, I was there," a rather subdued Laura called from the
bunk. Solitaire's vulgar language and tomboyish attitude were
increasingly irritating her. What was it the woman wanted to
prove? That she was tougher than most men around, even in her
line of business? To understand that, you just had to look her in
the eyes.

"Really, now? Funny, I can't for the life of me remember seeing
ya when things got a little hectic. Ignace?"

The chabin produced another sample of his wheezing hyena-
like laughter and shook his head.

"Well, let it lie. Ain't you hungry, Snow White? There's still enough of everything, onions galore, courtesy of the Toubib. A man's got to eat to keep his wits together. Same goes for our sex, ask the Toubib."

She pointed over her shoulder in the general direction of the galley.

"No, but thanks, no. And do stop calling me Snow White, if you don't mind. I hate that."

Very slowly and carefully, Laura let her torso sink back onto the bunk. How on earth had she strayed into these woods? She seemed to remember those lines from some Russian play she had seen with Robert in Hamburg. In her case, the answer was self-evident. She had no-one else to blame but her father. Had he not died so prematurely, he would probably have blurred his traces sufficiently for his past to rest with him in his damp Hamburg grave one day. For example, by selling the Yellow Dancer in good time.

On the other hand, there was still that quizzical figure of Sultan the Silent. As long as he was alive, he could have sunk Robert with no more than a phone call to the authorities, or the media, for that matter. He didn't even need a specific occasion or cause. Their lifelong enmity should have dictated such a move long time ago. Why hadn't he made it? Presumably because he enjoyed a Robert left in limbo, caught in an almost daily fear of his past coming to the surface like the bloated body of a corpse thought safely wrapped in chicken wire, weighed down at the bottom of the sea. Besides, a Robert doing time behind bars somewhere would not lead the Sultan to Penelope's present whereabouts.

"I'll go and suck on my pipe." The Doc rose from his chair, waved at César, and went on deck with the dog.

What was it they were waiting for here, Laura asked herself. The Yellow Dancer's repair works clearly would take months, if not years. Solitaire and Ignace could not possibly circulate freely on the island, fine. But as for Laura, she wasn't restricted in her movements the same way. And she had business to attend to, go to English Harbour and the bank and ask about the name and whereabouts of the recipient of Robert's obscure payments.

Then there was the matter of Penelope's letters. She got up and addressed her request to Solitaire and Ignace. The two of them heard her out patiently and conferred with each other in low voices and a quaint guttural language Laura had never heard before. When they had apparently reached their verdict, Solitaire nodded at Laura with the hint of her usual mirthless smile.

"Fair enough. I can understand you want to turn your back on the Caribbean and believe me, I would rather see the last of you, too. Unfortunately, it's not all that easy. See, the moment you go ashore, you are to report to Antigua immigration. And they will ask you where the hell you've come from in the first place, right. A boat? Which boat? The one shot to bits in Joe's yard? Or the one occupied by two of the most wanted figures of the Caribbean? What's a woman like you doing in the company of drug-runners? At best, they'll keep you in a dirty cell smelling of shit and crawling with rats and centipedes. You wanna risk that, be my guest."

"These islands had to fight hard for their independence and tend seriously to resent what they see as a violation of their sovereignty. As lax as they may seem on other offences, illegal entry is something they do not take lightly." Ignace added. "Can't afford to. With a population that small, it wouldn't take more than a handful of determined mercenaries with an agenda to tip the balance of power, occupy the place, for whatever reason. So, if you were thinking of by-passing immigration and taking the first plane home, don't. 'Cause when you turn up at the airport without an entry visa, you will be arrested. If you must go ashore, better let the Toubib watch over you and come back with you to the Pas de Deux, Sol permitting?"

"Yeah, alright, if she must. She had better go back with us to Gwada, anyway," Solitaire replied with a sigh.

"Better accept Chewy's advice and let the Frenchie follow you about. César can come, too. I'll bet he could do with the odd tree smelling of doggy do. Ignace will feel privileged to put ya ashore with the dinghy. The nearest bungalow-hotel is situated west of where we are, about half an hour's walk, tops. From there, ya can call a cab and do what ya have to. And, oh, yes, one more thing. We spotted the fucking sea-water pump dripping this morning. Get Joeye to drop by and lend a hand, today, hear. We need his expertise, so don't let him fob you off with one of his lazy-bone bums of mechanics. We want Joeye, in the fucking flesh, on the double. Feel me?"

Laura nodded and started dressing for shore leave. Just before joining César in the dinghy held ready by Ignace and the Doc, Laura saw Solitaire carry a plate of brunch dainties into Ti Martin's cabin. Despite her demonstrative toughness, the woman seemed to indulge in a few soft spots, Laura thought. One of them apparently bore the name of Ti Martin. The longer Laura chewed on it, the more she was convinced that, had it not been for Ti Martin's presence aboard the Yellow Dancer, Solitaire would have "let it lie".

SIXTH CHAPTER

1. Crossing the Line

Joe Grady was Jamaican born and bred. He had roamed the seven seas as a sailor and was convinced the world held no more surprises for him. As a rule, the cargo ships on which he used to serve did not belong to the most modern of their kind, to put it politely. Not downright floating coffins, either, but ramshackle old ships with run-down technical equipment forever prone to partial or total breakdowns. Since a black rastafa was neither the ship-owners' nor the crew agents' or indeed the sailors' unions' idea of a role model, Joe frequently had to accept sub-standard pay and had grown used to contemplating the unequal distribution of the world's riches from the wrong end of a queue lined up for the next job.

But Joe was no fool. Firmly persuaded that, one fine day, he would get his own back on society at large, he chewed the cud and patiently bided his time. Whenever repair works had to be carried out on a ship at sea or in port, he had quickly made it a habit to be there, looking over the mechanics' shoulders, giving them a hand, asking detailed questions, making notes and reading sun-bleached, coffee-stained technical manuals and indigestible directions awkwardly translated from the "Japaneesee". Thus, gradually, imperceptibly, like the oyster grows its pearl from a grain of sand, the ships he served in had turned the former rastafa junkie into a resourceful mechanic specialized in improvisation and stop-gap solutions.

One day, Joe had come to Antigua on board a Dutch high-sea tug, jumped ship and grown roots in Jolly Harbour. Here he could make good use of his technical know-how and no longer had to live with white mates cracking stupid jokes at his expense. He found Antigua a place that suited him fine, an island where everybody, irrespective of colour, creed, or favourite poison had a chance to live out their hallucinating dreams. Somebody as experienced and generally easy-going as Joe Grady fitted right in.

When he arrived, the boatyard had been pretty run down. Its original owner, a member of the multi-branch Antigua Bird dynasty, had lived up to the Russian saying, according to which work is no wolf, hence, no need to run after it. To himself and his family, the yard served primarily as one of many fronts for trafficking drugs and laundering money. The day the "Birdman" had to disappear rather suddenly at the outbreak of the financial crisis, Joe had squeezed through the window of opportunity and invested his modest funds in the yard, generally thought to be a doomed venture. A daring entrepreneurial move which had paid off. With some imagination and a lot of hard work 24/7, he had managed, in the course of only a very few years, to stem the financial tide and, to everybody's surprise, had succeeded in his efforts to turn the yard into a going concern. For example, by developing new original concepts like the hurricane holes he had created and rented out at substantial rates. It had not made him a rich man by any standards, but once salaries, taxes and miscellaneous other contributions had been skimmed off, he could still make a very decent living at Jolly Harbour. Which was more than could be said of the majority of the island's less fortunate inhabitants. Plus he had no bank breathing down his neck nor Russian thugs passing by now and then to collect arrears.

During his lunchbreak that day, Joe was happily dozing off in the shadow of his corrugated iron shed that served him as a combined workshop, warehouse, bungalow and smack shack. The sound of the rusty yard-portal hinges startled him. Through the gap of the half-open shed door, he had the gate as well as the Yellow Dancer's shambles in full view. Standing on her stilts she looked as if she had been put in the pillory for some outrageously blasphemous misdemeanour. The tell-tale "dotted lines" of her bullet-riddled hull had been provisionally roughcast first thing with generous layers of gelcoat. Thus, at least she was reasonably watertight again. Her insides were a different story. The delivery of the expensive teak and other wooden parts alone would take ages, Joe feared. Especially in view of the present juridical sea changes that rendered certain kinds of tropical wood hard to come by either legally or otherwise.

At first, he took the woman who he saw heading towards the shed to be Solitaire. He stooped, opened the bottom drawer of his metal tool cupboard, and took out an object wrapped in some oily piece of cotton cloth. He unfolded the rag and grabbed his Smith & Wesson 38, checked the chambers by spinning the cylinder with his flat palm, and tucked the gun in his belt right above the cleft of his buttocks. If someone of Solitaire's reputation exposed herself to the risk of strolling about like that in broad daylight, she must have a damn good reason, one which was likely to bode trouble for Joe.

As the woman was joined by a cinnamon-coloured dog, Joe realized to his relief that this wasn't Solitaire but the owner of the Yellow Dancer, who was perhaps hoping for a first progress report. Joe wrapped the cloth round the gun and slid it back into the bottom drawer. Then he rose from his rickety chair and, feigning a welcoming grin, walked out of the shed into the sun-baked yard.

Laura and the Doc had driven to English Harbour in a taxi. The old port with its many original 18th-century features still intact presented itself very much like the open-air museum it really was. After a lengthy search, the lady at the reception of the stately Admiral's Inn had finally found the package with the translations and handed them to Laura, who took a superficial glance at them and stowed them into her bag for later perusal.
Their lunch at the Inn had been excellent - Anglo-American rather than Caribbean. Laura had discussed the most recent events with the Doc and asked him what on earth had made him keep such dubious company.

"Well, as I told you on the Persephone: once you settle on these islands for good, you will be approached by assorted members of the local underworld sooner rather than later. Besides, my pension gone up the chimney, I had to make a living somehow or other. Right at the beginning of my Caribbean career, I made the acquaintance of a Gwada top gun who found it convenient to have a medical doctor in his general entourage, you know, someone who lent a tinge of respectability to his overall despicable operation. Long dead and gone, the man. As for myself, I was kept in the loop, somehow, probably because I was accepted as a harmless side show, a useful court jester hardly worth a bullet. Did cost me an eye, though, at one stage, I'll spare you the unsavoury details. Only goes to show the universal truth of the saying that there are no free lunches.

That said, and leaving Ignace out of the equation for a moment, Solitaire is not as vile an individual as you seem to make her out. I like to think of her as a fine musical instrument, say, a violin gone out of tune through neglect and blundering misuse by lamentably untalented fiddlers. You strike the right chords with her, you'll be surprised what tunes she is capable of. A better and more reliable friend you will never again find in your lifetime, believe you me."

After lunch, the Doc, César and Laura had jumped into another taxi to the island republic's capital St. John. Funny, Laura thought, that somebody like St. John, who was decidedly old school and had never even known of the existence of something like the Caribbean, seemed to be enjoying a slightly perturbing omnipresence in these parts. What exactly did he owe his popularity to in these parts? Maybe it was a collateral kind of consequence of the devastating hurricanes that could always be expected to wreak havoc here at irregular intervals. Over the decades and centuries, they may not only have caused great material damage but also engendered a fatalistic end-of-the-world mentality associated with the number one cryptic apocalyptic.

In the bank, Laura had brought all her charms to bear in a vain attempt at loosening the assistant director's tongue. In the end, Laura had thrown in the towel and prepared to leave empty-handed, when the street-wise Doc had cooled her visibly surging temper down and eased matters somewhat by lining the man's pocket with a bundle of presidents. A sad victory of mercantile utilitarianism over female charm, yes, but Laura took it in her stride. That way, at least she had learned that the money Robert used to transfer did not stay on Antigua at all, but was sent on to Guadeloupe and from there presumably to God knows what other choice destinations. All told, a rather elaborate ploy whose sole objective was to make it as hard as possible to "follow the money" and unveil the ultimate beneficiary's identity.

The town of St. John as such had proved the second disappointment of the day. Poverty presented its ugly face on every corner. Decrepit wooden houses, dusty shops and fly-blown cafés formed a scene of destitution. Had it not been for the Caribbean sunshine glossing over the squalor, St. John would have been a depressing place to visit. Under such circumstances, the junkie sleeping it off right next to the Disneyland effigy of the Bird dynasty's founder was an appropriate comment on the town's past and present, Laura found. Even the local lamp posts apparently weren't much to speak of. César sniffed around a few of them, but abstained from lifting his leg as if in fear of contracting an exotic venereal disease without having had the fun of sex.

So, the three of them had carried on to Joe's boatyard next to the Jolly Harbour marina. The place had seemed deserted at first sight but then Joe himself had materialised from a shed. Laura skipped the chit-chat and told him about the pump right away, whose type number Ignace had scribbled on a piece of paper.

"The friggin' sea-water pump again, is it?"

Joe pulled at his giant woollen cap, which would easily have accommodated a nursery of the stupendously big brown bats endemic on neighbouring Guadeloupe and no doubt capable of reaching Antigua as well, should they think it worth their while.

"I don't have this precise brand on stock, 'cause it's a European one. Let me see if I have some suitable alternative somewhere. Only recently, a whole lot of parts fell off a truck. Haven't had the time to sort them out yet. Don't go away, I'll be back in two."

He disappeared in the shed, where he was heard rummaging in some metal containers. Meanwhile, the Doc, who had run his hands over the patched-up parts of the Yellow Dancer's hull, had come to Laura's aid. Before long, the two of them heard a muffled cry of triumph from inside the shed and Joe reappeared with a cardboard box under his arm.

"Bingo. This should do the trick" He held out the box for the Doc to take it back to the boat.

"Fitting the son of a bitch shouldn't cause Ignace any headaches."

Laura shook her head energetically.

"Solitaire insists you handle this in person. The pump has been ailing for more than a week now, she said. It's killing her, apparently, and she wants the new one to fit like a hand in a glove. The least bit of precession, she says, and the pump's driving shaft will be bent and give again in no time."

Matters were not going Joe's way, so much was clear from his mien.

"Congratulations, you seem to have picked up some technical understanding already, not bad at all. However, I still have no end of work to do with the Yellow Dancer and a few other boats. I don't know where ya people have parked the Pas de Deux, but till I get back again to the yard, I'm sure I'll have lost all afternoon, Yamaaan. Changing a water-pump is no fuckin' brain surgery, precession or no precession."

"Okay," Laura replied and took the box out of the Doc's hands. "I'll tell her then that you have no time to spare."

With that, she turned and started walking away but came back as if struck by an afterthought.

"You see, I have only known Solitaire for a day or two but my impression of her so far has been that she's a very short-fused lady who doesn't accept refusal lightly."

Joe scratched his bonnet and took possession of the wandering box again.

"Yeah, tell me about it. Alright, then, I'll join ya, what the hell. I suggest we take my jeep so I got wheels to take me back home." About three quarters of an hour later, they had reached the bay and stepped into the dinghy that Ignace had run ashore for them.

"Hi Joey, glad to see you, bro. All's good in the hood? Laura, Toubib, done your chores?" Solitaire welcomed them aboard the Pas de Deux.

"Tell me, how's it hanging these days, Zion or Babylon? Can we offer you something to drink first, Joey boy? Ti punch, bourbon, vodka, a wee dram of cyanide, just say the word."

Joe shook his head and asked Ignace to start the engine. Then he went below to take a closer look at the damage. He shouted for the Doc to rev up the engine two or three times in neutral and came up again visibly bewildered, wiping his hand on the rag that always stuck in his back pocket.

"Ain't nothing wrong with your pump, folks, nothing at all. Working like miracle. What's the idea, what are ya stealing my time for?"

"Well, I'll be damned." Ignace looked questioningly at Solitaire, who sat at the table, drinking coffee, as if none of this had anything to do with her. They were joined by Ti Martin, who was already looking a good sight better, apart from a monocular hematoma round his right eye. Presumably he had been woken by the engine and thought they were leaving the bay.

"Did ya get that, Sol? Joey here says the pump ain't broken. Ya think we were a little rash asking him to come here?" As if by plunged in some thoughts pf his own, Ignace leaned against the door leading on deck and poked around his fingernails with the point of a huge combat knife. The big weapon seemed more suitable for cutting fingers off than for cleaning them.

"Silly us," he added, "But since ya're here, anyway, we'd much appreciate a little chat with ya, ain't that so, Sol?". Again, Ignace looked at Solitaire, who put her cup down, and gave Joe her cold calculating hangman's stare: the convict's size and weight, rope strength, size and positioning of the noose knot, and the like. Ignace knocked twice on the ceiling with the butt of his knife, whereupon the Doc, who had climbed up with César, revved up the still running engine and started hauling in the anchor chain with the electrically driven windlass.

It was only at this moment that the true nature of his predicament was dawning upon Joe, who slumped down on Laura's bunk. The way he held his cardboard box in his lap with both hands suggested a bewildered boy who had been dumped at the wrong children's birthday party by his forgetful parents. The Pas de Deux left the bay by a hair-raisingly narrow bottleneck between two rows of reefs almost forming a firm ring and headed for the open sea even before her anchor had quite surfaced.

"Ya see, we been crackin' our brains something awful on the attack on the Yellow Cancer, ain't that so, Ignace," Solitaire said. Her tone, though casual on the face of it, could fool no one. Even Laura had already learned that, whenever Solitaire called Ignace by his name instead of showering him with all sorts of insulting soubriquets, chances were, she was getting really cross.

"Could'a been a coincidence, I guess. Not likely, though, is it? Those silly buggers must 'a known she was expected in Jolly Harbour that day, n'est-ce pas? If ya didn't know better, ya'd be tempted to think somebody tipped `em off, eh, Chewbacca?"

Ignace seemed to enjoy their little game of ping-pong. Presumably, it wasn't the first time they played it out on a victim such as Joe Grady.

"Tipped them off?" he repeated in mock disbelief.

"Ya mean, sold Snow White and her two dwarves down the river, that what ya insinuating? Na, can't see someone stooping that low, I really can't. Mind, only very few people knew about it, after all."

"Ya gave it a name, bro. Five, all counted, I believe. And you, of course," Solitaire added, whilst pointing an accusing finger at the rastafa.

Joe shook his head and raised a hand in protestation.

"I got no part in it, Sol, I swear. Why would I do a thing like that? To some of my best customers, too."

Laura followed the odd interrogation with rapidly increasing concern, if not anger. Solitaire and the others had obviously used her as a decoy, so much she had realized by now. Had Ignace or Solitaire shown up at the boatyard, they would have taken an unnecessary risk to begin with, and Joe would have smelled a rat and tried to escape or resist capture. Laura's aura of manifest harmlessness was what had let him walk right into the trap. Ignace stepped up to Joe, lifted him off the bunk by his armpits as he had done with Laura in the Blue Lagoon and pushed him on deck. The cardboard box with the pump fell to the ground was picked up by Laura. The Pas de Deux had already covered a couple of miles and was beginning to adapt to the Atlantic swell again.

"No matter. What we're itching to know, Joey boy, is who exactly you sold 'em to. A name, Joey, give us a simple name, and you're off the hook, feel me?"

Joe protested his innocence once again. Ignace shrugged his shoulders, seized Joe's hands, forced them on his back and tied them with a piece of rope. Then he turned to Solitaire.
"Line celebrations?" he asked.

"Good idea, let's have a line celebration." Solitaire stood up and leaned against the doorframe.

Ignace tore Joe's T-shirt to pieces and threw the noose of another rope hanging ready over the taffrail round Joe's waist. The bitter end of the rope had already been fixed on a cleat at the Pas de Deux's stern. Ignace pulled out his knife and quickly made two superficial cuts into Joe's upper arms before Joe had even time to shout out with pain. The cuts were bleeding. Not so profusely as to put Joe's days in danger here and now, but steadily enough to catch the attention of any prowling predators of the sea. Then Ignace bent down, seized Joe's legs by the knees and threw the man overboard like a disposable garbage bag.

As he smashed into the water, Joe's body disappeared under the surface for a moment. When it re-emerged twitching and rolling, most of the slack of the rope had run out already. At the present speed of the yacht, it took about five seconds until the rope jerked taut with a nauseating sound. The noose slid under Joe's arms and ripped the man's body through the Pas de Deux's wake like that of a hooked marlin. The rope cutting into Joe's flesh must hurt like hell, but since Joe's head tore through the water with his body spinning round and round, his cries remained unheard.

Slowly, hand over hand, Ignace pulled the rope back in, very much in the manner of a big fish angler reeling in a line against the combined resistance offered by the sea and the struggling animal fighting for its life. Then he signalled the Doc to slow down and thus gave Joe a chance to turn belly up and catch his breath. He had nearly drowned and was desperate. There were no visible traces of blood in the wake. Didn't have to be since sharks, that much even Laura knew, don't track their prey with their generally weak eyesight so much as with their delicate sense of smell and vibration and could sense potential prey at amazing distances. A single drop of blood in the ocean seemed enough for these vampires of the sea to go for it.

Laura was getting furious and wanted to step back into the saloon but Solitaire effectively blocked her way.

"Sorry you have to witness this, Snow White", she said. "But why don't you take a lesson from it. Where I come from, treason is punishable by death, that simple. Treason, treason, has no season, as the old Caribbean pirate's code goes. Joe knew what he was letting himself in for. If word were to spread that he got away with it, any bounty-hunting son-of-a-bitch thinking himself lucky would soon try and make a fortune by selling us down the river. For that reason alone, we couldn't afford to let it go, see." Laura pointed her finger at Joe, who was again zooming through the Pas de Deux's wake since the Doc had accelerated anew.
"You profited from my ignorance and guilelessness to make me an accessory to the fact. That, too, is a form of betrayal, making you no better than him, conceivably worse, even."

"Better, better, put it in a letter. This ain't about high-flying ethics, it's about the code, our code, see. They call us outlaws, but there ain't no such thing. Just because we won't respect your laws, don't mean we have no none of our own. On the contrary. Ours may be a good deal less sophisticated, but I'll bet ya they are applied way more strictly than yours. No parole or remission granted here."

Solitaire seemed to be launching into what might be one of her favourite subjects.

"They are the result of centuries of malpractice and sanctions. It's our code, and we stand by it, live by it and die by it, if need be. Whoever poaches in someone else's hunting grounds will be expelled from the community. Whoever steals from his brothers and sisters loses an eye. Whoever betrays or sells a bro or sis down the river loses his life. No need to look at me with those reproachful dog's eyes, Snow White. I didn't make the code, see, all I do is trying to enforce it."

Joe's head was again under water. Before long he would drown for sure, unless the sharks got to him first. Blue sharks, or so Laura had read, can easily reach the cruising speed of middle-class cars and run rings around a yacht such as the Pas de Deux. Solitaire had the Doc stop the boat. Joe's lungs must by now be filled with water and spray in such quantities that he would have to grow gills fast to survive. Laura did not understand what it was that Ignace called out to him. But it probably didn't matter, anyway. The perverted dilemma of torture held sway again. In extremis, a suspect is ready to confess to anything his tormentors want to hear. The whole process serves no purpose other than that of confirming a foregone conclusion. The convict will systematically be broken and, in the very end, sincerely happy to have got something off his chest that he may never have committed in the first place.

Ignace pulled Joe to the boat again and lifted him onto the stern platform. Not a second too early, if the first triangular fins showing near the Pas de Deux were anything to go by. Joe's Jamaican "bat's nest", floating far behind for a while before suddenly being swallowed, must have whetted these undiscerning scavengers' appetite.

"There was this guy come to the yard," Joe gasped, coughing up gall, blood and salt water all at once. With his soaked dreadlocks, he looked like a black Davy Jones just leaving his locker for a breather of fresh air. If race discrimination was hell, Laura thought, hell would be proud to have its share of it.

"What guy?" Ignace asked.

"Dunno, dude with three gorillas and a bear cub, yamaaan. What could I do?" Joe kept coughing and wheezing, whilst blood was running down his arms and water was forming a light red puddle on the teak deck at his feet.

"Sounds more like a Barnum and Bailey's vanguard coming to town," Ignace sneered.

"Uncanny type. Spoke English with a funny accent. Threatened to set fire to my yard and kill all my workers. What could I do? So I tells him of the Yellow Dancer's transfer just to make him go away, I'm sorry."

"Don't be. What did he look like? How old was he? What kinda accent did he have?" Solitaire was looking at the miserable bleeding human wreck before her with disgust and spat overboard.

"Dunno. Head like a cactus, kinda egg-formed, pointed at the top. Age 60, 65, maybe. His accent? Dunno, never heard anything like it. Kept shoving in vowels where there aren't any. Hey, wait a sec."

He turned and indicated to Ignace to grope in his right back pocket. Ignace carefully pulled out a soaked piece of paper or card that was just about to be reduced to pulp. Laura had been all ears during the past few minutes. Joe's albeit fragmentary description of the person reminded her strongly of the man on the Yakamoz. Shouldn't she mention this here and now?

"That reminds me…" she started, but nobody paid any attention to her at this point. Laura felt like a child at a party of grown-ups, trying in vain to muscle her way into the conversation.

Ignace took the piece of paper from Joe with two fingers like a key exhibit in court proceedings and handed it to judge Solitaire. "That's what he gimme. 'Take good care of it', he told me. I had forgotten. Dunno what it's all about, believe me."

As far as Laura could make out, the slip of paper was a visiting card. Solitaire flattened it out on her palm and looked at it from both sides. Then she handed it to Ti Martin.

"I guess that concerns you, Ti Moun," she said and turned back to Joe without waiting for Ti Martin's reaction.

Solitaire appeared determined to put an end to this. It was obvious that they would not get more out of Joe. He wasn't holding out on them, but simply had no more to contribute. Solitaire cast a dark glance in Ignace's direction. The chabin heaved Joe from the deck onto which he had collapsed meanwhile, and braced himself to throw the rastafa overboard again, this time for good. That was the moment when Laura tossed the cardboard box with the pump she was still holding into the sea and stepped on Ignace's naked toes as hard as she possibly could, shouting "Parley!"

Solitaire looked completely nonplussed for once, while Ignace seemed divided between crying about his aching toes and laughing about Laura's seemingly nonsensical action. After a few seconds, though, the two owners of the Pas de Deux gave full vent to their mirth. Laura wasn't sure how to take that and started laughing aloud, as well. Joe had seen his last moments approach fast and was as taken aback as everybody else. So, he too, joined the others laughing hysterically in a mixture of fear, despair, and panic.

"Where did that come from?" Solitaire asked, when she had stopped guffawing and caught her breath again.

"Parley? Really? Where do ya think you're at, not in Pirates of the Caribbean, do you. Parley! I'll be damned."

César and the Doc, wondering what the din below was all about, showed their respective faces at the taffrail of the upper cockpit. César started barking with confusion rather than anything else.

"Captain Barbossa, Sir, kindly untie the prisoner and hand him a fresh pair of pants, if you will. Don't ya see he wet hisself," Solitaire called out to Ignace between volleys of laughter.

Laura had desperately looked for something to stop the murderous ritual of the execution. Where conventional means failed to take effect, only something so totally absurd and ludicrous as to cause complete confusion could break the spell. And, miraculously, it had worked. But she knew the effect would wear off quickly. So she had to profit from the surprise intermission, and fast.

"That's enough, now," she shouted. "It's not even a kangaroo court, it's murder, premeditated, cold-blooded murder. I cannot allow it. If you throw this man to the sharks, you might as well do the same to me. Joe has been punished enough as it is. He has looked death in the eye, that's no laughing matter. Do let him go now."

Solitaire wiped the smile off her face.

"Who do ya think ya are, Snow White? If it had not been for us, Ignace and myself, ya would now be lying on the bottom of the sea with eels nesting in your guts. And the one person ya would owe all of this to would be this shit-bag of Joe Grady, le sac de merde. If ya feel like practicing Christian love of thy neighbour, why don't ya start at home, in Hamburg, or wherever it is ya come from. In the Caribbean, it's an eye for an eye, ask the Toubib. We saved your sorry ass, now it belongs to us. As far as I'm concerned, ya aren't worth a dolphin's prick, mind. Be a good girl now and don't meddle with things ya don't understand. Maybe that will prolong your life by a few days. And never again slip into my shoes and tell my people what to do and what not. Ignace, Joey looks like he could still do with a bath."

At this critical juncture, something extraordinary happened. Ignace, who never allowed himself as much as a second's hesitation when carrying out Solitaire's orders, let go of Joe and started discussing with Solitaire in the same guttural language that nobody else aboard understood. Solitaire repeatedly shook her head violently and seemed to be getting increasingly angry. The exchange lasted quite a while, till Solitaire unexpectedly seemed to concede defeat by shrugging her shoulders.

"Well, like I say, Ignace has taken a crunch on ya, God help him," she finally addressed herself to Laura again.

"I swear I have no idea what he sees in ya. I am deeply convinced it's a mistake to waive the code and let this slimebag go. But alright, suit yourselves. I just hope I won't have to remind ya of this in a different context, soon."

She approached Joe, who had stood up from the floor, and seized his chin.

"Consider this the luckiest day of your miserable life, yamaan. I would even go as far as calling it your re-birth. Don't let it go to your head, or Chewbacca will one night wake you up to tell you he's cut your fucking throat. And don't disappoint us with the Yellow Cancer's repair, ya feel me, Babylon? We want her back shipshape and in running order. And don't bother to send us or Snow White here bills, either, hear. Untie the bastard. Let the Toubib dress his arm wounds, so he stops dripping blood on my deck."

"As for you, Snow White," she turned to Laura again and lowered her voice so it almost sounded like the hissing of a snake, "let me tell you one thing. Today, this has worked for once, alright. Not because of you, mind, but because of Ignace. The two of us, we share a lifetime of saving each other's skins and extricate each other from shit you couldn't half imagine. It makes us two of a kind, inseparable, feel me? On a superficial count, though, he has the better of me by a small margin. So, when he asks me a favour, I can't possibly refuse. That said, don't ever try to cash in on a moral debt I owe to a third party, feel me? Toubib, take us back to the fucking Antigua coast so we can dump that sickening snitch."

Laura took a deep breath of relief. For the first time since she had set foot on the West Indies, she had had it her way. This was not about her ego, though, it was about saving somebody's life. On a quest like this, there were no holds barred. It filled her with great satisfaction, despite Solitaire's words of warning. Her father would be proud… She did not follow the thought through. Half her life, she had tried hard to make her father proud, assuming that door to swing both ways. Now that all the pride she had ever felt for her father was eroding at the onslaught of acid mud and slime, Robert's presumed opinion about her was the least of her concern.

As she passed the table in the saloon, Laura glanced briefly at Joe's undulating visiting card, which Ti Martin had left it there to dry. It was perfectly akin to the one which Ti Martin had given Laura when they had first met in Pointe-à-Pitre. This one, too, bore the inscription, printed in elegant lettering, At the foot of the volcano, with a Paris address and phone number underneath. It appeared to be a nightclub frequented primarily by tapettes bien situées, well-off members of the Paris gay community, as the Doc had given Laura to understand during their lunch aboard the Persephone II. The somewhat pretentious name was meant to be reminiscent of Roman orgies in the shadow of apocalyptic annihilation by the frequent outbreak of volcanos such as Mount Vesuvius or Etna. Ti Martin had regularly performed in the nightclub and forged himself a reputation as a drag queen, it seemed. At the back of the card, someone had jotted down a quaint handwritten greeting: "Evil flowers wither too".

2. Withering Flowers of Evil

"Where are headed? Nobody tells me anything around here." Laura stood in the galley and made a valiant effort to prepare a palatable lunch from what paltry leftovers she had found in the fridge of the Pas de Deux. Shopping was something neither the Doc nor herself had thought of during their shore leave the day before.

"Straight to hell, of course. You saw the visiting card, didn't you?" The Doc was cutting onions and shed the odd tear. César was lying under the table waiting for dainties his master would hopefully bestow on him. Ti Martin took turns with the autopilot keeping the GRAND BANKS 49 on course. Solitaire was apparently sleeping on and Ignace was cleaning his favourite gun, a Glock 17 consisting largely of light plastic for the umpteenth time.

When he had set Joe down on the beach the day before, Laura had insisted on accompanying the two men in the dinghy. She wanted to make sure that no unfortunate last-minute accident befell poor Joe. Still very dejected, the Jamaican had thanked her for stepping in so courageously and promised to give priority to the Yellow Dancer's repair. Free of charge, as he had assured Laura once again. Early next morning, the Pas de Deux had weighed anchor and quickly left the Antigua coast behind.

"Yes, I saw it, but did not understand its message," Laura admitted.

"How would you. It's a coded message. For those in the know, an unmistakable one, though."

"What's it got to do with Ti Martin?"

The Doc wiped his crying eye dry.

"The card comes from the Paris nightclub I told you about the other day, remember. The one, in which Ti Martin used to perform at the time."

Laura nodded.

"He had originally come to Paris from his home town Marseille. Down there in the Midi, he had muddled through as a juvenile male prostitute, among other things. He had passed through the usual stages of petty crime and had made his experiences with drugs, first as a user, later as a dealer, nothing outrageously original. Must have been pretty much down and out, the lad.

Then, there came a dramatic twist. One of the Marseille drug barons claimed to have been robbed by one of "his own". A scapegoat had to be found and punished in an exemplary way to warn any potential copycats. Some hoodlum or other who probably hated Ti Martin's guts and more likely than not was involved in the affair up to his neck himself, threw Ti Martin's number in the hat. I am sure the boy had nothing to do with it, but these matters have a way of quickly acquiring a dangerous momentum, as you witnessed yourself yesterday. From one minute to the next, Ti Martin became a dead man walking."

The Doc dropped César a piece of pepper, but the dog treated it with the canine disdain it probably deserved.

"What? No veggies? A beggar playing chooser, I like that." César seemed unperturbed and continued sulking.

"Anyway. Ti Martin had spotted the writing on the wall and escaped his pursuers the hard way. On the huge Marseille victuals market, he found his way into a refrigerated truck with a load of fish and shellfish, oysters, the lot, you know, for the number one category of Paris écailleurs, fish restaurants. Can you imagine? The mind boggles. Anyhow, it was the one place where nobody would bother to look for him. For a reason, 'cause normally, Ti Martin would have frozen to death after only a few hours, of course. It's a pretty long way from Marseille to Paris as you probably know. Eight hours' drive, easily, not counting any pauses or breakdowns. It was touch and go. Word has it that Ti Martin, wrapped in thick clothing, of course, had cut open and disembowelled a huge bluefin tuna, crawled into its hollow carcass and crudely stitched the fish together again from the inside. Another hilarious urban legend, of course. What was corroborated by many witnesses, though, is the fact that Ti Martin reeked of rotting fish weeks after his arrival in Paris. They used to call him Le Martin-Pecheur, the kingfisher, for a while."

"Be that as it may, with his talents and experience, he had no problem getting a foot in the Paris door as well, once he had got rid of the fishy stench, that is. Night after night, he was a celebrated drag queen and main attraction of this or that nightclub of preponderantly gay denomination. The 'kingfisher' became an eccentric master of disguise, who would not have been recognized by his own mother, let alone by his former Marseille bosses. Still wears a silver tuna with small diamonds for eyes, kind of a lucky charm, as you may have noticed."

Laura said that she had. In fact, she had wondered about it at their first meeting, during their luncheon in the Café de Paris. A bespoke jeweller's piece, probably, something quite unique and valuable. The Doc added the peppers and onions to the stew whose first bursting bubbles proved it was coming to the boil. "Don't forget the other spices," he reminded Laura. "The older the meat, the more spices it wants, ask the Cajuns, or the Indians for that matter."

He started rummaging in the small cupboards above the stove, but did not find what he was looking for. Which wasn't so surprising, seen that Laura had hidden the worst offenders in the first-aid box. Considering that most of the Caribbean spices came with a Jolly Roger, anyway, she felt that place was perfectly appropriate.

"One day, Ti Martin and a young Moroccan, with whom he had started teaming up, were hired by a newly opened nightclub that quickly became the craze of the town: "Aux pieds du volcan", At the Foot of the Volcano. Ti Martin and this Moroccan partner of his called their sensationally lascivious act Les Fleurs du Mal, the 'Flowers of Evil', after the collection of poems by my celebrated fellow countryman Charles Baudelaire. Exquisite! The poems, I mean. You have to read them one day, French at its best. Baudelaire came to set the tone for a whole era, very much like the songs of certain ambiguous pop idols such as Michael Jackson in our day and age, really."

"Thriller?"

"Absolutely, who doesn't enjoy the funk of a thousand years and all the rest of it."

Laura's attention was distracted by the aroma of the stew, insipid as it was for obvious lack of punch. She thought she could suddenly pick up more than just an underlying whiff of rotten eggs, which was strange since there hadn't been any left in the fridge when she had looked.

"Ti Martin and Choupette, that was the name, or rather nickname, of the Moroccan, had been inseparable right from the off. They had rented a small flat near the Volcano and had the time of their lives, one would wish to think. Until young Choupette came under the influence of a much older Frenchman from the fashion world, stinking rich and rotten to the bones. When Ti Martin started pursuing him in his violent throes of jealousy, Choupette threatened to sell him down the river. Ti Martin realized that it had been a bad mistake on his part to let Choupette in on the more salient secrets of his past. Sooner or later, he was convinced, the Moroccan would act out his threats, come what may.
"Ever since his humble beginnings in Marseille, Ti Martin used to carry a sharp razor, never left home without it. One of those old-fashioned Sweeney Todd things with a mock mother-of-pearl grip and a wafer-thin blade sharp and deadly as a lancet. He applied it not only to his own unwanted body-hair, but also to some of his enemies' throats. A rapid, flash-like cut from one ear to the other and that would be it. Young male prostitutes share many of the risks of their female counterparts, as you can probably imagine. And in the drug business, a close shave is always in a day's work, anyway."

"The Marseille police had been wondering for years how come some of the corpses they had to collect almost daily in the harbour and the beaches along the Corniche showed cuts of almost surgical neatness. Not your crude Jack the Ripper job with sliced bellies and all those gory shenanigans. It was common theory they were dealing with someone displaying anatomical knowledge and surgical skills. Docteur Guillotin, as they called the unknown killer, became a local celebrity. Investigations obviously focussed largely on medical doctors and hospital staff, but to no avail. Nobody ever suspected Ti Martin. How should they? What anatomical knowledge he had was derived from animal rather than human carcasses. As a kid, he had helped his father, a taxidermist, with his work every now and then. As a kid! Some childhood, I bet. The rest was natural talent. Presumably, he would have made an excellent surgeon had he had half a chance."

"Or a first-rate taxidermist."

"For sure. So, you see, I was reminded of all this when I noticed the cut on your throat the other day."

"Terrific. You mean to say you saw my head stuffed with excelsior and hung on the Yellow Dancer's saloon wall like a trophy?"

"Something like that, yes. Anyway, soon, the Paris cops were hit by the same phenomenon. Docteur Guillotin had apparently moved up in the world. The metropolitan police are every bit as hardnosed and cynical as their Marseille colleagues. As long as Docteur Guillotin restricted himself to killing his own kind, they could not be unduly alarmed. A pédé crapuleux or paedophile low-life here, a verminous drug dealer there, so what. Saved the cops the trouble and relieved the overburdened justice system. Word on the street had it the authorities would have been disappointed had they inadvertently caught up with Docteur Guillotin one day."

Again, Laura refused to believe what she was told. This amiable, suave bird of paradise a stalwart serial killer? And the doc talking about him like he was a celebrated colleague of his?

"And you probably thought butter wouldn't melt in his mouth, now, didn't you?" The Doc had guessed Laura's thoughts.

"Well, need I spell out young master Choupette's tragic demise? I think not. The problem was, and is, however, that the Moroccan's father, a major operator in the Maghreb pègre, thinks he owes it to himself to avenge his son's untimely death. He put a rather substantial reward on Ti Martin's head. Flattering, in a queer sort of way, don't you think?"

"Dead or alive?"

"Quite. So, here was Ti Martin, having to perform another disappearance act."

The Doc had given up his search for the vanished spices and probably considered the entire stew as a culinary write-off.

"A frost-bitten ride inside a tuna wouldn't cut it this time. He had to change the planet. He bought a passage on a freighter to the French West Indies. In Pitre, where he once more had to start all over again, as a dishwasher no less, I made his acquaintance in the Café de Paris, granted him asylum on my Persephone and tried to keep his anatomical interests alive."

"I'm sure you did. And no bounty hunter ever smoked him out?" Laura suddenly remembered how Ti Martin had reacted at something he had seen while they were having their lunch at the Café de Paris. How he had taken a precipitous leave of Laura and literally vanished into thin air.

"I don't know, he won't tell, learnt his lesson from the days with Choupette, I presume. If anyone did identify him, they probably ended up in the mangroves with a severed throat. Now, whoever left this visiting card with Joe Grady appears to be fully aware of the risks of approaching him and seems to have a soft spot for poetry, to boot. He or she is asking Ti Martin for a dance on the island of the withered flowers of evil."

"Which one is that?"

"Don't you smell it by now? Women are supposed to have a better olfactory sense than men and I swear I could already sniff it halfway to Antigua."

Laura stuck her nose in the air, sifting through it like a dog. The stench of rotten eggs had indeed increased. Hydrogen sulfide, Mrs. Watson. Laura's face manifested a mild attack of disgust. Was the Pas de Deux heading straight for Hades? If so, there was bound to be one heck of a welcoming party with Solitaire and Ignace hitting the place.

"Why don't you go and join Ti Martin upstairs? You can see it better from up there."

Laura reduced the gas flame under the pot to a minimum and declared luncheon ready. Whoever felt hungry around noon could help themselves to a bowl or two of insipid stew or drop dead, as far as she was concerned. Then she used the remaining hot water to brew two mugs of strong black coffee and cautiously climbed up into the open cockpit.

Ti Martin gave her a welcoming nod and took the mugs off Laura's hands. A few miles ahead of the Pas de Deux, the stumpy smoking chimney of Montserrat's Soufrière Hills rose into the sky.

"Volcanos," Ti Martin said disdainfully, as he took a first sip of his coffee, "stinking geological pit bulls, forever ready to charge and kill."

Laura tried hard to keep the binoculars steady so that she could scan the coast of the island at ease. The population of Montserrat appeared sparse and very much limited to the northern part. Close to the island's north cape to the left, she could make out the contours of a yacht apparently just weighing anchor and hoisting sails. Seen at the present distance, the boat seemed to resemble the Yakamoz in size and rigging. Which would tally with the course she had taken after leaving the Rivière Salée, in fact. But for a laywoman such as Laura all sailing yachts would resemble one another once they were sufficiently far away for the details of their rigging to get blurred. Slowly, she kept scanning the hillsides till she reached the smoking top of the volcano, which looked like a hot beheaded breakfast egg steaming away in its cup. The long, thin trail of smoke from the volcano clearly to be seen against an impeccably blue sky, was drifting in the general direction of the Pas de Deux, hence the intensity of the smell.
"Doesn't look that bad, even unexpectedly green, at first sight," Laura said.

"Got to look more to the right. The last major eruption destroyed the former capital, Plymouth. You can still see the grey wasteland that used to be the town."

Laura moved the binoculars down again and started scanning the southern part of the island. On a slanting terraced plateau that had once carried the buildings of the capital at several different levels, a grey carpet of ruins and rubble, covered by mineral ashes, pumice and cooled lava spread across this part of the island. Almost like an artificial town shortly after a nuclear test strike somewhere in the Nevada desert, she thought, with the fallout having killed off all life.

Here and there, bits and pieces of brick walls appeared to have survived the catastrophe and stood up like so many antique steles meant to remind passing travellers of what had happened here in the mid-1990's. Plymouth had quite literally been reduced to ashes. Unlike the outbreaks of Mount Pelée on Martinique, the Montserrat eruption had not claimed any human lives, because it had been announced by several quakes and blasts, minor in strength but powerful enough to serve as portents. When the "big one" had finally come, the island had already been evacuated. Large parts of the population, descendants of the original Irish and English emigrants, had abruptly become homeless and sought asylum in Britain, which refused to repatriate them, the idea probably being that, what with the Union Jack streaming at such outposts as Gibraltar, the Malvinas or Montserrat, the illusion of the British world empire seemed still intact.

"We call it the ‚grey hell'," Ti Martin explained, as he put down his cup on the floor. After all she had heard about him from the Doc, Laura looked at Ti Martin with altogether different eyes.
"That story about you surviving inside a big tuna, is it really true?" she asked him.

Ti Martin glanced at Laura in surprise, but quickly found back to his usual ironic self.

"I see, the old fool has done it again, hawking rumours, ruining reputations. But what the heck. True or false, the tuna has become part of my personal myth, so don't expect me to debunk it."

Laura's next question was even more delicate, so she fought with herself for a few moments but she spit it out nonetheless.
"In your opinion, who was it wrote the message on the visiting card?"

Ti Martin shrugged his shoulders.

"Beats me, Laura. Somebody who finally wants to collect the reward that has been on my head for quite a while now. Maybe he waited for the sum to be increased once again. When that didn't happen, he decided the time to act had come."
"And what are you going to do?"

Ti Martin leaned back in his comfortable seat at the helm and swung his feet up on the instrument panel in front of him.

"Well, not run again, that's for sure. Done too much running in my time, already. I guess I'll confront the sucker head on. Won't be the first time I managed to convince a bounty hunter to quit following me, either."

What with the Doc's account, Laura had a more than vague idea what Ti Martin meant by "convincing".

"Surely not on your own? Not in your present condition?" She pointed at Ti Martin's bandaged head.

"It's between him and me. I won't draw Sol, the Toubib or Ignace into this. Least of all you."

"But you'll be signing your own death warrant."

"Don't worry, I know how to defend myself."

Yes, Laura thought, that he obviously did. Against a single opponent in a one on one. But confronting several heavily armed bounty hunters would be a different matter. And Ti Martin's ugly gash on the head could not have healed completely yet. It made him a soft target if not even something of an invalid. Reasonable odds looked somewhat different.

"Solitaire will never let it happen." Laura tried a different approach.

"Maybe so. I take it that, unlike the Toubib, you're able to zip your lip. I've let you in on it because I rely on your discretion, so don't let me down, please."

Laura silently watched the ominously smoking Montserrat drawing nearer by the minute now. The Pas de Deux was not much faster than the Yellow Dancer, yet did not heel to one side, but stayed upright like a dressage rider on his stallion. By and large, Laura had become accustomed to the rhythm of a yacht travelling at sea. To begin with, she had just found it slow, a waste of time, causing nausea on top of it. By now, she apparently had grown sea-legs, accepted and even started appreciating sailing as a very relaxing mode of transport, if and when you were not in a great hurry. She was fascinated by the hazy contours of the island gradually becoming sharper and ever more precise, due to the different shades of grey, which would then explode into all the colours of the rainbow during your final approach. There were parallels to be found there to man's gradual progress through different periods of his life, she was sure.

César was lying next to Ti Martin's seat and moved his legs again, dreaming. Laura wasn't sure whether she should feel privileged by the man's trust in her or whether she did not have every reason to be dejected by the moral dilemma into which he had plunged her. Ti Martin would never forgive her if she told Solitaire about his intentions and Solitaire would probably bear her a lifelong grudge if she didn't. How come Laura had such a fatal propensity for manoeuvring herself into blind alleys time and time again?

Ti Martin, probably eager to change the subject, pointed at the volcano.

"The smaller hill to the left of the smoke plume is called Chances Peak. Quite fitting, wouldn't you say?"

"Is there any port at all on the island?"

"Not really. Most ships and yachts drop their anchor in Rendezvous Bay, dead ahead of us now. From there, it's not far to Brades, the island's present capital up on the right."

"May I ask you one more question? When we were sitting on the terrace of the Café de Paris, in Pitre, you remember, I couldn't help noticing that you seemed concerned, as if you had recognized someone, a person who might have been on your tracks."

"What? Oh yes, I remember. I'm sorry about that bit of boorishness, especially since it was a false alarm."

Laura suspected this to be a lie. She thought of the floating body in the mangroves and the beetroot-red windbreaker that had never quite left her mind. But she decided not to insist.

"The permanent distrust, the constant need to look over your shoulder, doesn't it ever get to you? Always more or less on the run, never able to relax, to set your mind at ease?"

"Get to me it does. But then again, when it comes to the point, aren't we all on the run from something or other? All aboard this craft, for sure, including yourself, no offence. Anyway, it becomes something of a second nature. You stop being aware of it, only the people around you will notice, if they are perceptive enough. Always on your guard, always ready to disappear at a few minutes' notice. As soon as you step out of a building, you instinctively take in the situation. Who else is around? Who seems to be loitering with intent or acting in any way suspiciously? In the good old days of prohibition and rising drug abuse, head mobsters such as Lucky Luciano, Joe Masseria or Salvatore Maranzano practically never left their fortress-like warehouses and disused factory buildings for fear that, out there in the street, they risked getting massacred by some killers dressed as cops or waiters. At a single glance, outlaws have to establish who is harmless and who might represent a danger. Fortunately, bounty hunters or professional killers make mistakes, too, frequently due to excessive vanity, in fact. Their clothing may be just a mite too elegant, too expensive. Shoes tell their own story. Demonstrative lack of interest in you is always suspicious."

"Still, entering and leaving a building is critical. Before going in, you want to make sure you'll be able to get out again fast if need be. What emergency exits are there, how many, situated where and leading where to. Transport: taxis nearby yes or no, public means of transport available yes or no. Never turn your back on doors or windows longer than necessary. Watch out for moving curtains and flat rooftops. Funny thing people hardly ever look up, did you know that? An atavistic reflex, maybe. Danger for early man always came from the ground and, at worst, a tree or rock face, never from the air."

Laura remembered Robert's words of caution concerning "Dr Brutus." Now that she knew about her father's criminal past, she had a better grasp of his paradoxical spread-eagle position between trust and suspicion.

"And you know what? Cops have it very much the same way, elderly ones, anyway. The world of crime and punishment is a thoroughly paranoid one, believe me. It all starts with the blatant imperfection of penal laws. They ought to have them worked out by convicts, not DA's or politicians. Next, you have your corrupt police forces, your schizophrenic attorneys, your incompetent though well-meaning judges. At the end of the line, sadistic guards wait for you in cesspool penitentiaries. No joke, a criminal career. If you look at it from that angle, you should be happy to be here with us, because when all is said and done, you know where you are with us."

Laura nodded, although she wasn't sure she would have signed up to that light-heartedly. Not after the past few days' experience.

"At some point in time, you have to stop running. If a bullet has my name on it, inshallah. 'All is written', Choupette used to say, bless his soul. Tempting idea, though, in a way, to be born info a life already laid out for you by Allah, or God, Jehovah, whoever. The surrender of man's own free will with the redeeming effect of having guilt lifted off your shoulders, that's what religion infallibly amounts to. Suits the worldly powers that be suspiciously fine, doesn't it? I despise religion. What indescribable horror has been wrought in the name of something whose existence has yet to be proved. Makes your flesh creep."

He swung his feet back and stretched himself. Laura thought he looked very tired and beaten.

"Something the Toubib apparently hasn't told you is that I was diagnosed HIV-positive. My days are numbered, one way or another. So are yours, of course, nobody that we know lives forever, do they? Couple years earlier or later, what difference does it make? It's the quality of the years you were accorded that counts, ain't that so, Mrs. Forster?"

At noon, they had reached an anchor niche a little north of Rendezvous Bay and secured the Pas de Deux in front of a steep, gruff wall of volcanic rock.

"But only a goat can get ashore here," Laura lamely protested.

"Exactly, so nobody will be looking for us here, either." Solitaire had woken up and dressed. Now she was scanning the shore to the right of the yacht's anchorage.

"We'll wait for darkness to fall before we move the boat and Ignace and myself will take a closer look at the village."

Laura let go of César, who smelled land and couldn't understand why he was to be contented with staying aboard. Laura felt that this was the moment when she had to either speak up or forever hold her piece. Ti Martin, who had left the cockpit and joined them in the saloon, gave Laura a warning glance and slowly shook his head almost imperceptibly.

Laura remained silent. So what? She would have to live with it, that was all there was to it. Ti Martin had had all the time in the world to think it over and seemed to have drawn the conclusion that he would follow the invitation to dance on the volcano all by himself. Ignace and Solitaire were pink elephants on Montserrat as anywhere else. They could not afford to be seen by all and sundry. If it was a trap, it would be enough for one person to walk into it. Looking at it soberly, rationally, even a trifle cynically perhaps, Laura felt that Ti Martin was doing the right thing, suicidal though it might turn out

"There is this rusty old landing further south, near Plymouth. It forms the end of what used to be the Old Road. Ti Martin, the Toubib, and Laura can move the boat there. We'll meet you later, at the landing."

For the time being, Solitaire had stopped calling Laura Snow White. Laura dared hardly take this as a sign of her being accepted into the group, albeit as a precarious intern. Maybe Laura's spectacular intervention during the "crossing of the line" celebrations had left a deeper impression on Solitaire than she would readily admit. Ironic that now, when the ice between them seemed to be showing the first cracks, Laura had to hold out on Solitaire with regard to Ti Martin. Fat chance. Someone like Solitaire smelled a rat a mile away, how else could she have survived until now?

An ominous silence had fallen over the bay. The yacht which Laura had observed from far away but subsequently lost interest in, had vanished, sailed on to God knows what next destination. After lunch, everybody on board the Pas de Deux had some sleep to catch up with and lay in their respective bunks one deck lower digesting the insipid stew. All except Ignace, that is, who indefatigably mounted the watch like an experienced, ever suspicious sheepdog. He kept checking his weaponry while smoking one joint after another. Laura was anxiously waiting for Ti Martin to make his decisive move. Laura found her heart beating wildly and probably loud enough for Ignace to hear.

She did not have to wait for long. Ti Martin came strolling on deck, yawning and stretching his limbs.

"I think I'll take a little trip ashore, much too stuffy in here," she heard him say to Ignace in a very casual tone.

"Besides, I'm sure César needs to take a leak. He's getting old, the poor soul, and so is his bladder. Could you give me a hand with the dinghy?"

His request was addressed to Ignace, who took a long scrutinizing look at Ti Martin as if trying to get inside the man's skull. The chabin's suspicious instincts were never totally asleep. Obviously not. His life depended on them. Anything ever so slightly out of the ordinary made him stand to attention immediately. Maybe Solitaire had furthermore instructed him to watch out for Ti Martin's movements with special attention. Be that as it may, this sudden initiative of Ti Martin's, though harmless enough on the face of it, made him feel visibly uneasy.

"Sure?" he asked.

"Ya bet. What seems to be the problem?" Ti Martin asked back with his boyish smile that many had mistaken for simplicity of mind at their ultimate expense.

He had put a woollen cap like Joe Grady's on his head, covering his bandage. César's hearing seemed in working order, too, despite his age of some ninety or so dog years. When he caught the metallic jingling sound of his "harness", he was immediately all over Ti Martin.

"Alright, I'll be down in a sec." Ignace yawned, flipped the butt of his joint overboard and climbed down the steps backwards.

Ti Martin could feel Laura's eyes drilling into his back like two powerful laser rays. Without turning round, he lifted the seam of his colourful shirt with the stylized heliconias. Like that, Laura could see the butt and handle of Ti Jean's pistol, which stuck in his belt.

Laura had sometimes wondered about that curious difference in gun culture in Europe and the States. American men used to tuck their revolvers or pistols in the front with the gun barrel pointing right at their family jewels. Europeans on the other hand usually stuck their guns in at the back, where all they risked losing in case of a shot going off prematurely was their ass. Did Americans value their genitals less than Europeans and if so, why? "Some telltale differences in gun-carrying habits with men here and overseas", a doctoral thesis by Laura Forster, M.A.

Ti Martin would probably carry his razor in his trouser pocket. In Laura's estimate, though, he might not come close enough to his dancing partner to be able to make use of the blade. But you never knew. Ignace and Ti Martin prepared the dinghy for the landing operation and hung the heavy outboard engine in its bracket at the stern. Ti Martin and César climbed aboard.

"Wait a sec, I'll come with you," Ignace called out and tied the thin rope of the dinghy to a cleat on deck.

"I'll just go and get my favourite girlfriend."

Laura knew by now that by this he did not mean Solitaire, but his gun. Normally he would never part with it, even on board the Pas de Deux. A strange coincidence, maybe an omen that, for once, he did not have it handy at this crucial moment.

Ignace had hardly disappeared into the saloon when Ti Martin started the outboard. Curiously enough, it jumped into action immediately. Another strange coincidence, Laura thought, since normally it took at least four or five noisy pulls on the ripcord to get it running. The Buffalo Soldier took his leave from Laura with a gesture of mock salute and revved the engine up to full forward. When Ignace came running back on deck, Ti Martin was already out of hearing.

Ignace liked it less and less. He shook his head and looked at the dinghy's wake with a clearly disturbed and worrying mien. When the dinghy had disappeared behind a little rocky protrusion, Ignace entered the saloon and glanced briefly at Laura, who pretended to be dozing it off. The noise of the outboard had woken Solitaire and the Doc, who came up from their cabins below. Ignace gave them a short run-down of what had happened. Solitaire cursed him loud and blasphemously.

"I had a gut feeling he might try this. The little prick wants to get hisself killed, I'm telling you."

She turned to Laura.

"You didn't happen to known about this, did you?"

Laura shook her head as if to say ‚perish the thought'. Then she got up. She hoped Solitaire would not see her blush under the suntan.

"Well, alright then." Solitaire's voice did not seem to carry its usual conviction.

"I would have given you credit for a little more common sense, quite honestly." This was directed at Ignace, who looked like returning the compliment but apparently thought better of it and shut up.

"One thing is for sure, we can't swim after him. His mobile seems to be off. We have to trust he'll be at the landing tonight. Or else, we'll have to form a search party. In that case, I hope we'll find him in one piece. If we don't, I know one ugly mustee who'll be in all sorts of trouble, I swear."

3. The Dragon Den

All they could do now was kill the hours left till nightfall. Fortunately for them, the mile-long sulphuric smoke plume rising from the Soufrière Hills was deflected away from the Pas de Deux by the light but steady breeze of the Trades. Notwithstanding, the all-pervading rotten-egg stench was impossible to get used to, Laura thought. She tasted it on her tongue and her dried-out throat ached with it.

Besides, she felt sweaty, dirty and salty all over. A swim with a short rinsing shower afterwards would be what the Doctor prescribed. She asked around perfunctorily, but nobody seemed particularly interested in a dip. Solitaire, lost in thought, was staring at a chart and hadn't even heard Laura, or so it would seem. Only when she saw Laura pulling out her bikini and preparing for the swim, she looked up.

"I wouldn't do that, if I were you. There's no end of…Lemme show you something."

She got up, stepped on deck and waved Laura to follow her. At the stern of the boat, she opened a big locker, started furring through bits of ropes, bent plastic paddles, pieces of rusty chain, and other odds and ends, till she found what she had apparently been looking for. She pulled a heavy black bucket from the locker and tied a thin end to its handle. Then she pushed the pail overboard, tipping it sideways at the same time so that it wouldn't float but fill with water right away. She waited, till it was more or less full, then jerked it up on deck again without spilling so much as a drop.

Laura stared into the clear water, sloshing back and forth in the pail with the swell of the ocean. She saw nothing out of the ordinary and, looking at Solitaire, shrugged her shoulders. Solitaire's torso disappeared in the locker again. When she finally came crawling out again and straightened herself, she held up a pair of old swimming goggles, as if they were a trophy just won in a contest. The goggles had quite obviously not been used for a while. Their porous plastic was half-eaten by heat and salt whilst the glasses were almost as opaque as a pair of cataract eyes. Laura rubbed the goggles clean, put them on, adjusted them, took a deep breath and pushed her face into the pail. At first, she saw no more with the goggles than she had done without them. Then, gradually, she started discovering what seemed to be hundreds of tiny, glassy shapes moving languidly in the water.

"Baby jellyfish", Solitaire said, when Laura had re-emerged from the bucket. "Myriads of them. No sea wasps, more of a hair-shirt effect. They thrive in the lukewarm, sulphuric water around the island. Maybe your skin is thicker than mine. Me, they always give me allergic reactions, pustules itching like hell all over. Your choice, but we don't need any more trouble than we already have, I'd say."

Laura agreed and thanked her for the warning demonstration. Was there anything totally uncomplicated, not to say harmless in this deceptive Garden of Eden called the Caribbean? It sure didn't seem so.

"How can anyone live like that?" she murmured, as she handed back the goggles. It was a remark more than a question.

"A matter of perspective. And habit," Solitaire replied drily and slammed the locker shut.

"As you can see, if they need to, humans make their peace with practically anything, even with a stinking volcano. Nobody really forces them to settle under a smoke plume and always welcome the new morning with a deep breath of sulphuric air. Of course, many of them just don't have the means to go make a fresh start elsewhere. Anyhow, seems to me us humans are the only species on earth that adapts to shit like that. If you deprive animals of the habitat they are programmed for and feel at home in, they wither and die. Not us, no sir. We stay infinitely adaptable and persist no matter what. We may not like it at first, but the third generation at the very latest wouldn't dream of going elsewhere, any more. I guess that's the secret of our collective survival, our superiority over the animal world. But is it really something to be proud of, this reputation of being the most uncompromising opportunists in the universe?"

Laura smiled a little sheepishly. For the first time, she had heard Solitaire advancing an original thought of her own in something that came close to coherent speech. Apparently, this woman wasn't all animal survival instincts and brash reflexes but possessed a well-functioning brain not to be underestimated.

"Yes, you're right, I suppose. The Almighty must have been in two minds about us for a long time already. Probably decided to try again in another galaxy, this time without the evolution bit, maybe."

"Yes, he had better. Might drop sex altogether, how about that?"

"So men can do what we sometimes recommend them to - go screw themselves?"

Solitaire laughed at her own wisecrack but Laura could almost physically feel the woman's nervous tension. She was worried to death about Ti Martin and had every reason to. Laura thought of trying to side-track Solitaire's mind, lure it away from Ti Martin's lonesome expedition.

"Solitaire." Laura pronounced the name as she had just heard it for the very first time.

"So-li-taire. No offence, boss, but somehow, the name sounds to me like that of a hunchbacked fortune teller with a tasselled headscarf to cover her wild grey tresses and a hairy wart on the tip of her nose. Did you ever have another, I mean, a more common one, like,I don't know, Susan, Helen, Mary?"

"Watch that foul mouth of yours, Laura Forster," Solitaire laughed again. "But yes, or rather no. Not one name, many," Solitaire grinned and lifted her hands as if to start counting them down.

"Since I never had any papers that would have unveiled my identity, from my earliest days, I was baptized and re-baptized in every family or institution I happened to get to or spend time in. Those I can remember, anyway. I guess the idea was that, with every new name, I would be given a chance to become a new person. Didn't work, though. I stayed the same pain in just about everybody's butt, irrespective of what name they gave it."

Laura had no problem imagining an untameable young Solitaire going against all the rules or conventions in the book. Who could blame her? Given like circumstances, Laura might have come up with a very similar CV, even though all was not environment, or so they say.

"Later, I started enjoying the routine and changed names myself every other week or so. I scrolled up and down the alphabet, see. Like cyclones that used to be exclusively female at the time. Women equal witchcraft, the incarnation of evil, voodoo meteorology is what I call it. A depression remains a depression, never mind what name tag you stick on its toe. Listening to psychiatrists, I guess I should have ended up a schizophrenic nutcase. Maybe I did and am the only one around not aware of it, see, the Teddy Daniels syndrome."

"Teddy Daniels? Who's he?"

"Yeah, you know, that guy from the Di Caprio movie, Shutter's Island, heavy stuff. Anyway, that's for others to judge. No, seriously, I took frequent name changes as a kind of privilege. I mean, in a thoroughly regimented world, who else enjoys that kind of anarchic latitude?

"And Solitaire?"

"That's the one came to stick. Didn't even pick it myself, but was given it by the Black Queen, when I stood before her the first time: a ferocious, though bedraggled, tousled and starved she-leopard, who instantly reminded her of Solitude, as she told me later."

"Who's that?"

"Solitude? Never heard of her? Where have you been these thirty years? A mustee woman, Solitude was, a rebel heroine fighting slavery on Guadeloupe towards the end of the 19th century. She got caught, of course, thrown into a dungeon in Pitre and executed the day after she had given birth to a child. Hanged by the honest, law-abiding citizens of Pitre, who called her a murderous bitch. Had I been an ebony lass or at least cocoa, the Queen would have given me Solitude's name, she said. But a white woman wasn't entitled to bear it, that would have been a sacrilege, like, I dunno, a conchie being awarded the purple star, see. And so, Solitaire it was to be. Also, because when dealing with me, 'pears you have to have a lot of patience, feel me? I may be flattering myself, but I heard Solitude's bellicose spirit talking to me many times before I even got to know more about her life and times. She was said to have supernatural powers that enabled her to kill someone at a considerable distance. The remote-control pincushion trick, I suppose. That's one I haven't got the knack of yet."

"And yet she was unable to save herself, as it would seem. And who is the Black Queen? A chess player?"

Solitaire guffawed so loud that Ignace, who had silently been listening in on their conversation, jumped and dropped his joint on the floor.

"A round of chess with Porgy and Bess? Laura Forster, you are beginning to prove a valuable if slightly ridiculous addition to our little group of battered housewives. I think I like you. It's been a while since I had occasion to laugh so much in so little time. No, no, the Black Queen is a very, very old Garfuna, a black member of the Carib tribe. A very bad mother, too, take it from me. Not really the grandma type. By now, not even she would remember her real name, I guess – if she ever had one in the first place. Not many people on the islands have genuine birth certificates or authentic IDs of any sort."

"I didn't know Caribs were black."

"Well, how would you, never having seen one? Compared to a paleface, you might call them coloured alright, but not black. Over the centuries, they have mixed with God knows what other peculiar races and rampant tribes. Fortunately for them, I suppose, else they would have degenerated and died out centuries ago, like those Incas or Aztecs of Central and South America. Nature won't have anyone thriving on incest for long. Many of the Caribs still carry Arawak genes, in fact. They must have been a war-loving bunch, the Arawaks. Some Caribs shacked up with blacks, especially on the coasts of Venezuela, Ecuador or Brazil. That's where they had once come from to do their bit of Caribbean island-hopping. Their mustee offspring are called Garfuna."

"And what do they need a queen for? They live in a matriarchal society, one dominated by females??"

Solitaire laughed again.

"Thanks, I know what the word means. But then, who doesn't, when it comes to the point? Look at Muslims, for instance. Go out of their way to subdue their women, wrap them in black or blue rags till they are unrecognizable as members of the female sex, and yet, when push comes to shove, I bet it's their women who call the shots, at least on domestic affairs. And in-house battles stand for ninety-odd percent of family lives, don't they? There is something irrepressible in us bitches. Sometimes I feel pity for men, I really do. Compared to us, they are a sleepwalking bunch, hormone-driven zombies - present company not excluded," she added with a sidelong glance at Ignace.

"Anyways, back there on Dominica, where they live in the reservation, their official spokesman, local sheriff and mayor rolled into one, is chief Blade Johnson. Soft-spoken sun of a gun, very reliable, a natural with the machete. Maybe you'll meet him. And the Black Queen."

This time, it was Laura's turn to laugh at Solitaire's status report on the war of the sexes in the wake of the Eden meltdown.

"To me, the Black Queen was a substitute mother, a female tutor and companion all in one. My most significant person of reference, next to Ignace. Without either, I would have been swallowed by the quagmire that was my first life. When I first got to Dominica, by pure coincidence, mind, I was really finished, drained, flattened. She picked me up and became my Black Queen."

"Maybe she saw you already then as her possible successor, Solitaire the legendary Red Queen?"

"Who knows. I don't think so though. But even if she did, I wouldn't want to lead a people that would have someone like me as their queen."

Solitaire looked at her watch.

"You're nervous because of Ti Martin?"

"Hell, no, what gives you that idea? Up there, some bloodthirsty bounty hunters may be itching to butcher him. He's all by himself, not counting César who was never much of a fighter even in the prime of his life, the Toubib tells me. The bloody fool Ti Martin hasn't reported back for some five hours and switched off his mobile. Why on earth should I be worried about him?"

The charm of the little digression Laura had tried to create had obviously worn off. Laura took her shower and changed her clothes. The lukewarm water wasn't as refreshing as she would have wished, but it was better than close encounters with baby jellyfish. The Doc and Ignace kept alternating watches. The ticking of the saloon clock became louder by the minute. To take her mind off Ti Martin, Laura once again accepted the ungrateful role of cook. For supper, she prepared some fancy omelettes, which met even with the Doc's appreciation. Then, everybody went back to sweating and drowsing in frustrated silence. The men smoked, Solitaire did some chart-plotting of her own, and Laura cleaned the dishes.

At long last, the sun's rays lost their annihilating tropical force and the brief Caribbean dusk set in. The Doc climbed into the cockpit and started going through the routine that had become familiar to Laura. The engine jumping to life, the anchor chain rattling, the rumbling of the anchor coming on deck, Laura could by now attribute the respective functions to most of the sounds. Slowly, the west coast of the small island, lying in the red glow of the setting sun as if burning up from inside, passed in front of their eyes. While day and night routinely exchanged places, the first road lamps of Brades up on the green hills were being lit. The moisture grew with the soothing effect of darkness falling.

Somewhere in the east, or so the Doc had heard on the radio which he had been monitoring for a while during the afternoon, a whopper of a hurricane was in the making. The weathermen had baptized it "Alberto", because it was the first hurricane of the season and Spanish was first in line this year in the traditional rota of "New World" languages. A good thing German wasn't part of it, Laura thought fleetingly. A hurricane called Adolf would have a hard time gaining popularity.

"Ti Martin is probably already waiting for us at the jetty."

Laura's lame attempt at spreading optimism did not quite convince herself, let alone anybody else. She sounded more like a little girl whistling in the dark. Solitaire, the Doc, and Ignace checked their guns, reloaded them and secured them in their holsters. Also, they had changed their casual summer wear, T-shirts, shorts, and sandals for "fireproof" outfits, as if preparing not just for a climb up the steep hillsides but for a subsequent descent into the gaping maw of the blubbering volcano. Heavy boots with high-profile soles apparently conceived for stamping out forest conflagrations were passed all round. Laura reluctantly accepted the regulation combative ensemble handed to her and slipped into it half-heartedly.

"Will we be marching through plutonium?" she quoted one of her favourite Woody Allen lines, but again no-one so much as smiled. The farther south they went, the more intolerable the sulphuric stench became.

"Welcome to hell's inner circle," the Doc called out and tied a cloth round his mouth and nose. In this garb he looked like a surgeon who had just been called into the operation theatre and not been given time to change into the green butcher's smock usually donned by men of his profession. Above their heads, the permanently hissing volcano kept exhaling its evil black and grey billows of smoke. Laura was hoping they would soon get to the windward side of the smoke plume. But instead, the Doc suddenly cut the speed and had the Pas de Deux drift against some rusty old jetty with the last bit of momentum. Ignace elegantly hopped over the taffrail and tied the yacht to the jetty. Neither César nor Ti Martin were to be seen anywhere.

"If he was on his way here, he would signal with his torch or we would hear the dog bark," Ignace said.

When the Doc switched off the engine, they all concentrated on listening to any sound other than the waves splashing and the volcano hissing ominously. There was no man-made noise to be heard. They had not lit the yacht. Didn't have to, because, at that very moment, the half-moon, grotesquely blown out of proportion like a huge mirror image of Ignace' scar-strewn face, crept up behind the cone that was the volcano's caldera. The moon looked like it had been mangled by some greedy monsters of the deep and only narrowly escaped the red-hot eruptions of boiling magma. Its almost blinding shimmer shone on the slumbering ruins of Plymouth and let them come to life like the enchanted town of some long-forgotten legend. Staring at it like that, Laura could very well imagine a fire-spitting dragon to have passed over Plymouth and reduced it to cinders. The jetty here at the seaward end of the Old Road was one of the few things that remained relatively unscathed, albeit rusty and altogether useless, at that. The old capital, hidden under layer upon layer of half-solidified ashes, porous basalt and cooled-off streams of lava, lay to their right. Here and there, parts of buildings rose like unfinished crypts from the grey monotony of this theatre of destruction. Laura felt her bristles stand on end.

"What a ghastly place," she murmured.

"Ghastly, yes. But it does have its perks," the Doc replied. He switched on his torch and pointed its beam to a white sign a little to the right. It said "No entry beyond this point."

Laura wondered whether the poor souls of the damned were welcomed to Dante's hell by inscriptions like that, which reminded her of concentration-camp terminology: "Aryan sons of bitches only. No Jews allowed beyond this point."

"What's so perky about it, then?"

"The viper-pit principle. The less inviting a place, the safer it is for hiding or bartering merchandise of sorts. Only fools and volcanians venture into this hole..."

"Volcanologists is what you mean, I think," Laura interrupted the Doc.

"You see, the whole area from here to the south-eastern cape has been off limits these past ten years or so. Because from time to time you have minor eruptions accompanied by the ejection of pyroclastic torrents. That's round about 700° centigrade hot avalanches of dust and ash that come tearing down the hills at the speed of jet planes and kill off anything in their paths. When I say ashes, I don't mean the light black remains of burnt wood or paper. No, this is a deadly mixture of molten rock and almost liquid glass. Several smaller settlements erected after the 1995 eruption have already fallen victim to those avalanches and a dozen or so people have lost their lives. We are right in its drop zone, incidentally."

"Anyway, the uninviting character of the ruins is reason enough for shady riffraff such as ourselves to pay Plymouth a visit once in a while, fetch something or leave something else behind, whatever."

"A huge dead letter box, you mean?"

The Doc nodded.

"Yes. You could say that, in more senses than one, actually. A kind of secret trans-shipment area, an underworld free port. You would be surprised how many loving packages change hands here on a regular basis. Or how many bodies were discretely disposed of somewhere around here. Even the sea releases many of her victims, provided they dropped no deeper than roughly

250 feet. Those that do will never surface again, anyway. Bodies washed ashore, though, give rise to many questions. Once a pyroclastic avalanche has passed through, no more questions asked. Not this side of Armageddon."

"Sorry to barge in on your interesting discussion, but we got to get going, if we are to find Ti Martin alive. You'll be coming with us."

Solitaire pointed at Laura, who was shocked – not just at the sight of Solitaire, who, with her night visor and all, looked like a militant Martian prepared to conquer the blue planet. No, Laura was horror-stricken at the perspective of playing hide and seek amidst the nightly ruins of Plymouth.

"Why? What do you need me for?"

"Let me put it like this. I'm prepared to bet my Redhawk that Ti Martin told you all about his intentions during the voyage. I can't prove it, of course, but my gut feeling seldom lets me down. That's why you'll come with us. That way, if anything untoward has happened to Ti Martin, you can see for yourself what you are probably co-responsible for. If not, if you're not involved, it won't kill you but give you a little useful practice."

She waved to Ignace and briskly stepped across the swaying jetty as if it was a perfectly safe catwalk.

Laura staggered after her like a little dog, clutching the rusty, dusty railing with both hands. Ignace, also wearing a night visor, gave Laura a revolver, whose handling he explained to her under his breath while running after Solitaire, heavily wheezing, as always.

"This is a Taurus calibre 22, small, light, very little recoil, but with the hell of a punch at close range. Remember, only six rounds, like any revolver. If you lose count, better reload in good time. Here's a box of cartridges. Don't get caught out empty. It is loaded now and the safety catch is on. You move it like that, with your thumb. Don't forget that in the heat of the battle, else you can't fire and look stupid."

"And shoot only if and when I tell you," Solitaire added. "Aim at the widest part of the torso: the stomach or chest. And do try and kill only people you don't identify, that's a good principle to go by. Come on, get a move on, we haven't got all night."

Laura felt the cold metal of the snub-nosed little gun in her sweaty hand. It was almost a toy, she thought. Would she be able to point its barrel at another human being? She had no idea. There was no time for argument with her alter ego. Solitaire and Ignace hurried and scrambled ahead like two mountain goats pursued by a snow leopard. Without a night visor and totally devoid of any detailed topographical knowledge, Laura depended on keeping up with the other two. The beam of a torch, however, would have served as an all too easy orientation for snipers on the prowl.

Thus, accompanied by the perpetual hissing of the monster, the three valiant dragon-slayers were headed for the hidden nest of the slumbering beast, guided by nothing but the pale light of the rapidly rising moon, assuming its normal proportions with growing distance. They had to destroy the monster and its entire offspring, before the dragon woke at the first crack of dawn. Every step hurt Laura's legs. Her feet kept groping in vain for a hold in the mixture of ashes and loose rock. The sulphuric wisps crept under her clothes and spread over her skin like powdery mildew. After the virtual eternity of an hour or so walking uphill, they reached a ridge with petrified vegetation. To the left, a row of dead decapitated trees. To their right, a yawning canyon several hundred feet deep. Under different circumstances, Laura might have ventured a little closer to the edge of the abyss to see where it ended but now, with nothing but the moonlight to show the way, she didn't really feel tempted.

Suddenly, Solitaire made them stop and seek cover behind the split and slashed tree trunks. Solitaire and Ignace took turns at the pair of binoculars they had taken with them. Then, leaving the binoculars on the ground, Solitaire, using sign-language only, made Laura understand that she wanted her to stay where she was and wait for things to happen. While Solitaire slowly rose from the ground and disappeared to the right, Ignace picked himself up as well and sneaked away to the left.

When the two of them had been gone for about a minute or so, Laura took the binoculars and started scanning the area right in front of her. Again, the moon shed just enough light on the scenery for Laura to discern more and more detail. There was a group of three or four men standing on a rocky ledge, from which a single sooty tree stump rose to about twice the men's height. The figures were surrounding the stump like red Indians preparing a totem pole dance. It was only when the group's ranks opened for a few seconds at a time that Laura managed to catch a glimpse of the strange bundle at the foot of the stump. With a lot of imagination, it could have been interpreted as a person crouching or sitting on the ground, resting his or her back against the tree.

Laura had just put down the binoculars to wipe the sweat off her forehead, when a single shot rang through the night. It was the report of a big calibre, no doubt, probably that of Solitaire's Ruger. Quickly, Laura picked up the binoculars again. One of the "Indians" had been hurled against the rock face and collapsed there and then, dead or dying. The other three jumped from the ledge and scattered in all directions, but didn't get far, since Ignace and Solitaire were taking them out under their cross-fire. When the shooting stopped, all the "Indians" seemed to lie dead. Or maybe not all. The shooting resumed and bullets now started whistling in Laura's general direction, but too high to hit her. Laura was perplexed. Why would they be shooting at her? Then she got it. One of the "Indians", probably the last surviving one, must be running towards her unwittingly. With their gun fire, Ignace and Solitaire were practically driving him into what would be Laura's own line of vision.

What was she supposed to do? Already, it seemed to her she could hear the crackling of dry brushes and twigs accompanied by the wheezing of a man gasping for air as he was thumping and thrashing through the half-fossilized undergrowth. With bullets still whistling above her, Laura got up from the ground, hid behind a tree, pulled out her Taurus and switched the safety-catch, bracing herself for the inevitable.

When the man could only be yards away from Laura's tree, she lifted both her hands that clutched the handle of the gun and stepped out to the right. Fortunately for her, the man was just looking back over his shoulder, no doubt to see whether he had someone hard on his heels. Thus, he collided full speed with Laura, who hadn't even time to lower her arms and take aim. Instead, she was hurled backwards like a successfully tackled quarterback, fell on the ground and hit the loop of a big root sticking out of the ashy soil. She felt a sharp pang at the back of her head and passed out momentarily.

When she came to again, the "Indian" had disappeared and all was quiet as though nothing had ever happened. Her head hurt and her Taurus had gone, probably been flung away from her on impact. Laura got up from the ground, knocked the dirt and ash from her trousers and looked for her gun. Finally, she found it some five yards behind the place where she had lain. Then she climbed up the steep hillside to get to the rocky plateau.

Neither Solitaire nor Ignace paid any attention to Laura as she joined them at the "totem", where Solitaire was kneeling on the ground, still busy cutting the ropes with which the "Indians" had tied Ti Martin to the tree stump in a sitting position. The rope around the Frenchman's neck had served as a kind of garotte, as simple as it was effective. Ti Martin's head-wound had burst open again and coagulated blood formed clots in his "buffalo" curls. His mouth was wide open, as was to be expected with the strangulation he had suffered. Deep in his throat, the executioners had shoved the bloody cinnamon-coloured tail of a dog. On Ti Martin's chest, a cardboard sign bore another cryptical message: Save the last one for me, Yellow Dancer.

SEVENTH CHAPTER

1. The Greek Job

At the crack of dawn, Laura stood amidst the ruins of Plymouth all alone, her feet stuck to the ankles in the moist, sticky ashes. Solitaire, Ti Martin and the Doc sat at one of the tiny wooden tables of Drury's Irish pub, which consisted of no more than two low, half-collapsed walls. The three of them were playing poker, drinking rum and eating chicken wings from KFC boxes. César had sunk into the doughy grey mass so deep that only his head and wagging tip of his tail showed. The Doc was smoking his pipe, Ignace and Solitaire had each lit a joint.

Suddenly, a thundering rumble shook the ground under Laura's trembling feet. Then there was a huge explosion, the echo of which tore across the Atlantic like the first ripples of a tsunami in the making. Melting pieces of rock and glowing cinders were raining down on the Plymouth ruins. Black wallowing clouds of lava and ash straight from the earth's festering bowels came slopping over the rim of the caldera like hot coagulating pitch from a kettle boiling over and started rolling towards them at great speed.

The deadly avalanche of seething mineral sludge was only a few hundred yards away, but it seemed not to bother the three at the table a bit. As if sitting behind an opaque pane of bulletproof glass, unconcerned and seemingly untouchable, they were drinking to each other's good health, downed their rum in generous swigs and kept their eyes on the cards. Bloody gold-red rum was running out of the corners of Ti Martin's mouth in pulsating gushes.

Laura shouted a terrified warning, but the thundering clouds swallowed all other noises. At last, she turned and tried to run away, save her own life, but got stuck in the ashes as if wading through deep snowdrifts on an Alpine slope. The first wave of devastating heat hit her with merciless force and literally burned the flesh from her bones. The dust, pouring through her wide-open mouth, instantly turned her lungs into solid blocks of concrete. The end came with a big bang.

Crying and sweating, she woke up. The Pas de Deux was pitching through the Atlantic swell with calm, reassuring regularity. Laura's relief about the sudden end of her nightmare quickly gave way to the deep sadness and consternation about Ti Martin's cruel death. She turned and looked at the opposite bunk beyond the table. The last thing she remembered from yesterday night's desperate search was Ignace carrying Ti Martin's body all the way from the plateau underneath Chances Peak back to the jetty. Once back on board, they had wrapped the corpse in some bed-linen, and laid it on the free bunk in the saloon. A confused fluke wave hitting the yacht from the side only moments ago must have tossed the yacht's stern about with such force as to jerk the body off the bunk and onto the floor with a resounding thump.

Up in the cockpit, the Doc apparently had heard it too, because he came climbing down the ladder to see what had happened. With Laura's help, he picked up Ti Martin's stiff corpse and put it back on the bunk. Laura's heart went out to the Doc. He had lost his two most important companions at one single stroke and might now have to face a sad twilight dusk of life in agonizing solitude.

Laura got up and looked back. On the horizon, Montserrat resembled a big ocean liner going down over her stern after a deadly encounter with razor-sharp reefs. All that was left of the once mighty ship were her bows, the forward upper deck, and the first funnel, still puffing away pointlessly. The smoking volcano astern and Guadeloupe's steaming rain forests ahead, the Pas de Deux seemed to be cruising between two island-shaped figments of feverish imagination.

"How much longer to Dominica?" Laura asked the Doc.

"Three hours tops," the Frenchman replied coolly, casting another tender glance at Ti Martin's body that lay on the bunk like a mummy shoplifted from the depths of its secret pyramid tomb and hurriedly expedited to some New World museum. Whenever the yacht pitched or rolled, Ti Martin's head would shake as if in silent disbelief about the inconsiderate treatment he was being subjected to.

Dominica. Another place Laura had never suspected she would visit one day. The Sunday island presumably came as close to a home as someone like Solitaire would ever know, Laura thought. Refuge or asylum was more like it. Perhaps the last hole in the wall left to her kind in these parts. Solitaire would meet "her" people there. How many companions had she seen go down the same road as Ti Martin had? How did she manage to get over such losses time and time again without cracking? Had her heart eventually become as callous as her hands over the years? On their way back from Chances Peak to the boat, none of them had spoken a word. Solitaire probably blamed herself for not having anticipated Ti Martin's desperate move. Ignace obviously feared Solitaire's anger. And Laura was well aware of the fact that she had better try and keep an even lower profile during the coming days. If Solitaire seriously suspected Laura of holding out on her, it bode evil for their future relationship - to the extent that it did have a future. Strictly irrational, of course, since nothing would bring Ti Martin back.

Only when they were back on board the Pas de Deux, and the Doc and Ignace had finished with Ti Martin's corpse, had Solitaire spoken to Laura again.

"So?" she had asked her, "Where's your compassion now? An eye for an eye, that's our tune and the fucking Yellow Dancer, whoever he is, knows how to hum it. But let me tell ya this: the son of a bitch don't know who he's messing with. I'll give him a haymaker that will make him wish he had never even heard my name."

Laura was at a loss, yet again. Ti Martin's meaningless self-sacrifice as well as her own dubious role in it paralyzed her. From a legal point of view, Laura's share in the affair could be summarized as failure to render assistance, mitigated by the victim's own refusal to accept help. But for as long as his killer was at large, she risked getting reduced to the unrewarding part of the best scapegoat available. In her effort to accommodate everyone, she had once again made a mess of it and ended up with enemies all round, a chronic defect she would have to work on.

"What happened up there, after all? I knocked myself out on a root after colliding with the man running downhill?"

"Oh, so you didn't actually push him over the edge yourself, did you?"

Laura looked at the Doc for help and explanation.

"Well, we only heard his cry and took it you had somehow managed to shove him into the ravine. So it was more of an accident, then?"

"Yes, it was. I didn't push him. He must have lost his balance and stumbled a few steps back."

"One step too many, I presume."

Laura was relieved. At least she wouldn't have that one on her conscience. She had been instrumental in the man's death, yes, but that was manslaughter, or rather assault resulting in accidental death, at worst, justified by self-defence to boot. No judge would be able to send her away on those counts.

"Who could do a thing like that? I mean who is capable of such heinous abomination?"

The Doc shrugged his shoulders.

"In our world, almost anyone. Gratuitous cruelty is commonplace. Only he who shows himself consistently merciless has a chance to survive and stay at the top of the dung heap for a while, knowing full well we're all on borrowed time. It's a perpetual merry-go-round of cause and effect: accounts will be settled, territories conquered and lost again; there's never any shortage of motives. You know, this is no place for mentally sound people like yourself. I think you should really be going back to Hamburg on the first plane. The Caribbean air is rife with the stench of carrion, that's why it abounds with spices, to gloss over the scent. Don't let it get to you, corrupt you."

"God, I could kill for a cup of hot tea or coffee."

Solitaire had woken up and had climbed into the saloon unnoticed. Her uncanny feline ability to move about noiselessly kept everyone on their toes all the time. Which was probably the way she preferred it.

"No need for such drastic steps. We've already had enough killing as it is." Ignace had prepared tea and was pouring a few cups.

"Thanks, Ignace," the Doc said and filled his crooked pipe. It occurred to Laura that the Doc, though anything but taciturn, had a way of picking his "prey". Maybe it didn't mean anything, but as it was, he hardly ever spoke to Ignace. Laura wondered what would happen if by some odd chance those two ill-matched personalities were left alone on an island. It would probably come down to the size of the place. If it was too small for the two of them, they would probably fight it out right then and there with the odds in Ignace's favour, obviously.

"Well, ever since the attack on the Yellow Dancer, we racked our brains about who could be after us with such implacable intent. A situation not altogether new to us, mind. There are candidates galore. What complicates matters here, though, is your father's untimely death," the Doc explained.

"He must more recently have made quite a few enemies of his own that we strictly know nothing about. People with issues strong enough to pursue not only Robert but also his kin beyond his grave, as it would seem."

"My money would be on Suleiman the Silent," Solitaire advanced her guess.

"He certainly has the biggest beef with Robert Forster," the Doc agreed.

"How so?"

"Business. You see, shortly before his death, Robert learned that a consignment of Suleiman's was to be routed via the Aegean, like in the good old Leros days. Strictly speaking, the Turk had abandoned that line a long time ago, not least because of the changes in the very nature of transport modes. These days, everything is moved by container, whose routes have been programmed and clocked to the minute. You can follow your stuff about on your tablet or smartphone waypoint by waypoint, like an Amazon premium package. The old romantic times with their quaint analogue methods are bygones." He lit his pipe and took a careful sip of the hot tea.

"Every now and then, however, shit happens. A tiny grain of sand gets into the works and the lot comes to a grinding halt. A coordinated international DEA clamp-down, for instance, or some snitch co-operating with the law, anything at all. In such cases, the old routes are sometimes reactivated. Which sounds a lot easier than it actually is. Time hasn't stood still meanwhile, of course. You no longer have the most recent information at your disposal. Important waypoints have disappeared under new roadworks or buildings. Erstwhile perfect hide-outs have been transformed into banks or motorway junctions. Key personnel have gone on to the next world, and so forth. It is in such precarious situations that the beast sometimes will have to leave its cover and offer its flank. This is then the moment an experienced and patient enough hunter will pick to move in for the kill."

"The transaction at hand in the Aegean belonged in that one-off category. Robert had got wind of it and contacted me. The old enmity between him and Suleiman was gnawing away at both men's livers, I expect. Now Robert saw a good opportunity not only to harm the Turk financially but to discredit him as a businessman as well. A dealer who has zilch to deal when the time comes is out of the game for good. The drug business is not known for its readiness to forgive."

"To mount this sting, Robert needed reliable staff and since he knew I kept loose contacts to people such as Solitaire and Ignace…. The consignment in question consisted of a hundred kilos of heroin from sustainable growth with certificate of purity, so to speak, class A stuff. Expensive, too, of course. Some four to five million worth. More, if you blended it sagaciously. Twenty kilos were to remain with us, by way of remuneration for our services, the rest would go to appreciative Turkish competitors of Suleiman's, so they would be sitting on the fence for the duration of the action. A dangerous ploy with several volatile variables. Robert himself had long since retired from the drug business. So had Solitaire and Ignace. Had they been approached by somebody else, they would probably have turned the offer down, I guess. But for old time's sake…"

"An unfortunate multiple chain reaction," Laura summarized the Doc's long-winded explanation with sobering precision.

"So to speak, yes. Unfortunately, the execution of the plan was hampered by several fluky circumstances nobody could possibly have anticipated. As is frequently the case with reactivated routes, like I said."

"One such butterfly causing chaos with the flapping of its wing nearly cost Solitaire's life. To fight her way out, she had to kill three of Suleiman's thugs, a bad mortgage. Like I say, the Turk lost not only his dope and his men, but also had his reputation tainted. Which puts Solitaire and anyone close to her in Suleiman's black book. Does he have issues with us? Yes, I believe he does."

The Doc got up from his seat at the helm, thus making space for Solitaire, whose first watch had just started. She glanced at the instruments drowsily and tried to get her bearings on the blurred features of the Guadeloupe coastline. Then she fed the autopilot a few new data and waited till compass and plotter confirmed the new course.

"Why don't you tell Laura yourself about your Greek adventure?" the Doc asked her.

Solitaire did not seem to be in the talking mood. But in commiseration of the Doc's double loss, she apparently deigned to humour him.

"Yes, well, why not? You, too, think Suleiman followed us all the way to the Caribbean, then?"

"I couldn't blame him if he did. Like I say, he lost a small fortune because of us, and his reputation into the bargain. Thank you very much for putting this pit bull on our heels, Robert Forster."

"Funny, when you look back at it now. To think we were working for Laura's father. Anyway, like the Doc said, we could have refused; nobody forced us to accept the offer, tempting though it was. If I'd had any idea how things would go, I definitely would have said no."

"What happened?" Laura asked, quite happy for the conversation to move on to less mined territory.

"Well, the one hundred kilos were to be stashed by the Turks on a godforsaken rocky islet west of Lesbos. From there, it would be taken to Thessaloniki a few days later by some Greeks, to be smuggled on a cargo full of food aid destined for the Middle East. The food wasn't of the highest quality, of course, but still good enough to be side-tracked to some third-world discounter's chain stores. Not my headache. I was to go to the islet before the change of ownership went down and steal the stuff from under the Sultan's beak. Instead of going via Thessaloniki, eighty of the hundred kilos would be taken by Ignace, waiting on Chios, and myself to a place on the Turkish coast off Rhodes, where it would be received by some of the Sultan's worst competitors. Twenty kilos were for us."

"What would be the value of twenty kilos of heroin?"

"Why? Ya're tempted to muscle your way into the trade? Don't even think about it, you haven't what it takes. Price depends on a series of determining factors. Where does it come from, how was it cut, and, most important of all, how badly does your buyer hurt to get his hands on it? The theoretical market value of reasonable to good smack moves somewhere between fifteen hundred and twenty-five hundred dollars per ounce."

Laura gave a low whistle of appreciation.

"That's no net profit, of course. You need to skim off the overheads and all sorts of incidental expenditures I won't go into. But that you probably know all about yourself, anyway, being into logistics and all that."

"So, on paper it looked like a mere walk in the park. Had it not been for the one silly technical hitch. The screw of the motorboat I had chartered in the Aegean suddenly took leave of the rest, would ya believe that. I'll tell you something, Laura Forster. The Greeks have an eerie propensity for picking the one rotten apples in a basket full of rosy ones. You know what I believe? I believe that in the myriad workshops and industrial production hangars all over the globe, there always is one single container with the inscription Greece on it standing somewhere in a dusty neglected corner. As soon as the underpaid, exploited Korean contract worker bungles up her morning workpiece because the breakfast sushi is giving her indigestion, the rejected piece of workmanship goes into the Greece container. Zip fasteners, TVs, laptops, car tires, no matter what kinda shit, it all ends up in Greece, the world's largest dump site for industrial rejects."

Solitaire leaned over to the leeward side of the railing and spat out her tea.

"You want to poison me with this cuppa shark piss, Chewbacca? I always took you for a friend of mine. Looks like I have to rethink a few things. "

Laura felt she had to take The Chabin's side for once.

"The galley is one big mess, I'm afraid. Ignace may easily have picked the wrong box and poured the water over some dried chicken-broth. Or Greek tea, for that matter.",
Solitaire laughed.

"You see, I keep telling him he needs glasses. Just don't want to admit he can't see so good. One of these days, he's gonna shoot one of us by mistake, eh, Chewbacca? Well, don't forget to say sorry, at least."

She poured the contents of her cup into the sea.

"Here goes, all of you fish, delicious chicken shit, come and get it."

"Like I was saying, the screw took leave from the boat with a final ‚pleeeng', and was gone. Before I had even come to grips with what had happened, I was already knee-deep in water. Gushed through the empty tunnel of the propeller shaft. Fast, too. Next thing I knew, the boat sank from underneath my soggy backside. At the same time, the wind started picking up, naturally. Happens very fast and furious, in the Aegean, and always at the wrong moment. Even in meteorological terms, the Greeks managed to come up with a fucking blank."

"And so, I swam all night like one of those seriously disturbed channel crossers. Only I wasn't covered in grease from top-to-toe and didn't have a boat to pick me up when I was getting a little short of breath."

She went through some energetic crawl motions lest her audience might have no idea what swimming for your life looked like.

"The wind picked up more and more; the boiling sea was getting unmanageable. Don't ask me how, but I just about reached this goddamn rock of an islet more dead than alive. Fortunately, I had studied its contours rather precisely on the chart, as if I'd had a gut feeling things might go south. Thus, I recognized the rock when it sprung up in front of me in the early morning hours. For three days, I lived in a cave like fucking Wilma Flintstone, on rain water and crabs, and, oh yes, the remains of a snake, not to forget. Acquired taste, let me tell you. A bit like chicken, raw chicken minus the salmonella part. On the second day, I found matches in the bloody cave, that was a true relief from raw crab and shit like that."

Laura paled visibly. Solitaire's vivid account made her stomach churn. Solitaire seemed to have noticed. The woman never missed a beat.

"If ya're asking yourself here and now whether or not you would have survived an ordeal like that, Snow White, my answer, surprising as it may sound, would be no, you definitely wouldn't. You would've drowned, starved, died of thirst, stung by a scorpion, evaporated, withered, somehow vanished from the surface of the planet. Or else, Suleiman's three musclemen would have gotten to you, raped and massacred you. They'd been sent to the islet because the Greeks were still sitting in Thessaloniki, drinking their cute little coffees, waiting for the gale to die down, whatever Greeks tend to be doing if anything at all. The three men never knew what hit them when they reached the islet. Batwoman came down upon them like hell's fury."

The memory forced a grim smile on Solitaire's face.

"Yes, Suleiman has issues. Wouldn't be surprised if he was the instigator of all this - the attack on the Yellow Dancer, the murder of Ti Martin, and the killing of poor innocent César. Who knows what more he has in store for us."

"Under the circumstances, that's probably the easiest question of them all," Laura cut in, "kill every one of us, what else."

Solitaire seemed unmoved by the perspective. "That always takes two - one who wants to kill and someone else stupid enough to allow himself to get killed. If I ever lay my hands on him, I'll hang him from his balls and skin him alive."

2. A Kindhearted Captain

Laura woke literally oozing with sweat. Her limbs hurt and the chain gang of rock-splitting convicts was hammering away again behind her temples. She tried to sit up, but fell back on her bed as if made of jelly. Sun rays sharply contoured penetrated the narrow gaps in the wooden shutters of the two large bedroom windows like laser beams. Tiny particles of dust hovering in the close air of the room were forming dancing prisms, which changed shape with each of her movements. To snooze for just a few minutes longer in a bed fragrant with the smell of fresh linen after almost a week on board funky yachts came close to heavenly bliss here and now.

The somewhat pretentiously baptized "Hacienda del Sol", owned by a German acquaintance and former business partner of Solitaire's, no doubt counted among the more luxurious of the domains on rugged Dominica island. Feeling comfortable and snug for the first time in what seemed a matter of weeks if not months, Laura stretched out her numb limbs to the full and tried hard to round up the hammering convicts and march them back into their cells.

She felt the fingers of her outstretched right hand stroke a bulging leather handbag that had to be Solitaire's. It certainly wasn't Laura's. She could not remember ever having touched such an incredibly smooth silken surface texture. Strangely enough, she did not remember noticing the thing that must have lain somewhere near her pillow when she had gone to bed the night before. She kept caressing the leather and suddenly jolted up from

the mattress as if bitten by a tarantula. The handbag had moved!
When she turned her head to the right, she found herself staring
into the expressionless eyes of a big snake of lemon-yellow skin.
The reptile seemed to look her over quite dispassionately while
darting its forked tongue in and out of its mouth like the twitching hind leg of a dead frog it was just having for breakfast.
Laura's horrified cry did not seem to bother the snake a bit, virtually deaf as it probably was. To the extent that one could accuse it
of having emotions of any kind, it appeared curious rather than
hostile. Be that as it was, Laura didn't feel like musing on the
reptile's frame of mind. As she grabbed a clothes hanger and receded to the far end of the room, the glass door flew open and
the Doc, gun in hand, stormed into the room. Laura noticed small
bits of hard-boiled egg in his toothbrush moustache. Apparently,
he had been enjoying his breakfast on the terrace when Laura's
cry had alerted him.

In the twilight of the dimmed room, a scene of unspeakable
horror presented itself to the startled Doc. Still in her half-trans-
parent night-gown, Laura warily followed every one of the lemon-coloured reptile's languid movements. Having had infinitely
more time to contemplate the odd circumstances of their encounter, the snake on its part did not seem to pay any special heed to
its possible ramifications. With a bit of imagination, one could
even have credited the reptile with a slightly mischievous glint in
its otherwise expressionless eyes. The Doc took it all in at a glance
and, pocketing his Glock with the safety catch on, came out with
another one of his bleating guffaws.

"I see you're making friends with Ti Conrad. If it's his impeccable skin you're after, you'll have to wait a while, I'm sorry to
say. I suspect he has just shed the old one and was proudly pre-
senting his new outfit to a stranger without giving the adverse effect that would have on you so much as a thought. Conrad is the
uncontested number one in Solitaire's private wild life conser-
vation programme and I for one suspect him of being perfectly
aware of it too. He profits from the situation by taking all kinds of
liberties with unsuspecting guests of the Hacienda."

Again the bleating laughter. The Doc took Laura's clothes hanger, which she was unwilling to part with.

"May I introduce you: Conrad C. Constrictor, Laura Forster."

He put the clothes hanger he had finally wrestled from Laura's hands back into the cupboard, went to the bed and lifted the heavy, ten-foot-long reticulated python, about as thick as a man's arm, from the linen. Then, he took Conrad outside and placed him as carefully on the sun-flooded grass as if he was made of bone china.

"Here, my good fellow, you look like you could do with a bit of a tan."

The reptile shot out its tongue to test the changed décor for the scent of edibles and slowly, almost grudgingly slunk in the direction of the nearest patch of bushes.

"You will have to excuse Conrad. He's not his usual self these days, probably in the tight grip of the rut, hence, uncommonly excitable. Has been looking for a mate for some days now, or so I'm told. Maybe he found your female pheromones promising. All the harsher his disappointment, I suppose. Well, Conrad, that's quintessentially what life is all about, a never-ending series of great expectations and resulting disenchantments."

The Doc laughed out aloud again and signalled to Ignace and Solitaire, who had materialized from their respective rooms, that there was nothing to worry about. Once again, Laura felt ridiculed. Swallowing her wrath, she threw the white cotton dressing gown that she found hanging behind the door round her shoulders.

"What does the C stand for, Counsellor?"

"Excuse me? Oh, Ti Conrad. No, Charles, actually. Theo, the owner of the place, has this thing about animals' names, you see. Treats them like human beings. Once had a Collie he called Professor Thomas B. Preston, can you imagine. Used to call him Tommy for short, though, most of the time. Why don't you join me for breakfast, what's left of it, anyway?" the Doc invited her.

"Meals are best enjoyed with a good friend, I've always found. And you surely must be starved."

He had got that right, Laura thought and sat down opposite the Doc, rather surprised at his jocular mood after having been bereaved of two dear friends only 48 hours or so before. As a medical doctor, dealing with life and death on an almost daily basis, he had probably developed a philosophy or technique of his own that helped him overcome the frequent sense of loss and futility. From the corners of her eyes, she saw Solitaire shake her head and disappear into the main building of the Hacienda. Ignace, distrustful of the world at large and their present situation, in particular, apparently seized the occasion to go and scan the perimeter of the spacious premises.

"Constrictors such as Conrad C. are endemic on Dominica, as far as this part of the world is concerned, I mean," the Doc explained while pouring hot tea for Laura. He himself had finished eating and started filling his pipe.

"I'm sorry to have startled everyone with my hysterics. I hate snakes. Thank God Conrad isn't venomous."

"Well, the bad karma that tends to accompany snakes in our day and age is a thing that came with Christianity and is somehow associated with your sex, isn't it. Antiquity had a much more relaxed attitude towards reptiles. Snakes were even idolized, worshipped as soothsayers and experts in botany that could teach medical men the virtues or otherwise of this or that weed. The title of Pythia awarded to the respective virgin oracle of Delphi herself lives on in our lemon-coloured specimen, would you believe it."

He lit his pipe.

"Apostolos could have enlarged on that no end, I assure you. Anyway, Conrad is not poisonous, but not altogether harmless either, for that matter. As far as these islands go, you'll find venomous snakes only on Martinique and St. Lucia, by and large. They were deliberately imported by plantation owners some hundred-odd years ago. The idea was for bare-footed slaves to think twice before running away and hide in the rain forest. More effective than dogs, you might say."

He puffed on his pipe and tried to fan the smoke away from Laura with his hands.

"Constrictors are a more easy-going lot, even though pythons can get rather aggressive, too, if cornered. Besides, if you are bitten by a venomous snake, there will normally be antidotes around to be applied. But if and when a constrictor means business, you are quickly done for. You have no idea of the muscular power such animals pack. Even if someone rushes to your help, it is highly doubtful they can free you from the snake's deadly coils in time to save you from suffocation."

"Some people keep reptiles like that at home, till they gradually grow too big and dangerous. Then they release them somewhere in nature. That way, Florida has been inundated with pythons that have no natural enemies besides man and take on even adult gators."

"Sounds like the title of a horror film, Constrictors versus Gators."

Laura felt something with sharp edges in the pocket of her dressing gown. Cautiously, she searched the pocket and, to her great relief, pulled out a pack of Marlboro filter cigarettes instead of the black widow she had half expected to materialize. The Doc looked surprised.

"I didn't know you smoked."

Laura shook her head.

"I don't. But since everything around here seems topsy-turvy, anyway...."

The Doc lit a match for her. Laura inhaled the smoke and started coughing violently. The Doc gently slapped her back with the palm of his hand and told her to drink a sip of tea.
Laura did as she was told. The cough subsided and she leaned back in exhausted silence.

This was their second day on Dominica. After all Laura had read, it should be one of the most vestal of all the islands above the wind. Their approach to the long row of Dominica's cloud-covered mountain peaks had been spectacular to say the least. At first sight, the island probably looked every bit as pristine as it had presumably presented itself to Columbus and his men, hundreds of years ago.

When he was asked, upon his return to Spain, to give the nobility assembled at Court an idea of the island's topography, Columbus is said to have crumpled a piece of paper. When he let it go again, and the lump had somewhat unfolded again, he called that as close an approximation as his audience would ever get of the island's ruffled landscape.

After his first few promenades ashore, Columbus must have been able to give a vivid account of Dominica's many rivers and mysterious lakes, as well. The island belonged to those richest in water, yet most destitute in terms of economic activity. The fact that this held true even in modern times, was at least partially due to a devastating hurricane that had carried away most of the paltry dwellings and sparse settlements. Big cargo ships had been washed ashore like so much flotsam. Laura had noticed their rust-eaten, half-submerged wrecks when the Pas de Deux had anchored near the northern cape of the island. Immediately, two long dugout canoes had pushed off from the beach and taken the yacht's crew plus luggage on board. The luggage included Ti Martin's corpse, which had started smelling and needed to be buried as a number one priority.

Their welcome had been business-like, no flower garlands, no hugs and kisses, but no questions asked, either. Still, Laura sensed the respect with which the locals met Solitaire and her friends, including the corpse. Their canoes were propelled by powerful outboards, whose prolonged gas levers stood in as steering rudders as well. During the season, some thirty to forty yachts, all seeking to be custom-cleared, provisioned, and, in some cases, repaired, used to ride at anchor in Prince Rupert Bay. Now, shortly before the beginning of the first hurricane month, the Pas de Deux had the place all for herself.

On the Indian River, the locals had sailed them further inland under the natural roof of overhanging foliage of big, age-old trees with Spanish moss hanging from their branches. On a clearing with another ramshackle wooden jetty, two of Theo's jeeps had been waiting for them. On narrow, winding roads, they had finally reached the "experimental farm" owned by Solitaire's German connection.

At home, Theo, a former Berlin attorney, was considered a person with a soft spot for felons at large and drug traffickers, in particular. As it would appear, he thought of them more in terms of the inevitable fall-out of capital society. Many years ago, he had come to Dominica on holiday and had immediately fallen in love with the island. A year or so later, he had sold his Berlin law practice and made Dominica his new domicile.

The ambitious style of Hacienda wasn't exaggerated, not if you set it against the generally modest local standards. The whole complex of the mansion measured some 3,000 acres. There were strips of arable land as well as a splendid little park full of rare tropical trees, regularly pruned and lavishly fertilized plants, as well as a fanciful array of flower beds. A spacious barn, allegedly serving for the stocking of inferior corn and superior hemp, sat on top of a secret subterranean laboratory. Whatever Theo did with the corn remained his secret. Presumably, he sold it to some illegal local stills. The experiments carried out in the laboratory essentially served the one and only purpose to grow genetically manipulated hemp that yielded greater quantities of premium cannabis more resistant to fungi, vermin, and all sorts of exotic plant diseases. Consequently, the organically "clean" marihuana produced on the Hacienda enjoyed an excellent reputation far beyond the Dominica mountain ranges, but wasn't exactly a bargain, either. Whenever he went abroad, Theo placed his impressively furnished white bungalow with its red and violet Bougainvillea twines at the disposal of Solitaire and her friends.

Theo did go abroad a lot, mixing work with pleasure in an coolly remunerative manner. Ever since he had made the acquaintance of a Jamaican single mother of a five-year-old boy, he regularly took to the air in his single-engine Piper plane and left his estate vacant for many weeks of the year. "Vacant", that is, only if you discounted the unobtrusive laboratory staff and the regular if noisy passage of Indonesian cleaning ladies.

His financial commitment in the production and distribution of drugs had naturally led to Theo's bumping into Solitaire one day. By way of compensation for his generous hospitality, Solitaire brought her influence to bear so that her frequent host wasn't unduly bothered by emissaries of the local law. One good turn... It was Theo, too, Laura learned from the Doc, who had taught Solitaire some basic German. The few samples Solitaire had presented Laura sounded rather funny to her, since it had residual overtones of the characteristic Berlin dialect, a crude German equivalent of the City of London's Bow Bell cockney, so to speak.

"Every time Theo takes his plane to Jamaica," Solitaire had told her, "he packs some big soft toys for Brigitte's, his lover's son, that is. He always has one of those bright pink things sitting next to him in the passenger seat. I guess the flight pilots in the tower of Kingston airport must be wetting themselves every time they have to clear runway one for landing and watch Kermit, Gonzo, or Miss Piggy watch over the touchdown. It's one of two strategic crook's options, really. Either you do your damnedest to keep your doings under the blanket, or you make it so obvious as to render it ridiculously unbelievable. In his case, it's the latter. And it seems to work, since, as yet, nobody has ever wondered why it is that Theo's 'passengers' always book return flights. I guess Brigitte's son must be crying his eyes out each time his sporadic acquaintance with selected Muppet friends is curtailed again inexplicably. How is he to know that on their return to Dominica, the plush toys are stuffed with crystal meth and other drugs, which Theo buys wholesale on the Jamaican black market and retails here with a little kickback."

After breakfast, Laura took a leisurely walk through Theo's lush Garden of Eden. She was wearing Solitaire's tiger-head buckle in exchange for a portion of her violet nail polish, which Solitaire had found irresistible. The tiger's head would not normally have been Laura's first choice, but Solitaire had insisted that Laura take some accessory of hers in return for the polish. Faced with the alternative of, either, inadvertently shooting her toes off with Solitaire's hair-triggered Ruger Redhawk '44, or else putting on the much less risky tiger's head, Laura had opted for the picturesque buckle.

Most of Theo's plants had been set so as to surround a small pond, itself almost completely covered by a particularly beautiful species of waterlilies with white blossoms. Dark red and yellow heliconia, orchids in all colours of the rainbow, and "rattlesnake" calathea were all radiant with enchanting aromas tempting the visitor's olfactory senses.

Laura found a place in the shadow of a breadfruit tree standing on a small grassy bluff and sat down, leaning her back against the prickly trunk. The bluff offered a wonderful cascaded view over the colourful flowery splendour of the background panoply of the cobalt blue waters of the Caribbean. Somewhere between the pond and the horizon, the circular island of Marie Galante rose out of the ocean like a big anniversary cake with but one candle on a blue-and-white tablecloth.

Laura pulled out a package of neatly folded papers from her right hip pocket. It was the translations of Penelope's letters she had received at English Harbour, but had not yet had the time to peruse. In the wake of the turbulent events of the last few days, she had almost forgotten them, but had come across the package again as she was sorting out her luggage anew this morning at Theo's.

The translations were printed in a PDF format, small font, narrowly spaced lines, hard to read. All had been provided with dates, so that Laura could proceed chronologically if she so wished. As far as she could see, two whole decades had elapsed between the first and the most recent of the letters. Laura regretted not having so much as a smattering of Greek so she could have appreciated the flavour of the original. As reliable as the translations might well be, they would probably represent but a poor rendering of Penelope's very personal style and frame of mind.

In his cover letter, the responsible translator pointed out by way of a proviso that Penelope's Greek was that of the so-called Laz, ethnic Greeks who used to live along the Black Sea coast of Turkey. Their dialect was "corrupted" by Caucasian languages such as Georgian, which made it difficult to understand even for mainland Greeks. Hence, the translator could not and would not guarantee the detailed accuracy of his rendering but offered his work as the best he was able to do.

The letters were all addressed to Robert. The earlier ones bore the stamp of hectic disorder, the kind of grasshopper reasoning that Laura herself funnily enough had frequently been reprimanded for as a student. To all appearances, their female author wrote under great mental stress and time pressure. Nor could she avoid the obvious paradox of necessary repetitions and confusing interjections: had I had more time, I would have written you a shorter letter, Laura quoted her German teacher and smiled at the reminiscence. Some parts of the information clearly depended on the recipient's knowledge of the relevant context and were at best a matter of conjecture without it. Laura's only way to fill the gaps was by resorting to guesswork. Some of the shorter, truncated sentences and questions resembled desperate cries for help from the dark and dreary depths of a dungeon.

In the beginning, Penelope's most important message appeared to be an unrequited confirmation of her never-ending love for Robert. She wanted him to know that she had not followed Suleiman of her own free will, but had been forced to go to Turkey with him. Time and time again, she begged for information about her daughters and implored Robert to do everything in his power to find them and fend for them. A large, seemingly inordinate portion of her earlier letters was taken up by detailed descriptions of her immediate surroundings, as if she did not know exactly where she was and wanted to give as many clues as possible to facilitate and direct Robert's search for her. It was only later that she learned she had been taken to a place near Lake Van, in a remote, formerly Armenian-dominated part of Anatolia. Apparently, it offered an impressive view of Mount Ararat, on whose peak Noah's arch is believed to have touched down once the waters of the Great Flood had receded. Life there was full of hardships for her, an affliction of truly tragic dimensions, starting with the physical humiliations at the hands of the Sultan and, worse, always coming back to the psychological distress caused by the loss of her two children.

Laura's special attention was caught by a somewhat longer letter of this turbulent initial period of her plight. In it, Penelope described the Istanbul accident that Laura had already heard about from the Doc, and its consequences for Penelope and the baby girls. The letter's style was still a little awkward, but became more eloquent in the process.

The man on the helm of the boat had no luck, she wrote. He was catapulted out and probably broke his neck when he crashed down on the surface of the sea. The girls and I were flung into the water as well. Fortunately, they had put a lifejacket on me and so I was able, after a brief moment's shock and bewilderment, to pick up my floating babies and stay on the surface with them in my arms. But that would not have lasted long. The Marmara Sea was calm and warm enough alright, but the current was strong and would have carried the three of us away from the ship and washed us up the Bursa coast as floaters weeks later.

On board the cargo ship whose anchor chain our motorboat had hit, somebody must have heard the noise of the collision and felt the shock. A man came on deck and called out to me. I did not understand him. He must have seen the sinking motorboat and put two and two together. He threw us a lifebelt and then he lowered a small boat into the water. With that, he fished us out of the sea and took us aboard. I was unhurt, but totally confused. Eleni had a gushing wound at her left thigh, which was bleeding profusely. The man - he presented himself later as a Captain Boris Trigorin from Rostov - managed to stop the bleeding and disinfect and sew up the wound provisionally. Of course, Eleni cried as if she was being roasted on a spit, poor little bleeder.

The way in which he handled this and bandaged her afterwards made me think that he must have had some basic medical knowledge. He told me later that he had started studying medicine at Rostov university before deciding to go to sea, not least because of the financial predicaments that would keep on pestering him his whole life, he said.

Irini had been hit worse than Eleni. Her left arm was swollen and quickly turned a reddish blue. The captain said it had been broken several times and could not be properly taken care of with his primitive means on board the ship. She had to be hospitalized. I was afraid Suleiman would turn the whole of Istanbul inside out to find us and would most probably succeed too. As soon as he heard of the accident, he would be looking in the hospitals first, as a matter of course. That's why I asked the captain to do whatever he could in order to save Irini's arm.

Since broken limbs seem to belong to the more frequent medical emergencies aboard ships, the "Black Sea Rover" fortunately had everything necessary in her first-aid kit to set and plaster Irini's arm, at least. The captain said, though, that he could not guarantee that the arm would heal normally. Irini risked having it be broken again in a controlled manner, so that it could be reset properly once her skeleton had completely developed.
I asked Trigorin to be allowed to stay on board his ship for the time being. He said he had no problem with that, except that his next port of call was Odessa, on the Crimean Peninsula. I said I didn't mind, as long as I was as far enough away as possible from Istanbul and Suleiman.

When the rest of the small crew had come back aboard in the evening, the Rover weighed anchor and sailed up the Bosporus into the Black Sea. She was a tramp ship flying a Panamanian flag, the captain told me. He was the Rover's owner, too, always on the look-out for cargo of any kind. No matter what, provided it paid enough to keep the ship going. Istanbul had apparently proved a disappointment in that respect.

Trigorin was very considerate and generous at first. He placed his captain's cabin at my undivided disposal and kept his uncouth crew away from me and the baby girls. But the ship stank of diesel fuel, oil, cabbage, and worse. There were layers of dirt everywhere, vermin and rats living off the greasy galley rubbish. Trigorin asked me all sorts of questions. Where did I come from? Who was chasing after me? Did I know anyone in Odessa? Was there anybody he could contact on my behalf? Why he asked me all those questions, I only came to understand much later.

Somewhere in the Black Sea, a gale caught up with the ship and nearly finished me off. I got so seasick, I lay in my bunk and wished I could simply die. I would never have believed that seasickness can make you suffer like that. The babies didn't mind.

They probably felt they were back where they had come from, floating around in my womb. But their crying in general was nevertheless becoming unnerving, since I could hardly leave the cabin, which reeked of cheap vodka, for any length of time.
When we finally arrived in Odessa and the Rover had dropped anchor, I wanted to go ashore with the girls right away. I was sure that I could find my way west, somehow. But Trigorin would not have it. He said that if I was stopped without papers in the harbour area, I would be arrested and interrogated. In that case, he too would be in big trouble. The Rover would be staying at her present Odessa anchorage until he had found payload of sorts. He could probably procure some false ID for me, but that would take a few days.

He took some shots of me and the girls, allegedly to be used to produce false passports. I believed him and kept patient. The girls' healing process was advancing alright, but some more rest would be good for them, anyway. Eleni was likely to retain a rather big s-shaped scar on her left thigh. As for Irini, she could hardly move her arm. On top of that, the Rover had dropped anchor at about the same distance from the shore as it had done off Istanbul. Hence, even if I had wanted to escape, I could not get off the ship without a boat.

Some time later, I woke one morning and could not find Eleni. At first, I thought she had crawled out of bed and somehow left the cabin. But what with her wound, that was practically impossible. Someone must have taken her from me. But why? I was about to lose my mind under the mental stress of it all. Had it not been for Irini, lying next to me crying, I think I would have ended my days then and there.

Much, much later, I learned from Suleiman that the devious bastard Trigorin had soon understood what window of opportunity had opened for him when picking us up from the sea. He had realized right away that someone was after me. That's why, upon our arrival in Odessa, he leaked information about us, the girls and myself, making it clear that we were available to be exchanged for some reasonable consideration.

When his announcements had not produced any results for a
week or so, he changed his strategy. What if the person pursuing
me had lost interest, he must have thought. Or worse, was even
quite happy with this state of affairs and not eager in the least
to get me, us, back? So, Trigorin had to find alternative ways of
turning us into cash – and that's where the girls came in.
Trafficking in human beings, including illegal adoption, used to
be rampant in Eastern Europe at the time, not least in the Ukraine
as a bridge between east and west. That's what Trigorin pinned
his hopes on. Rightly so, as it turned out. Soon enough, he found
a Russian couple unable to have children of their own and so
much more open to alternative forms of acquiring offspring.
They had come to the Ukraine to find a girl of the ‚appropriate‘
age who might be available for an unbureaucratic adoption. The
normal official procedure would have taken them months, if not
years, and even then, they would have had no guarantee of being accepted, or so they feared. When they ran into Trigorin, he
showed them the photos and they chose Eleni like an item from
a mail-order catalogue.

This deal alone brought Trigorin more money than he could
ever have made with any sort of cargo, drugs being an obvious
exception, but also a much bigger risk.

I had no idea of any of this going on at the time and was simply devastated. With hindsight, Irini and I had actually even been
very lucky in the days following Eleni's disappearance. Trigorin
did not find any further adoption candidates, because most cou-
ples prefer boys to girls. And then, finally, both the Suleiman and
you had got wind of my presence aboard and arrived in Odessa
almost at the same time, by a strange coincidence.

Suleiman told me that the Ukrainians had detained him at the
airport for half a day because of some banal formality, a missing visa, I don't know. Else, he would have arrived hours before
you and the shoot-out between you and the Sultan's men would
never have happened. If Suleiman's arrival on the scene had any
good at all, it was his killing of Trigorin. I couldn't feel sorry for
the man, he deserved to die. Unfortunately, the Turk got hold of

me again first, took me off the ship and jostled me across the border back to this Anatolian lair. Hopefully, you managed to save Irini from him, even though you appear to have been shot, my valiant prince. If so, I have no doubt you will take care of our single remaining daughter, for as long as one of you is alive, my heart. Whether I shall ever see either you or her again is in the hands of God and the Mother of Christ, to whom I keep praying with all my might day and night in this country of heathens and barbarians. Not even an icon of the Panaghia have they given me, these faithless brutes. What remains is the memory of you and the two girls. The can never take that away from me."

Slowly, mechanically, like a robot only seconds away from power failure, Laura let the sheet of paper drop on the grass. What unfathomable drama! With what force and passion Robert and Suleiman had fought for "their" Penelope, who had paid such a high price for something not in her control. A price to be paid by herself and the twin girls, Eleni and Irini, who had become the pawns in this fierce, never-ending duel.

Eleni and Irini. She mouthed the names, as if half expecting them to appear before her thanks to some weird voodoo formula. A sudden ebullient emotion of bottomless sadness and unappeasable yearning surging up in her squeezed her heart with such force that tears were streaming down her cheeks and she tasted the blood of her chewed-up lips on her tongue.

She felt like Spanish director Alejandro Amenábar's single mother protagonist living with her two small children in a big, haunted house on a run-down estate somewhere out in the open countryside. Having vainly chased after the spectres that her children keep claiming to be meeting with regularly, she finally realizes that they, herself and her kids, are none other than the evasive "others", whereas the obtrusive "ghosts" are in fact the present flesh-and-blood owners of the estate.

In the Caribbean, too, reality and fiction were inextricably intertwined. Laura had been able to withstand the Doc's shocking revelations of these past days only because there had been this last refuge, this last-ditch rampart of reason and guarantor of normality called Frederike, whose memory helped Laura ward off the onslaught of generalized insanity. Now, Penelope's letters had brought this last firewall tumbling down, too. The picture of her mother she had kept in her heart had proved yet another a devastating illusion. Laura was the ghost, the only one, or so it seemed, who had no idea of according to what rules this game was to be played.

What had become of Eleni, whether she lived or had long since passed on, was something the letters would not disclose. Who and where Irini was at, Laura now knew only too well.

3. The Black Queen

"Speech, what speech? Oh, that speech. Glad you liked it." Rather embarrassed about the unexpected compliment, Laura felt she had to come clean and give the true author his due.
"Quite honestly, all I had to do was adjust the speech held by the reverend who administered my father's burial, to what little I know about Ti Martin. It's not something I should take credit for."
They were on their way to the Carib reservation. A good thing it had not grown dark yet, Laura thought. The narrow, constantly winding, abruptly rising and brusquely dropping rollercoaster road abounded with hair-raising hot spots and blind bends difficult enough to negotiate in broad daylight. Solitaire and Laura drove ahead in the first jeep, while the Doc und Ignace, less familiar with the island's funfair topography, brought up the rear in the second car. When Laura had broached the subject of gifts for their hosts' kids shortly before leaving the Hacienda, the only thing Solitaire had come up with were Theo's Muppet dolls. Fortunately, the Doc had remembered to remove the dope first, so that the Carib offspring would not mistake crystal meth for candy and help themselves to a mouthful.

Ti Martin's burial over and done with, it was a good thing they could profit from their visit to turn the page, as it were. Ever since their arrival on Dominica, his corpse had been an eerie presence in one of Theo's freezers in the basement of the Hacienda. In the course of this morning, their third on the island, Ignace and the Doc had dressed the dear departed in his white suit and dug a grave on a small hill overlooking the sea and some of the neighbouring islands.

"Ti Moun's gonna like it," Solitaire had commented approvingly and brushed aside Laura's scruples with her usual aplomb.

"I don't care what you people do in Germany. In these parts, you bury your next of kin when and where they drop dead, well, more or less - in your basement, under the lawn, in a flower bed, nobody gives a hoot. Theo shocked? You haven't met the man. Let me tell you, it takes more than an unexpected fresh tomb on boot hill to rock or shock someone like Theo. Surprised, maybe. It was none other than Theo, if I remember right, who once claimed that the history of these islands was not written with pen and paper but with machete and shovel. It's not as if we had dug a mass grave during his absence. Aesthetically speaking, I see it as a perfectly compatible addition to his estate. If he really objects, why, he's free to resurrect Ti Moun and pick another spot or consign him to the sea."

When they had lowered Ti Martin's mortal shell into the shallow grave, Laura had delivered her little borrowed speech, which Solitaire claimed had almost moved her to tears. Trying to remember the most salient points of the reverend's speech derived from some chapter of the Gospel according to St. John's, who else, Laura had experienced vivid flashbacks of Robert's burial. It seemed far enough in the past already so as to appear perfectly unreal. Even though she had followed the ceremony but through a veil of tears and behind a curtain of deafening silence at the time, the echo of the reverend's voice still lingered on like the persistent earworm of some inappropriate nursery-rhyme.

When Laura had finished, they all had taken a handful of soil and thrown it on Ti Martin's white suit. "It will never come out again," Laura had suddenly recalled Frederike's afflicted mother's cry, with which she would shame Laura whenever she came home dirty from a fall or a fight. For a second or two, Laura had felt seriously tempted to chuck Penelope's letters into the grave as well, as if to leave Ti Martin with some reading matter to while away eternity. But then she had decided to keep the letters, though not to share their contents with anyone. To begin with, she could not be sure they had been translated entirely correctly. But even if they had, they were nobody's business but her own. Chances were, no-one would be sufficiently interested, anyway.

Ignace had tried his hand at carving a rough crucifix and burnt both Ti Martin's name, his approximate dates of birth and unfortunate date of decease with the inscription "RIP" into its soft wood with the red-hot tip of his combat knife's blade. Probably not the kind of treatment he would frequently give to his own victims, Laura thought.

"I hadn't believed Ignace capable of such delicate feelings, such almost artistic aspirations," Laura said as an afterthought, half talking to herself.

"Why not? Just because he's a bit of an aesthetic mess himself? He didn't do his own modelling, ya know."

Laura bit her lips in anger, realizing she had been stupid enough to hand out something of a gauche compliment which had backlashed at her like the smarting whip of a willow wicker. How could she forget Solitaire's sensibility when it came to anything hinting at a lack of respect vis-a-vis Ignace, if only from afar? The fact that Solitaire herself called him all sorts of names was her exclusive privilege and an expression of her very personal way of dealing with the chabin's disfigurements. Ignace had come to understand and condone this, it would seem. In the course of the rough times they shared as partners in war and peace, they had developed their very intimate code of conduct and communication that was strictly off limits to outsiders.

"Did you and Ignace ever… I mean, was there ever anything more than…"

If she was to be honest with herself, the delicate question had been nagging Laura for so long now that, inevitably, the moment would come when it could not be held back any more, come what may. Much as she would have liked to, Laura couldn't hurriedly push it back into the bottle. Solitaire was too smart a woman not have felt it coming. She didn't reply for a while. Then she had apparently decided to meet this unrequited intrusion into her most private sphere with the condescending derision it deserved. She came up with another one of her bursts of mirthless laughter.

"You mean did we have sex? Before or after his close encounter with the manchineel tree?"

Laura gave an inaudible sigh of relief. Solitaire had not visibly taken offence at her manifest lack of discretion and even seemed ready to open the door to her soul just a crack. Laura had better profit from the occasion and slide her big toe in.

"No, no, I'm sorry, I mean, generally speaking, you know, no offence."

"None taken, though I fail to see what's it to you. But if you're dying to know, we are more like brother and sister. Which, incidentally, sometimes goes deeper than occasional sex, feel me? You got any brothers or sisters yourself? No? Well, he risked that mauled and messed-up skin of his often enough to save mine, and vice versa. I'm sure we'd both be happy to catch any bullet carrying the other's name on it. That's the stuff we're both us made of, not much you can do about it."

Laura was impressed. Chances were, Solitaire had just told her more about herself than she had ever done to anyone but Ignace, not counting that mysterious Black Queen of hers.

"How did you ever get to know each other?"

"What's this going to be, an official inquest? In our circles, asking personal questions is a taboo, big time, get it? Neither particularly smart nor very healthy, in fact. Most of us carry all sorts of scars under our steel armour. Look at your own father. Nobody is prepared to reveal more about themselves than absolutely necessary, lest it renders them even more vulnerable than they are, anyway. It might be used against them later. All of us have their skeletons in the closet, some more than others. Depending on who you come across, this kind of questioning of yours can cost you dearly, one day."

After that little speech of hers, Solitaire fell silent again. Laura thought the subject had thus been discarded for good. She had relied on her female intuition which said that women weren't made to withhold their most intimate secrets from fellow females for any length of time. But that was a preliminary conclusion distilled from a relatively small and entirely random sample. Still, she was convinced that, somewhere underneath that ruthless amazon image Solitaire presented to the outside world, there must be woman secretly yearning for a female confidante. Not necessarily another bird of a feather, but rather one of Laura's calibre, less streetwise but more emphatic and with superior social skills.

"At the Black Queen's place," Solitaire picked up Laura's question.

"I even suspected her of acting the matchmaker. But her motivation proved a different one. She had probably realized immediately that a mentally crippled humanoid such as myself would need a guardian angel of exceptional prowess to allow me to make thirty, at least. And the one she pulled out of her hat was an excellent choice, in fact, the best one available on the market at the time. Much later I learned Ignace had a reason to be on Dominica. Seems he had a baby boy with a young Garfuna woman who died only months later. What happened to their child, he would never tell, not even me. Can be very stubborn, my Chewy."

"And very rash. He nearly killed me."

"Yes, as you never tire to relate. Listen, had he seriously given that course of action a thought, he would have ended your days then and there. But you're right in a way, he's not squeamish, doesn't spare women or children, if need be. You were lucky he saw that little something in you that he thought worth preserving. Whatever that was."

"You know, I never understood why he had stayed on the boat at all when I arrived. As it seems, he had already moved the heroin. Why did you use the Yellow Dancer for your smuggling purposes in the first place?"

"Wow! You just won't let it go, will you? Like a Doberman bitch getting her teeth in somebody's shanks. Alright, you have one more for free. After that, no more questions, deal??

"Deal."

"The Greek job had been your father's call, a fact we weren't aware of. As loquacious as the Doc may seem at times, he never breathes a word about his clientele. Wouldn't work otherwise."

"Still, why the Yellow Dancer?"

"Like the surgeon said to the patient waking from his anaesthesia prematurely: just a sec, I was just about to fill you in. I had taken the dope to Chios in the motorboat, where Ignace and some other guys were waiting for me. From Chios, we took it to the Turkish border, because the food aid ship had left during the storm that had nailed us to the spot. On the Turkish coast, a Gület, one of those tourist boats, fetched the eighty kilos and took them to Marmaris. Our twenty kilos had to be shipped here somehow. On the island of Rhodes, we found a suitable cargo ship, with St. Lucia as her next port of call. The captain took us on board no questions asked. He liked the colour of our presidents." Solitaire was checking her freshly dyed "corns" with her right hand. Laura noticed that she had used Laura's nail polish, too. This female didn't just have a soft spot, this iron lady was on the warpath, would you believe it now! Laura couldn't wait to see which death-defying male was ready to shove his head between this tiger's fangs.

"The Doc came to fetch us at Castries, on St. Lucia, with the Yellow Dancer. She was an obvious choice because she used to stand vacant for long periods of the year and belonged to our principal, as far as this job was concerned. The Doc had sailed her there with Ti Martin, to take us aboard with the smack. We didn't even take the trouble of re-packing the heroin or hiding it in the crooks and nannies of the Yellow Dancer."

"Isn't that nooks and crannies, rather?" Laura threw in.

"Whatever. If some DEA guys had stopped us, their dogs

would have sniffed the heroin, sure thing. You can't hide much from a dog. But nobody showed any interest in us. Why would they? Drug-trafficking follows certain logical routes. Some of those lead from the Caribbean to the US or Europe, none in the other direction. Like carrying coals to Liverpool, see."

"Newcastle, I think."

"Whatever. So, we parked the yacht in the Blue Lagoon, where Ignace was to transfer the whole lot into the dinghy and take it to the Pas de Deux, waiting offshore. A somewhat delicate operation. With every shift of the merchandise you obviously increase the risk of discovery."

"But why was he still aboard instead of beating it, fast?"

"Well, believe it or not, I asked him that very goddamn question myself. He told me he had already had one foot in the dinghy, ready to push off and disappear, when he had heard one of the wooden logs of the frigging jetty squeak and crack. Following his instincts, as always, he had climbed back down the companionway and lurked in the dark. He wanted to see whether the Yellow Dancer was going to be visited by someone he had better take out there and then. Was someone on our heels? That's why he was hiding in galley when you came step-dancing down the companionway."

Laura smiled grimly. "Step-dancing" didn't quite cut it. Her coccyx still hurt. So those had been the beatings of the butterfly's wings. Laura remembered that one of the wooden logs had indeed broken under her foot, almost causing her to fall into the marina basin. She had managed to regain her balance - at the price of having her entire life coming to bits.

"Why don't you dim your headlights, you ugly one-eyed scarecrow! Dip'em or I'll rip'em.."

Angrily, Solitaire knocked against the jeep's interior mirror. The Doc tried to follow Solitaire's car closely, but every now and then stayed behind at a difficult junction and switched on his headlights to get his bearings again.

"Where's the party going to take place?" Laura asked.

"At Crayfish River."

"In the reservation?"

"No, Manhattan South. Where else but in the reservation? The Black Queen practically never leaves it. Her arthritic hips are giving her enough of a problem as it is, and there's no need. Whatever happens on the island, she'll be among the first to hear about it. So why sweat it? A great honour to be received by her. Not everyone gets that opportunity."

"No, I'm sure they don't. My own white queen was called Frederike," Laura heard herself say with some disbelief. Maybe she had spoken more to herself again than to Solitaire. Or maybe she had fallen into the same trap that had snared Solitaire. Either way, Solitaire would listen to her with one ear only, Laura was convinced, and certainly never use any confidentialities against her. That wouldn't be like her.

"Frederike, eh? How did you like her then? Was she as spinsterish as her Teutonic name?"

"She had Danish ancestors. Up there in the north, women are given strange names alright. However, my uncrowned queen was not much of a spinster. Strict but cunning and full of love and tenderness. Unrelenting but forgiving, full of the contradictory qualities that characterize our sex, according to men. An artistic soul, you might say, minus the eccentricity. That's a great misunderstanding, anyway."

"What is?"

"Artists being gifted eccentrics. That may exist, for all I know. But Frederike's example convinced me that art is ten percent talent and ninety percent hard work and iron discipline. She could draw remarkably well. Colours weren't her thing, though. Funny. Somehow, she seemed to see the world in black and white, like dogs or the early photographers. Up in our attic, she kept a dozen or so water-colour and oil rejects. They looked somehow off and badly disorganised, feel me?"

Solitaire smiled in the dark.

"Disorganised?"

"Yes. Paintings follow certain basic structures, with the two diagonal lines being all-important. And the centre, of course, where the diagonals meet. With a bit of practice, you can dissect any painting with an initial 'Y'-cut, almost like a corpse in the morgue."

"No shit?"

"No shit. But her drawings were excellent. She had a keen eye for detail, contours, profiles, things like that. In the evening, she'd sit down and draw the faces of some of the people she had met or seen during the day. Like musicians forever practising their fingerings so as not to lose their automatic reflexes. For her, it was a way of coming down and processing her impressions, I guess. I don't know how often she drew me, in fact. I found a whole box of sketches and drawings of me at different ages. Strange experience. Some of her drawings were published in magazines and newspapers. She would have made a great cartoonist, provided she teamed up with someone to colour her drawings. Her first book was to appear only weeks after her damning diagnosis, mammary cancer."

"I thought that was curable, these days."

"It is, these days. If you discover it before it has time to sow its offspring. At the time, therapy wasn't what it is today. And even nowadays, some women die, young ones, too."

"Wasn't she sad not to be able to see her daughter grow up?" She certainly would have been, had I really been her daughter, Laura thought.

"She didn't show it. She always exercised a lot of self-control, see. Never just blew her top like some people I got to know recently. I can't remember her ever shouting at me, let alone hit me, as much as I must have provoked her at times. Whenever she took issue with what you did or said or felt downright hurt, instead of turning against you, she would retreat into herself, kind of. That was worse than shouting at me or slapping me about, I found."

"Her death must have been a hard blow for you, then."

"It was, yes. Much as if she had been my biological mother, after all."

The truth was out. Solitaire had her right hand at the mirror again.

"I'll tell you. Just let me lay my hands on that Frenchman blinding me again, I won't be retreating into myself but… What was that you just said? As if she had been your…? What the hell do you mean, I don't follow?"

Laura started crying again despite herself. She hoped Solitaire wouldn't notice in the dark. Trouble was, of course, that this woman's life depended on her never missing anything around her. When she spoke, it was with an unusually soft, almost soothing voice.

"Listen. We have another twenty minutes or so to the reservation. Want to tell me about it? Don't have to, though, your call." She took off her bandana and handed it to the sobbing Laura, who nodded and wiped her face with the headband, which absorbed both her tears, snot, and a major part of her make-up. Then Laura started giving Solitaire a short account of what she had learned from Penelope's letters.

"Holy cow!" Solitaire exclaimed when Laura had ended.

"I don't know what to say, for once. A nice piece of work, your father. I'm not surprised this Sultan sticks to us like a fu… leech to a bare behind."

She took her right hand off the wheel, turned the mirror sideways to see what was going on behind them. Drawing her hand back onto the wheel, she ever so slightly touched Laura's thigh, as if by accident. A tiny gesture, hardly noticeable, but born out of empathy. Had it come from someone else, Laura would probably not even have noticed, certainly not have attributed any significance to it. But for this hard, unforgiving woman to bring herself to this small sign of compassion was very moving in turn. "Let me see whether I got this right. You are one of two daughters of Penelope's, who calls herself the Yellow Dancer. Ti Martin's killer apparently knew this. Now, he's inviting us to join him at her place, wherever that is. Sounds very much like the frigging Sultan to me, don't it? The inevitable Turk must have tracked your mother down by following either you or the yacht."

"Or both."

"Or both. And counts on us to find her too, before long. She is the linchpin in this whole charade."

Laura sneezed again into Solitaire's bandana.

"You're going to wash that thing before giving it back, aren't you?" Solitaire asked her.

The two women laughed. Solitaire leaned over to Laura's side and opened the glove compartment with her right hand, never taking her eyes off the road. After rummaging a little, she pulled out a neatly rolled joint, closed the compartment and lit the 420, striking the match with one hand. Then she took a few deep drags and passed Laura the smoking gun.

"Have some loco weed, you look like you need it. It's quality stuff, no bammer, Theo's own production. He always keeps some spares in the glove compartment, just in case."

Laura hesitated. She couldn't even remember when she had smoked her last joint and was afraid it might be a less than pleasant experience. But then she accepted it and inhaled the smoke a few times until her head slowly started reeling.

It was good stuff, though. She didn't feel sick but rather light, weightless in space. She handed the joint back.

"Honestly, I would rather keep your bandana, if I may. It's part of the great Solitaire legend."

"What else? My fucking buckle you already have. Now my bandana, tomorrow my string. You need close watching, Laura Forster. One day you'll wake up and address your mirror image as Solitaire."

"That would take more than just a few pieces of clothing. And have no fear, your string is not at risk. But if, one of these days, you could braid such cornrows for me as you wear them, I'd appreciate that no end. I tried to do it myself, but mine won't last long."

"Yes, I noticed. No problem. Was that it? Or maybe some manicure to go with it, a peeling or massage, anything? Don't hesitate, now that we are at it. But tell me one thing, Laura Forster. What do I get in return? What's my consideration?"

Laura reflected for a moment.

"Alright, you get to read the letters."

"Seriously? But those are highly personal shit, for your eyes only, so to speak."

"I don't mind. You don't have to, if you don't want to. Besides, I forgot, can you…"

"Read? No, I just follow the pictures."

"Rubbish. Read German, I mean."

"If it's printed German, yes, most of it, anyway. Theo saw to that. Handwriting in a foreign language is always a bitch, I find. Laura Forster, I am almost touched, you have warmed the cockles of my heart, as the sodding Irish say. Five or six months from now, and I might feel something close to sympathy for ya, if I'm not careful."

"Remind me about the letters when we get back to the hacienda."

"You can rely on that."

They were close to the reservation now. Laura opened her window. The moisture of the rain forest crept into the jeep's interior and wrapped her in a fine thin veil of cooling humidity. After the bleak sparseness of Antigua and the apocalyptic charms of Montserrat, Laura enjoyed the lush vegetation of Dominica with its hundred shades of green during the day and its nightly concert of myriads of noisy creatures of the dark. The flashes of the jeep's headlights were thrown back at them by the gleaming thickets and made the forbidding impenetrability of the forest even more dismissive. Here and there, they passed by small plantations with banana stalks whose tops had been wrapped into blue plastic bags like the heads of so many Mexican gang victims to retain the moisture and make the plants grow faster.

"Chiquitiquitá," Solitaire half said and half sung, in an uncommonly relaxed mood. You don't fool me, Laura thought, I recognize a rampant squaw on the warpath when I get to see one.

Laura wasn't sure exactly what she had expected. When they arrived at Crayfish River, the settlement at first sight did not differ dramatically from all the others she had seen so far on Dominica. Maybe the huts looked just that little bit more paltry. The chief, his wife, sons and daughters as well as the village folks at large awaited their visitors in front of the Carbet, a large wooden structure painted light green. It was the Caribs', or Calinagos' substitute for a town hall cum conference centre, where festivities of any kind used to be held. The welcome was hearty, as between distant relatives who hadn't met for a long time. Solitaire was in the centre of it all and was embraced warmly by the women and children like one of their tribe. Laura stood out like a sore thumb at first, but was soon accepted into the ring of boisterous friendliness. Communication wasn't all that easy since, to Laura, the Carib's guttural English truly sounded like the cooing of pigeons on the Hamburg town-hall gargoyles.

The chief asked the guests into the building, but the Doc held both Laura and Ignace back. Obviously, he wanted to give Solitaire a chance to be alone with the Black Queen for a short while. Laura smiled. You could count on the Doc's polite discretion and refined delicacy.

When Solitaire had disappeared into the Carbet, the Doc embarked on a conversation with the chief and his son. Their subject was Alberto, the approaching first hurricane of the season. As yet, it was spinning on its axis out there, in mid-Atlantic, gathering strength and flexing its muscles. Its precise trajectory and landing spot were anybody's guess. Laura was astonished to hear the men talking of the cyclone in the terms of a capricious human being, bestowed with a will of its own and a good portion of mischievous aforethought into the bargain.

"That's right," the Doc replied, when Laura asked him about it.

"Their incalculability accounts for a large part of the danger they represent. Precisely like some humans I happen to know. Sometimes, they seem to be heading for the West Indies, but then veer off and disappear in the Gulf of Mexico. Or they go ashore in Florida, hover above Miami or the Palm Beaches for a while, seem to get bored, turn back into the Atlantic only to come ashore in North Carolina or off Cape May. I remember a German sailing cadet ship in the nineteen-fifties that was sunk by a twister like that off the Azores. The cyclone had already passed, when it stopped dead in its tracks all of a sudden, like a dog that's caught hold of a strange noise or an interesting scent. It effected a neat curve and pounded on the ship. Only a handful of survivors were picked up in extremis days later. Let's hope Dominica will be spared this time. Another destruction of the banana crops would set the population right back to square one, economically speaking."

The difference in wealth between those West Indies islands still on the financial drip-feed of their former colonial masters and those which, like Dominica, were by and large left to their own devices ever since independence, was glaring enough, Laura thought.

"The Dominicans didn't grow bananas to begin with," the Doc continued.

"The chaotic mountainous topography doesn't exactly lend itself to cultivating plantations, or going for agriculture at large, for that matter. Much too jagged, no end of slopes and canyons. So, they'd much prefer to make a living off tourism, if they had an international airport to go with it, like Antigua or Guadeloupe. The lack of it, again, is at least partly due to the topography. Seen from above, the island must look like some corrugated iron roof after a meteorite dropped on it. Theo's muppets could tell you all about that, I guess. Indirectly, the Dominicans depend on the fruit grown by American companies around here. And on the fishing licenses they sell to certain Asian nations, for catching tuna and killing whales.

As for the Caribs, they are situated even a few notches lower on the food chain, in fact. Although their situation on Dominica, their last fall-back position, has dramatically improved more recently. There was a time when they would have been at best tolerated. Considering that they had been literally exterminated like vermin on all the other islands, that was a step in the right direction, I guess. Here, they now have a voice in local government, at long last. Solitaire used to put substantial sums into settlements such as Crayfish River. Dirty money, some would be rash enough to call it, blood money, even. But here it does good work and is appreciated, so what. All a question of perception and perspective. Well, I guess we should follow her in now, shouldn't we?"

Inside the Carbet, the women and older children were occupied preparing the food and laying the table. Laura saw large bowls with fruit and raw vegetables. It smelled of grilled corn cobs, cooked meat and undefinable, probably hot sauces and breadfruit or sweet potato mash. To drink, there was iced water and lemonade, rum, and Caribbean ale, fruity in taste and light on alcohol.

The sight and smell of prepared meat invited the unpleasant association of those gruelling legends of rampant cannibalism raging among the early Caribs. A foul reputation they hadn't been able to shake well into the 20th century, if at all. Nobody had ever presented undeniable proof of it, but seemingly primitive cultures are easy victims of long-lived rumours. Columbus and the sanctimonious Spaniards had been only too happy to exploit the convenient myth for their own purposes, mainly justifying their greedy seizure of territories and ruthless annihilation of the Caribs in the name of Christian humanity.

To the left of the entrance, Laura could make out the figure of Solitaire crouching at the feet of a rather obese black Carib woman with a wide-brimmed straw hat. That must be her, the Black Queen. Laura had not yet seen Solitaire in a position of such demure reverence. If she was prepared to take it, it would have to be interpreted as a clear and unmistakable sign of Solitaire's love and respect for the Black Queen. The old woman had bent her big torso forward as if about to plunge into an invisible pool head first. The brim of her hat was effectively covering her face. She had laid both her hands on the knob of a gnarled stick with knotholes galore. At a distance, it looked like something that had pushed up from the soil while she had been sitting there staring into the void. Laura felt irresistibly drawn toward the intriguing pair huddled in their enchanting intimacy.

Solitaire apparently had eyes at the back of her head too. Somehow, she must have sensed Laura approaching. She stood up, turned and nodded in Laura's direction with a somewhat embarrassed look, as if excusing herself for having been caught in this very private situation. The Black Queen was still looking at the floor. Maybe she was trying hard to read the tribe's future in the beaten dust before her eyes. Or maybe cataracts had taken their toll and she was blind as a bat. Solitaire bent forward and apparently introduced Laura, in a manner of speaking. Doing so, she employed the same Carib dialect in which she communicated with Ignace whenever the two of them went for privacy on a boat that didn't exactly favour any.

Infinitely slowly, like a bronze statue coming to life, the Black Queen raised her head. Laura was startled. She felt like looking at a medieval palimpsest of animal hide that had been written on and scraped clean again a hundred times. The Black Queen's dark leathery face seemed to have chronicled the thousand-year history of her people epoch by epoch. Her uncountable wrinkles were the hieroglyphs of those annals. At her unfathomable age, the old woman with her bloodshot eyes and still fleshy lips, gave Laura the impression of being in the possession of some secret potion which had helped her conquer the even more unrelenting ruler of the universe - Time Himself.

The Black Queen looked at Laura, unseeing. Then she waved at Solitaire to make her approach again and whispered something in her ear. Laura found that impolite and was slightly miffed. You don't have to bother, she thought, I can't understand a word, anyway. Then she saw the Queen discretely handing something to Solitaire that looked like one of the Doc's unsavoury tobacco pouches made of some larger animal's junk, no doubt. Solitaire pocketed the pouch without even looking at it. Obviously, she knew that, whatever it contained, it wasn't bull's balls.

"What did she say?" Laura asked when the Queen had ended. "Cut off Snow White's head?"

"No, she just wanted to know how much time the meat of a middle-aged European white would take to become medium rare on the spit. She hasn't got many teeth of her own left and consequently likes her meat tender and juicy."

The two women laughed and accorded one another a high five.

"You speak Carib that fluently?"

"Not at all. To the extent that it ever existed, the authentic Carib language has been extinct for quite a while, anyway. There are no written documents, nothing to go by. The last generation of teachers has died out. Even the Queen confesses to only a shaky command of it. Present-day Carib is a motley mixture of Creole, English, and Carib words and expressions. These days, I do have to concentrate very hard to understand half of what she's saying. A new set of dentures would help - her articulation, not my hearing."

The old woman imperviously knocked her stick on the floor as if to open a parliamentary session. Solitaire and Laura helped her up on her feet and supported her while she slowly slouched over to the table, where she held a permanent reservation next to the chief. The man could easily have been her grandson. Was, too, maybe. It took a while for her to settle, but that night, no-one seemed much of a hurry.

The banquet lasted an eternity and a half. Laura was familiar with such interminable ceremonies from Southern European occasions. Somewhere in the countryside, a huge table would be laid out under the discretely rustling olive trees. Benches a mile long and uncomfortable to sit on that could have accommodated half the local population, would be placed to the left and right of the tables. One delicate dish after another would be served by a whole platoon of servants, empty plates collected, new plates laid out, the waitresses' quickness of the hand deceiving the eye. First-class red and white wines would flow like small aromatic rivulets and clocks stop ticking. Sure, here in the reservation everything was a notch or two more modest, but the atmosphere of sheer delight, of enjoying each other's company was very much the same, notwithstanding.

Laura had noticed that Solitaire was not sitting next to Ignace but had crowded the chief's son suspiciously. The young man's age was hard to guess. Outdoor labour, sea air, and subtropical sunlight tanned Carib complexion fast and furiously, made these people age before their time. If his muscular body was anything to go by, he could be in his middle twenties, of sympathetic disposition, it would seem, and with open, self-asserted looks. Laura had expected him to be called something colourful like "Red Eagle" or "White Falcon" and was a little disappointed to hear that he answered to the pedestrian name of Jeremy. Still, she clicked her tongue as if appreciating a good wine. If she judged the nature of Solitaire's glances right, and she was rather sure she did, Laura would have thrown in her own thong for once in a bet that there was definitely something steamy going on between the two.

Ignace, on the other hand, was nowhere around. Maybe he had made enemies with someone or other of the Carib population he wasn't eager to meet? But then, why had he come here in the first place? Or perhaps he didn't want to frighten the Carib kids with his phantom's face?

When the banquet was finally over and most of the participants stepped into the open again, daylight had taken its leave from Dominica. Some of the Caribs had already huddled up around the camp fire, whose embers were fanned and swirled about so forcefully by the trade wind that it formed a twister column seemingly reaching the Southern Cross in the star-studded Caribbean sky. Everyone tried to find a place close to the fire, since it promised to become a cool, wet night for once. The Arawak braves must have once gathered like this to listen to the travelling Homers of their time and age who made them relive the forlorn battles of an even more remote and glorious past preceding the first landings of Europeans such as Columbus by entire millennia.

To climb up much higher in the Carib family trees was impossible, though, due to the deplorable lack of material. Uncounted volcano eruptions and earthquakes, it was to be feared, had lastingly destroyed irreplaceable clues. Now it was up to the Caribs, the Galibi and Caringo, to shape traditions of their own which, this time, stood a reasonable chance of getting handed down to future generations, provided there would be any.

"Are there any monasteries or convents at all in the West Indies, religious places run by nuns?"

Laura had addressed herself to the Doc with her question. The Frenchman had been immersed in his own thoughts and reminiscences of César and Ti Martin, no doubt. Laura had chosen not to tell him that she probably was Penelope's daughter. On the other hand, the letters contained other pieces of information that might be of interest and importance for Solitaire, Ignace, and the Doc. One way or another, Laura felt she wasn't entitled to keep such items from them. Among other things, they might lead them to the killer of Ti Martin and instigator of the bloody attack off Antigua. The Doc would be sensible enough to handle such revelations sagaciously before passing them on to the other two, who had a dangerous propensity to act first and think afterwards. Unless she proceeded cautiously, the consequences for all involved could be grave.

"Convents?" the Doc echoed with some obvious surprise.

"I don't see why not. Some islands such as Antigua are particularly religiously inclined, as you can see from the many placenames which rely heavily on the Holy Scriptures. But that is the same naive kind of bigotry you will find in the many states of the US. Each and every one of those who have ‚seen the light' will found a church of their own. ‚Church', mind you, not sect. That word is as much a no go in the States as a fart in the confessionary, beg pardon. Now, whether monasteries and convents will thrive in a climate as hysterically pious as all this, is over my head. Why the question? Have you decided to turn your back on the madding crowd after all and disappear behind convent walls forever?"

Laura had to grin.

"No, just so, out of general interest."

The Doc laughed aloud and shook his index finger at Laura.

"Just so, eh? Laura, no offence, you are a terrible liar. Whatever you do, never stray into politics. I have not known you for long, but long enough, I think, to know that you never say anything ‚just so'. Do me a favour and let me in on your agenda."

"Am I really that predictable? Shame on me. Okay, I had Penelope's letters translated the other day. You know, the letters I found on board the Yellow Dancer. In those of more recent date she keeps writing about her stay with the Holy Ladies. As if Robert had parked her permanently in some convent or other. Which is perfectly possible. After all, he used to transfer a kind of monthly alimony to the Caribbean. Now, if I put two and two together, I get Penelope living on that alimony in a convent some-where on these islands. Maybe he managed to wriggle her out of Suleiman's hands and…"

"Dumped her in a convent? Doesn't sound very much like him, though, does it. What's the precise wording of the letters?"

"With the Holy Ladies, always the same thing. I cannot read the original, of course."

The Doc sat musing for a while.

"Where and by whom were the letters translated?"

"In Hamburg, by a professional."

"What, if we are nevertheless victims of a mistaken render-ing? I don't know any Greek, either. But I know that in most of our European languages, innocent-looking prepositions are the source of astounding differences. At the same time, they are not always as explicit as all that, which places the entire responsibil-ity on the reader's shoulders, as it were. Chances are, modern Greek belongs to those implicit languages that allow speakers of more analytical languages such as German or English a world of options. It all hinges on the specific context, you see."

Laura did not quite get what he was driving at, except that he seemed to be on a promising track.

"Now, someone in Hamburg with a good command of Greek is not necessarily familiar with our Caribbean background, see. That makes him or her susceptible to committing mistakes."

"How? What do you mean?"

"Well, let's assume the preposition used by Penelope could be rendered as both in, at, with, or on, all at once."

"Yes?"

"Now, if I return to your Holy Ladies and translate them into French, I get Les Saintes Femmes, or Les Saintes, for short. That's the name of the small archipelago situated between Dominica and Guadeloupe. We passed it by on our way here from Mont-serrat. If you ask me, I think that's where you'll find Penelope aka the Yellow Dancer, if she is alive. Not with the Holy Ladies but on Les Saintes."

EIGHTH CHAPTER

1. The Hermits Ark

Alberto was approaching with giant strides. According to most meteorological calculations, the hurricane was heading straight for Puerto Rico. The beast was about to calve a nasty southern trough that could hit the islands above the wind in about 48 hours' time, at the latest. The ominously darkening skies should have been sufficient warning for everyone still out at sea to be looking for a safe hole or harbour forthwith. If time didn't allow that or someone felt lucky, they should at least give the Lesser West Indies as wide a berth as possible.

The crew of the good ship Pas de Deux had decided to be on their way to the Saintes archipelago, anyway. To begin with, the tiny archipelago was only a stone's throw away from Dominica. Second, a piece of massive anchor chain of the sort used by big cargo or cruising ships, had more recently been fixed to the bottom of the Bourg roadstead. It rendered the principal town's bay the best hurricane bet of the Saints archipelago, if not the wider Caribbean. The idea was for yachts to have their hooks slide under this heavy contraption anchored at a depth of some twenty feet or so and for their crews to keep their fingers crossed. It might not offer sufficient protection to survive a fully-fledged cyclone that meant business, but for the odd trough or tropical storm it would probably do better than Dominica's wide open Prince Rupert Bay, for instance.

And, last but not least, it was generally felt by Solitaire and her troop of three, well, two and a half, that, if scores were to be settled, this was as good a time as any to go about it. All dice, clean or loaded, appeared to rest in the hands of the Yellow Dancer, residing, as it would seem, on one of the Saintes. Solitaire would not let it rest until Ti Martin's murderer had been hunted down and brought to justice. To deter this irascible female, it would take a bit more than a pussycat trough.

And so, on the day following her crew's memorable encounter with the Black Queen in the Carib reservation, the Pas de Deux was riding at anchor in one of the most ravishing settings of the entire West Indies. Only a few months ago, the Bourg roadstead had literally been teeming with yachts and cruising ships. Which made its present deserted look somewhat creepy - a little as if you hadn't heard the news and were the only person wandering about wondering where everybody had gone, where a nuclear device buried there was to detonate in a matter of hours.

The topography of the archipelago provided not only for a sea- and landscape of breath-taking beauty, but also for a maximum of wind protection, since the place was surrounded by islets on practically all sides.

"What you're looking at right in front of us, is Terre-de-Haut, the horseshoe-like main island with Bourg as its largest and only settlement," the Doc was showing Laura with a swaying movement of his pipe, in a manner that suggested he had arranged all that himself on Laura's behalf only recently.

"To our left, the very small islet of Cabrit, meaning child in I don't remember what language. Behind us, the silhouette of Terre-de-Bas, the second in size of the archipelago. Not to worry, we're perfectly safe in here."

Laura had read that the group of islets with its surprising assembly of forts, ramparts, and fortifications had been selected by the Brits as a potential Gibraltar of the Caribbean. Since the British Navy was intensely busy further up north at the time, fighting the American rebels, they had to provide their smaller West Indian detachments with shore firepower daunting enough to deter the French competition. Hadn't really worked, though. The only battle of the area worth mentioning had taken place off Dominica, hence, way out of reach of the Saintes' canon. And the French defeat had turned out to be a Pyrrhus victory for the Brits, since their naval forces engaged here could not at the same time stop the multiple gaps of the strained English fleet along what was soon to become the eastern seaboard of the US. To have won the minuscule Saintes at the expense of the vast American colonies must have been a hard one for the Sea Lords to sell to Whitehall.

"There is many a would-be Gibraltar to be found in the West Indies," the Doc enlarged with a thin smile of disdain.

"You ought to see the walls of the two San Juan forts on Puerto Rico. They'd resist a major bombardment even nowadays, for quite a while. And yet, they couldn't spare the Spanish the humiliation of having to surrender the place to the new kid on the block."

"Neither here nor anywhere else did such local fortifications obtain any military significance to speak of. In the eternal race between gun smiths and stone masons, fire power is usually two steps ahead of wall girth, mostly due to the inordinate lengths of time it would take to build fortifications of the respective next generation - another example of hedgehog versus hare, you might say, though with inverted result. In war or peace, mobility always beats stability. That's what makes logistics such an invaluable asset. The vacant forts of the Saintes later came to stand in as prisons or quarantine stations. They had to serve some purpose or other if only to justify the forbidding overall expense, I suppose."

Laura was far more preoccupied with the meteorological safety of the place, but obviously did not have enough experience to judge whether the Doc's reassurances were to be taken at face value. The dark looming sky, the low clouds chasing across the horizon, and the violent gusts of wind and rain that had accompanied them on their way north clearly begged to differ, it seemed to her. The trough was a mere spin-off, but a very ambitiously focussed one that expected to be taken every bit as seriously as the hurricane itself.

At the same time, Laura was shifty with restlessness and curiosity. Would she really get a chance to meet with the woman face to face who, according to her letters, had every right to claim biological motherhood over Laura? Who else could have had any knowledge of the true causes of Laura's slight physical "handicap" that seemed to have bugger all to do with a motorbike accident? "Irini", Penelope had called her. As far as Laura knew, that was a favourite Orthodox saint whose name, encountered on every Aegean island at least once, simply meant "peace". Laura felt she could live with that.

But what would they have to say to each other, Penelope and her Irini? Blood being thicker than water was but a cliché whose essential message seemed sufficiently rebutted by the depressing fact that many murders, manslaughters, child abuse cases and all sorts of other abominable crimes were committed in what should have been an utterly protective family context. All things considered, the relationship between Penelope and herself was purely genetic. How much weight would that carry against the perpetual social, physical and mental proximity shared by a child and his or her foster mother? All of that, however, Laura had had with Frederike, whose genes she did not inherit but whose spirit and nature had been the single most important formative influence of Laura's childhood. Seen from that angle, humans weren't all that different from ducklings which, overriding what genetic information they would have received while still in the egg, will always follow the first creature they lay their eyes on upon penetrating its shell.

Maybe it would have been wiser to renounce at such a meeting altogether to avoid mutual disappointment. Time and time again, she had heard of art-sem children, who, later in life, made every effort to track down their biological fathers. What on earth for,, Laura had asked herself plenty of times. All the person in question had contributed was his semen, his genes. Exactly what did those children expect to discover that they had not already found in themselves - a few talents, a host of shortcomings, some virtues as well as heinous vices? Their genes being unable to communicate, chances were two perfect strangers would silently be staring at one another, questioning the ultimate sagacity of a meeting that promised little and yielded less.

Her companions had no part in this. The Doc and Ignace felt it their duty to accompany Solitaire on her campaign and follow the charade through to the bitter end. None of this truly concerned Laura, who was risking her life as much as any one of them, probably more so, given her inexperience in any kind of combat situation. Her one "kill" on Montserrat had been an accident. A further encounter of this kind would probably not have the same lucky ending for Laura. But to leave the three remaining Mohicans to their fate now would amount to treason, she felt. Irrespective of what the others thought about it, she was sure she would never forgive herself.

Solitaire suggested that the Doc and Laura should go ashore and do some cautious prospecting on the Yellow Dancer's whereabouts. This time of year, in the face of the approaching hurricane, they were unlikely to literally stumble over residents of Bourg. Local restaurant owners and shopkeepers had already turned the key weeks before and calmly retreated to Guadeloupe, the US, or France. But the four of them had to start somewhere, and Bourg was the best bid.

The short trip ashore in the dinghy came close to a rodeo ride on a furious bull. As much as the bay was protected against the wind, the Atlantic swell seemed hell-bent on making up for that weakness by visiting every corner of the roadstead. The sea in this kettle of roadstead was already running almost too high for a semi-rigid dinghy such as that of the Pas de Deux. Torrents of rain showered them from above, while bucketful upon bucketful of spray hit them squarely in the face and across the chest, the salt hurting their eyes and stiffening their hair. A good thing the Doc had insisted on the two of them wearing lifejackets.

Having climbed ashore and wiped the salt off her face, Laura was surprised by the prim orderliness of the small town in deep off-season slumber, as it seemed. None of that haphazard assembly of dilapidated shacks and warped cabins they had last sampled on Dominica. None of the chaotic architectural hodgepodge of Pointe-à-Pitre, either. Instead, a soberly structured blueprint settlement of colourful gleaming wet gingerbread houses, many of them made of stone however, with hurricane-proof shutters and hipped roofs made of tiles or screwed-on corrugated iron sheet. The odd garden gnome holding a joint and donning Jamaican headwear would have lent the place some nice Caribbean colour, though, Laura thought.

An immaculately asphalted road led up to the fort in winding serpentine bends. To the right, the same road climbed the much steeper hill crowned by the "donkey". This was a popular scenic lookout so high up in the sky that even the frigate birds had to turn on their sides or even roll on their backs in mid-flight to look at the tourists for once towering high above them.

"The Saintes are strictly speaking too small to make plantations of any kind profitable," the Doc said.

"And where there are no sugar-cane, bananas, or cotton, there's no need for black slaves either. Which is why, to this day, the population of Terre-de-Haut consists almost exclusively of whites, nearly all of them descendants of endangered species: Guadeloupe planters who escaped the guillotine during revolutionary years, emigrants from persecuted European minorities such as Flemings, Normans, Bretons, Huguenots and others. What held their heterogeneous community together, apart from the colour of their skin and their shaky refugee status, was their know-how and experience in the one single occupation most of them had practised back in Europe - fishing."

The Doc and Laura, somewhat at a loss where to turn to, sat down on the terrace of a café near the ferry landing. Rain trickled down on them through the swaying branches and rustling foliage of a huge flamboyant. Soaking wet as they were, the two of them hardly even noticed the water dripping on their hoods, forming rivulets on their way down to the rubber boots. The bearded owner of the café suddenly appeared out of nowhere and kindly asked them in. Laura wondered whether he had not yet quite realized the weather situation since he was wearing sunglasses of the mirroring kind. While he was preparing them a cup of coffee, he identified himself as the local padre, whose principal workplace, the church, looked like the hull of a ship capsized and washed ashore here by last year's hurricane.

The twice-daily ferry connections to Pointe-à-Pitre and Trois Rivières, the padre explained while expertly handling his espresso machine, had been discontinued as from this morning due to the hurricane. Cruise ships would be heading for less risky

Mediterranean destinations at this time of the year. The clergyman had never heard of a Penelope, he said. He did know the Yellow Dancer, though. Not the person, just the yacht of that name. He was not a sailor or fisherman himself, he explained, but had developed a keen professional as well as private curiosity in his preponderantly fishing regulars and occasional sailing walk-ins. That's why, from his house on the hill, he used to watch the Bourg roadstead with his astronomical telescope during the tourist season. Probably scanning the boats for naked sunbathing females instead of searching the skies for new comets, Laura couldn't help thinking. On several such occasions, the padre claimed, he had noticed the Yellow Dancer sticking out like a pink elephant with her yellow hull and had wondered whether her Daltonian owner was maybe cultivating this particular "difficult" heliconia species with better success than the padre himself.

"Somehow very fitting for a yacht dancing on the Atlantic billows," he added and referred them to a local character nicknamed Bernard l'Hermite, the Hermit Crab, who lodged in a primitive cabin halfway up the road to the fort. If anyone at all was able and probably willing to help them with their quest, this was the man, the padre said.

"Between the three of us," he had whispered as if he was afraid someone higher up the food chain might be eavesdropping on them, "Bernard is a very pious guy, in his own way, as you'll see. His popularity with the community is, well, negligible. Not only doesn't he do any fishing, which makes him a natural misfit on this island, but, strictly speaking, he doesn't do anything at all to earn an honest living. One of those birds in the field that don't sow..."

"Matthew six, twenty-six, I believe," the Doc cut in.

"Quite. I see you know your Holy Scriptures. Now, if Alberto were to scatter Bernard's cabin all over the place tomorrow, say, I suspect the villagers' general feeling would be one of good riddance. It's something of an eye-sore, as you will see for yourselves. So far, the Almighty has held his protective hand over Bernard and his sorry excuse of a cabin. Anyway, just like that, off the bat, I couldn't name a more reliable source of useless information than Bernard. If your Penelope is a creature of flesh and blood and not a SPECTRE haunting these parts, he's bound to know her."

A little later, when the Doc and Laura, steaming with sweat from the effort of climbing the hill in rubber boots hardly made for walking, had reached Bernard's crudely timbered hut, they immediately understood what the padre had meant by "in his own way". The cabin stood on the top of a steep cliff dropping some thirty feet into the sea. It had been wallpapered all over with naive posters and cardboard signs, all adorned with miscellaneous doomsday messages and dark metaphysical allusions, inviting passers-by to mend their sinful ways in good time and prepare for the inevitable. "Leave the motorway of Evil Falls at the next exit to Virtue Springs" seemed a sound enough motto, Laura felt. Bernard's peculiarly precarious set-up reminded her of the monasteries of Meteora in Greece, sitting high and dry on gigantic stele-like eroded rocks a bit like the Monument Valley mesas, though not quite as high and sufficiently rounded at the top to be habitable. The philosophy behind Bernard's hut on the cliff was identical with that of the monasteries: nearer, my God, to thee.

By way of proof that Bernard and Jesus were that close, the hermit had ventured to draw a portrait of God's son on his door. And even though certain features of it were faintly reminiscent of the mysterious Turin shroud, the overall impression was such as to make Laura hope that the authentic Jesus did not look quite as bushed and baked as all that.

"Praised be the Lord," Bernard cried as he finally flung open the plywood door with a solid kick as a reaction to the Doc's repeated knocking. To call the man dishevelled would have been a polite understatement. His long hair hung over his shoulders in ill-kempt dusty dreadlocks. His mat of a reddish beard almost reached to his buckle and bore material witness to the composition of his breakfast, in which cornflakes and baked beans must have loomed large. His hollow cheeks and baggy eyes betrayed the ascetic from either passion or dire necessity. He wore threadbare shorts and a discoloured T-shirt that had been holed by moths in several places. His bathing slippers were at least one number too small, probably complimentary footwear handed out by the low tide. As had been most of the materials used in the construction of his cabin, by the look of it. Flotsam and jetsam galore, all kinds of repatriated driftwood provisionally stuck together with ropes, rivets and nails - a Noah's ark in times of financial adversity.

"Ay, now and in all eternity, Amen," the Doc was quick-witted enough to complete what seemed to be the password motto.

"Brother, we have come to commend the soul of a poor, pitiable woman to the Lord's mercy," the Doc deftly continued on the spiritual note with the transcendental pathos of a lay sermonizer who had seen the divine light.

"God alone knows how often she has left the straight and narrow, Brother, ay, strayed in the most revolting manner, I will not keep it from you nor enlarge upon it unnecessarily. But in God's house, there is room for all and sundry in God's house, isn't that what the Holy Scriptures say? And the woman is ready and willing to mend her ways and return to the fold, so much can be said in her favour."

Laura felt the Doc was beginning to identify a little too much with his adopted role and wondered whether he had been a clergyman as well in one of his many former lives.

"What she needs in the black depths of her despair is a glint of hope, Brother, a little gleam of confidence. Your reputation as an assistant redeemer has found its way to us back in the European diaspora, Brother, and we were hoping you might be able to help us out."

Bernard's face showed pleasant surprise, something close to bliss, one might have thought. He was presumably used to dealing with much abuse and derision and enjoyed for once having to deal with such premium clients, remorseful though still a long way from redemption. He seemed to be visibly gaining a few inches in size and seized Laura's hand.

"Praised be the Lord. You have come to the right doorstep, Brother. I am but an unworthy instrument of God's mercy. But do let me know what I can do for this young lady. It's never too late to turn back as did the prodigal son. And yes, all sinners find a place in God's house if they so wish. Which reminds me. Why don't you come in out of the rain?"

He threw the door wide open and waved them in, but what general disorder and chaos they glimpsed from outside caused the Doc and Laura to turn down the generous offer as politely as they could.

"No, Brother, this is not her. This is sister Laura, a staunch pillar of our community. No, we are looking for a certain Penelope, also called the Yellow Dancer in some unsavoury quarters. I mean, Yellow Dancer, need I say more? What woman valuing her reputation would allow herself to be called that? Why not go all the way and call herself Happy Harlot? Unfortunately, we've lost her trail and were hoping you could put us back on her scent, if I may put it a touch lasciviously."

Laura suddenly had the strange but positive sensation of the ground under her feet trembling. If that was the first harbinger of an earthquake, Bernard's hut would be among the first constructions to go. One more reason not to follow his kind invitation and step inside. To appear in the Hereafter with unshaven legs and shaggy Bernard in her tow could give the Almighty a totally wrong impression.

"Yellow Dancer, you say?" The hermit passed his fingers through his hair and wrinkled his forehead. Then he pulled on his earlobes as if half expecting divine inspiration to drop like a pack of untipped Gauloises.

"The Yellow Dancer," he repeated the name.

"Yes, I've heard of her. A sinful woman, a loose woman, is that what you're calling her? I must admit, I'm mortified, Brother. In these parts, she enjoys the reputation of a magnanimous benefactress, a Mother Teresa of the West Indies, almost. Who knows, Brother, you can't look into the dark niches of a woman's heart, can you? Who knows what abominable sins she secretly hopes to redeem? But the Lord's mercy is not for sale. He is the supreme incorruptible being. Let ye that labour and are heavily burdened come to me, as long as the humiliated and insulted stay away. Praised be…"

"..the Lord," the Doc interrupted him with a touch of impatience.

"Penelope. D'you have any idea where she might be? Maybe here in Bourg?"

Bernard opened his eyes wide as if witnessing a case of unspeakable blasphemy.

"No, no, not here. Yonder, on Terre-de-Bas. Is said to own a small house there. A sinful woman, you call her? I have no words, Brother."

"Give it a name, Brother. Have you talked to her more recently?" The hermit shook his head so violently that his dreadlocks were swirling in the air, releasing a small cloud of greyish dust.
"Talked to her? No, what's getting into you, Brother! I've never set foot on Terre-de-Bas, as yet, and she doesn't seem to leave it, ever."

The tone of utter indignation in the hermit's voice suggested that he would rather venture on a guided Sodom and Gomorrha sightseeing tour than pay the neighbouring island a visit.

"If my information is correct, Penelope is on her way to total redemption, so don't worry," Laura opened her mouth for the first time. She found the Doc had gone a little too far. Nor did she want to leave the hermit with this kind of slanderous memory of her mother.

"Tell me, Brother Doc, am I hallucinating or did the ground tremble under our feet some minutes ago?" She asked on their way back to the dinghy.

"Did you sense that, too, Sister Laura? I am sure the Holy Ghost descended upon us at that very moment. No laughing matter. Persistent smaller quakes are the Lord's reminder, I suppose, that paradise has its price, too. A sea-quake with an ensuing tsunami would lay the entire archipelago waste and take our friend in his ark out into the Atlantic. Maybe that's what he is actually hoping for."

As if right on cue, the rain had started pouring down heavily again. Squalls whipped the long threads of big drops through the alleys like so many glass beads bursting on impact.

"How is it possible this man never visited the neighbouring island, incredible!"

The Doc raised a finger like a swot never at a loss for an answer. "Mental insular dwarfing," was his diagnosis.

"Dwarfing?"

"Islanders are peculiar people, in general. Their prolonged physical isolation leads to intellectual dwarfing as sure as smoking cigarettes causes lung cancer. I've read numerous treatises on the phenomenon. The more restricted my physical surroundings, the less marked my inclination to go beyond its narrow confines, albeit in virtual terms. Experts call it the Nissotic Syndrome. Add to this a certain socio-cultural divide as observed in this archipelago, tiny though it is. Whilst there are practically no blacks on Terre-de-Haut, you'll hardly find any whites on Terre-de-Bas. Instead, the offspring of escaped slaves from Guadeloupe and other places who settled here. They even grew a small artificial rain forest, which invited politically incorrect comments involving apes and trees, if you catch my meaning. In short, for the whites on Terre-de-Haut, Terre-de-Bas is a miniature Gwada and for the blacks of Terre-de-Bas, Terre-de-Haut embodies what they or rather their ancestors once ran away from.."

2. Solitaire's Colleges

"None of us will hold it against you if you don't come with us." Solitaire interrupted her plaiting of Laura's hair into tiny cornrows and took another critical look at her work. What with the heavy swell which the Pas de Deux had been exposed to for hours now, she had to support herself with her free hand on the rest of Laura's chair.

"Whoever is waiting for us over there wants our asses, not yours. If it really is the Sultan we're dealing with, he probably hasn't entered your name in his black book yet. So, as long as you keep sitting on the fence, he has no reason to take it out on you."

Laura looked at her watch. It was only a few minutes shy of midnight. She had handed Penelope's letters to Solitaire shortly after her return from their reconnaissance tour and had reminded her of her promise concerning the cornrows. Since Solitaire had not been able to sleep either, she had quickly transformed a corner of the saloon into a hairdresser's-cum-beauty parlour, fixed a small mirror on the wall, collected her brush, comb, hairpins and other necessary utensils and started working on Laura's hair. It was the most peculiar hairdresser's Laura had ever been to.

The GRAND BANKS 49 was pitching in the waves with such fervour as though she felt reminded of her ancestral North Atlantic fishing grounds. Time and time again, she would tear at her anchor chain with sudden violent jerks that made Laura wince and cringe. How long would the weakest link of the chain withstand such permanent strain? The gale's uninterrupted fierce howling round the yacht's superstructure was enough to put fear in the heart of the most seasoned salt, let alone that of a landlubber such as Laura. Raindrops in two minds about whether to turn into hail soon kept pelting the yacht's deck like buckshot. How on earth Ignace and the Doc managed to get so much as a shuteye in this crazy turmoil was a mystery to Laura.

"It's awfully kind of you to leave the decision to me," Laura replied, ever so cautiously taking off the bandage with which the Doc had covered her wound on the forehead.

"But after all we've been through together so far, you don't seriously believe I'd withdraw from the game now and leave the grand finale to you. Besides, I'm probably the only one of us who has any idea of what Suleiman looks like. I mean, just in case it's him, the perpetrator, and we have to identify him in a crowd."

Solitaire, who had continued plaiting, stopped again.

"How so? Have you seen a picture of him or met him?"

Laura told her about the Yakamoz on the evening of their wait at the south end of the Rivière Salée. Her description of Suleiman was of needs rather fragmentary. Solitaire listened attentively, then shook her head impatiently.

"Why didn't you say so earlier?"

"I tried to, but nobody paid any attention. Besides, I wasn't entirely sure and didn't feel like making a fool of myself yet again.

After all that's happened these past few days, I look at things differently and wish I had insisted."

Laura took a sideways glance at Solitaire but could not detect any signs of genuine irritation. Maybe it was better to change the subject anyway, before they started quarrelling for good. That was the last thing she needed now.

"How did you get onto this slippery slope, generally speaking," she asked Solitaire with a spot of calculated ingenuousness.

"I mean, can you remember anything at all from your early childhood?"

Laura wasn't sure Solitaire would want to talk about this here and now. On the other hand, a better opportunity than this might not present itself again in the foreseeable future. Or maybe ever. "The stale stink of orphanages and reformatories," Solitaire murmured, after a few moments of silence. Apparently, she found it hard to bring episodic flashes into some rudimentary chronological context. She wasn't the only one battling with that problem, Laura thought.

"A mixture of damp linoleum, pungent floor polish, sweat, shit and cabbage, all rolled into one. And then there are the noises. Hysterically crying children, shouting guards, squeaking rubber soles on endless corridor floors, tunics whooshing past. The slamming of doors, the metallic whizz-bang of iron bolts shooting shut and the tinkling of massive key rings. Individual high-pitched voices, bits and pieces of incomprehensible languages. There they are, my memories, more like associations."

Again, she stopped dressing Laura's hair as if listening to a prompting voice inside herself.

"Russian, Finnish, Swedish, I dunno. A never-ending series of kindergarten set-ups, run-down orphanages, and ghastly juvenile detention centres. No idea how I got from one to the other. The one thing I do know is that I never met my parents. Maybe they had already passed on by then or had somehow been separated from me for good. Possible they just abandoned me like a puppy that was growing much faster than expected, occupying too much space. I hope for them they perished. If they didn't, they ought to thank God for every day that goes by without them bumping into me in some dark alley."

"Why Russian orphanages?"

"I really have no idea, a complete blank. Looks like my parents may have been Russians. I can still speak a few phrases, expressions like the ever-present davai, davai, 'get going', 'come on' and ne nado, don't do this, don't do that. In more recent years, many Russians have found their way into the Caribbean like maggots into a cake. For them, it probably makes a pleasant difference from passing their summer holidays in such places as Irkutsk, Semipalatinsk or Omsk, I suspect. Even from bloody freezing Moscow. Anyway, they have revolting manners, an uncivilized bunch, and usually carry thick bundles of dollar bills in their pockets like spare rolls of toilet paper. Big thing for Russians, toilet paper, they keep nicking it from wherever they can get it, if only by force of habit. Their whores tend to be cheaper than the vodka they down all day long. Barbarian hordes, if you ask me. Nomads who should have stayed in their steppe yurts. Whenever I hear the language, I feel like I've accidentally stepped into some time machine that has beamed me back to their Goddam hard-labour orphanages."

"Not what one would call a carefree childhood then?"

Solitaire laughed.

"Hardly. Come to think of it, I don't know what carefree feels like. Frequent beatings, lice, bed bugs, fucked-up toilets, and no end of potatoes. Hard to tell what's worse. You can't imagine the quantities of potatoes that will find their way into a Russian. I once read that an average human being consists of up to something like 80 per cent of water. I don't know who found that out and how, but I do suspect the method doesn't apply to the Russians. My guess is they consist of up to 90 per cent potato starch. The rest is probably cabbage rolls and borscht, thin red shit that reminds you of a woman's menstrual bleeding, vile stuff. Gets its own back by making you fart for hours afterwards, too, mind. They must sweat borscht through their pores. I can't stand the smell."

"What, of the borscht or of the Russians?"

"Both."

Solitaire staggered across the saloon and took two bottles of water and a couple of chocolate bars from the fridge. When she came back, she handed Laura one of each.

"If we're going to make it a white night, anyway, we might as well live it up. Ti Martin's luscious buttocks!"

She held the bottle in the air, almost toppling over in the swell, and drank half of the water in one big swig.

"The disgustingly sweetish stink of overcrowded dormitories still lingers in my nose. So does the infernal noise. Nobody had any papers, so they always had to guess both childrens' origins and ages. There just wasn't space enough for separating the sexes either. All got corralled together in one or two huge dormitories. The slightly older boys had just discovered their dicks could do more than piss and were rubbing the things day in, day out. Enough to make you a lesbian or join the convent," she continued chewing on the chocolate.

"One night, I overheard a gang of young offenders who were planning to escape from the Russian detention centre near St. Petersburg or Leningrad, as it was then called. Kids, really, but already as hard-nosed as Ignace, I swear to God. They caught me eavesdropping, of course, and threatened to kill me if I delivered them to the guards."

"Well, I kicked their leader in the groin and, as he bent over in pain, hit his chin with my knee, probably breaking his jaw along with his balls. That kind of sobered them, revolutionized their views on the weaker sex. They left their knocked-out leader behind and made me their capo di capi. Smart move on their part, don't you think?"

She giggled at the memory of it.

"I didn't trust them, anyway. That must have been the time when I started carrying a knife on my person. Always. I must have been what, six or seven, I guess."

"During their forced labour in the woods and swamps around Leningrad, the boys had collected logs and secretly knocked up a primitive raft, which they kept hidden in the high reeds of a stretch of Baltic coast. It even had a small mast with a big linen sheet for a sail. That was the Mayflower on which they intended to cross the gulf to capitalist Finland. Obviously, it must have been totally unseaworthy, even for a relatively short voyage such as that, bože moj, some sixty-odd miles. At the time, however, it felt like the QE 2, minus the food buffets and the luxury cabins. Provisions they had stolen over many weeks. Much of it had gone mildewed and mushy, meanwhile, bread loaves full of miniature animal wild life. But that made it but marginally worse than the meals we used to get in the institutions."

"Did the raft have a name? Papillon, maybe?"

Solitaire laughed and drank another swig of water. She wasn't used to such a long uninterrupted speech, it seemed to make her thirsty.

"No, we baptized her Bomž. That's what they call the homeless in Russia, who, for ideological reasons, have always been an even more embarrassing presence there than anywhere else. Their mere existence is sufficient proof of socialist theory not working in practice."

"Then, one night, we stood out to sea. Must have been in the middle of summer. It just wouldn't get dark. But we felt we had waited long enough and with the weather promising to remain calm, it was to be now or never. You could almost smell the Finnish skerry coast. Fir and birch trees all round. With any luck, we'd make it in a few days' time. The water was tepid okay, the sea unruffled, no wind to speak of. We took turns at the coarse oars. There were eight of us, so we did two-hour tricks each."

"What scared us most were sharks. To discourage attempts at escape like ours, they kept telling the kids that the Baltic Sea, which most of us had never set eyes on before, was teeming with man-eating sharks. It was only after we hadn't spotted any fins for many hours that it dawned upon us we'd been had. The Russian coastguard apparently had other things to attend to than chasing after a handful of kids doomed to drown, anyway."

"We rowed and rowed till we all had burst blisters on our palms and fingers and had to give in to cramp. Our navigational skills were slight to non-existent. But that didn't matter in so far as we couldn't miss the Finnish coast even if we had tried. We made an effort to stay on the direct course with a boy scout's compass, whose trembling little needle was spinning round and round at every movement of the raft. Currents were unknown to us and, fortunately, rather negligible in the Baltic, which has no tide to speak of in those eastern reaches. One Siberian boy had a fair idea of the most prominent night sky constellations. He showed us the faintly glimmering polestar, which we tried to keep in front of us.

When the third or fourth morning came, the first lighthouses on the Finnish coast were already clearly standing out against the blue sky. Suddenly, a cargo ship seemed to be steering right into us. Our mast had long gone overboard by then. Even with what little swell there was, we must have been practically invisible and had no means of attracting the crew's attention other than shouting and waving our arms about. My guess is, there was no-one on the bridge of that ship, anyway. They had activated the autopilot and were snoozing it off in their bunks. We were the proverbial lame duck in the water. The freighter missed us by a hair's breadth, alright. But its wake put paid to the raft. Bomž just gave up on us and disintegrated. We all plunged in the water, the QE 2 had been sunk on her maiden voyage."

Solitaire took a last swig of the bottle and belched aloud. "Sorry, I always gulp too much air. Lifejackets were a luxury we hadn't been able to afford. I managed to seize one of the bigger logs and held on to it for dear life. Fortunately, what little wind-generated current there was pushed me towards the shore and not away from it. That would easily have been the end of me. Well, it was to be that of my friends, who could swim no better than me. I waited till I had come close enough to the outer ring of skerries and half paddled, half climbed ashore like some antediluvian marine creature discovering there's more than water on the globe. The rocks in the skerries are round and smooth, less forbidding than those of the Mediterranean, for instance. Slippery, though. You don't hurt yourself that much, but find no easy foothold, either. There are no urchins to munch the algae, only

medusas, harmless ones, and poisonous algae, disgusting stuff."
"For a while, I roamed the Finnish birch woods and lakes like
an ever-ravenous wolf-cub separated from its pack by hunters.
There were isolated summerhouses, bungalows, huts and sheds
all over the place, most of them vacant and the locks easy enough
to pick. So, I had both drinking water and food, could even sleep
in a bed on occasion. What nearly killed me were the mosquitos. We'd had them in the wilderness around St. Petersburg too,
of course, but nothing as numerous and blood-thirsty as these.
There were whole clouds of them coming down on you, especially whenever you had something edible on you, which was
not so often in my case, fortunately. Without protective balm or
a beekeeper's net you risked getting devoured by them before
even the wolves had time to get at you."

"When I finally got caught by an elk hunter, after I don't know
how many weeks, I had infected mosquito bites all over my body
from the perpetual itching and scratching and had almost lost my
fucking mind. Since I knew no English then and he didn't understand Russian, I could not communicate with the man other than
by sign language. If I had had half a mind, I could have stabbed him
or grabbed his rifle and shot him, but for what?. So I let him hand
me over to the local police who took me to yet another orphanage,
this time somewhere near Turku. That wasn't a great deal better
than the Russian ones I already knew, a little cleaner, though. The
Fins eat fewer potatoes and wouldn't touch borscht, but they drink
as if there was no tomorrow. More than the Russians, and believe
me, that takes some doing. Their language remained a mystery to
me. I never even came close to speaking it, except for a few everyday words, such as kiitos, thanks, or kyllä, hello."

That was something Laura could well relate to. She had once
spent a few weeks in Helsinki and had tried to "pick up" some
Finnish, but had lamentably failed. The peculiar inflation of vowels, many of them doubled, yet all entitled to be pronounced in the
name of the "phonetic writing" doctrine, necessitated a different
breathing technique reminiscent of apnoea diving. Normal Europeans could not pronounce words such as hyvää pajvää, a good

day to you, without soon turning blue in the face. Lacking motivation, Laura's crush on Finnish had quickly subsided.

"I had to get away from there, the sooner, the better," Solitaire continued.

"The personnel we were exposed to would normally be drunk by early afternoon, at the latest. Since it was frequently getting dark then, anyway, they probably felt entitled. Some of these people I don't think I ever saw on or off the job. That vastly facilitated my escape, of course. I climbed aboard a freight train to the nearest harbour one night and jumped on a ferry to Stockholm, as a stowaway. After the gruelling experience with the raft, I felt like a virtual princess aboard that huge ship scraping along the Stockholm skerries so frighteningly close at times I thought she did it on purpose to get her barnacles taken off. Ships began to fill my little galaxy. I decided to go to sea, somehow or other."

"While other kids went to school, I was doing the grand tour of all major ports in Europe and overseas, mostly as a stowaway, to begin with. I wasn't particularly tall, lean, thanks to the measly orphanage food, with crew-cut hair and dressed like a boy - again, very much in the orphanage tradition. On top of that, I adopted a boyish walk that I found hard to lose again later in life. If you'd run into me somewhere back then, you'd probably have taken me for a country boy bandy-legged from counting swine. I could make a cat look clumsy when it came to slipping in and out of the weirdest tiny niches aboard ships. Soon I knew every potential hide-out on any kind of freighter or tanker, let alone passenger ships. They're the easiest. Now that they are getting as big as floating towns, no-one on board has any means of knowing the entire population, obviously. If you go about it with some skill and discretion, you can stay on virtually for months on end without ever being discovered. I learned how to pick container locks and hide in there, too, even though that was more dangerous. If they had ever re-locked the thing while I was asleep, I might have suffocated. Happens to refugees ever so often. You don't notice it, just fall asleep and never wake again. Knocking on the container walls won't help. At sea, on big ships like those, no-one will hear you."

"Anyway, to say ships were my home would not quite cut it. There was something mystic about it. On a ship, hidden away somewhere in the hold or engine room, I felt absolutely safe, like being inside a whale, you might say. The warmth, the smell of oil and fuel, the noises, it all reassured me. My heart adopted the slow, regular beat of the engine's pistons. I was perfectly at rest, untouchable, while the whale would be moving on to yet another port. It had a magic of its own."

"Were you never caught?"

"Oh yes, plenty of times. They would slap me about, shout at me and make me clean the dishes and toilets for the rest of the voyage. My impression from the beginning was that, most of the time, they looked upon me as a godsend, cheap labour, you see. So, getting caught was bad luck but not then end of the world. On one passage from Le Havre to Fort Lauaderdale, for instance, they discovered me hidden in a lifeboat. One of the sailors had brought a dog aboard, can you imagine? A fucking dog will sniff you out any time, no matter where you choose to hide."

"The Norwegian captain who looked me over took me for a boy, of course, and grew uncannily kind. I had learned a crude sort of English by then. Reading and writing was a bore, but for my purposes, what little I had learned seemed sufficient. I never attended a normal school, ships were my colleges. Sounds weird, doesn't it? Well, anyway, whenever I see people who attended first-rate public or private schools and universities and yet are as thick as a short Irish plank, I guess I didn't get such a raw deal after all, what say you, Mistress Forster?"

"Anyway, the Norwegian's English wasn't much better. Halversson, he was called, Thorstein Halverson. Quite a mouthful compared to Joe Grady. So, we communicated well enough and had a good time till, one day, he tried to get into my pants, I mean, literally. I must have been about thirteen, in the throes of puberty. I already saw my virginity flying out of the porthole, but as it turned out, Captain Thorstein and myself, we were both in for a big surprise. You see, he was a stalwart Viking from the wrong side of the fjord. I'll never forget his disappointed face when he realized I was a dickless boy. Pity he never met Ti Martin, I bet they would have had the time of their lives."

"The day came when I had grown old enough to seek job opportunities on ships officially. I still had no papers, so, strictly speaking, I didn't even exist. A precarious situation, indeed, but one which has its advantages too. When the respective shipping agents, ships' pursers and captains I approached or was interviewed by realized what vast treasure trove of knowledge about ships I had already acquired over the years, they would normally procure some papers or others, just to have me on board. To begin with, they usually took me for a despicable liar and braggard. But the kind of information I had on my fingertips, I couldn't possibly have collected from books or magazines, so they invariably ended up believing me."

"I found my way onto any cargo ship or passenger liner in no time. Besides, I was a specialist for smoking out stowaways. After all, I knew their preferred hide-outs beforehand. All of this led to my getting jobs that used to be reserved for boys, at the time, and I was mighty proud of myself, too."

"So that's how you came to the Caribbean then?"

"Later, by more devious routes."

"I had frequently been to some of the local ports and harbours around here, in fact, including Pitre, but had never stayed for any length of time. In Antwerp, I had met a guy and fallen in love with him, like a poodle puppy feeling a crush for a grown-up bull terrier. A Spaniard, twice my age, and irresistible for a sweet seventeen-year-old such as yours truly at the time. He seemed to know everybody who was anybody in Diamond City. Never short of cash, either, the uncrowned king of the harbour's red-light district. Our affair was tainted by a desperate lop-sidedness. More likely than not, he had ten girls like me for every finger of his right hand. But for me, it was the first time. Trite, really. I was blind and he used me, full stop."

Laura was listening attentively, but didn't detect any bitterness or sarcasm in Solitaire's voice.

"One of his bros happened to be looking for a drug-runner to replace one who, as they put it, had just retired. They call them mules in the business. Asses would be more fitting. It sounded disgusting, but I did it, five or six times, just to humour my Spaniard. I was lucky, never got caught. Nor did I end my days in some ghastly run-down hotel room with a burst condom in my guts, like some of the retired colleagues."

"When he finally kicked me out, anyway, I continued in this line of quick and easy returns. Only from then on, I took greater care what I fed my monkey. I would insist on clean stuff, none of your denatured shit cut out of recognition that goes round killing off destitute junkies. I abandoned my maritime career and wriggled my way further into drug-trafficking circles instead. Much of the stuff is regularly smuggled on ships and with them I obviously was a dead ringer. Wherever you can hide as a stowaway, there's ample room for dope, too. Even though nowadays, they go as far as to weld metal cases filled with the stuff to underwater parts of the hull, can you imagine?"

"By and large, the drug sale and distribution follows the same rules as any other trade with high-value goods. There tends to be greater fluctuation, though, due to consignments defaulting or markets restructuring. Whenever the dominant position on sections of the Dutch, German, or Belgian and French markets fell vacant, for whatever reason, there would be fierce wars between the gangs aspiring to fill the gap. To survive in a habitat like that, you need warriors who will shrink back from nothing. I happened to be unscrupulous in a naive, childish but totally impassionate, deadly way, you know, like one of those African child soldiers. Even without any military service behind me, I could shoot like an experienced sniper and was fast with the knife. Blades had been my best friends ever since my childhood days. In short, getting me on their payroll was a smart career move for anyone hoping to climb up the ladder."

"So you killed people even then?"

"That I did, I'm sorry to say. You got to remember, this is a trade where killing replaces redundancy. It's like terminating someone's contract. Mostly, the guys I was dealing with were the basest of lowlife who should have known better than wriggling their way into the drugs business. Sometimes poor bastards who hadn't thought of the longer-term consequences of their actions, because thinking wasn't their strongest point anyway. People who were suspected of cooperating with the law, or had misappropriated funds or drugs. Sometimes, they were just in somebody's way up or happened to belong to a competing chapter. Such folks would be living on borrowed time. Pity? I don't know. Whoever makes his living by drug trafficking one way or another is familiar with the rules, or should be. You can't rely on anyone and must be aware, at every step you take, that you may get shot, stabbed, burned, buried or baptized at any moment."

"Baptized?"

"Dumped in a tub or barrel filled with acid, works wonders with dry skin."

Laura felt her flesh creep. She thought she had heard enough, more than enough, in fact. But she had broached the subject and now she had to hear Solitaire out.

"Like I said, I belonged to the killer elite from an early age. But no one is so good as to be invulnerable. Inevitably, you'll be running into someone even better, faster, deadlier. I was always aware of that and felt I had almost reached the end of my tether. In this line of business, you die young. It was only a question of time till I caught a bullet or walked into a hostile blade. It was at that point I met the Black Queen. Thanks to her, my life took yet another unexpected turn, not unlike that compass needle on the raft."

Laura had closed her eyes, listened to the pleasant sound of Solitaire's voice and felt the workings of her deft fingers in her hair. When Solitaire fell silent now, Laura opened her eyes again and saw that the new day was dawning. A day that might prove to be her last, all things considered. The feeble daylight was having a tough job trying to pierce the thick, dark clouds which covered the visible part of the sky like an ominous work of Alberto's making.

"Meeting the Black Queen became something of a rebirth for me. Whoever had given me my first life, she gave me my second. Thanks to her, I managed to break the vicious circle of my addiction and gratuitous violence. To think that, at the beginning, I had wanted to massacre the woman. She locked me up in a hole in the ground with gratings for a roof. Once a day, she had someone place a bowl of water there, in which she had dissolved God knows what freaking herbs and shit. Tasted like rat's piss, obviously, caused me diarrhoea and hallucinations. Swell combination, you ought to try it some time, just for laughs. But since I didn't get anything else for a week or so, I had to swallow it or die of thirst. I felt more badly treated than a pig. Probably was, too. The only thing that kept me alive, I guess, was my resolve to get my revenge and slit that woman's gizzard."

"The Carib kill-or-cure treatment worked, though. After some weeks, I was totally emaciated and somewhere in outer space, hallucinating. I didn't remember where or who I was. You see, she had deleted my hard drive so residue-free that she could gradually start creating a new one for me. She gave me more and more solid food and normal water. No more funny weeds. Very slowly, I started recovering and came to my senses again."

"She persuaded the village teacher of Crayfish River to teach me some of the ordinary things you learn at school. Most of the extraordinary ones I had taught myself on ships already. The man had a superhuman patience and was stupendously well-read. Died some five years ago. Good man. Well, for all it's worth, Crayfish River was my rebirth."

"They ought to call you Phoenix. Some story of re-socialisation."

Solitaire shook her head.

"Not really. I didn't get back on the path of virtue, as you may have noticed. For all her wisdom, the Black Queen would not have known how to even spell that word, socialisation. No, we both of us have the crime gene in our system. You don't wash that out like poison in a kidney dialysis. Yet nothing but the feeling to be accepted by a group of people, maybe loved for what you are despite what you have done, helped me get back on my feet again. The one truly destructive element about drugs is not the addiction or the necessity of or greed for more and more money. No, it's the degrading exploitation and abuse of all by everyone.

Once you fall into that trap, you start perceiving human beings only in terms of their usefulness. What are this or that person's weaknesses and how can I exploit them for my own criminal purposes? That's what corrupts you because it reduces your fellow human being to a mere object while you yourself turn into a mindless robot devoid of emotion."

"Now you sound like an investment banker suffering from burnout." Laura laughed. "And yet, you did not leave the business altogether."

"Well, we all have to live with our little inconsistencies, don't we? It's all I used to be really good at and what allowed me to make a decent living, in a manner of speaking. Otherwise, there'd only be prostitution, the basest form of livelihood. Thanks to the Black Queen's advice and help, I made enough money and saved most of it seriously enough to consider retirement. In fact, had it not been for the one-eyed Frenchman, I would have already retired."

"You think you could live in Europe, in a civilized country?"

"Maybe in Hamburg?" Solitaire laughed.

"No, I'm afraid I'm a burnt-out case for the European scene. The first meter maid trying to give me a ticket there, would find her scalp gone. Pickpockets coming anywhere near me would lose their fingers and burglars leave the house feet forward. I would quickly become a Ma Baker of Blankenese."

"Or a very popular communal politician, who knows."

They both laughed aloud.

"Well, what do you think. I believe you'll make a beautiful corpse, now."

Solitaire took the small mirror off the wall and tried hard to show Laura the result of several hours' work from all sides. Solitaire's pains had paid off, Laura found. Chain upon chain of corns huddled to her scalp, just as did Solitaire's to hers. At a distance and in the grey twilight of a rainy day, the two women might have been mistaken for sisters, nay, for twins. The main difference was in the eyes. But for anyone to notice that, they would have to come closer than either woman would allow a stranger to do.

"Thank you very much, Miss, you can look forward to a big tip."

Momentarily, the rain seemed to have stopped and even the gale-force wind was taking a breather. A deceptive silence had fallen over the bay. Like being in the eye of a cyclone, Laura thought.

3. The Fervid Ferryman

"In answer to your question, no, on the contrary, this gale plays right into our hands."

Ignace stopped packing his large watertight bag, which was already bulging with guns and ammunition. Laura had asked whether it might not be better to postpone Operation Overlord till tomorrow or to such a time when Alberto had passed and the general meteorological configuration become more favourable for outdoor events. Ignace obviously didn't share that opinion a bit.

"The gale is our best ally," he repeated and started wheezing with excitement.

"It offers us the element of surprise. Maybe those enemies of ours on Terre-de-Bas aren't counting on us landing today, not under these adverse circumstances. But even if they do, hard wind and pouring rain will give as much of a hard time to them as it does to us. Incidentally, the weather situation in the English Channel was pretty bad on D-Day, too, if I remember rightly."

"You sound as if you had been there," Laura laughed. But she knew he was right as far as the weather was concerned. "If the Allied landing had turned into a catastrophe as it very nearly did, weather would have become even more of an issue than it had done, anyway."

But she renounced at enlarging upon that thought, so much more so, as the Doc and Solitaire declared they shared the chabin's view. Laura quietly gave in and stepped into the open, where a hefty squall that seemed to have been waiting for this golden opportunity, seized her and well-nigh blew her overboard. At least her hair resisted the gale. The corns would not block her view during the skirmishes that were to come. What colour lipstick should she choose for the battle, blood-red, maybe?

Laura's handgun-to-go, the Taurus 22, had been taken apart and re-assembled again four or five times by her under the expert eyes of Ignace, the gun surgeon. Not once had she been left with any of those "superfluous" parts that never seem to belong anywhere. Not a mean achievement, even given the uncomplicated build of that Brazilian small-calibre gun built with fierce favela door-to-door fighting in mind.

All four of them had slipped into baggy camouflage battle tunics and bullet-proof Kevlar vests and prepared the hooded capes which were to round off the combat attire. The Doc had gone the extra mile and donned his black beret as if only too ready to provide snipers with a privileged target. Also, he had insisted on them smearing their faces with black shoe polish to darken their features and blend in with the soil, as it were. That kind of rendered the lipstick issue facetious, Laura thought. Solitaire had given her ankle holster with the combat knife to Laura and helped her to strap it on. Laura wasn't used to such an appliance stuck to her leg like an electronic tag and found it gave her a "duck walk".

"Ready for a shopping spree in downtown Aleppo," Laura shouted, making an effort to appear carefree despite herself. She had absolutely no idea of what lay ahead of her. But even with her newly-acquired killing experience, she still wasn't sure she would be able to fire a shot in cold blood at another human being, let alone dig her knife into someone's chest or belly. Perhaps it would have been better for all concerned if she had stayed away. Not that she feared for her life, well, not all that much. In the course of her Caribbean weeks, death had become something of a familiar figure, though anything but a close friend. Somehow, it seemed to have lost its sting. But she didn't want to slow the others down or get in their way, either. Not when speed and agility were of the essence.

"Like hunting a shark in the dark," she thought as she clung to the taffrail of the yacht dancing on the waves. The wind was whistling round the stubby radar and radio mast of the Pas de Deux while the sea was pounding against her hull. Something was missing, she found. What was it? The birds, of course! The sky was about to turn black again as with a total eclipse of the sun. Seagulls, frigate birds, herons, terns and cormorants had withdrawn into the jungle of black mangroves or into trees or under rooftops to sit the gale out. It was a game of hide and seek. Alberto had counted to three and Nature herself had squeezed into the remotest corner of the Caribbean not to be found out.

Their view from the yacht was restricted by the whipped-up spray, but on the Bourg beach yonder, somebody appeared to be on the move. By the look of it, the padre would be true to his word. During their little exchange with him yesterday, the Doc had asked him whether he would be prepared to act as their ferryman and take four people plus heavy luggage to Terre-de-Bas. The man of the cloth had had his qualms, what with the weather situation and him being no fisherman. But the Doc had succeeded in dispersing the man's burgeoning doubts by showing him a solid package of pale green bills. The church was in dire need of a new pulpit: if at all possible, one of hardwood that would last till Doomsday, at the very least. The local community's collection bag returns alone would be too slim to defray the costs.

The padre's "Saintoise"-type open boat was pitching like mad in the churning sea of the bay and made only little headway towards the Pas de Deux. Every time a wave lifted the boat's stern out of the water, the outboard engine's screw would fan the air instead of propelling the boat.

"Don't worry," the Doc, noticing Laura's concerned face, explained to her, "boats like his have stood the test of time. During World War Two, at the time of the French Vichy government, they fetched men from Trois Rivières, Guadeloupe with the Saintoises,, and took them to Dominica. From there, the poor blighters were shipped to the European battlefields and probably soon wished they had never left the Caribbean. Anyway, very seaworthy boats, the Saintoises, believe me." The Doc had stepped behind Laura and put his right hand on her arm.

"Whatever happens over there, try and stay close to me, d'accord?"

Laura nodded. Despite her wearing a woollen cardigan under her battle dress, she felt cold with fatigue, chronic lack of sleep and wind chill. The Doc could feel her tremble and pulled her back into the saloon.

It took the better part of half an hour for the Saintoise with the peculiar name of Rancho to come alongside and be tied to the Pas de Deux's hull. She couldn't stay there for any length of time, though, because the boats were being smashed against one another so hard by the swell that one of them, probably the Rancho, would be the one to give. So, the four of them chucked their bags into the Saintoise and were helped over the Pas de Deux's taffrail by the padre, who gave them, one by one, what he jocularly called a mixed blessing. He wasn't wearing his sunglasses, which made him look surprisingly older than he had appeared back at his café, Laura found. What fascinated her were his fiery eyes which belied his uncertain age and seemed to be sizing his passengers up like those of an experienced undertaker trying to determine what size caskets he would have to prepare for this lot.

They pushed off. The outboard engine was howling as if trying hard to drown even the wailing of the wind. The sea tossed the padre's passengers from one side to the other and back again. Then the Rancho shot forward with a jerk and lurched into the seas bucking and lunging like a bronco suddenly let loose to scamper and gallop into the arena. Time and time again the boat was literally buried in spray so that it didn't take long till everyone had been drenched to saturation point. The fiery-eyed helmsman seemed to be keeping them on course. Laura wondered whether the Doc had gone against pertinent conventions and paid the ferryman yesterday at Bourg, already.

"We'll fight them on the beaches..." she quoted cigar-smoking Churchill but was the only one able to hear herself. Rancho. Was there no end of bizarre names people would give to their boats?

Maybe it stood for some farm or ranch the padre had owned, a piece of land he had cultivated until that moment God had manifested himself to him and advised him to change the smock for the frock, as it were. It didn't seem the right moment to go into that. If this bronco-riding went on much longer, their enemies on Terre-de-Bas would wet themselves with laughter at the pathetic sight of four heavily armed "seals" puking their guts out big time upon setting foot on the island's beaches.

Solitaire handed Laura another drum for her revolver.

"Don't panic and don't waste it all at once, Snow White," she admonished her as if she had just given her her weekly pocket money. Even in the turmoil of sea and gale, Laura noticed with some satisfaction that, as pronounced by Solitaire, her nickname, insulting at first, had gradually turned into an expression of albeit slightly ironic esteem. Given a few more weeks, it might yet develop into something of a battle cry striking terror into the hearts of Caribbean scoundrels and riffraff of all sorts. Especially so when Solitaire was around too. In fact, probably only when she was around, too.

"Do count your shots," Solitaire continued, "and in case of doubt, reload immediately, swap the drums, lest you suddenly come up empty, feel me?"

Laura nodded. Nothing to it, like counting sheep from the passing train, she thought. Meanwhile, the sky above the Saintes had turned an even darker shade of velvety black and the wind seemed to be picking up by the minute, reaching solid gale force. Rain whipped up the surface of the sea, whose level seemed to be rising fast. Laura glanced back at the Pas de Deux. Solitaire and Ignace were loath to be abandoning their yacht, their home, to the destructive forces of the hurricane. The padre promised to keep a watchful eye on her, though there wasn't much he could do from shore if ever she broke her chain and went adrift.

Other, less devoted ferry men might have wondered about the bizarre foursome they were taking to Terre-de-Bas and might perhaps ask themselves whether the world had gone to war again without it having seeped through all the way to the West Indies. Not so the fierce-eyed padre, who seemed totally preoccupied with his old decrepit pulpit that risked giving in to his body weight any day now, as he had told them, maybe during his next projected sermon on the subject of the Apocalypse. Not a welcome omen for a community of staunch believers, a clergyman going to hell in his own pulpit.

"The worst thing about a hurricane for the coastal population is not the wind or the interminable rain, but the storm surge," said the Doc, sitting behind Laura in the canoe-like Saintoise.

"The water level rises and rises and there is absolutely nothing you can do about it but take to the high ground and watch in horror. Boats and ships are washed ashore and broken in two. Nothing is quite as destructive as a mass of water coming ashore."

First details of the coast of Terre-de-Bas became clearly discernible. The Rancho was apparently heading for a small bay, which was bounded to the southeast by a cape protruding far out into the sea.

"That's Petite Anse," the padre called out in a stentorian voice, "the ideal landing place, if you ask me."

Laura gave him an appreciative nod but didn't have much time for appreciation. To the left and to the right, the green waves washed over two primitive rockfills serving as moles.

It was between those two that the padre manoeuvred his rolling and careening boat. The small shallow basin between the moles had once been the main landing of the island, the clergyman explained. After an earthquake in more recent years it had assumed the aspect of an abandoned and flooded quarry. Large parts of the beach had already been covered by the rising sea, so that several fishing boats pulled ashore by their owners were adrift now and threatened to break away from their mooring ropes any minute. The Pas de Deux would have suffered a similar fate had they tried to anchor her somewhere in the neighbourhood.

The padre turned his Rancho with its bows into the wind. He seemed to prefer keeping a safe distance from the shore. His four passengers in their drenched battle dresses and ridiculous small hats of the same make with brims hanging limp like mushy biscuits, grabbed their bags and slid overboard. The padre shouted something Laura didn't understand, made a hasty sign of the cross and backed his Saintoise out of the landing. If he preferred another of those gallant, nerve-racking rides through the furious sea to staying on Terre-de-Bas, Laura thought, that was proof of his anticipating a lot of trouble that he had better avoid. As the Rancho veered to get on course for Terre-de-Haut again, the fiery eyes of the ferryman seemed to burn themselves into Laura's head as if determined to leave a lasting imprint.

Standing in the water up to their hips and being pushed forward by the incoming tide, the four "mercenaries" quickly waded ashore and, seeking cover from any possible sniper fire, threw themselves behind one of the few boats still lying on dry land. If their enemies were waiting for them here and now, the fight would be over before it had begun, so much was clear even to Laura.

But nothing happened. The scenery had a distinctly unreal touch to it, Laura couldn't help thinking. Some sad skeletons of boats as well as a couple of vacant, half rotted-away huts seemed to have survived the hurricane before this one and were now waiting for am almighty squall strong enough to put them out of their misery. Behind them, Laura could see the beginning of the gently rising asphalt road leading to the village. The interminable series of showers had transformed the road into something of a cimarron.

Protected a little from the wind by one of the ramshackle huts, whose rattling boards were unlikely to see the storm through, they opened their bags and took out their guns.

"I hope those knives of yours have stainless steel blades," Laura tried again to contribute to a relaxed atmosphere.

"Solingen quality," Ignace confirmed.

"Stick it in and turn it, so the wound won't heal that easily," he added, looking at Laura. He pulled out his knife and showed her how to do it.

"Feels like a Halloween pumpkin, human flesh does. The heart sits under the left nipple, about here," he was pointing at his left breast pocket filled with a gun magazine.

"The rib cage tends to be quite tough, you need to force it in with some conviction."

From the corners of her eyes, Laura saw Solitaire suddenly freeze as if she had spotted a ghost. Laura followed her stare. A single black man none of them had noticed when stepping ashore was standing still and motionless like a largely uninvolved and totally disinterested spectator at the opposite hut's doorframe. How long he had already been there remained a mystery. It was a man in shorts and a flimsy T-shirt. The discoloured nature of his clothing and his black skin had worked like a natural camouflage and made him invisible against the darkish wall of the hut.

Solitaire's right hand had immediately taken hold of the grip of her Redhawk. But since the man obviously carried no weapon and made no mien to run away, she let her own gun slide back under her belt and slowly walked towards him. The man opened his arms wide and turned his lighter palms upward to signal that he was unarmed and meant no harm. Ignace would probably have shot him anyway, just to be on the safe side, but Solitaire deliberately blocked his line of fire with her body.

She exchanged a few words with the man and came back.

"He says strangers arrived yesterday," Solitaire rendered the gist of what she had learned from the man.

"Six or seven men, with bags not unlike ours. They drew some considerable attention in the village, obviously, but that didn't seem to bother them. Checked into the Salako hotel, which is normally closed at this time of year, must have re-opened for this very occasion only."

"One of them, probably their boss, had a little bear on a leash. That's literally what the man says. A small bear. More probably a big dog, maybe a trained man tracker. No woman with them, of that he was positive."

"Doesn't sound like a true morale-booster." Laura would have liked to check in next to the strangers and asked to be woken when all was over and done with.

"Depends on how you look at it. At least now we know the nature of the beast," Solitaire retorted.

"I suggest we bypass the village and approach the hotel from the side of the rainforest. They won't expect us coming from there."

"Unless your friend is telling them about our landing this very minute," Ignace said.

They looked round. The mysterious black man had profited from their momentary distraction and stolen away unnoticed. Ignace was about to run after him, but Solitaire stopped him dead in his tracks.

"Let him go, he won't be selling us down the river, I don't think. Somehow, he rather gave me the impression of being on our side, for whatever reason. Alright, are we done here?"

She looked at her troopers, who gave her the thumbs up. Laura was full of admiration for Solitaire's self-control and resoluteness. She had cut off the legs of their pants to be less hampered in her movements no doubt. Laura, who had not seen Solitaire in shorts yet, was a little envious of her leader's well-formed, athletic legs. The woman could have made the catwalk her career. Maybe she would not have been tall enough, though. Lack of height was an exclusion criterion for models. As probably was the tattoo of a black panther's head she wore on her right thigh. From where she crouched on the ground, Laura thought she discovered a strange but unmistakable "s"-shaped scar running right across the panther's forehead.

NINTH CHAPTER

1. Baron Samedi

Four shadows were chasing up the hill like a small vanguard commando that had accidentally strayed behind enemy lines and was now desperately trying to secure the high ground fast. Sticking to the extreme right of the asphalt road oozing water that formed ever larger falls gushing seawards, the group made sure they could vanish into the thicket at the first sign of an ambush. After a sharp bend to the left, the road seemed to be leading straight into a dark tunnel. Above their heads, the dense wet foliage of tropical trees effectively cut off what little daylight there was. From the entrance of the "tunnel", a steady river of rainwater kept coming at them with such force that it threatened to wash them all the way back to the beach. At the end of it, the contours of the first huts and houses of the village just about showed through the steaming mist.

Solitaire clenched her raised right fist and all four of them bent down low and dove into the bushes. Panting, slipping, and stumbling, they ran through the undergrowth in a wide arch, keeping the houses to the left at about the same distance all the time. The village proved larger than Laura had suspected. Cursing her father in a low voice, she made every effort to stay hard on the heels of the others, but repeatedly skidded on the muddy, slippery slope of soaked black soil. Time and again she fell like a log and had to helped up again by the Doc or by Ignace. Her cape and battle dress soon took on the dark colour of wet dirt, and her arms looked as if she had unearthed a whole family of bog mummies with her bare hands. Laura laughed out loud. In view of this stuck-in-the-mud exercise, the Doc's recommended shoe-polish camouflage act really seemed a little superfluous. Wrapped in their bulky capes, the three figures running in front of her were hard to identify. Except for Solitaire, of course, who kept in the front all the time.

Every now and again, the cloud cover would spring a crack and the rain cease for a few minutes as if momentarily fatigued or surprised, only to set in again soon with a vengeance. The gale was still picking up, Laura felt. A blinding flash of lightning hit the ground not far behind them, followed almost immediately by a deafening clap of almighty thunder. Heavy squalls were tearing through the tops and crowns of the higher trees. Their trunks were swaying, bending, and breaking under the strain. Thorny twigs of head-high thickets left and right backlashed into their faces and forced them to run a painful whipping gauntlet, while all around solid branches crashed through the underwood and thumped onto or into the soft ground like "blind" shells someone had forgotten to provide with explosive charges.

After the best part of an hour, they reached the border of the small artificial rainforest. They stopped, panting, coughing, wheezing, but glad they had made it so far without getting shot at.

"Bushed, but not ambushed," Laura tried another wisecrack that fell flat. The two women squeezed the water out of their cornrows and everyone wiped their faces dry. They held up their weapons and once again checked the magazines and chambers as if afraid the bullets might not have made it all the way up here. Laura verified there wasn't any dirt in the barrel of her pocketed Taurus. Then they hid their half-empty bags with the spare guns and ammo under a Russelia bush, easy to spot because of its low-hanging panoply of twigs, studded with fiery red "squibs".

Solitaire inculcated them briefly with the three rendezvous points they had fixed in the case that their little group was forced to split up and scram in all directions: the Petite Anse, the airstrip, and this Russelia bush on the border of the rainforest on the village side. In that order. They test-ran their walkie-talkies, which Ignace had found in the further recesses of the Pas de Deux's locker. They weren't exactly state of the art, more like technical museum exhibits, but on the whole twice as reliable as mobile telephones prone to fall into dead radio spots. Finally, they adjusted the shoulder straps of their submachine guns and cautiously took to the road.

Squeezing along the houses left and right two by two like the animals of the ark, they approached the village centre, their guns across their abdomens, ready to wreak death and destruction. Laura's light submachine gun was empty, though. To handle a deadly device that dispenses 800 rounds per minute, is not something to be picked up overnight, Ignace had found. In Laura's hands, a loaded submachine gun would have been a far more dangerous threat for her own companions than for the enemy. Like a run-away garden hose, her weapon risked developing a life of its own, spraying the countryside with full metal jacket hollow-point projectiles indiscriminately. That would have meant a lot of holes, not all of them strictly appropriate. Hence, so long as the enemy wasn't aware of this little ploy and Laura kept her pokerface, their bluff might not be called.

With every house they passed, they could sense more and more eyes on them, even though for them, not a soul was to be seen. At any moment now, somebody could open fire at them from a window or terrace, possibly without them even hearing it coming since the eerie howling and roaring of the gale was practically drowning all other sounds. The rain was pelting furiously on the glistening black tarmac. Loose slabs of corrugated iron from the roof-tops were swirling about like huge bionic bats with dysfunctional radar cells. A lonely metal dustbin came pitchpoling down the road like a robot gymnast performing an Olympic floor exercise. Its contents had long been scattered and gone with the wind. Most people caught in cyclones, Laura had been told, do not perish because they are sucked into the chimney of the twister and blown to high heaven, but because they get hit by low-flying debris.

The thunderstorm kept going strong with earth-shattering fury. The bolts of lightning were streaking away like Martian spaceship's laser guns. Papers, cardboard, wooden slabs and all sorts of loose rubbish were blown along the empty road and across the lawns, hit the houses or smashed into the trees. The entire village breathed the atmosphere of the forgotten props of some B-class western movie produced years ago on a shoestring budget. The film crew probably had not bothered to take the stuff down, but had left the props to rot or be used again in another horse opera with black and white cowboy hats and heavy period guns. Meanwhile, the invisible inhabitants must have sought shelter in a more solid brick building, the school maybe, and would be plunged in devout prayer for this apocalyptic visitation to pass.

Suddenly, Solitaire held up her left hand and clenched her fist again. The group stopped. Solitaire put her left index finger to her closed lips. A somewhat paradoxical gesture considering the deafening din around them. They were now standing between two oblong wooden houses proffering temporary protection from the wind. Listening hard, Laura, who had teamed up with the Doc, caught a strange metallic squeaking sound amidst the roar, the thunder, and the pelting of the rain.

What had probably intrigued or alarmed Solitaire was its striking repetitiveness. By and large, nature is incapable of such pendulum precision. It sounded very much like the grating in the wind of a heavy wooden sign Laura had once seen hanging from some rusted cast-iron arm at the door of Falmouth harbour's Dog Watch Tavern - the kind you would expect to be frequented by invalid sailors stomping time with their wooden crutches and carved whalebone prostheses. Since nothing was to be seen along the road, the strange noise had to come from the back of the house to Laura's left, across the road, the one that Solitaire and Ignace had just been about to pass when Solitaire had stopped them. Solitaire gestured that she would stalk to the back of the house with Ignace clockwise and indicated Laura and the Doc to do the same the other way round.

When Laura and the Doc had crossed the road and reached the house's rear side, they very cagily peeped round the corner. Neither of them could believe what they saw. Like a bored old-age pensioner or maybe the abandoned village idiot, an elderly black man was sitting in a porch swing, pushed back and forth by the wind with such momentum that the man kept using his feet as brakes so as not to be hurled on the ground or even catapulted on the lawn. He wore a black silken top hat which he had drawn far down over his forehead and had donned a black, greasy frock whose tails were flapping ferociously in the wind. On his thighs, he clasped a wooden walking stick with an ornamental skull as a knob. The red paint on the wall behind him had peeled off in several places and hung down in flakes torn off by the wind one by one. The porch under his feet showed numerous holes and dangerous gaps. The wood was so rotten that this colonial version of Count Dracula must repeatedly have crashed through the boards like through thin spring ice. The porch swing had quite obviously been exposed to the elements during all kinds of weather for many years and clearly showed the results of the wear and tear. Its original upholstery had probably been torn up by cats, much of the stuffing having subsequently disappeared to bolster bird's nests and rodent burrows. All that was left of the panoply tissue were a few wind-blown rags and the iron frame. The hinges had rusted to such an extent that they would squeak at every single movement of the swing.

The sight of the four heavily armed people suddenly popping up from his left and right did not seem to upset the old man in any way, although he did stop the seesaw movement of the swing by jamming the tip of his walking stick through the rotting wood. Then he got up, bowed and described a half-circle in the air with his top hat in an elegant stage flourish, while his frock tails rattled in the wind like a rotten sail come loose at the foot.

"Antoine Jolibois, at your service," he shouted. Then he started laughing, loud and piercingly, for no apparent reason other than maybe the ridiculous comment on the decrepit surroundings his name seemed to offer. He pushed his top hat back over his forehead with all his might so that, to claim the man's headwear, a cyclone would have to rip off the man's scalp into the bargain. The black mad hatter sat down again, pushing the frock tails under his buttocks. The rhythmic squeaking of the swing started over. Laura tried to fight her terrible suspicion that this black scarecrow of a man might conceivably represent the local community's mental average. Which, if it were true, bode ill for the Yellow Dancer.

"Bojou," Ignace addressed the old man in his truncated French.

"We seem to have lost our way somewhat. Would you be so kind as to…"

Before he had time to finish his unlikely opening, the old man started laughing aloud again as though in anticipation of a punchline he had heard before and, raising his walking stick, pointed it at something beyond his surprise visitors, all standing transfixed by his bizarre vaudeville act. At the same moment, the ominous metallic clicking of gun slides made the four figures in front of him freeze. Then a man's high-pitched voice was pitted hard against the wind.

"Maybe I can help?"

The slow, pointed, though slightly outlandish pronunciation and an unmistakably menacing overtone formed a glaring contrast to the seemingly polite, casual nature of the question. Laura had to think of her first meeting with Ti Martin. Solitaire was the first to overcome her startled paralysis. Very slowly, she took her submachine gun off her shoulder with one hand and let it drop on the ground where it landed with a wet squishing sound. This was probably her way of signalling to her people not to try anything foolish. If that had been the message, it was fully understood, and they all followed Solitaire's example. Then they lifted their hands above their heads and slowly turned on their heels.

A medium-sized man in a black hooded cape covering his features with the single exception of a long beak of a nose stood some ten yards away, holding Solitaire and her companions at bay with his gun. In his uncanny facelessness, he could have been an impersonation of the Grim Reaper who would not let a simple hurricane come between his mission and the lost souls that, by all rights, were to be his. The submachine gun he carried in lieu of the standard-issue scythe could be shrugged off as a personal whim or a recently effected upgrade. Even though she could not see much of him at all, Laura was positive that this was the man she had watched at the helm of the Yakamoz when they passed through the Rivière Salée together.

Next to his left leg, an excitedly panting big, muscular Schwarzenegger of the canine world with disproportionately small, round ears the shape of headphones seemed to be itching for orders to tear those four pathetic humans in front of it to pieces. Whenever it rose on his hind legs, Laura thought, it probably stared its master right in the eyes. Behind this peculiar twosome, no less than five tall, massively armed bald gorillas stood in a semi-circle, pointing their guns at Solitaire and the others, yet keeping their boss out of their respective lines of fire. Not even their bulky capes could dissimulate their broad shoulders and arched chests. In their big grizzly's paws, their submachine guns looked like something fallen out of a chocolate Kinder egg.

For the length of maybe ten heartbeats, the two groups with their light and dark capes and hoods stood facing each other in total silence. The unreal scenery gave Laura the impression of a secret gathering of some exceptionally militant Franciscan and Benedictine monks having met at this unlikely place with the single purpose of deciding the age-old quarrel about the sex of archangels once and for all by means not usually in the monastic repertoire. At last, the "black abbot's" voice broke the spell.

"What unpardonable rudeness on my part. I seem to have forgotten to present myself," the man continued in his strong accent with the odd misplaced vowel. In his effort to leave no doubt about his firm grasp of the English language, he used unwieldy expressions that marked him even more as an autodidactic foreigner. Besides, he would squeeze in the odd "phantom" vowel whenever two or more consonants threatened to collide, which gave away his Turkish origin.

"My real name will probably not ring a bell, but I'll mention it anyway, for good order's sake: it's Suleiman Özgül. Yes, I thought so, never heard of it, have you? In some circles to which you are presumably familiar, they call me Suleyman the Silent."

The Turk bowed with the clumsy stiffness of a man who spends most of time sitting behind a desk, or at a bar. Subconsciously, Laura registered that the squeaking of the porch swing had stopped. If the black scarecrow had been allowed to withdraw to his private quarters despite the Sultan and his men immobilising everybody at gunpoint, that could only mean the Sultan and Dracula were in cahoots with each other. Maybe the black Baron had orchestrated the whole rigmarole and cast himself as a dead ringer for the role of a decoy. Solitaire turned her head only slightly in the direction of Ignace.

"Suleyman the Silent... what? Sucker? Never heard of him. You, Ignace?"

Ignace gave the impression of a man hectically filing through the yellow pages of his mental directory. Then he looked up blithely, sighed and shook his head as if to insinuate that the names of, say, the five last Tudor kings were more familiar to him than that of Suleiman. But the Turk did not lose his composure that easily. He seemed not altogether devoid of humour, Laura thought.

"What's in a name, right? Then again, the sequence of recent events ought to corroborate that I deserve my handle. But let's not give it any more thought. Since we are on the question of names, I take it you have found my message and are on the noble quest of unearthing the lady they call the Yellow Dancer, am I right? Of course I am. Or would that be yet another name you never heard of?"

Solitaire's main fuse, none too resilient at the best of time, had reached breaking point.

"What in the blazing hell is this supposed to be? Why this stupid questioning? What did you kill Ti Martin for and why have you lured us on this godforsaken island with your silly charade? To play a round of Snakes and Ladders?

"Patience, dear Solitaire. As they say, all comes to him who can wait. As for Ti Martin now, his killing was a favour for a distinguished customer's friend. And if you try hard to be objective, you will have to agree that Ti Martin had been overplaying his hand for quite a while already. As for you," he was pointing at Laura, "I have known you all my life, in a manner of speaking. But you won't remember me, I'm afraid, you were too small then. Meanwhile, you seem to have developed very well, my compliments. Your choice of friends you'll have to work on, though, I'm afraid. Well, none of us is perfect, are we?. Not even Korkmaz here," he stooped slightly towards his dog who would probably have pricked up his ears had they not been small and round.

"Water under the bridge. I'd like to invite you all on a little leisurely walk, if I may. The weather being what it is, the fun will perhaps not be totally unmitigated, but I think I can guarantee you will not regret your coming."

"May we take our arms down, my hands have lost all feeling. Besides, it's easier to walk hands down," Solitaire asked, while Suleiman's gorillas were frisking them and collecting all hidden weapons and the walkie-talkies.

Suleiman shook his head and clicked his tongue apologetically. "That may be so, but no, please keep them up a little while longer. I wouldn't want to end my days like three of my closest collaborators on Kavaloura."

"Kava.. what?" Now it was Solitaire's turn to feign ignorance. "What's that? No, don't tell me, a ship?"

"Close, but no cigar. No, it's a small insignificant islet in the Aegean, where I had deposited a consignment of dope destined for Europe. First-class stuff. When my people came to fetch it, the only thing they found were three rapidly decaying corpses playing poker. One of the stiffs packed a royal flush, I was told, another had an ace stuck up his short-sleeve. The humour of some people….Sick, wouldn't you say? Anything you might contribute to elucidate the deplorable episode would be most welcome." "No idea what happened to them, nor to the 100 kilos of your smack."

Suleiman stopped in his tracks and turned around to face Solitaire, who was already well aware of having committed a blunder.

"Funny, I don't recall mentioning heroin, nor the precise quantity of the merchandise now, did I? "

Solitaire shrugged her shoulders.

"Must have heard it somewhere, small world, you know."

"So they say, so they say. Mehmet here," he pointed at the gorilla walking in the middle of the phalanx, "is a brother of Ali's. That's the skeleton with the royal flush. I could imagine Mehmet itching to be alone with you for an hour or so. But pleasure has to wait. What's that the Toubib keeps telling his dog, break step! And, oh, yes, you can take your hands down, now, after all, I think."

Suleiman pointed in a direction that would take them out of the village's confines. His bodyguards nodded to signal that they had stripped the group of all weapons concealed on their bodies as well as their Kevlar vests and were ready to move. Suleiman took the lead and kept his dog on a thick leather leash fixed to a spiked necklace that made Korkmaz look like a regular Warcraft pet.

"And yet another thing,"

Suleiman stopped again.

"Do me a favour and keep walking at an even pace. Remember, gentlemen never run, anyway, if we are to believe Mr. Siting. Korkmaz tends to get jumpy whenever he sees someone making sudden moves. The hunting instinct, you see, there is nothing I or anybody else for that matter could do to hold him back."

He continued the march.

"As you will have noticed, Korkmaz is a Kangal, an Anatolian sheepdog. The similarity of this particular variety with bears is not accidental. In Turkey, such dogs were bred and trained to guard herds and had to be capable of taking on any predators, since their armed masters, the shepherds, could not always be around. The small ears of this Kangal are meant to offer next to no hold for the paws, claws, and fangs of attacking wolves or bears. To notice such predators approaching a herd at night, an animal with a fine olfactory sense has practically no need of hearing. Men stand no chance against a Kangal, anyway. And even with a gun in hand, you would have a hard time stopping Korkmaz once let loose. Should you ever be confronted with a Kangal, unlikely as that may seem given the present circumstances, you better stand still or sit down and don't move a muscle. Remember, dogs go straight for the jugular, it's in their genes."

The guards and their prisoners did a right turn at the farthest corner of the village. Hanging their heads, Solitaire, Laura, and the two men trotted along like half-drowned kittens, while Suleiman marched in front as proud as the proverbial cock of the roost. The thunderstorm had at long last moved on to more promising territories. The bouts of tropical showers had given way to a lighter, if annoyingly persistent rainfall. Capes or no capes, everybody was soaked. The gale was apparently approaching its climax, tearing at houses and huts as if determined to remove both village, island, and archipelago from the map. Even though Alberto's eye followed a track much more to the east, it seemed at least to be squinting at the Saintes. Laura bit her lips till she drew blood, a habit of hers when feeling stressed. Despite Solitaire's careful planning and preparations, the four of them had been taken like rank recruits. Without their guns and generally outnumbered, they were pretty much helpless against Suleiman and his men. Why had he not shot them right away? To relish his triumph, make the most of it?

"Where the hell are you leading us?" Solitaire, probably angry with herself for having put her foot in it with the Kavaloura story, burst with impatience.

"Relax, we're almost there. Right about!"
They were veering onto a flooded lawn and sank into the grass up to their ankles.

"Halt! We've arrived."

They stopped. Suleiman had led them to the village churchyard, whose graves formed slightly undulating rows behind a rusty cast-iron fence.

"If I may go first…"

Suleiman kept his dog on an even shorter leash and strode through the squeaking gate. His gorillas wedged in the prisoners and pushed them on like lambs herded to the slaughterhouse.
"Beyond this point, only you, please." Suleiman was looking at Laura. At his sign, Solitaire and the two men were held back by the bodyguards. Some thirty feet further on, the Sultan and Laura passed by a rather wide and deep, freshly dug pit pretty much filled with opaque rain-water the colour of clay.

At last, Suleiman stopped in front of a single, well-tended grave, which displayed all the signs of housing a recently departed member of the local community. The casket six feet lower down must still be intact, since the big molehill of soil above it had not caved in yet. The grave was framed by a low marble rim that ran all round its oblong shape. The headstone was of the same material, its inscription partially covered by a fresh bouquet of yellow heliconia. The flowers stood in a vase itself almost completely buried in the ground so that the flowers wouldn't be blown all over the place.

"May I present…the Yellow Dancer." Suleiman stooped and plucked the vase with the flowers from the ground with a squelching sound, so Laura could read the simple inscription. Penelope Z, 1945 to 2015. RIP.

Suleiman displayed remarkable tact by taking a few steps back to grant Laura a moment of silent composure. Laura, standing beside herself, looked at her biological mother's grave with a mixture of sadness and confusion. The gale had continuously torn and ruffled her corns with such force that by now, the loose strands of her wet hair were being blown about her face like so many Nepalese streamers. She felt as if the earth had stopped turning, while the atmosphere around it continued to move, causing this interminable, seemingly untiring wind. How many times had she more recently tried to imagine what to say, how to address her mother, and had finally left it entirely to the spur of the moment. The natural enough thought that she might be standing over her grave, however, had never really crossed her mind, even though the possibility of something like that occurring had never been as remote as all this.

"You missed her by a few weeks. We both missed her, that is, and now we shall have to content ourselves with her dear memory. Of which you will have very little, if any at all, I presume." Suleiman, who had stepped up to the grave again, touched Laura's arm.

"She must have filled any number of spectacular financial holes around here with Robert's money. That's what I was told, anyway. That's apparently how she came by the honorary nickname they gave her, Yellow Dancer. Dancing in paradise with Robert now, I take it. May Allah hold his hand above her forever, huzur içinde yatsın, as we say. You know any Turkish, no? Pity, a beautiful language, believe me, very ornamental, loaded with tradition and Oriental mystery. Anyway, we both loved her most passionately, both your father and myself, that is. Each in his own way, of course."

He put the vase with the helicona back on the ground.

"The true irony of it all is really another, you know. I did my worst to deny Robert Penelope, and he made every damn effort to keep you away from Penelope and vice versa. Maybe he had the honest intention of bringing Penelope and you together one fine day. I doubt it, though. She had become a bad debt for him, you see, a millstone round his neck, if you see what I mean. By her very existence, she would have revealed his past by and large and brought his house of cards down. And so, he had to hide her from you and you from her. Life is a tale told by an idiot, isn't that what Shakespeare said? It would make a nice inscription on her headstone. On anybody's headstone, for that matter."

For a while, all three of them remained standing like biblical figures turned to pillars of salt by God's wrath or blind fate's spite. Laura felt neither pity nor sympathy for the vindictive Turk who had been a mortal enemy of her father's for most of his life and, when all was said and done, had to be held responsible for the turmoil of this sad Levantine tragedy. On the other hand, there was no denying that the very same Turk, albeit as the very incarnation of evil, had become part and parcel of her confused family chronicles like some distant, ill-famed relative who nobody liked to have around but who it was impossible to ignore and avoid altogether.

"Enough of grief and mourning, the here and now beckons us on with unrelenting urgency."

Suleiman seized Laura's arm and pulled her away from the grave. With his free left hand, he waved at his gorillas, who were still training their guns on Solitaire, Ignace, and the Doc. As far as Suleiman was concerned, the three of them had more than outlasted their usefulness and could be disposed of without further ado. That's what the rain-filled pit must be for, it flashed through Laura's mind. Maybe Solitaire would be spared for a rendezvous with Mehmet before joining the two men. And Laura herself? Suleiman had no beef with her other than she was an awkward eyewitness better silenced.

She had to lift herself out of her trance-like daydream, and fast. Her thoughts were racing, as she racked her brain for the next move. "Parley" wouldn't cut it, she was certain. More likely than not, the Turk wouldn't know what it meant. If he did, he would be unlikely to respect and adhere to the terms of an extinct outlaw code.

Laura and the Sultan had hardly put ten feet between them and Penelope's grave, when, behind them, an eerie creaking sound like that of the heavy door of an overgrown, forgotten crypt turning on its hinges was to be heard. Using the shocked, stupefied reaction of the Sultan's gorillas as a mirror, Laura gathered that some gruesome spectacle of sorts must be in the making behind them. Before she had time to turn, though, a deep, hollow, bone-chilling laughter seemingly coming from the earth's womb mingled with the rustling of the foliage above them. Immediately, volleys of shots were being fired, bullets were whistling in all directions, in short, a messenger from hell must be paying a long-awaited visit. Submachine-guns spat out myriads of deadly projectiles both from the direction of the grave and from that of the nonplussed gorillas. Ignace, the Doc, and Solitaire had taken cover by diving behind whatever little stump and bump promised them survival. Suleiman had flattened himself on the ground and rolled sideways, not to get caught in the crossfire. Laura jumped headlong into the prepared mass grave, the muddy water softening her impact. Korkmaz yelped once or twice and then took to his paws in a frenzy, his leash flying in the air like a snake that had dug its fangs in his throat and refused to let go again.

Laura dared not lift her head. Burning hot shells were raining down on her like drops of lava, seething as they hit the muddy water. Without the experience of the attack on the Yellow Dancer off Antigua, she might have lost her mind in the pit that could so easily become her grave. As it was, she succeeded keeping her nerves under control tolerably well. Whoever was using Penelope's grave as a dugout and kept firing at Suleiman's thugs, must be an enemy of her enemy. It wasn't him she had to be afraid of, but the bodyguards.

One way or another, the moment would come when the shooters would have to reload their guns. Not all at the same time, of course, but in sufficient number perhaps to allow Laura to try and escape the infernal encounter. That would work only if she knew beforehand where to run. Any hesitation or lack of orientation was bound to cost her dearly. She threw off her cape and cautiously lifted her head just an inch to steal a glimpse over the edge of the pit.

Penelope's tomb was wide open. The thick wooden lid that had covered it had been flung aside with some force. The big lumps of soil that had covered the lid, making it heavy to lift, were now spread all around the grave and started dissolving in the rain. A little further back, the bullet-riddled headgear of Baron Samedi, standing in the tomb and firing away with his ancient Kalashnikov had ended up in a deep puddle. Had Suleiman's bodyguards bothered to bring but a single hand grenade to the churchyard, that would have put paid to the Baron and all the rest of them. Fortunately, they hadn't deemed it unnecessary. The special circumstances of his sudden appearance had caused general confusion and thus given the Baron what little edge he needed to marginally improve the awesome odds he was up against. Obviously, he would not be able to kill the gorillas all at one stroke. But he had apparently succeeded making impressive inroads into the enemy's phalanx. The remaining bodyguards defended themselves with some vigour and shot back till the barrels of their guns were steaming in the rain.

The shooting never let up. Bullets dug themselves deep into tree trunks with a soft thudding twang. Others bounced sideways like billiard balls and continued as deadly ricochets. Crosses, stones, vases or lamps on the graves literally exploded and hurled their splinters and debris in all directions. The images of some of the departed ones were punctured, their owners symbolically killed anew, as it were.

Then, suddenly, there was the very faint hint of an intermission that Laura had nervously been waiting for. She had already dug in her feet in such a way as to allow her to jump out of the pit and roll behind the thick trunk of a chestnut tree she had picked as her next cover from her dugout. She pulled herself up on the remnants of a branch shot in two. Then she ducked, half counting on being caught out by some stray bullet any time now, and ran towards the remote rear part of the churchyard. Keeping her head down, she almost collided with the low fence delimiting the area on that side. The shooting had started anew and the full-metal-jacket envoys were reducing the boards of the fence to her left and right to splinters and sawdust. With one leap that would have stood any Paralympic contestant in good stead, she jumped over the fence. Her veins bursting with adrenalin, and splinters and shrapnel still whizzing round her head like angry bees, she ran towards the rainforest without so much as looking back.

2. The Stalking Iroquois

Somebody was sneaking through the undergrowth. Like a tiger on the hunt, he or she seemed to be taking infinite care to tread noiselessly. Yet Laura's delicate hearing had caught a feeble squelch like that of a sponge getting squeezed dry. Laura was huddled motionless on the boggy soil smelling of marsh grass and vanilla. Vanilla had been her father's favourite flavour in almost everything: ice cream, biscuits, desserts, whatever, no problem if only it was vanilla.

Laura didn't share that passion. Too sweet, too velvety, too vanilly. Instinctively following her first impulse of flight, she had run on and on head over heels, uphill and down, then uphill again, leaving the churchyard far behind. Then, soaked to her bones by the rain and the muddy water in the pit as well as bruised all over by thorny bushes, birch-like twigs and razor-sharp sawgrass blades, she had forced herself to stop. She had to bring her racing pulse down to normal and try to listen and watch closely instead.

Her self-imposed discipline and innate reflex of self-control seemed to pay dividends now.

Above her, more branches broke off and crashed down like slain chimps dropping out of the trees. Smaller twigs whistled through the thicket like arrows shot by well camouflaged redskins. The din around her, though gradually fading, was still strong enough to drown any suspicious stalking noises. Yet, as soon as Laura's "sonar" had picked up a repetitive sound of a certain frequency and amplitude in a generalised turmoil, it would cling to it, home in on it like a bat on a moth. Presumably, some lingering atavism inherited from our troglodyte ancestors. A measly echo of the somnambulistic gift of infallibility with which some females of the animal kingdom are apt to catch the feeblest, most pitiful croaking of her starving young in the ear-splitting cacophony of a herd, pack or colony.

Laura's weak sense of orientation, however, was lamentably failing her again. The same moment she had entered the rainforest, she had been lost. Originally, the little artificial jungle had been planted very much like a densely wooded park with discretely marked paths for tourists to follow. Yet rain and gale-force winds had almost turned the facility into the true McCoy, a well-nigh authentic rainforest complete with landslides, uprooted trees, and thickets torn asunder and piled upon one another. Laura's walkie-talkie had fallen into the hands of the Sultan's men, so that there was no more communication between her and Solitaire's soggy pants gang or what was left of it. Laura had to find the Russelia bush, under whose branches studded with blood-red blossoms they had hidden the remaining weapons for precisely this kind of contingency.

There it was again - that spongy squelching sound of soles partly dissociating themselves from the sticky clay of the bog. Then, the soles were pressed back deep into the mud by a bigfoot's considerable weight. Too heavy for either Ignace, the Doc or Sol. Very likely, one of Suleiman's gorillas. Was that a shadow to her right? Or just a figment of her feverish imagination? Laura felt that, during the past weeks, she must surely have suffered five hundred of the one thousand deaths a coward is generally said to die.

Ever so slowly, she crawled on all fours like an Iroquois squaw on her desperate search for the remnants of her scattered tribe. A real redskin would already have fabricated a bow and arrows from what material the rain forest abounded with. Yellow-feathered Laura didn't even have a pocketknife which could have served her as a tool and weapon.

The ugly metallic clicking of a gun's cock, a sound she had come to despise deeply by now, made her freeze. The shadow to her right had not been a spectre but a very real person, the guy Suleiman had introduced as Mehmet. He suddenly appeared from the bushes only two or three steps away from her and levelled the barrel of his gun at her head.

Mehmet, of all people, Laura thought, as if that made any difference now. Too late to run for it. If she so much as flexed a muscle or twitched her brows, the Turk would squeeze the trigger. Despite her precautions, Mehmet had proved the more skilled stalker. His left shoulder was bleeding profusely. Presumably he had been hit by one of the stray bullets from Baron Samedi's Kalashnikov AK 47. A graze had ripped his right earlobe off, which made his growing likeness to Korkmaz even more striking. Blood was running down his face and neck. Without saying a word, Mehmet raised his gun hand, which he had dropped a few inches in a fit of pain or indecision. Laura hung her head, rested her upper body on her arms and closed her eyes in silent resignation. By way of consolation, the Doc had explained to her, back on Montserrat, that she need not fear the pain of getting shot dead. No, it wouldn't hurt at all, since, more likely than not, she would not even feel the impact of a bullet travelling at a muzzle velocity of several hundred miles per hour.

"The moment it hits you, you drop dead before the sound of the explosion reaches your ears or your synapses have time to pass the sensation of Pain on to your brain."

So when she did hear a noise now, it wasn't that of a shot but something like a metallic singing very much like that of a scythe being brandished through dry wheat stalks at the height of summer. Then, an object of just about the size and weight of a coconut thumped down on the wet soil next to her, followed by something infinitely heavier crashing into the lower bushes and coming to rest on the carpet of flattened sawgrass.

"Praised be the Lord," she heard another familiar voice call out. She opened her eyes. In front of her stood Bernard, the pious hermit of Terre-de-Haut. His hair no longer stood up as if hit by lightning, but hung down his head and shoulders like a soaking wet mop. His long beard had gone, which took some ten to twenty years off his age. At his present state, he even bore an uncanny resemblance to the pot-smoking Son of God as portrayed on the door of his ark. In his right hand, he held a machete of the kind that had been used on these islands for centuries to cut sugarcane and coconuts. With the notable difference that this blade wasn't dripping with juice but with blood.

"Now and for all eternity, Brother," Laura, still kneeling on the ground, replied mechanically and thanked the hermit for helping her get up on her feet.

From the corners of her eyes, she saw that the object which had landed by her side bore a striking resemblance to Mehmet's skull. A headache less, she couldn't help herself thinking. The torso of the bodyguard lay stretched out peacefully as if asleep on the branches of a bush, whose leaves had saw-teeth like Solitaire's knife, though a few sizes bigger. Excitedly paddling fire ants were using Mehmet's rapidly coagulating blood streams as a welcome means of transport.

Laura wanted to shake the hermit's hand and thank him once again for saving her life, but Bernard was already busy collecting Mehmet's weapons. He picked up the submachine gun which lay under Mehmet's headless corpse and handed Laura the handgun he had found in the man's armpit holster. Laura took it and, thanks to her newly acquired expertise, immediately identified it as a Makarov IŽ-70, the same kind that Ti Martin had packed on his last campaign.

So now she had a gun, at least, and one she was sure she could handle, which was a reassuring improvement on her sleep-walking situation. What bothered and baffled her at present was the perpetual shifting of the goal posts. Who was friend and who was foe in this confusing struggle. The locals were apparently on Solitaire's side, as the example of the black Baron had amply illustrated. But what was the hermit doing here? Had she run into him minutes ago unexpectedly, she might have shot him. Not in cold blood, of course, but rather by accident, as a natural reflex, before he could have identified himself as the ally that he appeared to be. Whence this inexplicable yet determined partisanship? How and why had the hermit overcome his seemingly intense dislike of Tere-de-Bas and come to her rescue? Why had Baron Samedi put his life on the line to bail them out at the churchyard? Whatever the answers to those questions: for the time being Laura contented herself to accepting any help she could get.

After the episode with Mehmet the Headless she could continue her search for the others. Think, think, she kept calling herself to order, trying to use her brains despite her exhaustion, her thirst, her weariness, and despite the pain that surged through her every time she moved her limbs. Her wits, not the Makarov, were her most formidable weapon, but only if she decided to use them. Which of the agreed rendezvous points could she possibly reach fastest from where she stood, without bumping into yet another of Suleiman's men? She only hoped not to come across Korkmaz. Without his master, he would probably be perturbed and all the less predictable. Smelling her fear, he would probably charge.

The Petite Anse! She had to get back to the bay where the padre had set them ashore. That would be her safest bet. The hermit could probably have shown her the way, even accompanied her, but it was too late for that now. He had disappeared again like a ghost. Through the roaring of the gale and the swooshing of the treetops, she thought she sometimes heard distant shots, but it could also be more branches being broken off by the wind. Not so much as an amiably smiling cat around to indicate to her which way to turn.

Finally, she remembered where she was, what kind of place she had set foot on. Terre-de-Bas was a little speck of an island on the chart she had seen aboard the Pas de Deux. Hence, when push came to shove, it didn't really matter a hoot which way she turned.

Before long, she would of needs leave this dug-up, washed-up, fucked-up rainforest and inevitably end up on the beach. Following that, clockwise or anti-clockwise, as her whim or the prevailing wind direction might dictate, she would reach the bay. She shook her head at her temporary insanity and ran straight on.

The cool metal of the Makarov in her hand was perhaps more of psychological than of practical importance. Laura took not a little pride in the fact that she had not lost her head after all, but had analysed her predicament in relatively cold blood. The thought of her three companions and their possible fate had contributed to sobering her up. Was Solitaire still alive? Laura was pretty confident that this relentless amazon of a woman she had recognized as her biological sister only a few hours ago would be able to hold her own, even barehanded. Ignace the Terrible could take on a whole regiment on his own, anyway, so he was the one she did not have to worry about. The Doc was slow but cunning enough to reason his way out of a paper bag any time.

The dark green veil in front of Laura seemed to grow more and more sparse. She thought she could already hear the thundering surf ahead. She had to bend the bushes and low-hanging branches back a few more times until, finally, she emerged from the lush vegetation and the sea lay right in front of her.

What a sight! This sea had very little in common with the somewhat bumpy, but still perfectly manageable element it had been that morning. The waves beyond the surf reached the height of a two-storey building and came on rolling furiously like a herd of stampeding buffalo. In the narrow strait between the two main islands of the archipelago, hissing breakers came rushing in to pound the coastal sands with roaring thunder as if trying to penetrate the earth's brittle crust. The gale drove the white foam over the surface in long, fraying stripes, whipping the fine velvet sands up to form whirling and swirling yellow clouds like dunes in a desert storm. The neighbouring islands had disappeared behind a curtain of mist, foam, and sand. The dark grey sky seemed forever merging with the leaden sea to form a firm shroud covering the archipelago.

As far as Laura could judge, the level of the sea had not risen any further. That would be an unmistakable sign that the gale, fierce as it still felt, had finally passed its peak. Laura took off her heavy combat boots and ran along the beach on her bare feet. The fine thin sand was blown up and down her back as if propelled by a hundred high-pressure valves. Her toes were bleeding but her concern for Solitaire and the others effectively blocked out the pain for the time being. The cape on the northern edge of the bay would be less than half a mile away, she reckoned. Immediately behind it was the rendezvous point. Always assuming it was the right cape. If it wasn't, she would have to make for the next one. Or the one after that.

The report of the shot from the rainforest to her right was drowned by the thunder of the white frothy surf. Even though Laura did feel something hitting her right shank, she was nevertheless surprised when her leg suddenly gave in and refused to bear her weight. She swayed, tumbled and dumped down on the wet sand and rolled a few feet into the foaming surf, which covered her immediately. It was only when she noticed her blood billowing in the water that she realized she had been shot at.

The sniper had aimed too low and wounded instead of killing her. Right now, he was trying to correct his mistake by taking pot shots at her. Projectiles hit the sand and whipped up small, fast approaching fountains in the sand. Lying in the shallow water, Laura didn't present aa easy a target as standing up, that was the good news. On the flip side, she couldn't allow herself to recede further into the sea for fear of being drawn into the groundswell's deadly pull. If the sniper kept on practicing, however, he was bound to finish her off sooner or later. Which left Laura with a bit of Hobson's choice: be drowned or get shot

As it happened, though, the man appeared too impatient and unwilling to waste more time. He left the cover of the thicket and came straight for Laura to put her out of her misery. Laura saw he carried a submachine gun. That probably accounted for his poor target record so far. At any distance at all, a short-barrelled gun like his could do a lot of damage all round but would not be accurate enough to hit a single "difficult" object. Had the sniper used a rifle instead, Laura would have been dead.

When he had come close enough, or thought he had, the sniper raised his gun and pulled the trigger. But there was no bang. A fortunate dud, or else his magazine was empty. The man cursed his unreliable weapon aloud, let his magazine drop in the sand, and knocked in a new one. Then he raised his gun again. The report of the shot raced across the beach. Laura shuddered, wondering at the same time what was going on. If she was to believe the Doc's prediction, she should never have heard the shot. Nor did she feel hit, even though the sniper could not possibly have missed her at such close range.

Standing halfway between the beach and the rainforest, the man dropped his right arm with the weapon, as if it had become too heavy for him. Then he staggered forward a step or two. His knees caved in, he slumped on the ground like a depleted sack of rice. One more time he picked up his gun. Again, the echo of a shot rolled across the sands. The man had just managed to raise himself when the bullet hit him from behind. Where his face had been seconds before, a shapeless mass of blood-red flesh was turning skyward now. Finally, the man fell forward on his gun and lay still.

For quite a long time, or so it seemed to Laura, nothing further happened. She paddled ashore, tore a strip of tissue from her shorts and tried to stop the bleeding of her right shank with trembling, jittery hands, while squinting nervously in the direction of the rainforest. She had no way of knowing who else was hiding there. Except that it couldn't possibly be one of Suleiman's gang which the sniper must have been a member of.

When Laura looked up again, she saw a human skeleton slowly stepping out of the first row of trees. Hallelujah, Baron Samedi had survived the shoot-out in the churchyard. Without his top hat and frock he was reduced to the sorry bag of bones someone had drawn on his black overalls and shirt. As he came running towards her, Laura noticed a couple of red blood stains on the white of the sketched-out rib cage. A bleeding skeleton was an anatomic novelty, something that underscored the man's voodoo powers.

Laura breathed a deep sigh of relief and lifted a welcoming hand to the Baron, thanking him for his invaluable intervention. Then she tended to her wound again. When he reached Laura, the Baron dropped his Kalashnikov, which had probably already seen action during the Cuban revolution and had a look at Laura's shank. The exit wound showed him, as he was gesticulating to Laura, that the sniper bullet was a lucky through-and-through. At first sight, anyway, the bullet had missed both the bone and the artery. All they could do here and now was try and stop the bleeding and guard against inflammation.

Only a few weeks ago, Laura would probably have passed out at the sight of so much of her own blood being shed. But what with the adrenalin pumping in her veins and her thoughts focussing on Solitaire, the gunshot wound worried her as much or as little as an accidental cut in her finger with a kitchen knife.

The Baron draped another strip of tissue from Laura's "shorts" round her right groin to slow down the blood supply to the leg, and tore his own shirt into two narrow strips which he wrapped round the wound for additional protection. Then he invited Laura to put her arm round his shoulder, which she did with great pleasure, as she was beginning to feel the pain on her leg. She pointed at the cape. The Baron seemed to understand. Thus, Laura hobbled along the beach, supporting herself on a voodoo skeleton. The effort of each step strained the muscles of her thigh so much that the tight bandage cut deep into her skin. She would have liked to ask the Baron what had made his friends and himself take sides with Solitaire and her group. But the communication would cost more time and energy than Laura felt she had at her disposal. Each step cost her an almost superhuman effort and gave her pains flashing through her body like high-voltage shocks. The gale was slowly subsiding, it seemed, but its squalls still packed enough force to throw Laura off her feet, had she not been supported by the Baron.

As they approached the cape, Laura realized that the sea level had risen altogether too much for her to wade around the cape even with the Baron's help. The path on the shore side, however, led uphill, back towards the rain forest. That would be both taxing and hazardous. Laura had no way of knowing how many of Suleiman's men were still around. Couldn't be all that many, all told. But a single sniper, albeit wounded himself, lying in wait up there somewhere would have been sufficient to take out both the Baron and Laura. That's how she would have proceeded, anyway, had she been one of Suleiman's bodyguards.

The water, on the other hand, would carry her and take the weight off her thigh and shank. Sure, the mighty groundswell risked smashing her or pulling her out to sea irresistibly. On the other hand, she was an excellent swimmer taking comfort in the memory of having once been very close to a nomination for her college team in the varsity Olympiad, had it not been for a silly cold that had wrong-footed her.

Either way, she didn't have one more minute to lose. Solitaire's life was at stake. The life of a woman for whom she had begun to feel sisterly love even before she had realized, that very morning in the Petite Anse, that she was in fact her biological sister. The "s"-shaped scar on her right thigh had identified her as the very "Elenii" with whom she had shared Penelope's womb for the duration of nine long months. With hindsight and having come to know the belligerent spirit of her sister by now, she wondered how they had existed in such a confined space without coming to blows even then. After having been separated from her so shortly after the first months of their lives and being re-united with her by the most unlikely of coincidences, it would be cruelly inconsiderate of fate to make her bury Solitaire on Terre-de-Bas before she even knew that Snow White was her sister. Taking him by surprise, she kissed the stupefied Baron on both cheeks and, before he had overcome his amazement, waded a few steps into the sea and threw herself headlong into the thundering surf.

3. Death of a Guardian Angel

Sharks! The thought shot through her mind while she was tossed about by the waves like a helpless wounded seal. She had to mobilize all her remaining strength just to hold her head above water and take a quick breather every now and again. Being totally absorbed up by her worries about Solitaire and the others, she had unwittingly neglected her own safety. As far as she was aware, sharks dangerous to humans rarely ventured into the shallow waters close to the beach, but there was no guarantee of that never happening either. Not far from New York's Atlantic harbour entrance, sharks had once even followed a river upstream and had attacked unsuspecting swimmers.

Sharks were quick and infinitely adaptable learners when it came to exploring new sources of food. Laura's bleeding shank might work as bait and attract the attention of a man-eater loitering about the Saintes with intent. With one leg almost immobile, her progress in the water was painfully slow. Very gradually, inch by inch, she succeeded putting enough distance between herself and the tip of the cape so she could round it without risk of being hurled against the towering rocks and smashed to pieces. The good news was, she could be reasonably sure that she was practically invisible from the shore. It felt like hours until she could finally change direction and profit from the impetus of the waves instead of constantly hammering into them with all her might. From the crests of the frighteningly steep billows, she could make out the handle-like contours of the Petite Anse.

Details were another matter, though. For one thing, her eyelids had almost been gummed up by the brine. For another, the moments of relative calm between her steep uplifts and downhill shoots were too brief to allow her to take in the dramatic scenery. Everything, herself very much included, was in constant motion, turning her topsy-turvy for seconds on end to let her go back to normal the next moment. The one thing the sea didn't was allow her to get anywhere nearer the beach. That's how it seemed to her, anyway.

At long last, she thought she had caught a glimpse of somebody sitting on the ground, with his or her back leaning against what had once probably been a flagpole and stood out like an ugly tooth broken in half. It seemed to Laura that she was looking at the figure of a woman, possibly that of Solitaire, facing away from the sea. Maybe that was no more than wishful thinking on her part. In the crazy stop-and–go ride forced upon her by the tug of war between the waves pushing her torso towards the beach and the strong undercurrent pulling her feet away from it, she felt like a disoriented whale being inexorably driven towards a beach on which it does not belong and where it will eventually be crushed by its own weight. "Pull yourself together, bitch," a panting Laura desperately shouted at no-one in particular. At present, the surf was getting a little weaker, more manageable, so she regained control over her limbs and tried to brace sherself for the imminent crash-landing.

It had to be Solitaire on the beach. Yet the way she was leaning against the pole, out in the open, completely exposed, she made an easier target than a Solitaire in full command of her mental and physical powers would ever have allowed herself to become. Either she was seriously injured and had just made it to the flagpole where she had collapsed, maybe fainted. Or else a hidden sniper had wounded and deliberately placed her there as a decoy and was now waiting to take pot shots from the comfort of his cover at anyone rushing to her help. Laura knew this to be a ploy used in combat ever since the dawn of mankind.

Wherever the sniper was hiding, he would hardly be paying attention to the only side from which no friend or foe was to be expected - the sea. That was Laura's chance. Unfortunately, she could only seize it if the sniper was careless enough to give away his position before Laura would be flung ashore. At that point, she would be a sitting and probably rather battered duck without so much as a shred of cover. To hit anything while still being tossed about by the surf would have been hopelessly ambitious even for a crack shot, let alone a mediocre one such as Laura.

She had just raised both arms in front of her to cushion her landing somewhat, when she thought she saw the bloody skeleton of the Baron emerge from the bushes at this beach end of the asphalt road. During the minutes Laura had needed to round the cape swimming, he had apparently skirted the Petite Anse climbing and walking. The sun peeping through the clouds for the very first time that day briefly flashed, on the barrel of the Baron's Kalashnikov. Then there was a shot. The skeleton stopped dead in its tracks, staggered backwards and slumped onto the tarmac. It all happened very suddenly and fast, but had just lasted long enough to given Laura the opportunity of noting approximately where the shot had come from, before the next wave washed over her head. The single shot had been fired from behind a large boulder some ten or so yards to the right of Solitaire. Presumably, the big chunk of rock had been rolled here by some recent earthquake. For the sniper, it offered excellent cover, at the same time blocking his view of the sea, though.

The impact was even harder and more painful than Laura had anticipated. She just managed to roll sideways on the concretelike sand, then she must have lost consciousness for a few moments. When she came to again, she was hurting all over and at a loss as to where she was and what was going on. Fortunately, the burning pain in her shank brought her back to the harsh reality of things quickly enough. She bit her tongue to stop herself from crying out loud and crawled towards the boulder on all fours. Halfway there, she suddenly noticed the bald head of the sniper pop up over the top of the volcanic rock. It was Suleiman's head, clearly, unmistakably. The funny cactus stubble on his skull gave him away. Why he had chosen to show his head at that crucial moment would remain his secret. Maybe he felt it necessary to change his position after the tell-tale shot he had fired at the Baron. Or perhaps he wanted a clearer field of vision between himself and Solitaire. Who knows, maybe the man's instincts had warned him that, even though there was little risk of someone approaching from the sea, that eventuality could not be discarded altogether, either.

What with the din of surf and wind, he could not possibly have noticed Laura's touchdown. But under present changed circumstances he could hardly help discovering her presence any second now. Laura had to give it a shot here and now, literally.

She was lying on her stomach, her breathing and pulse almost back to normal. She raised her head and lifted both hands clasped round the handle of the Makarov, which had fallen out of her pocket during her crash landing. She raised the gun to the level of her eyes, hoping that no sand had found its way into the moveable works. To hit the cactus head at this distance with the only shot she was likely to get, wasn't easy. Exhaustion, fear, and the irregular squalls tearing at her arm made Laura's hand tremble and sway. Caustic saltwater kept trickling from her scalp into her eyes. She saw the contours of Suleiman's head as if through a moving veil. She flipped the safety catch with her thumb, breathed normally, not too deep nor too shallow. When all the air had left her lungs and her body had become totally relaxed, she pulled the trigger between two heartbeats. Gently, with just as much force as was necessary to overcome the Makarov's pressure point without so much as twitching the barrel, exactly like the Doc had taught her during their one-off shooting exercise on board the Pas de Deux.

The bullwhip-like report of the shot and the singing whizz of the projectile had not yet reached Laura's water-stopped ears, as the cactus disappeared behind the rock as if jerked down by invisible strings. "Bull's eye", Laura murmured and picked herself up. Yes, by the look of it, she was perfectly capable of not only pointing a gun at a human being but of actually shooting him, if sufficiently desperate. With a loud groan, she hobbled across the beach towards Solitaire. Her sister was conscious, had maybe just been woken by the shot. She glanced at Laura briefly with weary eyes.

"Well, if it isn't Snow White. What kept you?"

Laura smiled. A joking Solitaire couldn't be in such a bad state.

"What can I say, traffic is a killer around here. And, oh yes, your cornrows," she pointed at her hair, "Sloppy job, didn't make it through the gale. Forget what I said about the tip."

Solitaire giggled and groaned, as Laura felt her sister's torso with her fingertips. A bullet had apparently smashed through Solitaire's right shoulder and put her out of action. She must have lost blood, but at least neither her lung nor any major blood vessel seemed affected. Her face was waxen and pale, though, her T-shirt and pants drenched in water and blood.

"I've been shot, too," Laura said with almost child-like pride pointing at her own conspicuous badge of courage on her shank.

"How are you? Where are the others?

Solitaire forced a wry smile.

"How am I? Swell, Laura Forster, real swell. In fact, I was just considering going for a swim, anyhow. Where the other two are, I couldn't tell. Communication has been down more recently. I guess I was too busy getting killed myself, see…"

Solitaire tried to straighten herself. Directly opposite the flagpole, a bleeding Ignace came limping out of the bushes. When he saw Solitaire and Laura, he stuck his gun back into his belt and crossed the road that separated him from the two women. Blood ran from the blade of the machete in his right hand. When he reached the Baron who was lying motionless on his back, he kneeled down and briefly felt the man's pulse at the jugular. Then he raised himself and slowly shook his head. Samedi, or so it seemed, had finally exhausted his treasure trove of voodoo conjuring tricks. Ignace got up again, threw the machete aside and helped Laura get Solitaire back on her feet. As both were turning their backs on the boulder that had served Suleiman as cover, Solitaire's surprised cry was the only warning they ever had.

Ignace dropped Solitaire to the ground and, without turning round, flung himself into Laura's arms. Thus, Suleiman's bullet, which would most likely have got Laura in the chest, slammed into the chabin's back instead. Ignace was propelled against Laura by the impact of the projectile and very nearly brought the two of them down. He grabbed Laura even tighter, painfully digging his fingernails into her biceps. Then, his vice-like grip suddenly relaxed. Like the full moon setting, his disfigured face slid down before Laura's eyes. She could not hold him as he fell heavily on the ground, pulling Laura half down with him. A thin trickle of blood was running out of his mouth as he groped for Laura's hand.

"Admit it," he whispered, "you were in on Ti Martin's caper." When he saw Laura nodding quietly, he grimaced a grin and pressed something round and metallic in her hand, clasping it tightly.

"You owe me one..." were the last words Laura heard. The next moment, a wave of blood gushed forth from his lips. Then his eyes grew rigid and his view turned inwards.

Another shot rang, this time fired by Solitaire who, with amazing presence of mind, had seized the Beretta from the dying chabin's belt as he fell. Suleiman had been caught empty at the wrong moment and not been given time to finish reloading. He hit the boulder sideways and rolled behind it, out of Solitaire's and Laura's sight.

All too eager to come to Solitaire's aid, Laura had forgotten to make sure she had truly killed the Sultan. A beginner's mistake, but one that had cost Ignace dearly.

"Didn't I tell you. He had a crush on you," Solitaire whispered as she dropped the Beretta. Laura realized that her sister needed immediate medical help, lest she died then and there on the beach of voodoo island because of her loss of blood. She grabbed Solitaire under her arms to pull her further away from the flagpole, just in case Suleiman the Indestructible had survived yet one more time. Only then did she cock her Makarov and limped towards the boulder to finally make sure.

At about the level where Suleiman's head had suddenly emerged, Laura noticed a small fresh dent in the rock with spots of blood in the resulting grove. It would seem she had not missed him. On the ground, there was a small puddle of blood. The only thing nowhere to be seen was the rest of Suleiman's bullet-proof body. Having been hit in several places and clambering for his life, he would not represent any immediate danger and could probably be neglected for the time being. By herself, a desperate Laura, injured herself, would never be able to carry her wounded sister all the way up the hill to ask for help in the village.

Suddenly, she thought she heard a hectic kind of panting like that of a dog seeking to cool its body down after a prolonged run across the countryside. Very slowly, she pushed aside the twigs of a large bush to her left. Right in front of her, no more than a few feet away, his trembling tongue hanging out of his half open mouth sideways and raising the short bristle-like hairs on his neck, stood a snarling and wheezing Korkmaz, pulling back his fleshy flews and baring his awe-inspiring fangs.

TENTH CHAPTER

1. The Yellow Dancer

"Mais tu's ou là, espèce de brute?" The Doc's voice somewhere in the thicket beyond Korkmaz had a wondrous effect on the dog. Korkmaz seemed to calm down almost instantly and stopped snarling. His menacing attitude was miraculously transformed into the model mien of man's best friend, happily wheezing away and wagging his tail in joyous anticipation. Laura's right hand, which was still clutching the unlocked Makarov, relaxed and disappeared behind her back. Without taking her watchful eye off Korkmaz, she stepped a little backwards before calling out for the Doc in a shaky voice. Only then did she notice the wound on the dog's right hind leg. He had apparently been grazed during the shoot-out and handicapped to a point at which he was still able to bare his awe-inspiring teeth, but perhaps no longer capable of following up on his threat.

Seconds later, the Doc came cursing through the crashing undergrowth. His attention seemed devoted entirely to tracing the dog so that he took no immediate notice of Laura's presence.

"Ma fois, am I glad to see you both in good shape. Good dog, nice dog. So Korkmaz found you, after all. I was hoping as much. But you look injured! Where are the two misfits hiding?"

Laura wasn't quite sure who had been found by whom, but that was a moot point. At least to the extent that Korkmaz contented himself with limping after them peacefully. She led the Doc to Solitaire, who was sitting up on the beach, holding Ignace' head in her lap. The Doc kneeled beside her and put two fingertips to the chabin's carotid artery. When he had ascertained that there was no more hurry, as far as Ignace was concerned, he took a closer look at Solitaire and came to the same conclusion as Laura.

"She has to be carried up to the village right away. We'll be needing some sherpas. I'll try and get help from Guadeloupe later. The hospital at Pointe-à-Pitre has a chopper, as far as I know. I hope it's in working order for a change and the pilot sober. Whether it can lift off with this wind-force still raging, is a different matter. Your shank must be taken care of, as well, or both of you will die at my hands. That would take some living down, first Ti Martin and César, now Solitaire and you. They'd be calling me Doctor Death as from today, really can't allow that to happen."

"And Suleiman?" Solitaire whispered, while she stroked the dead chabin's wayward dreadlocks.

"Bugger him. We'll get him some other time. He won't go far, anyway, if he is as badly shot as Laura tells me."

Laura sat down next to Solitaire and put her arm around her shoulder. Solitaire looked at her with eyes that at least momentarily seemed to have lost their glint of steely resolve. Did she have a presentiment that Laura and herself were much closer than ever suspected? Hardly. She had had no time to peruse Penelope's letters yet. But that didn't matter now. During those days spent together, Laura felt they had found a unique intimacy of souls. That was more important and infinitely more valuable than the identity of their respective genetic codes.

"I had told Ignace to play your guardian angel rather than mine, this time. That's what he did."

"Yes, that's what he did." Laura nodded.

"To think that he was about to cut my throat when we first met..."

"Where did you get this scar on your thigh?" she asked Solitaire, who seemed puzzled by this question totally out of context, as it must seem to her.

"No idea, what does it matter. Has been there for ever. Maybe I was born with it. A blunder on the part of the midwife, a brandmark of the devil, who knows. No, I guess some childhood accident of which I myself have no recollection. There was no-one to ask about it, either. I once wanted to have it removed surgically, but the Doc advised against it. Told me it would be too much of a thing and, with any bad luck, risked looking worse than now. So I let it rest."

Laura said no more about it. This was not the right moment to delve into Solitaire's lost childhood once again. If she wasn't looked after on the double, she would forfeit her future as well. Alberto seemed to have continued his lonesome stroll north by northwest. The rain had exhausted itself and the tropical storm was running out of steam. Cormorants, seagulls, frigate birds, and other feathered species lifted their heads from underneath their wings, craned their necks, sorted out their ruffled feathers and ever so warily left their nests and hiding places. Slowly, as it were probingly, the hard core Caribbean wild life woke from its stupor. Voices and the patter of many feet were to be heard from the asphalt road above the Petite Anse. A few moments later, a motley dozen or so locals carrying a picturesque array of arms appeared on the scene. They seemed to be led by the bizarre spectator who had been questioned by Solitaire shortly after their landing.

The men weren't slow to realize that their help was once again asked for but apparently held different opinions as to how they should proceed. At that moment, an ancient pick-up truck turned around the corner and stopped in front of the women. Bernard the hermit and another local got out and released the loading flap.

"Anyone for a ride?"

Laura raised her arm. The blacks got hold of Solitaire, Ignace and the Baron, lifted them up onto the pick-up and helped Laura to get on the platform and sit across so that her legs came to rest on Solitaire's and the two corpses' feet. The Doc and Korkmaz got into the front, Bernard took the wheel again and off they went up the hill as fast as the slippery road would allow.

Through waves of pain, Laura couldn't help smiling at the picture of the unconscious Solitaire squeezed between two dead bodies, all three heads rolling left and right at every bend the pick-up had to negotiate. Laura closed her eyes. The swerving truck made her seasick. Whenever Bernard accelerated, Laura had to hold on tight not to fall off. She couldn't even remember when she had last eaten something. Small wonder she felt nausea surging up inside her. She wondered how the Frenchman had succeeded in "turning" Korkmaz, making him his own pet. The poor beast had probably listened to him for a while and then decided there was no antidote against loquaciousness in the conventional canine toolbox. And so, he had just given in at some stage and resigned himself into his fate. Laura opened her eyes again and noticed with relief that they had reached the first houses of the village.

The truck stopped next to the red house at whose rear side they had first made the acquaintance of Baron Samedi. Bernard helped Laura down. Her shank now hurt fiendishly, the bumpy ride hadn't exactly helped. She clenched her teeth and looked at Solitaire who was manifestly worse off. The second the car had stopped a small crowd of black women had come running out of the red house to take care of the dead and wounded. They placed Laura on the terrace and carried Solitaire inside with the Doc hard on their heels. The corpses of Ignace and the Baron, were sat down on the porch swing, where they would have struck any uninformed passer-by as two retired freaks, bizarre but harmless, tired and fallen asleep after their prolonged walk down memory lane.

Probably deemed in no immediate danger, Laura was left alone for the time being. She had no problem with that but sat weak and absent-minded on the mouldy stairs of the porch. The Doc obviously was in a hurry to look Solitaire over and call the helicopter from Pôle Caraïbes airport.

The few men around, exhausted from fighting, running and carrying were having a well-deserved break with beer and cigarettes galore. Korkmaz had hopped down the truck and lay down next to Laura, wheezing as if to complain about this scandalous lack of attention vis à vis a pedigree specimen of Turkish kangal, arguably a Sultan of the canine world.

Laura caressed him behind his small ears and talked to Bernard, thanking him for saving her life and now that of Solitaire, if all went well.

"Pa ni pwoblem," Bernard replied, smiling at his vain effort at emulating Gwada patois.

"The ways of the Lord…How's your leg, what happened?"

Laura sketched out the sequence of events that had occurred after they had parted company in the rain forest. Bernard nodded and pointed at the porch swing.

"I guess the locals will be taking care of those two, bless their souls. Well, if there's nothing more for me to do here, I'll be off then, been hanging around on this island for much too long. If there's anything I can help with later, you know where to find me." With that, he shook Laura's hand and sat in the truck which soon sped off

Laura suddenly remembered the round piece of metal the dying Ignace had slipped into her hand. Down on the beach, she had pocketed it quickly without examining it, seen there were so many other things to attend to simultaneously. Now she took it out to have a closer look. It was a kind of ancient gold coin, rather solid, on a silver chain to hang round one's neck. Funny enough, she couldn't recall having seen Ignace wearing it. The front side of the coin bore the portrait of what must surely be some conquistador or other having forged his career in the New World, so long as that had been dominated by the Spaniards, anyway. At the back, the coin showed an eagle with its wings spread cormorant-like and his profiled head turned to its right. As she felt the knurled edge of the coin, Laura noticed it had a very fine kind of groove running all round it. She tried to press her thumbnail into the groove and lo and behold, the two halves of the coin moved. In fact, it didn't flip open but rather, the two parts shifted in relation to one another in very much the same way you opened a mango or an avocado. Inside, the photographic portraits of two persons stared Laura in the face. One was that of a young woman displaying all the characteristics of a Garfuna girl as Laura had come to meet them on Dominica. The other one showed a boy age three or maybe four. It was the boy's features that fascinated Laura most. The longer she looked at them, the more they seemed to take the shape and expression of Ignace. Not the Ignace Laura had known, scars and all, but the young Ignace before his disastrous encounter with the Manchineel tree or even before his descent into the criminal underworld. Why had he given the coin to her and not to Solitaire?

Laura closed the medallion-coin again and decided to limp inside. If she didn't insist on some competent medical help here and now, she might end up losing her leg. The Doc knew his way around relatively uncomplicated gunshot wounds. As for Solitaire's injury, his means were too limited to give her the kind of treatment called for.

It took a while till Laura had managed to wriggle her way through the excited crowd of women; her eyes had problems adapting to the dimmed light of the bedroom, into which she was jostled by the human tide. At first, Laura thought she had strayed into an orthodox church by mistake. The air was heavy and stifling with incense, aggressive detergents, sickeningly sweet blood, and the general humidity caused by sweat and drying clothes. Laura had heard of the allegedly anti-inflammatory qualities of frankincense, won from the rather rare Boswellia tree, a valuable commodity since antiquity, but had not counted on it thriving in subtropical regions. As far as she was able to see through the noisy "congregation" huddled together, some icons of the Virgin Mary with and without baby child hung from the otherwise bleak walls, probably for extra coverage in case the local species of frankincense proved less effective than its European or Middle East counterparts.

During a two-week holiday on the isle of Crete, Laura had dabbled in the theory and practice of icon painting, which enabled her to recognize different representations of the "life-giving," "protecting" or "guiding" Virgin on sight. Fine thin vapours of incense, which started getting her high, emanated from a small lamp-like barrel hanging from the ceiling over a wide double bed that must have seen some lively action in its time. A Greek Orthodox crucifix was fixed to the wall on the far side of the bedroom. It had the characteristic square format that sets its species apart from the Roman Catholic or Russian orthodox varieties. The crucified Christ looked down with sincere concern on the big billowing pillows of the bed, presently occupied by the wounded Solitaire. She had been stripped down to her slip and looked sweaty and bloody. The cage of her chest and shoulder had been bandaged heavily with a white cloth that displayed a rapidly spreading red spot. Some of the black women were busy applying compresses to her forehead. The only other white woman except Solitaire sat on a rickety wooden chair by the head of the bed.

The elderly woman wore a black headscarf, which only just covered her long, thick hair. The grey meshes protruding here and there like layers of soot in the scarred rock face of a muted volcano, would certainly have been retouched by Laura's Hamburg hairdresser, she was convinced. Yet when the woman turned her head so that Laura could see her face, she realized that the woman's hair had better be left alone. It was perfectly in keeping with her sharply contoured, barely wrinkled "southern" features, which showed remarkable similarities with the icons. Maybe she had once served the anonymous artist as his favourite model. Except, perhaps, for her eyes, which betrayed a glowing passion that would be unbecoming in a portrait of the Holy Virgin supposed to be impervious to the temptations of the flesh. Despite the woman's relatively advanced age, her underlying flamboyant beauty had left more than one trace in her pleasantly uneven features.

When her eyes fell on Laura, the woman released Solitaire's hand, which she must have been squeezing for quite a while already. She stood up and took a step away from the bed so that Laura caught a glimpse of the bunch of yellow heliconia which stood in a vase on a small white night table behind the woman. She was a few inches shy of Laura's and Solitaire's height. Her long black dress didn't allow any detailed verdict other than that she was certainly neither obese nor skinny, by any standard. The penetrating view with which she looked Laura over was almost identical to that of Solitaire, albeit without the latter's withering coolness. Otherwise, the similarity was so striking as to be verging on the ridiculous. Laura needed no formal presentation to realize that she was facing Solitaire's and her own mother who had recognized her by the same token, as she could be expected to, irrespective of the many years of separation.

"Oh, good you're here at last, Snow White," Solitaire groaned from the bed. "This crazy mumbling bitch who almost squeezed my hand to pulp claims to be my mother, would you believe that? I have the fever and she does the hallucinating. Maybe you can convince her that I'm the child of a Siberian she-wolf and a wandering Russian evangelist. One way or another, I just want her to leave me alone."

Solitaire interrupted herself and was looking on with a mixture of mild horror and utter bewilderment. Penelope had pushed her way through the confused helpers and had embraced Laura with a fervour that suggested she would never let go of her again. While both women started crying and sobbing, an uncanny silence fell over the small crowd of watching blacks. Then, one of them started slowly clapping her hands, probably more for lack of a better idea than anything else. Another woman joined her and yet another, till the entire congregation turned into an audience rewarding the protagonists with a standing ovation.

"Well, thank you, that went well, didn't it? I tell you, bitch, you will have to make up your mind whose mother you want to be, mine or Snow White's," an even more bewildered Solitaire cut in, when the applause had subsided a little. "Can't have it both ways, see."

Laura raised her head from Penelope's shoulder without relaxing her embrace and nodded reassuringly at Solitaire.

"Yes, she can, believe me. Of all people, she can."

Solitaire was seriously weakened from the loss of blood and perturbed by the spectacle unfolding in front of her eyes. Laura followed her sister's painfully slow cognitive progress as reflected in her face. For a week or two, Laura had been Snow White, the naïve, ignorant deadweight on board the Pas de Deux. Now, it was payback time. What little triumph she derived from watching amazement, disbelief, contradiction and general speechlessness take turns in her sister's perturbed attitude, she was determined to enjoy to the full.

Penelope let go of Laura and, holding her by her arms, stepped back a little again as if not quite satisfied with her first preliminary scrutiny. After all the possible and impossible scenarios of this first meeting with her mother which Laura had tried to imagine, she had deliberately discarded the one where Penelope was going to say something like "My, my, haven't you put on weight, Sweetie."

Fortunately, she didn't say it. In fact, she said nothing at all, wiped her face and eyes dry and led Laura to Solitaire's bed. Before Laura had realized what her mother was doing, she found herself pushed gently on the bed next to Solitaire. Then, Penelope squeezed herself in between her daughters. She stretched out her arms to her right and left and caught hold of both her girls' heads. Now Laura understood. Penelope was turning the clock back. This very instant she was going back some thirty years, to the moment when she had last held her injured twins warm and safe in Captain Trigorin's shoddy cabin on the Black Sea Rover, before being so brutally separated from either.

"The chopper is coming. I just wanted to give Solitaire another shot, so…."

The Doc almost dropped his syringe at the sight of the three women in the bed. But it took more than that to perturb a cosmopolitan Frenchman like Jack aka the Toubib. Probably still largely at a loss as to what was going on, he injected Solitaire with another dose of sedative. He had hardly finished the job when the deafening sound of a helicopter's chopping rotor blades above Penelope's house rendered further conversation impossible. To remove the bullet from Solitaire's chest was a delicate operation that had better be carried out in a hospital. Besides, Solitaire needed banked blood urgently. The soaked lawn in front of Penelope's house was just large and firm enough to serve as a landing and starting spot for the chopper.

While Solitaire was being carried out, both the Doc and Penelope urged Laura to join her sister so that her shank wound could be taken care of in the hospital as well. When she had made sure that there was indeed enough space in the helicopter, Laura accepted the offer with some relief and thanked the emergency doctor for the painkiller he gave her. Penelope and the Doc stayed behind with concerned faces and waved the chopper goodbye. Korkmaz was still lying on the porch, protecting his sensitive ears from the din with both his mighty paws, or so it seemed.

During their flight through no end of turbulences and squally wind, Laura held her sister's hand. Somehow, she envied Solitaire her deep slumber. Thus, her sister was at least spared the trouble of having to listen to confusing morsels of the Forster family saga before her operation. Once her surgery was over, she would have all the time in the world to read Penelope's letters and try to piece the detailed puzzle together herself.

The helicopter was already preparing for touch-down at Pôle Caraïbes, where flashing blue lights signalled the presence of ambulances, when Laura thought she saw a single white sail on the horizon. She asked for the pair of binoculars, adjusted them to her eyesight and pointed them at the yacht that seemed to be steering due east. The few weeks she had spent on both the Yellow Dancer and Pas de Deux had not been sufficient apprenticeship to turn her into a sailing expert. And yet - here and now, she would have wagered her majority share package in ROLA Inc. on the lonesome sail out there being that of Suleiman's Yakamoz.

2. Penelope's Odyssey

"Thanks to their rubbing shoulders with humans for thousands of years, dogs have come to be almost as shameless opportunistic as we are. That's what makes them susceptible to manipulation, again, very much like us. All you have to do is put yourself in their place, study their ways, and re-programme the hard drive."

The Doc pulled his pipe from his pocket and stroked Korkmaz, lying at his feet. The dog's hind leg had been bandaged expertly. Fortunately for Korkmaz, it wasn't broken.

"In Turkey, kangals used to be deliberately trained to accept as members of their pack only a very small group of familiar faces and attack any outsiders. But the Caribbean is not Anatolia, thank God, Suleyman is no shepherd and Korkmaz a dog young enough to learn the odd new trick. He had been cut off from his master by the shoot-out, got totally confused and hurt into the bargain. Suleiman's fault. If you want a dog to react correctly in a gun fight, you have to take him to the firing range so he doesn't scare that easily. Like a police horse, same thing. When I picked him up in the rainforest, he gave me the impression of being completely at a loss. His genetically bequeathed system of coordinates had exploded, no new one in sight. I started feeding him a new set of apps and seem to have succeeded, eh, Korkmaz? And the way things stand, he is not likely to run into his former master in the immediate future, so…"

"Now all he needs is a proper name," Solitaire suggested. . Korkmaz sounds like the popping a cork. An alcoholic bum might feel at home with a name like that. A dog of his stature deserves something a little more…classy."

"How about Attila?" The proposal came from Laura, who had just been musing on which parts of the Doc's analysis of canine behavioural patterns could be applied to her own present situation.

"Not bad, not bad at all. I like it. Attila! Has the right kind of noble ring to it. Besides, as he is the heir apparent to a César, no less, it would be very fitting, wouldn't it? Which reminds me. You know what I believe, Laura? I believe, no, I'm more and more convinced, César was the only one to sense from the very beginning that you and Solitaire are siblings. I guess he could smell it somehow. You remember him licking your face on your first morning on the Yellow Dancer? In my humble opinion, he must have mistaken you for Solitaire, even though he had only met her once or twice. A dog's memory consists essentially of recorded scents and maybe voices. So when you started shouting at César as you woke up from your dream, he probably heard he had been mistaken."

Laura laughed at the idea, but would not have discarded it altogether herself.

"But what about you? How come the similarity between the two of us didn't strike you from the start, when so little else escaped your attention??"

"Why should it? Solitaire and I were in relatively close contact, yes, but we actually met in person only very seldom. The remote possibility of Solitaire and you being sisters, twins even, in the face of such diametrically opposed characters living in such totally different worlds alien to one another somehow never invited such a thought. Besides, it's a well-known phenomenon that there are any number of would-be doubles roaming the streets. People who, though they may look like mirror images of one another, have absolutely nothing in common, certainly not their respective parents. I myself always looked upon Solitaire as one of a kind, anyway. Same applied to my notion of you, Laura. No, I didn't have a clue and, what's more, I'm not even totally convinced now."

Penelope, the Doc, and Laura were sitting on the deck of the Pas de Deux in the Blue Lagoon, having a well-spiced clam chowder for lunch that would have done Ti Martin proud. Nothing in the peaceful picture-postcard panorama of the Lagoon suggested that a tropical storm had torn through these parts only days before. No roofless houses, no uprooted or palm trees stripped of their crowns. Only the miscellaneous debris and flotsam slopping about in the harbour basin was a little bulkier than normal. Due to the massive anchor chain on the bottom of the sea in the Bourg roadstead, the yacht had survived the storm surge. But the chaos inside the Pas de Deux still bore sufficient witness to the awful beating the Pas de Deux had received at the hands of hurricane Alberto or, more precisely, a distant relative of his. Broken china, tumbled out drawers, and slapping cabin and cupboard doors all told their sorry tale of destruction. Whatever hadn't been nailed down, tied, or otherwise secured, had been spread all over the saloon and cabin floor by the merciless thumping of the waves. Compared to the damage a possible total loss of the yacht would have caused, however, such superficial damage done to easily replaceable household items was hardly worth mentioning.

Solitaire had recovered surprisingly quickly from the surgery she had undergone at the Pitre hospital. On the third day following her operation, a troika of strong stage-coach horses couldn't have held her back in the ward. "Hunting accident" had been the official cause of the gun wounds in both Solitaire's and Laura's cases. Which wasn't all that far from the mark as it sounded. Not if you disregarded the fact that nobody in his or her right mind would have gone hunting amidst the passage of a hurricane trough. Any burgeoning doubts were effectively dissipated by the more than generous donation the financially hard-put hospital had received in Solitaire's name. "Pa ni pwoblem".

On Terre-de-Bas, operation spring cleaning had been carried out with almost Teutonic thoroughness. The most obvious traces of the shoot-out on Terre-de-Bas had been removed or glossed over, the churchyard been given a new fence and six dead body-guards buried in the spacious pit that the Sultan had originally reserved for Solitaire and her group. Baron Samedi and Ignace shared Penelope's alleged tomb, from which the voodoo master of ceremonies had emerged in such spectacular manner. Future archaeologists, hitting upon this little provincial cemetery by accident, might find it a little hard to sort out the hodgepodge of loose ends that presented itself here.

Solitaire wouldn't readily admit it, but she was still weak, of course, even though she did everything in her power to appear her normal self. It had taken several serious exhortations on the part of the Doc to convince her of the necessity to have some rest. Now she lay tucked up on the free bunk in the saloon of the Pas de Deux and deigned to be served by the "Greek bitch", who enjoyed her combined role of nurse and mother, pouring Solitaire iced water for the analgesics she had to take, kept applying cold and hot compresses on her forehead as the Doc had instructed her, made her take all sorts of vitamin supplements, minerals and food additives and peeled apples and oranges for her - in short, she did anything to pamper her Eleni. More likely than not, Laura thought, this was the very first time her sister enjoyed this kind of tender care so commonplace in the fold of "normal" family contexts. The kind of treatment she apparently had been given by the Black Queen didn't come anywhere near that, if Solitaire's account was anything to go by.

Laura's leg still hurt, but was on its way to healing without any awkward complications expected. Neither dirt nor contaminated seawater teeming with germs had caused inflammation, which, in the Doc's learned opinion and long experience, was an almost greater miracle than Solitaire's quick recovery.

Even though Laura had already had some extensive chats with Penelope on several occasions, her thirst for information hadn't been quenched yet, not by a long chalk.

"How on earth did you manage to mobilize those people on Terre-de-Bas against Suleiman?" Laura started a new interrogation round. Penelope shrugged her shoulders rather more violently than the harmless question seemed to warrant. Her frequently exaggerated gestures betrayed her general state of excitement as well as her southern European origins.

"Mobilize? I didn't have to mobilize anybody, pedin mou."

The three of them had come to a mutually acceptable agreement consisting in Penelope's calling her daughters by the Greek names she had originally given them whilst her daughters would call her Penelope or Penny for short, to avoid the awkward title of "mother", at least for the time being. As for Eleni aka Solitaire, she had finally shelved her matricidal schemes given the attenuating circumstances of Penelope's rough-and-tumble CV but would, in her own words, rather eat her thong than call Penelope other than that or, alternatively, the Greek bitch, all according to context and occasion.

"People on Terre-de-Bas respect me, adore me for what I have done for them over the years, you know. Irrespective of whether I co-financed the higher education of a local boy, gave money for the renovation of a poor family's decaying home, or paid the medical bills of a neighbour afflicted by some cancer or aids. It made me a godmother of the village, perhaps of the island. Not that I ever coveted that privileged status or abused it in any conceivable way, ever. But these folks feel morally indebted to me and were only too happy to wipe the slate clean with their fight against Suleiman and his thugs, who meant absolutely nothing to them, even though they had promised them money."

"You knew the Turk was coming, then?"

"Well, your father had learned his lessons from the feud with the likes of Suleiman and spun a net of what he called sensors around me. Like a seismic early warning system, he used to say. People in his confidence would alert him as soon as they got wind of someone or other seeking information on either Penelope or the Yellow Dancer."

"The position of those sensors in the net showed him how close the respective suspect had come to me and, consequently, whether it was imperative to do something about it quickly - ultimately move me to yet another place. On the other hand, none of the sensors knew much more than my name and hence could not have given away anything about me or my whereabouts. So he had it all lined up for me. What his early warning system failed to register, though, was Robert's own end approaching. That's something he hadn't provided for. So, when he died, the spider's net was torn to bits. I had to re-organize myself fast. I chose the Doc as a replacement for Robert, well, in a manner of speaking. Had I been aware of Laura's existence and known how to contact her, I would of course have asked her to step in for her father. Meanwhile, as long as the Doc wasn't sufficiently familiar with this new role of his, I had to improvise, as you may have noticed. Bernard on Terre-de-Haut, the one you call the Hermit, signalled the pending arrival of both Suleiman and Solitaire to us here. Antoine, also known as Baron Samedi, had the brilliant idea of letting me pass on and resurrect with a bit of voodoo fireworks while making Suleiman believe he was on his side."

Penelope took a swig from the water bottle and stroked Solitaire's cheek. Maybe it wasn't for the worst, Laura thought, that Solitaire and herself had not grown up together. If Penelope's sympathies were as clearly attributed as it seemed, that was probably not just due to Solitaire's greater need of care at present. What with her education and her sober mind always alert and her unwavering affection for her stepmother, Laura could not but appear more remote, maybe even a little alien to Penelope.

Penelope put the bottle down and let out a solemn belch. Korkmaz aka Attila raised his massive head reproachfully as if silently remonstrating against such bad table manners. Maybe Suleiman had been more taxing about such things. Since nobody else seemed to be taking offense, he dropped his head on his forepaws again with the kind of deep sigh that only dogs seem apt to produce. It had something of an ultimately damning verdict on mankind, Laura felt.

"I presumed Suleiman still to be hard on my heels. After all, it had become an obsession with him over the years and decades. How he managed to unearth me here, at the other end of the world, remains a mystery to me, because, like I said, Robert was very meticulous when it came to questions of safety and secrecy. Not least in his own interest, I might add. Now I realize, of course, that Suleiman followed the movements of the Yellow Dancer. He had no way of knowing that Robert had unwittingly ordered his own daughter to steal Suleiman's heroin via the Doc's mediation. It was the Yellow Dancer that finally led Suleiman to my daughters and the Turk who had been the chief instrument of our separation, now became the catalyst of our reunion. Maybe poetic justice does exist, after all.

Laura's thoughts strayed into Faustian dimensions: what with the spirit who, however malicious his aforethought, always ends up inadvertently doing good. That, too, must be a source of some considerable frustration, come to think of it.

Penelope fanned away the clouds of blue smoke rising from the Doc's pipe and smacked her hand down on the Glock, which Solitaire had cleaned, dismembered, and re-assembled some three or four times, already, out of sheer boredom. Presumably, without even being aware of it, though.

"Do you mind, Eleni? You give me the jitters. As for Antoine, the Baron, he had been a policeman on Guadeloupe for some thirty-odd years. He was very much into anything other-worldly, spooky, in an obsessive kind of way. Insisted on calling me his Brigitte, can you imagine. I guess he was in love with me, the Baron was. I seem to do that to people, well, to men, anyway. Okay, to some men, then," she added with a sidelong glance at the Doc.

"Do we have to take it then you had the odd fling on the side?" Solitaire asked her with feigned severity, holding the unloaded Glock in a way to have its barrel point at Penelope by pure coincidence. "Shame on you, Yellow Prancer."

Penelope laughed, pushed the gun aside and pinched Solitaire's cheek.

"Fling? Well, if you wish to put it like that. Let me briefly remind you, pedin mou, that Robert only showed up here every three or four months, see. A woman of fifty has her sexual needs, too, as you will discover soon enough yourself, if you live that long, not least a full-blooded Greek woman, at that."

"Fifty?" Laura asked, after having done a quick calculation. "Are you sure? How old does that make us? Thirty or thirty-one?"

"Thirty-one, obviously. If your papers say otherwise, they'd be lying. Anyway, Antoine drummed up a platoon of volunteers with some rudimentary combat experience of sorts. Their weaponry was basic: machetes, old hunting rifles, the odd World War One Mauser, left here by the occupying German forces towards the end of World War Two. Antoine told me that the Mauser as used by the Prussians, Turks and God knows who else, could still penetrate modern Kevlar vests as worn by the police forces. A Kalashnikov bullet doesn't penetrate a coconut, on the other hand, relies on number, not punch. Quality product, the Mauser: beautifully balanced, too. No visor to speak of, he said. You have to take aim looking along the barrel. And you have only one shot at a time, of course.

As for his Kalashnikov, Antoine had helped himself to that from the evidence room in Pitre, shortly before his sixty-fifth birthday. It was his idea of a suitable parting gift for a retired policeman. Anyway, with the armoury that Suleiman's men were kind enough to take to our island, I guess we're in for a serious upgrade of the local arsenal."

"Then you showed up and put up a smokescreen. The result was a generalized FUBAR that could have been the end of us all, hooya. I hope you are aware of that, my dear friends. I had heard of Solitaire and Ignace. They are, were, living legends of the West Indies. But I had never actually met them in the flesh, so I didn't know what to expect. When I heard from Bernard that another woman was among Solitaire's entourage, I had no idea where she came in. And even though I had never given up my hopes to see Irini again one day, I didn't make the connection. How on earth was I to even suspect that my twins were heading my way without knowing about one another or about me?"

She was overpowered by her feelings and wiped her face dry with the sleeves of her blouse.

"How did Robert manage to wrest you from Suleiman's sticky claws?"

Penelope blew her nose rather noisily in the paper napkin the Doc had handed her and shook her head vigorously.

"Is that what he claimed? Well, he had his own view on reality, let's be kind to the dear departed and put it that way. 'Wrest from the Sultan's claws'? I like that, even if it falls a damn sight short of the truth." She blew her nose once again and took a sip of water.

"I suspect Robert would have preferred me to have remained a permanent member of Suleiman's serail next to Lake Van. However, that's a service I could not render him. Over the years, I had scratched a petty sum of money together without Suleiman noticing, you know, I called it Operation Squirrel. Suleiman had become a trifle sloppy over the years, probably could not imagine I would take it upon myself to cross the better part of dusty Anatolia on foot like some frigging Lawrence of Arabia, for no better reason than to escape the abominable Turk and his pathetic tribe. I managed to escape one night, with nothing other than what I had on my back at that moment, no food or water either. I couldn't risk being caught sitting on packed suitcases, so to speak. How would I have explained that to someone even less clinically distrustful than Suleiman?"

The memory of her painful Odyssey made Penelope pale even now. She folded her hand as if praying and raised her arms.

"Escaping, though, is one thing. Surviving out there all alone, with nothing to go by and everybody you meet potentially hostile, is quite another, I can assure you. At night, I used to walk along narrow country roads, winding mountain paths and smelly sheep runs, the mighty Panayia is my witness. First I went north, towards the polestar, until I came close to the Black Sea coast, where I was born and was confident of finding my way around.

From there, I made west, always towards the point on the horizon where I had seen the sun set. Venus and Mars was there for me at night. I took them for my little daughters, see. Couldn't really imagine them any bigger than when I had last seen them. During daytime, I used to hide and sleep somewhere in barns or in the open, behind bushes or trees. Tried to tend to my bleeding feet as best I could. A couple of times I stole the reeking galoshes men had left on shelves next to a mosque, even though I never found anything my size. I stole washing from the lines of isolated houses, God forgive. Hunger wasn't the worst. I found roots, rotting potatoes left in the fields, things like that. I dared not approach lambs or sheep. They were too well guarded by shepherds or their dogs like Attila here. Plus I would have to kill them somehow and light a fire to roast their flesh, much too difficult and risky."

"Kurdish shepherds I bumped into would sometimes allow me to share their meal, you know. An enemy of a Turk is their friend almost by definition. A miracle I didn't come across vagrant poachers or the dreaded Turkish jendarms, bloodthirsty sadistic killers who spare neither women nor kids. I feared them more than the wolves, which I regularly heard at night but never saw so much as a tail of. I bet they kept an eye on me but thought little of a prey so emaciated as not to offer enough food even for their cubs."

At the mention of wolves, Attila raised his head again as if all too eager to hear more about that aspect of things.

"The worst was the perpetual thirst. I licked dirty water from puddles, like a frigging animal. I also tried drinking my own urine, get out of here! Disgusting. I wonder how long you could survive on nothing continuously recycling your own piss, beg pardon. No thank you Doc, on reflection, I think I don't want to know. The closer I came to Istanbul, the easier it got to thumb down a diesel or climb on a tractor. I'll never forget the two or three hundred miles I did sitting among horrified pigs on a two-storey cattle trailer en route to the slaughterhouse, one hell of a ride, believe me. Women on the run like that were few and far between in Turkey at the time. Nowadays there may be different ways, but Anatolian years count like dogs' years: one year in civilisation make seven years in Anatolia. Anyway, with the things I had stolen here and there, I dressed up like a man and tried to talk in a deep voice, if at all."

By way of proof, she changed the pitch of her voice by at least one octave right in the middle of her sentence like an old vinyl disc turning at the wrong speed. Then she stood up and mimicked the typically macho walk and gestures of male adult Turks scratching her virtual balls in such a deceptively realistic way that her audience almost wet themselves with laughter. It was obvious to Laura that Penelope would have made an excellent act on stage, had fate, or Suleiman, or Robert or God knows who allowed her to embark on that kind of career.

"When I finally arrived in Istanbul, I managed to contact your father after many unsuccessful attempts. He activated his old Turkish connections and provided me with a place to stay. Then he paid me a voyage to Europe on a cargo ship. He probably feared, and rightly so, that Suleiman had the airports under observation and would have intercepted me. In Hamburg, Robert put me on another cargo ship to Halifax, then one to Boston, and so on, till I ended up here, at long last. To follow that kind of devious track, even the Sultan's legs were a little too short, in a manner of speaking."

That a woman such as Penelope with this kind of background should have taken a special fancy to a daughter such as Solitaire, could surprise no-one, Laura thought. She had no way of competing with that kind of hallucinatory curriculum. Not until very recently, that is.

"How on earth did Robert manage to arrange all this under the authorities' eyes, I wonder?"

The Doc intervened with a knowing smile.

"Falsification of documents is an essential part of smuggling, always has been," he answered in Penelope's stead.

"Robert must have been in contact with first-class experts who would fake and forge anything under the sun: bills of lading, invoices, declarations of tax or import duties paid or to be reimbursed, insurance, you name it, all complete with stamps, seals, authentication and confirmations. Birth certificates, passports, driver's licences or other forms of ID would sometimes be more difficult but eventually didn't pose any insurmountable challenge for such people either. All of this Robert had under his control, as long as…"

"…as long as Frederike played ball," Laura completed his sentence.

"Exactly. Frederike must have been in the know and condoned his devious doings. She took it with her to the grave. If I try and judge her by what Robert told me about her, Laura was probably more important to her than anything else in her life. My guess is she would have done anything not to lose the privilege of watching her grow up. Maybe Penelope was lucky not to cross Frederike's path, in fact. I hate to think of what might have happened. Frail as she may have been, Frederike was of Viking origin, remember? I bet she could have swung a poleax if hard pushed."

Laura was startled about the Doc's daring hypothesis, which didn't seem to match the Frederike she had known and cherished. Although… But there was one question that interested Laura more than any other.

"Wouldn't you love to return to Greece?"

Penelope did not answer right away. It was obvious that she must have already asked herself the very same question many times without having come to a clear conclusion.

"Where in Greece? I am Greek alright, though born on the Turkish shores of the Black Sea. Yes, I am Greek with my heart and soul, but my proper home came to be the Fener quarter of Istanbul. Thereto I cannot return, however. Not as long as Suleiman is alive and not as long as the political situation works to the detriment of minorities like mine. On a windy Greek island with frocked clergymen and fly-blown kafeneia, I would probably take to the bottle or throw myself off a cliff like so many of my ancient forbears. Athens or Thessaloniki perhaps, yes. Thessaloniki, in particular. That's where Robert and I had the prime of our lives, and where I got pregnant with the awesome twosome here."

She laughed and smacked the next compress on Solitaire's forehead, as if killing a cheeky mosquito.

"Had I known at the time what kind of personalities you would become…"

She didn't finish the sentence and wiped her nose clean.

"Fact is, I wouldn't want to let my people here down. Especially not now that they saved both my life and yours. I owe them at least as much as they owe me. To just leave them in the lurch would seem a trifle heartless."

"Yes, I can relate to that. But, no offence, maybe it would do them a world of good to have a new, dynamic Yellow Dancer as godmother or queen. One they could rely on in whatever situation and predicament. One that would defend their interests irrespective of what the odds or who the respective opponents."

Penelope looked up in surprise.

"None taken. But what extra-terrestrial being do you have in mind?"

Laura pensively stroked the healing wound on her forehead. Then she shrugged her shoulders.

"You know, I'd be surprised if the person I am thinking of hadn't seen me coming."

"Yeah, I saw you coming a mile off, Snow White," Solitaire interrupted Laura from the bunk and waved her hand at her in a weary gesture of denial.

"You mean well, as always, I'll give you that. But if you take anything at all with you from your stay in the Caribbean, which, incidentally, I seriously doubt, it should be the fact that here, it is each sorry sucker for him- or herself, first. Either that or you go under. We cannot afford your European starry-eyed idealism. Besides, you may remember I had a somewhat problematic youth myself, likely to catch up with me one way or another any day."

Laura laughed out loud.

"Yes, Your Honour, I think we'll plead for mitigating circumstances on account of extraordinary juvenile hardship. Not despite but particularly because of this tainted past of yours, I should think. It's what lifts you way above all other applicants for the job."

"Such as? Show me some. I don't think there are any."

"Doesn't matter, don't you sidetrack me. Why won't you look upon it as an opportunity to redeem yourself in the eyes of society at large, how about that? And consider this: what would have become of you if the Black Queen had adopted the same attitude of indifference when confronted with you? You wasted a lot of your talents. Not entirely your fault, I concede. But so far, you cheated your way through life like a cardsharp by never assuming responsibility for anyone, least of all for yourself. One big pathetic case of self-pity and fault-finding with others, that's what you are. About time for you to grow up, Eleni Forster."

Solitaire raised herself on the bunk with such force that Laura almost dropped her wine glass.

"Call me by that name once again and Penelope will yet have to bury one of her daughters after all."

Laura realized she had mocked the tiger in his lair and decided to back off.

"I'll always support you and, well, let's call it your people by anticipation with all I have, materially, financially, whatever. You can always count on that. Deal?"

"I don't need your alms, sis." Solitaire's eyes still had a dangerous glint in them as she glanced in the direction of the table. With her right hand, she pulled something out of her pocket that looked like a bull's scrotum. It was the leather pouch the Black Queen had handed her quickly, furtively, but not fast enough by half for Laura to miss it.

"You see this? Uncut diamonds. Ignace and I never accepted cash, only diamonds. It's a relatively safe, inflation-proof currency. I learned that from my Spanish lullaby companion in Antwerp. This should last a while."

Laura smiled. She had managed to direct Solitaire's attention away from the question of principle to the details of modality. It was a trick Robert had taught her. Once you were down to details, the game started following your rules, invariably. Solitaire would rise to the bait – even if for no better a reason than simply to prove to Laura that she was perfectly capable of handling a challenge like this no matter what.

"But even if…" During the short but intensive exchange between her daughters, Penelope had stared at the vegetation of the Blue Lagoon somewhat absent-mindedly and came back now to the question of her future domicile by way of a confusing non sequitur.

"Even if I was to go to Thessaloniki, what would I do there? I no longer know anyone there, and would be surprised if anyone there remembered me."

Laura had figured that out too.

"That's right. You'd be needing a reliable companion. Someone who could help you to establish and maintain the right contacts, a social network of sorts. No sensor, but a seigneur maybe, a true representative of the old school who respects and protects you."

As if by mere coincidence, Laura's eyes came to rest on the Doc, who happened to have finished his pipe.

"I don't know," Laura addressed herself to him, "but have I ever told you of my time as a hobby archaeologist in Greece? No? Wonderful country, Greece. People are a laid back bunch, the climate was specially conceived for geriatric needs, sailing opportunities galore, and one of the oldest and noblest cultural pasts of mankind to muse on."

It was possible to take the Doc by surprise, but not to render him speechless.

"Greece, now? Isn't that the country that only produces junk?"

Solitaire on the bunk broke into such laughter as to cause Penelope change her compress hastily.

"Imports junk. Domestic production is limited to goat cheese, olives, and hot air, anyway. But production and multiplication of income isn't everything in life, now, is it? West of Lesbos, for instance, I happen to know a romantic little rocky islet, apparently goes by the name of Kava… something or other. Might just have space enough for a small house. Or take Leros, with its stately Italian villas standing vacant. The dog you'll have to leave behind though, I'm afraid. Dogs barking in Turkish won't go down well with the Greeks."

"On the contrary, Laura, on the contrary. Penelope, could you imagine the two of us going into dog-breeding? A kennel of sorts? Starting with this beautiful model of a canine stallion, we might be able to build up something economically viable. I would be prepared to sell my Perséphone II and use the proceeds as starting capital."

After all Penelope had gone through with heterosexual men, Laura thought, she might be prepared to give it a try with a gay Frenchman.

"And now, that you have attributed appropriate roles to each of us, the only thing that remains for you to find is a convenient enough place for yourself."

Laura had come to know Solitaire too well not to sense the irony in her voice.

"You may not be aware of it, Doc, Penny, but when there started being talk about her taking over from Robert, Miss Forster here was scared shitless, pardon my language. Understandably so, since she had only spent ten years at some of the most renowned universities. How could you expect a girl so ill-prepared to manage an already flourishing business venture!"

"Don't you worry about that. They'll be hearing from me back in Hamburg. And if things were to go pear-shaped, one day, I hope I can count on the help of a resolute consultant from overseas, whose mug sticks on many of the wanted posters between here and Curaçao."

"You can wager our Greek mother's collection of incense bowls on that, Laura Forster."

"There's still one more question, however. I mean, I've already popped it on several occasions," the Doc hesitatingly took the floor again.

"Meanwhile, a thing or two has happened, so I'll pop it again. What are your plans for the Yellow Dancer, once Joey has finished the general overhaul of the yacht?"

"I suggest, we let her sit out the rest of this hurricane season as well as the next one, if need be, on Antigua," Laura replied. "Come winter, we'll see whether I want to leave her in the Caribbean, take her across to Europe, or sell her. But I suspect Penelope will want to have her say in that, too."

The champagne that the Doc had kept pouring rather generously seemed to have gone to Penelope's head somewhat.

"Sell the Yellow Dancer? Over my dead decaying body. The yacht is all that's left of our life together, Robert's and mine."

"Not counting us for a moment," Solitaire ironically threw in.

"Yes, of course. Sorry about that. But I mean, Robert and I roamed these waters so often in her, she was close to becoming our permanent home, had he not died prematurely. I'd rather set fire to her than leave her in the hands of some new owner. Where would we be today, all of us, without the Yellow Dancer?"

"Me, I'd probably be in Hamburg, in my snug Bauhaus-style office, happy and contented, and with a scar or two and one bullet hole less, I might add," Laura replied.

"Well, not a lot you're missing, then, is it. You can have most of that again tomorrow or the day after, even though I'd love to keep you with me a lot longer."

Laura smiled and pulled out a gold coin on a silver chain.

"Tomorrow? No, not really. There's something I still have to do here. A recently deceased friend of mine left me some serious homework, you know. I wonder whether the Doc and Sol might be willing to accompany me to Dominica one more time."

"Me, I'd be lying on a beach on Puerto Rico with Ignace smoking pot and shooting iguanas, or vice versa, whatever," Solitaire cut in. Apparently, she hadn't heard Laura's question.

"Accompany you to Dominica, why, certainly, no problem at all, Laura. Apart from that, to answer Penelope's rhetorical question, I guess I'd be looking forward to another one of Ti Martin's inimitable gumbos with César at my feet on the Persephone," the

Doc concluded the ballot. "You see, there you have it, that's precisely what I mean," Penelope shouted and slammed her palm on the table so hard that some of the empty glasses and chowder bowls, staunch survivors of the hurricane jumped, toppled, and fell to the floor.

3. Three Gentlemen in Black

The three gentlemen in their elegant black suits, silvery grey neckties, and shining black lace-up shoes are in a hurry, there can be no doubt about that. The leather soles of their Italian designer shoes discretely squeaking on the freshly polished floor, the men are scurrying breathlessly through the arrival hall of Orly airport. Two of them have clenched their baggy calfskin briefcases under their elbows like deflated Irish bagpipes, whilst the third carries his by the handle. In front of the large electronic panel, they stop dead in their tracks. They put their briefcases down and pull out their reading glasses. Myopic as they are, they seem to have considerable difficulty trying to keep up with the relentlessly scrolling lines of information on places, airlines, arrival times, delays, and cancellations. At last, they manage to nail down the evasive, since continuously revised, ETA of Caribbean Air flight number 2335 out of Pointe-à-Pitre.

Dr Sanders, the leader of this spontaneously formed welcome committee of ROLA Inc., is absolutely not amused. The day before, he inculcated his two colleagues to make every effort, irrespective of the admittedly somewhat early hour, to meet him on time at the Hamburg ROLA office building so that the driver could take them to Paris in the company car. The declared twin objective of the mission: to fetch Laura Forster from the airport and to make her the unsuspecting target of a coordinated surprise attack by convincing her to renounce her claim to any leading role in the company, no less.

"ETA Paris 10.30 a.m.," Answering Sven Larsen's ridiculous question, Dr Sanders added with almost military precision "Local time, of course, what did you think?"

And yet, they were late, of course. Larsen, the fiscal expert, complained about chronic matutinal indigestion. Probably the first ulcerous harbingers of a looming burn-out. And as for Hansen, he seemed virtually unable to keep early appointments in a state of perfect sobriety, anyway. After his second or third divorce war of the roses he seemed about to lose control. Which is why he frequently spent the night sleeping in his office. And still managed to be late for early meetings.

"Baloney, gentlemen," Dr Sanders swept their respective pretexts off the table. After all, their trip to Paris was no mere polite gesture, but a major bid in the refurbishment of the corporate structure that, as always, went hand in hand with a solid power struggle.

Enough was enough. Again and again, Laura's return had to be postponed for no obvious reasons other than the apparent fickleness of women, something you couldn't possibly have in business contexts. No, the time had come for some hard decisions. During their trip back to Hamburg, Dr Sanders would submit a carefully concocted document for Laura to peruse and sign. With this signature of hers, Laura Forster would declare her renunciation of any future intervention in the running of ROLA's business transactions against a steep consideration in the form of an annuity to be converted, if so wished, into a golden handshake, a one-off lump-sum payment.

In view of the necessary dress rehearsal of the negotiation to be expected, it seemed extremely deplorable – if not downright irritating – that Larsen did not let a single toilet which they encountered on the German and French motorways pass untried.

"God Almighty, Larsen, do you live in Hamburg's one and only pharmaceutical black hole? That's no more than routine contingency provision for people at our age and in our position: appropriate remedies against hangover, diarrhoea, migraine, libido insufficiency, looming heart attacks, that sort of thing."

If only he had gone on his own, Dr Sanders thought. Time was money, after all. Not that their coup was levelled at taking Laura off her guard, perish the thought. Her handshake wouldn't just be gilded, after all, but consist of solid nuggets. It would allow her to spend the rest of her life in circumstances for which the term "comfortable" must have been invented. And yet, knowing Laura and her chronic indecision, they must prepare for the difficult task of convincing her. Hansen, Larsen, and he himself would have to "triangulate" her simultaneously to quell all attempts at resistance at the earliest possible stage.

"Maybe you are a little too soft for the business, after all, eh, Larsen, if this little transaction is giving you such a stomach ache?" Dr Sanders, his usual caustic self, couldn't help himself insinuating.

"This isn't an attempt on her life, you know. Besides which, we have your interests in mind, too. Think about it during your next date with the john. Show us what you're made of; that despite present appearances, you're not full of shit."

After a moment of chuckling reflection, he added, "Or perhaps better don't. Let me do the talking. I know how to take her, have known the spoiled brat for, what, I don't know, ever since her birth, it seems to me. If we play our cards right, Laura will be out of business before we even pass Fontainebleau."

"We won't be passing Fontainebleau," the driver, failing to recognize the purely rhetorical quality of the geographical remark, threw in, thereby drowning the point of the squib.

That said, the driver's general nervousness was more than understandable. On this Friday morning, the usual bumper-to-bumper traffic on the Paris ring roads had slowed down even faster than normally due to extraordinarily many pile-ups, only to come to a complete halt in a perfectly entropic scenario. So shortly before Whitsun, some unfortunate locals were still bound for work, while the larger part of the matutinal "pelotons" were already heading south to their respective holiday resorts. Add to this the inevitable accidents, harmless as they might be, and what you got was the average Paris traffic chaos multiplied by a madness factor of three.

Consequently, when the company car finally drew up in front of the arrival hall at Orly, Laura Forster should under normal circumstances have already landed half an hour before. But the gentlemen in black were lucky. Laura's plane had taken off with a considerable delay because of a heavy mid-Atlantic storm and had not been able to catch up on its original flight time, despite the jet stream's favourable influence on west-east flights. And so, on balance, the three slightly transpiring gentlemen unexpectedly found themselves almost an hour early instead.

Not a little relieved and in good humour, all of a sudden, Dr Sanders invites his colleagues for coffees.

"Camomile tea for Mr Larsen," the attorney jests, as he pockets the check to complete his travel expense statement. The ceaseless comings and goings in the arrival hall dulls the men's perception of detail.

"Like a refugee camp," Dr Sanders sneers, while knuckle-crackling Sven Larsen has not yet overcome his shock about the lack of hygiene in the public toilets. He attributes it squarely to the lax French attitude, their inexorable laissez-faire. The airport restrooms, he complains, look like Mongol yurts and smell like tiger cages. Dr Sanders won't have this kind of sweeping attribution of blame. Even though he himself, on one occasion during their trip here, tried in vain to hit the tiny hole in the ground of the disgusting motorway stand-up facility.

Whenever you put your feet parallel on the low pedestals, holding your pants with one hand and balancing like a tight-rope walker with the other, your faeces were likely to land on your heels, at least partially. If you leaned forward to accord yourself a little leverage, on the other hand, you risked falling with your pants down or else propelling the shitload at the ceramics on the wall behind you. The ideal ballistic curve of an average-sized human turd, Dr Sanders enlarges, can very probably be calculated rather precisely by dint of a formula containing such fixed variables as the height of the respective person, shoe size, and the average intensity and frequency of the peristaltic movement - child's play, in a word. And yet one obviously couldn't expect that degree of precision of people who had already made such a mess of their ballistics at Verdun now, could one?

"And do take it from me, gentlemen," Dr Sanders winds up his little digression, "in the whole of Istanbul I haven't come across toilet facilities as filthy as those. To add injustice to injury, the French have the nerve to call their disgusting shit-holes Turkish toilets, would you believe, such an unholy allegiance of ignorance and arrogance? Muslims are almost obsessed by physical cleanliness, that's no more than a fact. By comparison, true Turkish toilets are a marvel of scatological sophistication, a mixture of toilet and bidet, in fact, where you..."

He interrupts himself, realizing he has lost his audience at this unappetizing crossroads. Larsen and Hansen are knee deep in their files again. Dr Sanders seizes the opportunity and runs the most salient points of the draft contract by his colleagues yet again. In between, the legal eagle several times grabs his mobile phone to instruct his Hamburg secretary, making her responsible for whatever deficiencies and faults he finds. A lacking third or fourth copy, the awkward formulation of seemingly trifling variants, it all lands on her shoulders. Like so many caterpillars, such textual passages would unveil the full beauty of their true ramifications and repercussions to the legal entomologist only much later, after many weeks of analysis and heart searching. Someone like Dr Sanders was liable to couch a death sentence in such innocuously seductive terms that any ignorant or naive delinquent would be only too happy to put his signature on the dotted line. The question being whether or not some generally sharp kid such as Laura would allow herself to walk into that trap.

Suddenly, Dr Sanders looks up from his laptop and listens attentively. The landing of flight CA 2335 out of Pointe-à-Pitre seems to be on. In the general din of the arrival hall, the voice of the man on the loudspeaker sounds like that of a muezzin suffering from aa serious bout of cold.

"The acoustics around here are abominable," Sven Larsen calls out. "That's exactly what I'm saying, the French just can't find their ass in the dark when it comes to engineering."

"Maybe your knowledge of French isn't quite what you made us believe it was when you submitted your job application," Dr Sanders can't help remarking.

"Immaterial. Just as an afterthought, do you have any idea, by the way, how long we men wait for the representatives of the weaker sex? I don't mean wait till we have her in the sack. No, what I mean is, wait for our wives or girlfriends to renew their make-up, shave their legs, polish their nails, gel their hair while you and I are waiting for them in the car or wherever. Any bids?" The other two stare at him blandly.

"A whole year! Someone's taken the trouble of calculating that, can you imagine. That's a rough average, of course. In other words, there are unfortunate men out there having to waste maybe up to two years like that. Flight delays not counting, since they disregard sex."

The three gentlemen in black shake their heads and pocket their files and laptops. Then they start cutting their way through the crowd of colourfully dressed and boldly coiffed black and brown grown-ups and their mustee kids chasing each other through rows of waiting stressed and sweating whites.

Hansen wishes to learn his colleagues' opinion on what to expect. For instance, would Laura still be wearing her mourning attire?

"How would we know?" Dr Sanders retorts.

"I mean, on Guadeloupe she probably slipped into something more comfortable and less hot, I should hope. Now, for her return flight, she may have dressed in black again. After all, in Robert Forster's case, the conventional period of mourning is far from over, or is it? Either way, you will have to hold the sign up a little higher if you want Laura to notice it."

With that he is referring to Hansen, who was holding a cardboard sign with the inscription, in printed letters, ROLA Inc. welcomes Laura Forster in front of his stomach and hastily lifts it up to his chest. Sven Larsen had suggested sending a somewhat more cheerful message, but had bitten on granite with his colleagues who stood for a slightly more detached welcoming culture.

"This isn't a family reunion, you know," Dr Sanders had re-
marked caustically.

Which of the passengers of several recently landed planes
come from Pointe-à-Pitre and which from other cities of half a
dozen Atlantic and Pacific destinations is difficult to surmise,
with nothing to go on other than the luggage stickers hard to de-
cipher at a distance. All passengers are exiting through the same
green "nothing-to-declare" customs channel, brushing past the
snouts of two mildly interested French DEA dogs.

And so it does not take long till the attention of the three weary
men sags considerably. For them, the passing of so many indi-
viduals creates an endless flow of dark-skinned or sun-tanned
figures who are recognizable, if at all, by their backpacks, trolley
cases, and hazardously bound and glued packages of all sizes
and colours rather than by their individual physiognomies. Not
surprisingly under those circumstances, the three gentlemen in
black don't heed a lean, middle-aged woman approaching them
with a limp that, even though rather pronounced, doesn't seem
to slow her down all that much.

This lack of attention seems forgivable for two principal reasons. To begin with, the woman's appearance does in no way
correspond to their legitimate expectations. Her clothes are light
years away from anything that could rightfully claim the title of
"mourning attire". She wears a pair of light blue jeans in youthful
tatty design, adorned by a broad black leather belt with a double
row of ornamental silver rivets and a striking trophy buckle in the
form of a tiger's head, whose wide-open mouth packs an awe-
inspiring double pair of fangs. The ends of her madras blouse
are tied together with a knot above her tummy, and her wide-
brimmed straw-hat has been pulled deeply over her forehead.
On top of that, she has covered the top half of her face with a
big pair of sunglasses, which gives her the appearance of a giant
insect calmly scanning its surroundings for food and predators.

Second, and conceivably even more confusing, she is accompanied by a small boy five or six years old, one should think. The
child is dressed in the summer clothes of his age-group complete

with shorts, sneakers, polo shirt, and wears a small straw hat as well as a knapsack on his back. His deeply tanned mustee features are exotic, to say the least. If Dr Sanders had thought such a thing at all possible, he would have felt tempted to call the boy a Caucasian negro, something of a fluke of nature.

Dr Sanders feels decidedly awkward. What business does this bizarre twosome have with them? Maybe the woman is myopic and wishes to take a closer look at Hansen's cardboard placard, hoping it holds some message for her? Or she is still fighting the after-effects of fighting her fear of flying with an alcoholic antidote and is going to ask them, no doubt in a slurring voice, where the ladies' restrooms might be. It's only when the woman plants herself right in front of them, lets go of her trolley, case in one hand and the boy on the other, pushes the brim of her sun hat up and takes off her sunglasses, that the unbelievable truth is dawning upon the three gentlemen in black.

So, Laura Forster is not wearing mourning clothes. In fact, meeting her there in the arrival hall, nobody would even suspect her of having suffered a terrible bereavement only very recently. Her long dark hair is braided in such a manner as to form French plaits, tied closely to the left and right above her temples. Some would argue that the coiffure takes five years off her real age. The effect is not palpably affected by numerous bruises on her cheeks and forehead. If anything, it adds to the overall rather ferocious image the woman is apparently hell-bent on rendering and constitutes nothing, at any rate, that the passage of time and a good make-up could not make disappear rather quickly.

Dr Sanders' restlessness gives way to open confusion. Has Laura - if this is indeed her - suffered a traffic accident? Did she temporarily fall into the hands of indigenous tribesmen? And what about that scar over her right eyebrow, didn't that sit on the left side when he last saw Laura shortly before her departure?

The woman smiles as if perfectly satisfied with the impact her apparition has made. More precisely, her lips go through the smiling routine while the rest of her face seems unaffected by even the slightest sign of mirth. Those eyes of hers! In spite of himself, Dr

Sanders takes two steps back, nearly tripping over his briefcase. Ever since he first got to know her, Laura Forster used to have a rather gentle, slightly introvert look. The eyes of this woman, however, signal an unhealthy dose of self-confidence and unforgiving toughness. Whoever wishes to eat a bowl of chowder with this lady had better bring a very long spoon.

"Laura, Laura Forster?" Dr Sanders asks as if welcoming a mutant. "Would the real Laura please stand up and manifest herself…". He coughs nervously, afraid that his voice might fail him. The woman nods and seems to be looking down on the members of the reception committee, although, from a purely anatomical point of view, she is no taller than any one of them. Then she stretches out her right hand, or paw, and distributes a round of long and surprisingly hard shakes. Finally, she speaks.

"I'm glad to see you again, gentlemen. You must excuse my repeated postponements, something happened on the way to the beach, so to speak. Which reminds me. Gentlemen, I wish to present Ignace. Ignace, be a good boy and say hello to these gents, they have come to drive us home."

Like a well-raised child, the boy stepped forward and, instead of shaking the three hands stretched out in his direction, just touches the brim of his straw hat with a perfectly disarming smile.
"Ignace is the son of a recently deceased friend of mine, who I owe a lot. My life, among other things. So Ignace has effectively become an orphan. He'll be living with me in Hamburg for a while in view of a possible adoption if all goes well. I'll tell you more about it some time," Laura continues. "Meanwhile, if you would be so kind as to take care of my luggage, please." This last sentence is addressed at Hansen, who mechanically grabs her suitcase and follows everyone like an obedient dog.

"Very considerate of you to fetch me here in Orly." Dr Sanders finds her voice is almost as hard as her handshake.

"That's very convenient, in fact. During the long flight, I tossed some ideas about concerning the company's management restructuring. I'd like to present them to you first thing tomorrow morning. Here are a few notes I should like you to have sent or mailed to whomever it may concern, today, or rather yesterday. Shall we?" Laura points in the general direction of the exit. Sven Larsen hands the embarrassing ROLA Inc. welcoming sign to a surprised-looking kid sitting on top of a heap of suitcases and stuffs his glasses into his breast pocket.

Dr Sanders' heart contracts several times rather painfully. He can still feel the handshake of this woman who claims to be Laura Forster. It didn't cost her more than an ironic look and a few casual remarks to reduce his draft contract, a masterpiece of legalistic fog-screening elaborated by no less than four men in the course of a week, to ashes.

On the way to the car, he wonders whether his wife isn't right urging him, time and time again more recently, to let it all go and retire before it is too late. After all, there are plenty of beautiful places they can still visit together, so long as their state of health permits. The West Indies, for instance. If he was to trust the glossy holiday brochures and flyers the wife kept coming home with, the Caribbean would seem a safe enough bet, yamaaan.